The
NOVEL
ADVENTURES
of
NATALIE
DAUGHTRY

Treasures of Halstead Manor

The Rare Jewel of Everleigh Wheaton
The Novel Adventures of Natalie Daughtry
The Hidden Key of Brooke Sumner

"Prepare to swoon! *Charlie's Angels* meets *National Treasure* in this enthralling new contemporary romance by Susan L. Tuttle. The perfect balance of adventure and romance, *The Novel Adventures of Natalie Daughtry* chronicles an empty nester's quest to find a rare children's book and, in the process, determine if her marriage is worth saving. As Natalie and her two friends travel the world in search of the book, she leans into her faith and faces the truth about what went wrong with her husband. Tuttle's layered plot, compassionate voice, and warm humor will keep you turning the page for more."

Jill Kemerer, *Publishers Weekly* best-selling author of
The Cowboy's Christmas Compromise

"*The Novel Adventures of Natalie Daughtry* is a beautifully written novel about the complicated intricacies of marriage and about God's redeeming love. We get the perspectives of each partner, lending great insight into how they drifted apart and felt bound by misunderstandings of one another. A quiet suspense builds alongside this narrative, turning into a globe-trotting great adventure. Ultimately, we see the lengths God will go to weave restoration into a broken marriage. A fantastic read for anyone looking to revive their faith in the power of love."

Tina Shelton, author of *This Ain't No Promised Land*

"*The Novel Adventures of Natalie Daughtry* is well crafted, with a fascinating plot that will keep readers turning pages well into the night (ask me how I know). If you love mystery, adventure, history, or books, Susan L. Tuttle's latest offering is right up your alley! Add in some sweet, swoony romance and some unique, colorful characters, and you have a book that will transport you straight to Wonderland."

Amanda Wen, award-winning author of the
Sedgwick County Chronicles

"A dash of history, a mystery to be solved, and a relationship to be healed all entwine to make Tuttle's characters leap from the page. Literary fans will delight in this tale of intrigue, romance, faith, and friendship. An engaging, unforgettable read!"

Jill Lynn, Carol Award–winning author

"*The Novel Adventures of Natalie Daughtry* is a delight from start to finish. Full of exciting twists and unexpected detours, it never disappointed. And the engaging cast of characters made me feel right at home even as we jetted around the world. Don't miss this one!"

Liz Johnson, best-selling author of *The Red Door Inn*

TREASURES OF HALSTEAD MANOR

The NOVEL ADVENTURES *of* NATALIE DAUGHTRY

Susan L. Tuttle

KREGEL
PUBLICATIONS

The Novel Adventures of Natalie Daughtry
© 2025 by Susan L. Tuttle

Published by Kregel Publications, a division of Kregel Inc., 2450 Oak Industrial Dr. NE, Grand Rapids, MI 49505. www.kregel.com.

Library of Congress Cataloging-in-Publication Data
Names: Tuttle, Susan L., 1974– author.
Title: The novel adventures of Natalie Daughtry / Susan L. Tuttle.
Description: First edition. | Grand Rapids, MI : Kregel Publications, 2025.
  | Series: Treasures of Halstead Manor ; 2
Identifiers: LCCN 2024039827 (print) | LCCN 2024039828 (ebook)
Subjects: LCGFT: Christian fiction. | Novels.
Classification: LCC PS3620.U885 N68 2025 (print) | LCC PS3620.U885
  (ebook) | DDC 813/.6—dc23/eng/20240830
LC record available at https://lccn.loc.gov/2024039827
LC ebook record available at https://lccn.loc.gov/2024039828

ISBN 978-0-8254-4860-7, print
ISBN 978-0-8254-7188-9, epub
ISBN 978-0-8254-7187-2, Kindle

Printed in the United States of America
25 26 27 28 29 30 31 32 33 34 / 5 4 3 2 1

To my favorite (oldest) daughter.
Your arrival added another beautiful chapter to my world. In so many ways,
you've made my story richer with your sensitivity, tenderness, and empathy.
You love big, but always remember that I love you MORE.

CHAPTER ONE

Luciana Perez, age eight
Lekeitio, Spain, 1922

MOST OF HER FRIENDS DISLIKED the night, but Luciana Perez regularly declared it her favorite time of the day. When the sun touched the ocean's edge and the prettiest color of pink filled the sky, Mamá would put the baby to bed while Papi would tuck Luciana and her younger sisters under their covers. He'd snuggle a chair close by, lean near, and read them stories with the silliest of voices. There simply was nothing better than story hour.

She, Marisol, and little Emilia would each be allowed to pick one book. Luciana always chose *Alice's Adventures Under Ground*, knowing that sometimes her pick would result in more than one tale being told. Papi loved to recount how the book had been written just for their family many, many years ago. No one else even had a copy like theirs. Mr. Carroll had carefully crafted the keepsake for Luciana's great-grandmother. He'd wrapped his words and illustrations inside a deep-green cover held together by a beautiful golden spine. Best of all, Papi would point out on the first page where Mr. Carroll's handwriting inscribed a kind message to help Great-Grandmother remember her daughter who'd died. Papi said this book brought his grandparents happy memories to help lessen the sting of the sad ones.

Luciana supposed that was why she loved stories so much. They always seemed able to make her laugh, even when she felt unhappy. They let her wander to places she'd never actually visited. They made her feel courageous and curious and adventurous all at once. Sometimes she wished she could live inside the pages. In fact, once she'd spread *Alice's Adventures* out on the floor and tried to jump into it. Papi had arrived right as her dusty toes had landed on the pages, and while he was cross she'd torn the edge of one, he'd smiled and claimed she was as audacious as Alice herself. Luciana didn't know that big word, but she loved the sound of it.

"All right, girls," Papi said as he closed *Pinocchio* and picked up Luciana's choice, "it seems we're to read another of Alice's adventures. Which one would you like to hear tonight?"

Emilia was too little to say anything other than "rabbit," which was all she remembered about the book. Marisol was only a year younger than Luciana, however, and she loved the silly poems inside because Papi would read them in a singsong voice. Luciana would much prefer to hear about the Queen of Hearts herself, but arguing would waste precious time.

"You choose, Papi." Luciana scooted up in bed, excitement thrumming through her.

Papi closed his eyes, opened the book, and placed his finger on a page. Opening his eyes, he looked down. "Tonight, we read about Alice and a cat." Clearing his throat, Papi spoke in the voice he only used for Alice. All too soon he'd finished the chapter.

Marisol and Emilia had fallen asleep, but Luciana was much too awake for Papi to stop reading.

"Please, Papi, one more chapter?" She played with the shiny gold bookmark that fit into the spine. It was one of her favorite secrets, for if one didn't know it was there, they'd never discover it.

Papi took it from her hand, slotted it into place, and closed the book. "I'm afraid not, my child. I have a guest in my study who is waiting for me."

"Please?" She blinked up at him, doing her best to win him over with a pleading look. "You always say patience is important. Can't they be patient?"

Papi chuckled and ran his hand over the top of her head. "He already has been." Papi stood and tugged on her hand. "Come. Let me tuck you into your own bed, where you can tell yourself stories until you fall asleep."

Begrudgingly, she followed him across the room. "My stories are not nearly as wonderful as Mr. Carroll's."

"And why not?" Papi folded back her blankets and motioned for her to climb into her pink sheets.

She shrugged and settled under them.

Papi wrapped her in tight, then leaned down close. "You can tell any story you like, Luciana. Be anyone you want to be. You get to create your life, and it's only limited by your imagination, so dream big."

The necklace he wore dangled free from his shirt, and Luciana grasped for the long rectangular charm. Like the bookmark, numbers were engraved into the golden piece. She much preferred the bookmark, but Papi claimed this to be half the key to his heart. The other half, he'd whisper whenever she asked, belonged to her.

Her fingers rubbed the shiny metal. "Then I shall dream of one day living a story as grand as Alice's."

"Even grander." With a tap on her nose, he placed a kiss on her forehead. "Good night, mi joya."

"Good night, Papi."

He blew out the lantern, and darkness shrouded the room. She desperately wanted one of the new electric lights Papi had added to many of the rooms downstairs, but he said it would be some time before he added them up here. If she had one, she could try to read another chapter herself. She still stumbled over some words, but more and more she recognized enough of them to enjoy books in a whole new way.

Instead, she lay in bed, looking at the dark ceiling as she spun stories in her mind. It wasn't the same though.

An idea hit. She rolled over and reached for where Papi had left *Alice's Adventures Under Ground* on the small table beside her. She stood and tucked the worn book under her arm, then crept across the floor. In the hallway she looked to the nursery, where she could hear Mamá's whispers to baby Paloma as she rocked her. Turning, Luciana tiptoed to the stairs, avoiding the squeaky step at the bottom.

She stole across the wood floor toward the library, where Papi had recently added one of the new lights beside the cushioned window ledge where she loved to sit. Mamá had even placed a blanket there for rainy days . . . or cool nights like this one. Summer was nearly over, and soon Luciana would have to open the only type of books she didn't like—schoolbooks.

Her lips scrunched up at the distasteful thought.

As she pressed forward, her glance caught on the door just beyond the library. Papi's study. Not closed all the way, the tiny opening allowed voices to drift through it. Luciana tipped her head, curiosity pulling her closer so she could peek inside.

"My work with Empress Zita is none of your concern, nor should you make it anyone else's."

Luciana perked up at Papi's mention of her new friend's mother. Only days ago, while playing with Adelheid, Luciana had learned that Adelheid's mother had given some of her jewels to Papi. Neither of the girls understood why. Adelheid's mother shouldn't have jewels to give. And Luciana's papi tended grapes in their family vineyard. What would he want with other people's treasures?

She pressed closer to listen for anything that would feed her curiosity or she could tell Adelheid.

Another man, whose back was to Luciana, responded. "It is my concern when you refuse to pay me. This is not what we agreed upon." He sounded similar to when Papi was pretending to be the mean Queen of Hearts. A deep pitch just scary enough to cause Luciana to shiver with a different fear than Papi's villain voice produced.

But then Papi spoke, and the strength and calmness of his tone erased her worry. "It's not, and for that you should be thankful. What you brought me is fake." Papi stood in front of a painting of a white lighthouse standing tall along a beach's edge. He tapped his chin as he studied it. After a moment he turned toward the stranger.

Luciana pressed against the wall so Papi didn't see her.

"A very well-made reproduction of Seurat's work, but a fake nonetheless." His footsteps echoed through the room. "If you would like me to fully uphold my end of our agreement in light of this knowledge, I still can."

"N-No, sir. I'm fine." Suddenly, the stranger sounded like the frightened subjects of the queen. "I'll go."

"Ah yes, I thought you might. However, before you leave, there is something I need you to give me."

"Yes?" The word cracked.

"The name of who made this." When the man didn't answer, Papi continued. "I assure you, if you're wondering who you need to be more concerned with angering, it is me."

Luciana flinched. Of all the voices she'd heard Papi use, she'd never heard that one. Cold and hard, like the jagged cliffs outside.

The man spoke a name Luciana wasn't familiar with, but Papi seemed to be. Then he scurried toward the door. Luciana ducked into the library, her pulse skittering. Of all the stories she would have made up tonight, this wasn't one of them. Papi was her hero, but to the man now rushing out of their home, he seemed to be an enemy. That made no sense, and it made her tummy feel funny. Or perhaps her heart.

Luciana closed her eyes. Papi told her she could make her life anything she could imagine if she just dreamed big enough. She pictured herself with Papi on a sunny day, walking among the grapevines. His laughter. Him reading her a book. Mamá and Luciana's sisters happily playing nearby.

Her puffing chest slowed, and her breathing eased. For the first time ever, she preferred her own story over Papi's, because whomever he'd been in his study had to be a character he played. Not her real papi.

CHAPTER TWO

Present Day

SHE'D BEEN LIED TO.

Absence did not, in fact, make the heart grow fonder. In Natalie Daughtry's experience, it only made it cooler and more detached. At least that was what seemed to be occurring between her and her husband of almost twenty-three years.

Natalie sighed as she slowed for a stop sign. After she'd left two voicemails on this sunny Friday morning, Mason had finally called while she was on her way to her new job. "It's fine, Mason. There's no sense driving home if you'd simply have to head back there Sunday for another game should you win tonight." Though most of the boys on his high school team and their families planned to make the two-hour return drive from Peoria.

"If gas prices weren't so high . . ."

Natalie's mind drifted while Mason offered his excuses. There'd been a time when he'd been a broke college student who'd scrounge up change to drive three hours to see her. True, their bank account now wasn't plump by any means—thanks to two sons in college and their move back to Kenton Corners, Illinois, which had required giving up her dream career—but they certainly weren't hurting so badly that they couldn't afford a tank of gas.

Seemed what Mason couldn't afford was to spend time with her. Though he had no problem investing oodles of it with his teams. Ironic, since he used to call her his number one teammate.

"Nat?" His frustrated tone said he'd called her name more than once.

"Sorry." She navigated toward downtown. "Traffic." Not a complete lie. She'd recently passed a car going the opposite direction. "You were saying?"

"Never mind." Voices raised behind him. "I have to go. The boys are finishing up in the batting cages."

As the athletic director at their alma mater, Kenton Corners High School, Mason had originally signed on as football coach and PE teacher. Then this spring he'd agreed to also serve as the baseball coach until the school found a qualified candidate. No doubt if they asked him to take the role permanently, he would add it to his already full plate. Mason was happiest interacting with a sport. Any sport. Especially when his teams were winning, and right now the KCHS Cougars had made it to the quarterfinals of the state playoffs.

"Good luck on the game. Let me know how it goes?"

"Sure. I'll text you." He hung up with a simple goodbye. No *I love you* or any term of endearment. Not that she'd offered one either, but she'd long ago become tired of saying the words first, only to hear him mindlessly repeat them.

Reaching the Golden Key, the small downtown bookshop, Natalie steered into one of the diagonal parking spots. When she'd left her job as head librarian at the Cincinnati Public Library in Ohio so Mason could become the athletic director here, she'd taken a part-time position with the Kenton Corners library system. While it felt like a demotion in both skill and pay, at least she'd still been able to work with books. Unfortunately, at the first of the year, budget cuts had forced KCL to consolidate with a nearby county, and since she was the newest hire, she'd been the first fired.

Or "let go due to budget constraints," as they'd so kindly put it.

As such, she'd been on the lookout for another job this past March when she'd received a mysterious note from someone named Caspar, beckoning her to Halstead Manor. He'd invited two other women as well—Everleigh Wheaton and Brooke Sumner. Accepting his summons had led to extra income which had gone toward her sons' bills at Purdue and Cornell. More importantly, his unexpected job offer had brought new friendships and an intriguing distraction at a time when she greatly needed both.

Mason spent more hours with his students than with her, and Reed and Hunter had decided not to come home for summer after all. She couldn't blame them. Their once lively home now echoed with memories rather than the sounds of new ones being made. She didn't want to be there either, and obviously neither did Mason.

Which begged the question—why were they continuing to play this charade of marriage? Their boys were grown, so it certainly wasn't for their benefit.

She met her eyes in the rearview mirror, the answer staring back at her. The only thing holding her to Mason was the commitment she'd made before God on that fall day years ago when they'd both been young and in love. Their youth had evaporated right along with their love, but their vow remained. It was the one constant she couldn't navigate around.

Though lately she questioned if God really intended for her to stay in a marriage that was a pitiful representation of him. After all, marriage was meant to show a picture of God's love for his people. They certainly weren't bringing him any glory with their union. It felt as if God's heart was breaking right along with hers.

Movement from inside the Golden Key dragged Natalie's attention to its entrance. Behind the evergreen-colored door with a large window, owner Harry White waved. Natalie smothered the smile that always wanted to lift at her boss's appearance. His bushy white hair rarely saw a comb, but the wayward strands balanced his dimpled cheeks and rounded chin. His shockingly green eyes always held a sparkle, and his lips rarely frowned. But his physical appearance stood in stark contrast to his attire. Harry White loved bow ties and plaid suits. Today he wore one the color of chives, with hues of pink forming wide, intersecting lines. His bow tie matched the pink, as did the silk scarf in his breast pocket. The contrast between his unkempt hair and impeccable suit created a visual portrayal of Harry's personality to a T. Simply put, Harry White was a charming dichotomy of a man.

A little of the gloomy weight that seemed to follow her lately lifted. Working here around Harry and books paired perfectly with her other position with Caspar. In their own ways, both jobs reawakened the adventurous spirit inside her that Mason had once stoked but motherhood had quieted. The moment she'd held Hunter in her arms, she'd feared leaving him an orphan. That feeling intensified when Reed came along.

During those years, reading had provided the chance to still explore, but in a safe way. Her love of story had led to a fulfilling career as a librarian while also allowing her to flourish in her role as wife and mom.

And flourish she had. She'd poured her all into ensuring Mason and the boys reached their goals, because she adored her family. The story they'd been writing together was her favorite of all time, and they'd now reached the point where Reed and Hunter had begun their own narratives. It was hard, but her mama's heart knew this day would—and should—come with her boys. But she hadn't expected Mason to do the same.

All the changes in this past year highlighted her encroaching loneliness. Making new friends as a girl was hard. Making new friends in her forties? Practically impossible, especially with her boys grown. Children came with built-in friendship opportunities in the form of other mothers. That was why when Caspar's invitation had arrived, along with two new female acquaintances, Natalie had jumped on it.

Unfortunately, work with Caspar still left spaces in her days. Case in point, he'd mentioned another assignment but had yet to fill her, Everleigh, and Brooke in on any details. Rather than waiting in her quiet house, Natalie had accepted the job with Harry. Today would involve her first hours working solo after being trained by him yesterday. Speaking of, he remained at the entrance, watching her.

Opening her car door, she exited into a wall of heat wafting up from the asphalt. Summer had arrived early and in full force this year. Most people thought the Midwest dodged the season's intense temperature, but she'd endured plenty of scorchers growing up here.

"Come in, come in." Harry stood with the door wide open to greet her. "Before that dastardly heat melts you."

"It is sweltering out there." Natalie strode past him into the air-conditioned store. She inhaled the scent that only books produced, the smell as familiar and comfortable as the jeans she wore. Layered underneath the lovely aroma floated notes of lavender and mint from the diffuser Harry constantly ran at the counter. "How's your morning been?"

"Oh fine, fine." As he spoke, he scurried past the oversized chairs planted near the windows. A bright fabric embroidered with books and mugs in a myriad of blues, greens, and purples covered the chairs. What most would consider garish somehow worked in this space. Harry paused beside the front counter. "And yours?"

"Fine as well." Minus Mason's phone call. "Better now that I'm here. This place carries a contagious joy, and you are a huge part of that."

Harry purposefully stocked titles that always ended in hope, while also doling out that emotion along with kindness to every person who walked through his door.

His cheeks reddened and lifted as he smiled. "Sarah often said she'd caught the joy bug working here."

His last employee had recently married and moved to Nashville. She and Harry had shared a special friendship, and Natalie could tell he missed her. "Have you heard from her?"

"She rang me this morning. Sounded jovial, like a newlywed should." A faraway look filled his eyes. "It's a peculiar thing to have lived here long enough to watch not only your own children but others—like yourself—grow up, get married, and move away. Though you've since returned." He slapped his thigh. "And you're not here to listen to me bemoan the passing of time. Come, come. There's a project in the back." He waved her to follow him.

She did, and they ducked into the stock room that also functioned as their break room. The cozy, welcoming feel of the bookstore extended to this area. Extra titles lined shelves. An armoire provided space to hang her purse. A round table took up one corner with comfy chairs to sit and eat. Thick rugs warmed the concrete floor, and a desk with a lamp and computer invited her to research.

A stack of four old books perched on the corner of the desk. Natalie approached them. "You went to another estate sale."

Since returning home, she'd reestablished her regular visits here, and she and Harry had developed a friendship of sorts. She knew one of his favorite pastimes included shopping estate sales for treasured stories, a hobby he seemed especially talented in. They'd bonded further over their love of antique books. He'd shown her his collection and pointed out a few titles he'd purchased years prior from an estate sale at Halstead Manor. That had brought up her own connection with the house, and Natalie had inquired if he recognized the name Caspar, but much to her dismay, it was unfamiliar to him.

"Indubitably, Natalie. How absolutely astute of you to notice, though

I'm not surprised. Not surprised at all." Harry lifted the top book. The cover was a deep navy blue with a gold-embossed little boy and bear, and Harry presented the offering to Natalie. "It's signed. I believe it to be real, though I wanted your opinion."

Her nerves hummed as she carefully cracked open the cover. A map of the Hundred Acre Wood greeted her, and she studied it before turning the page. She made note of the publisher and copyright—E. P. Dutton & Company, 1926—before flipping to the title page to find A. A. Milne's signature. Natalie had once immersed herself in Milne's work and familiarized herself with his signature—she'd been tasked with authenticating several of his books for a museum exhibition in Cincinnati. All those details remained clear in her mind.

In all honesty, retaining information posed no difficulty for her, and his wasn't the only author's handwriting she'd familiarized herself with. Coming in contact with collectible books as often as she did in both her work and hobby worlds, learning to spot forgeries proved a valuable talent. Harry certainly seemed to agree.

Natalie traced her finger over the small illustration of Pooh Bear alongside Milne's autograph. "Remember, you can always text me a picture when you're at a sale. While I might not be able to provide a definitive answer from a photo, there are times I can absolutely conclude what you're looking at is fake." She closed the book and handed it to him. "This signature, however, is very real."

"Fantastically good news." Harry clutched the book to his chest. "Though I'm quite certain even if it weren't veritable, I would have purchased this lovely anyway. Books should never face the fate of spending the rest of their days in a box." He shook his head. "All that wonder, lost. No, I simply could not abide it."

"I understand." She loved words and stories as much as he did. "But you do need to be careful you're not taken advantage of."

He leaned close, as if sharing one of his life's secrets. "As long as the story remains unchanged and able to be shared, then naught is lost." He straightened. "You can see this wasn't my only acquisition yesterday. I believe allowing these books their time in the sun is only fair, as they've been sequestered far too long. Thus, today's project entails our front window. Are you up for the challenge?"

"I am." She peered at the other three titles on the desk, then to those remaining in the box beside it. "Though some might benefit from being in the display case inside rather than exposed to sunlight."

"I am quite sure you'll know which to place where. Quite sure." He reached for his worn leather bag, which accompanied him everywhere, should he meet a book in need of rescue. "I'm off to the bank and then lunch with Winnie." His sister, and no doubt part of the impetus for his love of Winnie-the-Pooh collectibles. "If you need me for anything, I'm only a block away."

"I'm sure I'll be fine." She highly doubted there was a book here she wasn't at least somewhat familiar with, and learning his point-of-sale system had been a breeze. Harry maintained an old-fashioned gold cash register with heavy round buttons, which added to the charm of this store. He also, however, had a tablet for anyone who wished to pay with their phone. "Take all the time you need."

"Time, yes . . . that reminds me." He rested a hand on his belly. "Have you heard from your Caspar when you might be needed again?"

During her interview, she'd informed Harry that her other job often required strange hours. Sometimes even last-minute trips. He hadn't seemed to mind, but he would need to know her availability before making any of his own plans. Especially as she was his only employee.

"Not yet, though I believe he'll be in touch soon." At least she hoped. Not only for Harry's sake, but she'd feel much more settled herself when Caspar finally called. She hated wondering if he'd forgotten about them or simply moved on. That the job he'd offered and the friendships it had brought could already be fading. This season marked by leaving was unsettling. She wasn't ready for one more thing to walk out of her life, even something so new. "I'll let you know the moment I'm aware of any conflicts so you can plan accordingly."

"Good, good." Harry's familiar repetition snapped her back to the moment. "Simply keep me aware. I'm as flexible as Tigger is bouncy. I don't care which hours I work—just that I don't work them all."

Bidding her adieu, Harry slipped out the exit that led into a small alleyway. Natalie worked to haul his finds from yesterday to the front counter. There, she could leisurely sort through the titles, catalog them into the computer system, and contemplate a creative way to display them in the window. One of the charming things about Harry's store was how he mixed old books in with the new ones.

As she settled near the register, the bell over the door dinged and a young mom pushed a stroller inside. A baby reclined against a blue plaid blanket, and a toddler with blond pigtails held on to the mom's shirt.

"Morning." Natalie greeted.

The mom lifted tired eyes to Natalie and bestowed an exhausted smile on her. "Good morning. We're here to look at the Gerald and Piggie books. If you have them?"

"We most definitely do, along with the Pigeon books. Have you read those?" At the shaking of their heads, Natalie waved them along. "If you love Gerald and Piggie, you'll love their friend the Pigeon."

Pointing out the comfy reading nooks along the way, Natalie escorted them to the children's section. After showing off the large selection of titles Harry kept on hand, Natalie stepped back so they could explore. The mom knelt to help her daughter find old favorites, along with new tales, while also rocking her son in the stroller.

Natalie smiled, remembering those days of entertaining a toddler and simultaneously protecting the slumber of the baby. Moments when both children were in their happy place and peaceful felt, at times, as rare and fleeting as a shooting star. If only someone had told her how those years would fade away faster than that star flying through the sky.

No one had prepared her for this season. There'd been bridal showers and baby showers and crazy amounts of advice on how to navigate the toddler to teen years, but people had been conspicuously quiet on what to do once you raised your children and your marriage sputtered into complacency. So here Natalie sat, seeking to fill the spaces she hadn't known were being carved out.

The toddler giggled as her mom expertly voiced Gerald and Piggie and their silly antics. Natalie ducked away to return to the task awaiting her. A short time later, the mom purchased three new books—one of which featured their new friend Pigeon.

Natalie worked straight to lunchtime, happily pointing out new authors right along with old classics to customers who meandered in and out on this sunny day. There was something wonderful about pairing a person with the perfect read. Typically, with a well-placed question or two,

Natalie discovered where to direct them. Sending people on their next adventure, helping them find an encouraging word, or even deepening their knowledge on a subject was a joy she didn't take lightly. Quite simply, there wasn't much that submersing oneself into a new book couldn't cure.

Her stomach growling, she nabbed her salad from the refrigerator in back and set it at the counter. Now to find her own next title. Harry kindly allowed her to treat the store as a library. He proclaimed it was one of the perks of working here, and she gladly partook in it. She'd already devoured the recent releases from her favorite authors, which meant today she was on the hunt for her own new friend.

Her arms were full of possibilities when the bell over the door jingled yet again. She peeked around the romance section to see a tall, thirty-something man with olive skin, black hair, and dark eyes enter. He looked like someone who frequented gyms more than bookstores, but who was she to judge her fellow bibliophiles?

Natalie set her books down and greeted him. "Good afternoon. Can I help you find a book?"

He looked up from the thriller that had caught his eye. "Just browsing." He tilted his head as he studied her. "Have we met?"

"No. Not that I know of." She was good with faces, even better with names. Mason always relied on her to supply them because they frequently slipped his mind. This stranger wasn't anyone she recalled having met.

His perusal of her intensified. "I'm sure I've seen you someplace." Then he snapped his fingers. "Halstead Manor, right? You've been out there?" He must have noted her confusion, as he added, "I was recently there with a crew doing some work for . . . John, I think his name was?"

There'd been some men leaving as she'd arrived the other day. They'd been fixing siding on the house, but she'd been so focused on what had been happening with Everleigh that she hadn't given them much notice.

"Yes, right." She held out her hand. "I'm Natalie."

"Matt." He clasped her hand. "That's a pretty interesting place. Does it belong to your family?"

"My boss, actually."

He looked around the space. "This owner owns the manor too?"

She shook her head. "Nope. Different boss."

"Oh." He nodded before holding up the book he'd been checking out. "Happen to have any other titles by this author? I love her signature twists and turns."

Natalie was familiar with the author of suspense. "Sure. Follow me."

They chatted while he chose a book, then they made their way to the front counter. While she'd been assisting him, Harry had returned from his lunch. He checked the register and now waited patiently as she rung up Matt's purchases.

As the door closed on Matt's exit, Harry turned her way. "Stupendous, Natalie! Your first morning alone, and you've made several sales. Nicely done. Nicely done."

She often wondered if Harry even realized he regularly repeated himself. Everyone—including her—found his quirkiness charming. "I'd like to take all the credit, but it's more of a testament to how you've made this a place people love to frequent. Though I'm not sure what draws them more. You . . . or the books."

"Oh, poppycock." He tugged on the corners of his bow tie as if straightening it, though it remained forever cockeyed. "I am nowhere near as interesting as any of the books here."

"Tell that to your customers. Nearly every single one asked about you or told me to pass on a hello." She nodded to the window, where Matt could be seen sliding into his car. "He was the only person who actually knew me. Strangely enough, I had no clue who he was."

"Hmm." Harry squinted toward the front window at the man's retreating back. "I didn't recognize him either."

Unusual. Harry knew practically everyone in town. "He said he'd seen me out at Halstead Manor, so I wonder if he's a part of Stew's Crew. They've been working there recently." That was who John had used, based on the van in the driveway that day.

Harry shook his head, causing his white hair to stick out farther. "I'm acquainted with all of Stew's boys, and he's not one of them."

"Maybe he's new?"

Again, he shook his head. "I had them out the other day to fix the awning over my door, and that man was not with them. I'm good with faces. I'd have remembered."

Natalie stared at the door Matt had exited through, her curiosity piqued. The only people she'd bumped into out at Halstead Manor, besides her new friends, had been that work crew. If Matt wasn't one of them, how did he know her and her connection to the manor?

CHAPTER THREE

"You didn't have to do that." Natalie accepted the toffee nut latte Everleigh handed her as she walked into the study at Halstead Manor. After nearly another week of waiting, they'd finally received a call yesterday to assemble this morning. Their meeting with Caspar would start in a few minutes.

"I know, but I wanted to." Balancing more cups in one hand and guiding Gertrude Levine with the other, Everleigh moved farther into the room. Retired FBI agent Gertie had become a part of this new little group of friends that had formed when Caspar had hired them to help Gertie find the Florentine Diamond—a gem that had eluded her most of her life. She was a spitfire of a woman who refused to allow her diminishing eyesight to slow her down.

Everleigh worked as her live-in caregiver and also happened to be dating her nephew, Niles Butler. They'd fallen in love while searching for the diamond these past few months. The newness of their relationship highlighted the worn edges of Natalie and Mason's.

Not ready to sit, Natalie strolled the room's perimeter. It was again Friday, and Mason had been home since Sunday night, but they'd hardly seen each other this week. His baseball team had won their quarterfinal game, which secured them a spot in the semifinals starting tonight. Between his navigating the last few days of the school year, final exams, and extra practices, Mason had only been home to sleep. Natalie had picked up hours at the Golden Key to fill her days, which she did enjoy, but she was more than ready for this next distraction from Caspar.

Stopping beside the massive fireplace, Natalie ran her fingers along the intricate details carved into the marble. This was her favorite room in Halstead. The bank of windows faced east, allowing sunshine to stream in from the moment it crested the horizon. Bookshelves lined the opposite wall with enough open space to hold every title she owned and then some. She'd happily spend an afternoon cozied up reading on the couch, but the only time they were in the manor was when they met with Caspar.

Of course, that only happened via speakerphone. John Doyle played their go-between with the boss she, Everleigh, and Brooke had never met in person. To the best of their knowledge, neither had Gertie or John. He was simply a lawyer also hired by Caspar, and another part of his job was to ensure everything pertaining to their ventures with Caspar remained aboveboard and legal. The elusiveness of their boss bred curiosity, and she, Everleigh, and Brooke, each in their own way, had tried to find a picture of the man. Not knowing Caspar's age or even his last name, they hadn't had any luck.

She'd hoped that with more interactions, Caspar would unknowingly reveal clues about himself. Unfortunately, that hope was dwindling. John had been brought on board six months ago. Three months after that, Caspar had found her, Everleigh, and Brooke, and there wasn't much they'd discovered other than the Florentine Diamond. Though the deeper they'd delved into that search, the more they'd felt Caspar had a solid idea of where the gem was and simply had been leading them to it.

They couldn't prove that fact, and much about Caspar remained a mystery, but one thing they all felt sure of was that they could trust him. He'd never asked them to do anything nefarious. He'd paid them as he'd promised. And he hadn't resisted when they'd suggested returning the diamond—worth millions—to the Viennese government. So when he'd asked them to work one more job, they'd agreed. Today he planned on providing the details.

Everleigh held out a coffee to Brooke. "Americano, blond roast."

Brooke accepted and arched an eyebrow in surprise.

"What?" Everleigh shrugged as she passed John his drink. "I know your order because I listen when you place it."

Brooke nodded her appreciation.

"Thanks," John voiced his, then took a sip as he rounded his large mahogany desk. "Good to see you, Gertie."

"Can't say the same, but it is good to *hear* you," Gertie quipped, with a tinge of humor. "Hope you don't mind me crashing the party, but Niles was off working a case, and tagging along with Everleigh seemed far more interesting than a quiet house."

"You're always welcome to join us," Natalie responded for the group, knowing it was their consensus. They'd all come to love Gertie during their search for the diamond.

"Good, because I'm mighty curious about what Caspar is sending you after next. My being here will save Everleigh a conversation later."

Everleigh laughed. "With you, yeah. Not with Niles." She settled onto the couch beside Gertie and across from Brooke.

Brooke's blond hair was pulled into a sleek ponytail, and she wore all black, the only color she seemed to own. Rather than jeans and a leather jacket, however, she sported a pencil skirt, fitted sweater, and collared shirt, evoking an almost vintage look.

Crossing her legs, Brooke met Everleigh's gaze over the small table between them. "You do know one coffee is not enough to get back on my good side."

Natalie swallowed her sigh. A month ago Everleigh had run off alone on the final leg of their diamond hunt, and that action had proved damaging to the trust they'd all been building—especially for Brooke. Though Everleigh's own struggles had caused her solo flight, and she'd returned with heartfelt apologies, Brooke battled to regain her footing in their friendship. That would hopefully come with time, especially with the efforts Everleigh seemed to be putting forward.

"I understand," Everleigh responded. "But just so you know, it's not a bribe. I promised I'd put actions with my words, and this is me doing that."

Brooke tipped her head. "In that case, next time bring me a muffin too. Cranberry orange."

If Natalie wasn't mistaken, humor laced Brooke's directive.

Everleigh reached into the bag she'd slung over her shoulder, pulled out a small paper sack, and wordlessly handed it to Brooke.

This earned her an eye roll along with a full smile. "It's a start."

While Brooke indulged in her muffin, Natalie decided to satisfy her curiosity. She turned to John. "Have you had anyone other than Stew's Crew out here working?"

His forehead wrinkled. "No. Why?"

After her conversation with Harry, she'd suspected that might be John's answer. "There was this man I bumped into at the bookstore." She'd made them all aware of her second job. "He introduced himself as Matt and said he'd worked on a crew out here and that he recognized me. But Harry knows all those employees and said he doesn't remember him. I thought maybe you'd had another group out here."

"I haven't. And Harry's right—none of those guys were named Matt."

Finished with her treat, Brooke unwrapped a piece of gum. "That's strange." She popped it into her mouth and started chewing, a sure sign she was thinking.

"I know," Natalie agreed. "Especially since someone has been following Everleigh."

"Had been," Everleigh amended. "I haven't seen anyone since we returned from Vienna. I'm fairly sure that had to do with Palmer anyway."

Her ex-employer *had* been causing her trouble, but that was over now.

Gertrude tapped her cane on the ground. "We don't know for sure. Niles couldn't find any connection to prove it was Palmer."

"He also couldn't disprove the theory," Everleigh countered.

"It's probably nothing," Natalie said. Because there was no reason it should be something. "With John opening Halstead Manor up again for Caspar, there's a lot of reemerging curiosity in town over this place. For all we know, that guy was looking for some good gossip to offer over coffee at the Corner Café. He probably saw us coming and going and was too embarrassed to admit he'd been watching the place."

"It wouldn't hurt to ask Caspar about it," Gertrude suggested.

There was no reason to divert today's conversation. They'd waited too long for the details they hoped Caspar planned to reveal. "Let's wait to see if I bump into him again."

John's iPhone rang from its place in the center of his desk. "Everyone ready?" At their nods, he swiped his finger over the screen. "Hello, Caspar. We're all here."

"And how is everyone?" Caspar's digital voice filtered across the open line. "Rested after your trip to Vienna?"

"Yes. Thank you again for sending us and providing an extra day to sightsee." Natalie still couldn't believe some of the places she'd recently traveled to, and Vienna had been one of her favorites.

"Of course. You all earned it."

She imagined she heard pride in his computerized tone. In every dealing with Caspar, he used some sort of synthesizer. Their best guess was that one of them would recognize his voice, so he felt the need to disguise it. They had no real proof, but it was their current theory.

"So what's next?" Brooke asked, never one to beat around the bush.

A rough chuckle sounded before Caspar's synthesized voice responded. "No small talk then. I'll get right to the point, since I've made you wait." A pause for some clicking, then, "There's a book I need you to collect for me."

Natalie's interest piqued. He was speaking her language. Plus, if he wanted them looking for a book, chances were it was rare, old, or both. He wasn't simply speaking her language—he was speaking it fluently.

"What is it?" Natalie leaned in.

"A handwritten and illustrated copy of Lewis Carroll's first attempt at *Alice in Wonderland*, which he titled *Alice's Adventures Under Ground*."

The thought of a handwritten manuscript by Lewis Carroll vaulted Natalie out of her seat, but before she could speak, Brooke jumped in.

"That doesn't make sense. Carroll gave that first edition to Alice Liddell, the little girl everyone believes inspired the story. That copy is now on display at the British Museum."

Brooke owned a pawn shop and immersed herself in antiques. In fact, she'd once been an antique runner, acquiring pieces for wealthy collectors. Her knowledge and background often overlapped with Natalie's, but no one knew history and literature quite like Natalie. This instance was case in point.

She looked across the room as she addressed everyone. "True, Carroll did give a copy to Alice, but it's been rumored for years that he wrote an even earlier version that's been lost since before Liddell's copy was given to her."

A line formed between Brooke's perfectly manicured eyebrows. "I've never heard that theory."

"It's not well known, and many believe it to be myth. I can send you a link to the few articles I've read." Natalie had no trouble recounting the periodicals' names, article titles, or publication dates. Her memory simply worked that way. If she engaged with something once, she didn't forget it.

Brooke nodded, seemingly content with that answer for now. Natalie wasn't offended by the need to prove her statement. Over the past few months, she'd come to know Brooke and her desire for concrete answers. Natalie couldn't say she blamed her. Right about now she'd love some solid solutions to her marriage.

"Natalie's correct," Caspar said. "This is a rumored copy, yet it is very much real, and I have a lead on its location. It seems a collector named Edwin Hollis purchased it a few decades ago, and it's now a part of his estate."

Somewhere during the conversation, Brooke had started strolling the room. Now she stood in front of a reproduction of Van Gogh's *Café Terrace at Night*. Replicas of several famous works hung around the manor, and Brooke often inspected the pieces whenever the three friends visited. She seemed as drawn to Halstead's collectibles as Natalie was to its vast book collection.

Not turning around, Brooke filled the space with her question. "If you know where it is, then why do you need us?"

A whirring sound filtered through the lines, along with more clacking. "Hollis recently passed away, and his butler, who's been left in charge, is overwhelmed with organizing the property. He can't locate the book among all the man's keepsakes. He's agreed to allow you to search for it if, while you're there, you help him empty the estate."

Now Brooke turned and speared the phone with a wide-eyed glance. "We'll be glorified cleaning ladies?"

"I call the mirrors." Gertie perked up. "It's a job I could really see myself doing."

A collective groan made its way through the room.

"Do you ever run out of puns, Gertie?" John asked.

"Speaking as someone who lives with her, no." Everleigh patted the old woman's knee. "And I'm hoping she doesn't."

Brooke moved to the window and balanced on the ledge. "Back to this job. Why not wait for the butler to go through the place and eventually find it himself? Why send us?"

"That could take months, and I'm anxious to have the book in my hands.

Yet even if I could exercise patience, my concern is he doesn't understand the value of the book, and with the large scope of work in front of him, he could accidentally overlook the copy, give it away, or worse—throw it out." Caspar paused, and clacking occurred again in the background. "That won't happen with you."

"Is the estate that big?" Natalie asked.

"Yes," Caspar said. "And Edwin Hollis was also quite the collector, or so I'm told."

Everleigh leaned forward, elbows on her knees. "How long do you think this job will take?"

"A week, possibly more. It depends on how things look when you arrive and how quickly you locate the book." Another pause from Caspar's end before, "I will pay your travel expenses along with a flat rate for your time."

"What exactly is the going rate for cleaning ladies slash treasure hunters these days?" Brooke asked.

"Twenty thousand. Apiece."

"Geesh. You really want that book." Brooke spoke what they were all undoubtedly thinking.

"Yes."

Oh, Natalie wanted to know why, but Caspar wasn't one to offer explanations. He did, however, offer handsome paychecks, and this time was no exception. Natalie didn't have to think long or hard about her decision. The chance to track down such a special book would entice her even without such an impressive payday, but the money sealed the deal. It felt good to contribute to the boys' college funds and to her and Mason's retirement. Though spending their retirement years together seemed less and less likely. They'd once kept a bucket list of things they wanted to do once the boys were grown. She didn't even know where that list was anymore.

Everleigh and Brooke met her gaze. They both needed the income too. Everleigh continued to pay off the loans she'd taken out for college and to help her mom with medical bills before she'd passed away. Brooke, meanwhile, remained on the edge of losing her fledgling antique business. They both nodded their desire to take on the job.

"We're in," Natalie said.

"Wonderful," Caspar responded. "Are you able to leave Sunday?"

Brooke said she needed to schedule people to cover her store.

Everleigh and Gertrude needed to be sure Niles and Burt—Gertie's old FBI partner—could cover her PI firm.

"And I need to call Mason. His team is playing tonight, so the earliest I'd connect with him is tomorrow." Not that she anticipated any issues, but if Mason won tonight—like he expected—he wouldn't be home until late Sunday. That created a solid chance she wouldn't see him before she left. There'd be details to iron out, such as care for their dog, Wilson, and ensuring Mason could meet the air-conditioning guys scheduled on Tuesday. "But it should work."

"Let John know once you've all confirmed, and he'll book your flight with the pilot."

"Flight?" Excitement began a beat inside Natalie's heart. The bucket list she'd shared with Mason might be lost, but she'd recently started penning her own. It contained multiple places she longed to see, and she wondered which one she might cross off next. "To where?"

She could practically hear Caspar's smile as he responded. "Colmar, France."

CHAPTER FOUR

THERE WAS NOTHING QUITE LIKE the home one grew up in. Friday evening Natalie parked in the driveway of the small ranch where she'd spent her birth to college years. Dad and Mom had updated the shutters, front door, and trim to a matte black and then painted the brick a soft white. Inside they'd torn down a few walls to open up rooms so their growing family could better fit in the space. Her parents adored when she, her three older brothers, and the thirteen grandchildren they'd collectively provided all descended at once—like tonight. Dad's seventy-fifth birthday party.

The home overflowed with people. Sam and Brenda Riggs loved well and were well loved in return. Natalie supposed it was what had made them so great at pastoring their local church until Dad retired ten years ago. A big reason she didn't want to come clean about her failing marriage was she didn't want to disappoint or embarrass them. Her. A pastor's kid with a broken marriage.

Natalie grabbed Dad's gift from her passenger seat and sucked in a fortifying breath. Walking in alone would garner looks and a few questions from her brothers. She hadn't told her family that Reed and Hunter weren't returning home for the summer, and they'd want to know why. Short answer—her boys liked their jobs near their campuses. Long answer— their once tight family unit was breaking apart, leaving her to often fly solo.

She'd hoped moving back here, where Mason had experienced his best days and they'd fallen in love, would rekindle that part of their relationship, when they'd penned their story together. The outline they'd created

33

in those early days included future chapters with Mason as a head coach at a university and them working side by side to realize that dream. In the past few years, Mason had edited her right out of that draft. Their stories diverged, and she'd thought returning to the beginning would help them land on the same page once again.

It hadn't.

Exiting her car, she stepped into the humid summer air and breathed a sigh of thankfulness that she'd changed clothes prior to coming. With temps in the upper eighties, she'd donned shorts and a loose sleeveless blouse. Seemed even thinking of heat caused her to sweat these days.

Crossing Dad's meticulous lawn, Natalie stopped to give hugs as she passed old friends and neighbors who milled around playing games. Most knew that the Kenton Corners baseball team had won last weekend and had their semifinal game tonight in Peoria, so they didn't ask why Mason hadn't accompanied her. A few inquired about Reed and Hunter but easily took her response that they were working for the summer. Finally, she made it inside.

"Happy." Her mom's warm voice wrapped around the familiar nickname, the endearment hugging her before Mom's arms did. "You look adorable. I love those shorts on you." Mom always had a compliment or encouragement on her lips. She released her daughter and peered around. "Are the boys still outside?"

Natalie added her gift to the pile on the table. "Actually, they've decided to stay on their campuses for the summer. They each have great jobs, and school is so expensive—even with the help we've given them."

Mom's blue eyes roamed over Natalie's face. "I'm sorry, hon. I know you were looking forward to them being home for the summer. You've always loved having your people close."

Pressure built behind her eyes. "I do, but those two went and grew up on me." As much as she tried to prepare for this whole "grown and flown" stage, watching her boys fly away from her was proving harder than she'd anticipated.

Mom pulled her in for another hug. "I know it feels like it, but they haven't left you. They'll be back, and you'll have an even deeper relationship with them. It'll be different, but oh, so good." She rubbed Natalie's back, her words and soothing touch calming like only a mother's could.

Then Mom held her away so she could look Nat in the eye. "In the meantime, it sounds as if you and I have some empty hours to fill with coffee and shopping."

Natalie choked out a laugh. Better than a sob. Mom and her constant looking for the sunny side. "That does sound great. Though I did just accept a job at the Golden Key and . . . I'm traveling to France."

"France?" Dad stood at the screen door leading to the backyard. "Didn't you just go to Vienna?"

A familiar figure wearing a huge grin stepped up alongside Dad. "What are you, a world traveler now?"

"Lorne?" Natalie couldn't hide her surprise as she moved to hug him. "What are you doing here?"

Lorne was her dad's oldest and dearest friend and had been since before she was born. As such, she couldn't remember a time in her life when he hadn't been part of their family, even though he'd moved to the UK years ago. A confirmed bachelor, he visited as often as he could, and he'd attended all their biggest milestones, so really, she shouldn't be surprised he was here.

"I couldn't miss this celebration, Happy."

Natalie brushed aside an unsettled feeling at hearing her nickname again. She couldn't remember where the moniker originated. All she knew was that it had been a long time since she'd felt like the carefree little girl who'd earned it.

Lorne's comforting warmth enveloped her. "It's your father's seventy-fifth *and* the chance to remind him he's older than me. I had to be here."

"Careful. I'm still strong enough to knock you out of the way if you keep stealing my hug." Mirth filled Dad's words. "I might have a few more years than you, but I've also got more muscle."

"I believe I beat you in our last arm-wrestling match."

"But who benches more?"

"And this is where the family competitive streak comes from." Enjoying their familiar teasing, Natalie stepped from Lorne's embrace into Dad's. "You know you're my favorite."

"Yet you hugged him first," Dad groused.

"Because it's been three years since I've seen him." Though they had kept up via emails, texts, and phone calls.

"It's been too long," Lorne noted.

"I agree." She took stock of the changes time had brought to him. He still styled the waves of his thick brown hair off his forehead, but now hints of silver threaded their way through those strands. A few new wrinkles deepened his laugh lines, but his green eyes hadn't lost a bit of their sparkle. "How long are you in town for?"

"A couple of weeks. I have some business that happened to line up with the party." He often traveled to nearby Chicago for work. Another bonus of moving home to Kenton Corners meant she'd be here when that happened.

Like now. "Perfect timing."

"Exactly." He looked past her. "Are Mason and the boys here?"

She shook her head. "They'll be sorry they missed you."

"Maybe we can do dinner while I'm in town."

"I'll definitely take you up on that, but the boys are staying on their campuses for the summer." She should have brought a bullhorn to announce Reed's and Hunter's plans to everyone all at once.

Mom wrapped her arm around Dad's waist. "You need to mingle."

Dad, ever the extrovert, puffed an exaggerated sigh tempered with his toothy grin. "If I must." He pressed a kiss to Natalie's cheek. "Come find me once he's done monopolizing your time."

She laughed. "Will do."

Mom and Dad headed deeper inside the house, while Natalie and Lorne stepped outdoors. Snagging an iced tea, Lorne nodded toward two open seats on the deck. "Happy to be back by family?"

"Definitely." Especially as her marriage deteriorated. It would be hard to talk with them about, but she'd need their support if things with her and Mace didn't improve.

She followed Lorne, her muscles relaxing. This remained her favorite spot here. Old oaks created a canopy of shade perfect for resting under. Mom's flower beds lined the deck and offered the sweetest aromas and a colorful display. Best of all, a small creek bubbled along the edge of the yard. She and her brothers used to catch frogs out there during long summer days.

Speaking of her brothers, Joe, her oldest, called from the yard. "No sitting down. Get yourself out here, Happy. You too, Lorne." He held a bocce ball in his hand, and her other two brothers stood beside him.

As with most traditional four-person games, Dad had long ago created a set big enough for their six-person family to play. Natalie turned to Lorne. "Ready to take them on?"

"Always." He motioned for Natalie to precede him, and they joined her brothers in the yard.

"None of your guys with you today?" Steven, the brother closest to her in age, asked.

Peter tossed the small white ball in the air. "We knew Mason had a game, but where's Reed and Hunter?"

Definitely should have brought the bullhorn. She hauled in a long breath and contemplated just sticking a note on her forehead so she wouldn't have to keep repeating herself. "They're staying on their campuses for the summer. They both love where they're at, and they have amazing jobs."

Joe wrapped an arm around her shoulder. "Welcome to the Empty Nesters' Club, sis."

"Might feel strange right now," Peter joined in, "but trust me, you and Mason will quickly realize it's pretty great to have all that privacy back again. Right, bro?" He shared a look with Joe.

"Ah, man." Steven groaned. "She's still our little sister."

"Don't worry," Natalie assured. "Mason's never home anyway, so things truly are private around my house." Even when he was home, she couldn't remember the last time they'd been affectionate toward one another. "Toss the ball, Peter, and let's get this game going." Because she didn't want to stand here talking about her nonexistent love life with her brothers, of all people.

Peter started things off, and they dove into play as Natalie caught up with what her nieces and nephews were doing. Three rounds in and the conversation circled back around to her life.

Joe sidled up beside her. "How was Vienna?"

Steven focused on his throw. "Still couldn't believe it when Mom told us all the traveling you've been up to. I remember a time you refused to board a plane."

Her family hadn't missed how motherhood had transformed her into a homebody. Before Hunter and Reed arrived, she and Mason regularly traveled. During the boys' first few years, Mason still tried to book trips, but eventually he gave up after her continued refusal.

Natalie aimed her red ball. "Times change. In fact, I'm going to France for the next week." She honestly wasn't sure which excited her more—the opportunity to see more of Europe or the possibility of discovering a rumored book.

Oh, who was she kidding? Definitely the book.

She felt the weight of her brothers' gazes and looked up. It was as if her disclosure had pressed Pause on the moment and meeting their gazes hit Play. Words tumbled from them.

"France?"

"Seriously?"

"Who are you?"

Her brothers' voices melded together, but it was Lorne's that stood out. "You'll love it there."

She smiled at him. "I hope so."

"What does Mace think about all this?" Joe asked.

Good question, and maybe if she and Mason were talking more, she could do more than guess. He'd never understood her fears of leaving the boys and apparently hadn't believed her when she'd claimed that yes, she still *wanted* to travel—when the time was right. Well, that time had arrived, and she'd invited him to Vienna, but then he'd turned her down because it hadn't worked for him. He'd scored tickets to a White Sox game during an unprecedented winning streak.

Maybe that was part of their problem. Their timing had been off for so long that they now lived on different schedules. It definitely felt that way with the possibility of her leaving before he made it home. "I haven't told him about this latest trip yet, but he's seemed fine with everything so far."

"Really?" This from Steven.

She heard the disbelief in his voice. "I mean, I think so. At least he hasn't raised any concerns, but he's rarely home, so we're not talking much."

"Obviously." Joe completed his turn. "Or you would have told him about your upcoming trip."

Peter chuffed. "Or maybe not. This is Natalie we're talking about."

She stiffened. "What does that mean?"

Her brothers all looked at her, their eyebrows lifted high. It was Joe who finally answered. "You're a great listener when it comes to everyone else's lives, but you rarely talk about your own."

"At least not in any detail," Peter added. "We get the periphery, if we get anything at all."

Steven nodded. "You don't exactly wear your feelings on your sleeve, Nat."

Really? All three of them? She propped her free hand on her hip. "Yet you call me Happy."

"Yeah, you let the easy ones show," Steven said. "But when it comes to the tough stuff, you tend to clam up."

"And we might be reading between the lines here, but it sounds like things with you and Mace are a little tense?" Peter guessed.

She barely heard Peter's comment because Steven's remark had hoisted her defenses the rest of the way. "I do not clam up. I have no problem telling people how it is."

Her brothers laughed. They actually laughed.

"You have no problem keeping people in line when necessary or defusing difficult situations," Joe said. "But, Nat, come on. You're like Fort Knox when it comes to your thoughts and emotions."

She couldn't be more baffled than if they'd held a mirror in front of her face and she hadn't recognized the reflection. How did they see her so incorrectly?

Or was *she* the one viewing things wrong?

Frustration buzzed under her skin. "Can we just play the game, please?"

Another shared glance between her big brothers, who then shrugged.

"Sure thing," Joe said. "Your turn, Pete."

Her brothers stepped away to get the ball rolling again.

Lorne had remained silent through the entire conversation, and now he edged in close. "They mean well."

"I know." She watched them make their tosses. "But they also don't have any clue what they're talking about because they don't have any clue what's going on with Mason and me."

"Hmm . . ." His light hum split the air between them.

Natalie peered through her peripheral at Lorne, who stood there, arms casually folded across his chest. He'd already taken his turn while her brothers had been talking to her.

"Agh!" She puffed out air. "Fine. Point taken."

"I didn't say anything."

"Didn't you?" She faced him. "Because I distinctly heard you say, 'Well, Natalie, that's because you haven't told your brothers what's going on with you and Mace, which effectively makes their point.'"

Lorne chuckled. "That does sound suspiciously like something I'd say." Now he also turned to face her, growing serious. "Whatever is going on, it's all going to be okay."

She peered up at his warm gaze. Like Mom, Lorne was an eternal optimist. "How do you figure?"

"Because you're no quitter."

Before she could respond, her brothers called out that it was her turn. Her first throw landed far from the mark. Recalibrating, her second landed within centimeters of the white ball.

"See?" Lorne grinned. "You don't give up."

Then Steven took his turn, and he knocked her out of contention.

Natalie turned to Lorne. "It's not always about how hard you try, especially when there are other players in the game."

"True, but marriage isn't a competitive sport. That other player is your teammate, which means you *both* need to communicate or you both lose." Lorne headed to collect their balls before the next toss. "Come on."

If only he—and her brothers—understood that she agreed with them, which created the heart of her concern. Marriage *was* a team sport, but Mason had effectively benched her. How long before he kicked her off his team completely?

❖ ❖

Someone was in her house.

Natalie sat up in bed and willed her heart rate to slow. She reached for her phone. Midnight. She'd only been asleep an hour. Maybe she'd dreamed the muffled bump she'd heard. Sitting still, she strained to listen over her thumping pulse and reached for Mason's spot in bed to find it empty. Right. He was in Peoria for baseball. Frustration lit inside. He should be here so she could shake him awake.

Instead, Wilson lay pressed against her legs. The Bernedoodle blissfully slept. That had to mean something, right? If there was an intruder, Wilson would bark. He never let a squirrel pass by unnoticed, so there was no way he'd miss a human being.

But there it was again. A creak from that floorboard in the kitchen. The one that always made a noise when someone walked across it.

Oh, she should not have been reading that Jessica Patch thriller before bedtime, because now all she could picture was a serial killer in her home.

Phone in hand, Natalie stood on wobbly legs. She'd have 911 on with five quick presses to the side button, but she didn't want to call in a reader-induced false alarm. Wilson lifted his head, watching her curiously, but he didn't move. The only weapon in this room was a firm king-size pillow that Mason compared to a rock. She picked that up and sneaked to the door to peek out. She had an unobstructed visual down the hall to their open family room and kitchen. The area appeared clear.

Tapping her leg for Wilson to come, she slid her stocking feet along the wood floor, doing her best to remain silent. It took a second to realize that Wilson hadn't followed her from the room. The big oaf could scare someone with his size if he weren't such a scaredy-cat himself.

She reached the end of the hall and peered around the corner toward the sunroom. No one there either. Leaning against the wall, she closed her eyes and pulled in a calming breath. Bed. She needed to go back to bed because she was obviously so tired that she was hallucinating.

Opening her eyes, she turned just as a figure walked straight for her. Screaming, she launched her pillow at him. Except, it wasn't her pillow she threw—it was her phone. The device bounced off the intruder's face, and he yelped. Having lost her ability to call for help, her fight-or-flight kicked in, and she raised the pillow to nail him with it next. Wilson came charging from the bedroom, barking. Maybe an attack dog did live inside the lovable lump.

The intruder's hands rose to block her pillow attack. "Nat! Stop! It's me."

Mason's familiar deep voice reached through her panicked haze but not fast enough to stop her blow. The pillow smacked him upside the head, and he snatched it away from her.

"Mason!" She cupped her mouth. "I thought you were someone breaking into the house."

"And you came at me with a pillow?" He flicked on the lights. "What were you thinking?" He leaned around her to look at Wilson. "And some attack dog you are."

"Leave him alone—he must have known it was you." She patted Wilson's head, her heart still racing. "Unlike me. You're not supposed to be home yet." KCH had pulled the final slot of the night, and Mason had been confident they'd win their game. That meant he'd be gone through Sunday.

With a hefty sigh, he bent and picked up her phone, then handed it to her. A red mark marred his forehead where it had nailed him. "Why don't you ever read your texts?"

She narrowed her gaze, opened her phone, then showed it to him. "Why don't you remember to actually press Send on yours?"

"Oh." He dragged a hand through his messy brown hair. He'd always liked it a little longer on top. "Sorry. We lost, and a couple of the boys went after each other on the way to the locker rooms. I thought I'd hit Send, but I guess I got distracted."

Nothing new there.

"That's why you're home? You lost the game?" He'd been so sure of their win.

"Yep." His jaw tightened, but his shoulders slumped with his deep sigh. "Which means baseball season is officially over."

Though football practices would start soon. It was a never-ending sports cycle with Mason.

They stood staring at each other for a long moment. Natalie broke the silence. "How's your head?"

"I'll survive." He rubbed it, a glint of humor in his eyes. "Nice throw. Maybe I should have you come coach the boys, since whatever I'm doing isn't working."

"You made it to the semifinals."

"And lost."

Mason was notoriously hard on himself. A competitive perfectionist, losing wasn't in his playbook. After all these years, he still didn't know how to handle that outcome—other than spiraling into frustration, which he turned inward.

She worked to pull him out of his downward turn. "You won far more games this season than lost. It's the best record the team's had in years."

"Thanks, Nat." Right words. Wrong tone. Her encouragement hadn't made a dent in his mood. "Think I'll go watch some ESPN."

His continual rebuffing of her efforts hurt. Used to be, Mason would sit and talk out his losses with her—ones that occurred both on and off the field. Somewhere along the way, things had changed, and she had no idea why. The status of their relationship unsettled her, and she hated feeling unsettled.

"I really am sorry you lost, but it's nice to have you home." That last part felt awkward on her lips, but it was what a wife should say. Another attempt that didn't bolster his attitude. She didn't want to stand here and continue feeling the uncomfortable space growing between them. "Um, I'm going to go back to bed. Did you lock the door when you came in?"

Of all things, *this* made his dimple deepen? "Worried you might have to go after another intruder with your pillow?"

"You're the one who said the thing felt like a rock."

"To sleep on, not to take out a man who outweighs you by sixty pounds."

He either was blissfully unaware of the extra padding she carried in her middle or wise enough not to mention it. "It worked, didn't it?"

His hand on her arm stilled her, along with her surprise at his seriousness. "No, Nat, it didn't. All teasing aside, if you really thought someone was in the house, you should have called 911 and not gone after them yourself."

The concern in his voice squeezed her heart. It almost sounded like he cared. He was giving her whiplash tonight. Aggravation and exhaustion removed the guard from her words. "Seeing as how I was here by myself, I didn't have much choice."

Any softness in his eyes dimmed with her harsh response. "Right." He hooked a thumb over his shoulder. "There's a game starting. I'll be to bed later."

With a nod, Natalie returned to her room alone. She shouldn't have bit at him when he was already down, but her emotions had become increasingly uncontrollable when it came to Mason. Like when her boys once had temperamental toddler moments, every thought seemed to escape before she could capture it. Unlike them, the behavior wasn't in any way cute.

As she climbed into bed, Wilson hopped up to snuggle against her. Thoughts chastised her, making it hard to sleep. She was upset when Mason brushed her off and upset when he attempted to show concern. Seemed they both were all over the place with their emotions, and her response to his worry hadn't been warranted. It definitely hadn't helped the dynamic between them. Maybe that was irrevocably broken.

With a huff, she flopped onto her side and tried every relaxation technique she knew. Deep breaths. Counting sheep. Quoting Bible verses. One must have finally worked, because at some point she drifted to sleep. She woke to sunshine streaming in her window and a still-empty bed, but at least it looked slept in.

After brushing her teeth and slipping into her robe, she headed for the coffeepot. The kitchen and family room remained empty, which meant Mason was out for his morning run. He'd tried for years to coax her to fall in love with the sport like he had, but she'd yet to grasp a firm understanding of why a person would run on purpose.

She was sitting at their table with her mug of coffee and toast when Mason walked through the back door. He crossed to the sink and poured himself a tall glass of water, then added some green powder to it before joining her.

"Good run?" she asked.

His phone beeped a text, claiming his attention even while he answered her. "Five miles."

Not that his response made sense to her question, but that wasn't unusual. Lately it felt like they spoke different languages.

Still too keyed up from last night's adrenaline rush, Natalie opened her recent sigh-worthy read rather than the thriller she was halfway through. Kindle in one hand, toast in the other, she let the story transport her to a small beach town in Maine. The hero had fallen for his best friend, except she didn't notice his feelings, and his green-eyed monster came alive at her announcement of a date with a doctor she'd recently met. The banter was just getting good when Mason interrupted.

"So," he said as he set down his phone, "what are your plans for the day?"

She swiveled her glance to his. He never asked what she was up to anymore. Though she did need to bring him into the loop on her upcoming trip. "I'm meeting Everleigh and Brooke to do some antiquing, but I'm sure we'll chat about our next job for Caspar. We met with him on Friday, and he gave us the details."

"Oh?" His tone wasn't quite surprise, nor was it pleasure. "Will it involve more travel?" His question, however, held a note of wariness.

"Yes." She paused, the narrowing of his eyes catching her off guard. When he remained silent, she continued. "He's sending us to France, and it looks like we're leaving tomorrow. I arranged daycare for Wilson if you can drop him off and pick him up each day." Her Kindle shut off. "And I can drive myself to the airport. We'll be flying private again."

Mason crossed his arms over his chest, his running shirt pulling taut over his muscles. He stared out the window into their backyard for a long moment before returning his gaze to her. "How long will you be gone?"

Strange question when they rarely spent time together. "We're not sure, but hopefully no longer than a week."

His nostrils flared. "You've traveled a lot for this job."

Why on earth did he sound put out? "More than I anticipated, but that's not a bad thing. Especially when Caspar is covering all the costs."

Mason sniffed. "Sounds like you have everything handled."

"If you don't want me to go, Mason, just say so."

"No, it's fine." He stood. "I'm taking a shower." Then he headed down the hall.

Natalie sat there stupefied. What on earth did he have to be upset about? Certainly not that she was leaving for a week, because he wouldn't even notice her absence. It didn't matter if she was in their living room or a continent away—Mason did his own thing and she did hers. In fact, it was almost easier to be thousands of miles apart. At least that provided a plausible explanation for his distance from her. The loneliness of Mason choosing work over her carved deeper when he was just down the hall.

She waited until he exited their room before getting ready herself. Towel drying her hair, she was thinking through her packing list when her phone dinged a text from Mason.

Left to pack up my classroom.

Home for dinner tonight?

I'm meeting Trey.

His best friend from high school. They'd reconnected since she and Mason had returned to Kenton Corners in the fall.

All right.

His plans weren't a surprise, and they meant she could make—or not make—whatever she wanted for dinner, since it would only be her. While she missed family meals around the table, she didn't mind not having to come up with dinner menus each week.

Natalie grabbed her purse as her phone dinged again.

How about lunch?

Knock her over with a feather. Mason was asking her to have lunch with him? That hadn't happened in . . . she couldn't remember how long. Curiosity welled inside.

Where and when?

1 at Olive Garden?

That used to be her favorite restaurant, but she'd cut back on carbs this year in hopes it would help balance her juggling hormones and reduce some excess pounds creeping onto her hips. Either she hadn't told him, or he hadn't been listening.

Her brothers' words from yesterday nudged her. Perhaps she hadn't told him.

She had told him about France though, and for whatever reason her plans upset him. Could it be he sensed the growing distance between them too? This invitation to lunch felt like an attempt to head in her direction, and while she fully understood how dangerous hope could be in this situation, the least she could do was meet him halfway. And if that involved a plate of fettuccine, well, she'd take one for their team.

She tapped out her answer.

See you then.

CHAPTER FIVE

IT DIDN'T MATTER HOW MANY years he'd been a coach—the stale smell of sweat and grime always churned Mason's gut. His first few years he'd added air fresheners to locker rooms, but all they did was woefully mask the scent under a cloak of floral undertones that made things worse. Instead he'd learned to breathe through his mouth. The habit marginally helped.

Mason flipped on the lights to his office, situated in a hall behind the lockers. The end of baseball season had filled every extra hour in his schedule, and he hadn't found a moment to pack things up for summer. Not that his summer was a long one. Conditioning started next week for anyone who hoped to make the football team. Tryouts would occur in July. He'd have his roster set by August, with practices filling up that month.

Still, he needed to toss all the stale snacks accumulated in his drawer, along with the empty cans and coffee cups. The mere fact that his office looked like his sons' rooms when they'd been in the throes of their teen years attested to how crazy life had been these past few weeks. All his energy had gone toward playoffs—and it hadn't made a difference. Once again he'd come up short.

With a grunt, Mason swept a pile of junk into the trash bin beside his desk. He'd been so sure they'd win the title. Same as his football season, which had ended just shy of top seed. Clinching a state win would help bring him another step closer to becoming a college coach. He'd never anticipated it taking this long, but the dream remained in reach. Lately he wondered if it were only that though, a dream. If he couldn't even coach a high school team to victory, why did he think he had the chops to lead a college team?

An oppressive weight of inadequacy pushed against him, and he fought the familiar emotion as he cleaned his office. If he were honest with himself, his personal life wasn't much better. Natalie hadn't attended one baseball game this season, and he could only remember her coming to two football games. She used to be his biggest cheerleader, and man, he missed that. Missed her seeing him as something to be celebrated. She'd become as nonexistent by his side as the trophy he'd hoped to bring home. Granted, he didn't mind her not viewing his losses, because all he wanted was for her to be proud of him. See him as a success. Her equal. That desire pushed him hard at his job. He'd even turned down her invite to Vienna so he could stay back and work with the guys to ready them for the playoffs. At least that was part of the reason.

Mason scrubbed a hand through his hair. He'd yet to meet her new friends, but they seemed—like so many of Natalie's friends and colleagues through the years—to run in an entirely different stratosphere than him. One Natalie navigated comfortably through. He'd known since the first time he'd seen her in high school that they weren't on a level playing field, but that hadn't stopped him from falling head over heels for her.

Two years his junior, Natalie Riggs had been in the library when he'd first spotted her. He'd gone to meet some teammates and found them giving one of the cheerleaders a hard time. Before he could step in to stop them, this wisp of a sophomore bolted up to defend the girl he'd once watched torment Natalie. In all his eighteen years, he'd never witnessed someone go after a bully for a bully. From that moment on, he couldn't get Natalie out of his mind. Or heart.

He still couldn't believe she'd married him. Lately, he worried she regretted their years together. Especially with the changes he'd witnessed in her since she'd been working for this Caspar and company. She'd ventured to multiple locations these past few months. When they'd first started dating, he'd had to coax her into adventure and travel. Somewhere along the years she'd stopped saying yes to his invitations. He figured she'd lost her carefree spirit. Seemed more like she'd lost her desire to adventure with him.

A knock on his office door pulled him from his spiraling thoughts.

Typically, the building remained fairly quiet on a Saturday, but with it being the end of the year, most of his colleagues were cleaning out their rooms right along with him. He looked up to see his friend and principal, Trey Winters, standing there.

"Hey," Mason greeted. "What has you daring to journey into these parts without a gas mask?"

Trey chuckled. "It's not that bad."

Mason lifted both brows.

"Okay," Trey admitted. "It is that bad, but you rarely get service in here, so I figured you wouldn't get my texts."

"True." He cleared off the chair in front of his desk and motioned for Trey to sit. "What's up?" They had plans to meet for dinner, so this impromptu visit had to be work related.

"First off, I wanted to congratulate you on finishing strong this season."

"We lost."

Trey nodded. "But you lost in the state semifinals. That's something to be proud of."

They obviously had a different definition of the word. "And that, my friend, is why you are the principal and I'm the athletic director."

Another chuckle from Trey. "You have always been too competitive for your own good and way too hard on yourself. You had a near spotless record going into the playoffs. Don't those wins count for anything?"

"Doesn't matter how many wins there are if I don't clinch the most important one."

They sat in silence a long moment. Trey bent his leg, resting an ankle on his opposite knee. He crossed his hands over his stomach. "I just got off the phone with a friend of Sarah's. Actually, she's friends with his wife, but that means I'm friends with him."

Yeah, he and Natalie had acquaintances like that. In fact, Natalie had become friendly with Sarah because of his relationship with Trey. "Did you two have a nice chat?" Mason inquired dryly.

Trey tilted his head. "Actually, smart aleck, it was, especially where you're concerned." He brushed something from his pants. "I can come back though, if you're busy."

Intrigued, Mason sat forward. "Spill it."

"This guy's name is Craig Hoffner, and he happens to be head coach for Ogden University's football team out in Utah. They're a Division III school, but he's looking for an offensive coach, and I might have been bragging you up the last time I was out there."

So many thoughts ping-ponged through Mason's brain that he wasn't sure where to start. He grabbed one and voiced it. "You're just telling me about this connection now?"

"I didn't want to get your hopes up."

"Should they be?"

Trey nodded. "Cautiously up. Craig's interested enough that he'd like to fly you out. I mean, that's no guarantee, but it's definitely a foot in the door."

And he'd take it. "When?"

"I'm not sure exactly, but my guess is in the next week." Trey leaned forward and dug a slip of paper from his pocket, then placed it on Mason's desk. "Told me to have you watch for their call."

Mason picked up the number. "And you're okay with this? I've only been here a year."

"I knew when you came what your end goal was." Trey stood. "And just because you're going out there doesn't mean I'm losing you. Let's cross that bridge when we get there, okay?" He stopped in the doorway. "Think Natalie will be okay with it?"

Trey was the only one aware of the tension in Mason's marriage. Mason had opened up to him in the past few months, and Trey had provided a firm sounding board.

"I think so." Hoped so. "Me coaching a college team has always been the goal." Though this last move had brought more strain than he'd anticipated. He'd promised it would be their last for several years, but honestly, he hadn't thought an opportunity would open up this soon. Surely she'd understand their possible plan change. Natalie had always supported his dream to coach at a college level. She'd be excited for him. Maybe even proud of him again, because lately he wondered if his lack of achievement was part of what had driven a wedge between them.

With a nod, Trey left. Mason returned to cleaning his office, a buzz of anticipation under his skin. This job could be the win he'd been waiting for.

Two hours later, Mason asked for a booth tucked into a corner at the back of Olive Garden. He'd purposefully arrived early so he'd have time to think through what he wanted to say to Natalie. Reality overshadowed the excitement of his news.

Not only was this a potential change to his promise, but if he got the job, it would be the fastest turnaround they'd made to date. One that came on the heels of her giving up a job she'd loved. This time around it wasn't only her work he worried about, but she'd recently gotten their new house the way she liked it. She'd even asked again, before investing in new paint, if their timetable remained the same. He'd assured her it had. He'd been telling the truth, and he hoped she believed him. This interview had arrived unsolicited, but he'd be a fool to not pursue it. Natalie would understand, wouldn't she?

It certainly couldn't hurt that they were at her favorite restaurant. Plus, dropping the news in public was far better than the silence of their home. Those thoughts didn't quell his swirling gut.

Dragging a hand through his hair, he bounced his knee. Natalie walked in, and he waved her over. She had on jeans that showed off her curves and a green tank top—his favorite color on her because it brought out that deep shade in her hazel eyes. Her brunette hair brushed sun-kissed shoulders, and a gold necklace gleamed against the dip in her collarbone. For all that was strained between them, his attraction to her had never waned. There was no woman on the planet more beautiful than his wife, and her sweet nature only intensified her appeal. Could they get back to where they'd once been?

"Hey," Nat said as she slid into the booth across from him.

"Hey." He sat back down from having stood at her arrival. "You look nice."

This brought out her wide smile, though her forehead wrinkled too. Almost as if he'd taken her by surprise with his words. "Thanks."

When was the last time he'd complimented his wife?

He slid a menu her way. "They have a few good lunch specials."

She took it and scanned the list. "I'll probably just do the fettuccine."

"I was thinking spaghetti."

They sounded like two teenagers on their first date, only they had less to talk about. They already knew everything about each other, and with the boys no longer at home, they didn't even have their kids to fill in the silent gaps.

Natalie set aside her menu and took a sip of water. Her eyes tracked to a nearby server. As if feeling her gaze, the woman turned and headed to take their orders. She hustled away, and awkward silence settled over the table.

Clearing his throat, Mason opened his straw and sank it into his soda. "How was antiquing?" A pastime he'd never understand. Picking through glorified garage-sale fodder didn't land the bottom spot on his list of possible things to do.

She twirled her wedding band around her finger. "We had fun. Brooke found a few things for some of her clients. I found a first edition of an old English dictionary."

Words excited her and terrified him. They were the bane of his dyslexic brain.

They both played with their straws as their conversation dried up. He grasped for a fresh topic. "Tell me more about this next job with Caspar." At least that subject might take them until their food arrived.

"Right. Like I said, he's sending us to France." Her hazel eyes lit, their gold specks sparkling, and her bright smile spread. This glimpse of the Natalie he'd fallen in love with sat him back in his seat. He missed her. What was it about this Caspar, this job, that brought out the old Natalie, when nothing Mason did seemed to even capture a flicker of that woman?

Natalie had mentioned not knowing the age of her mysterious boss, and she'd never met him in person, but he'd somehow managed to re-awaken something inside her. Perhaps it was because Caspar seemed far more cultured than Mason. His office probably smelled of cigars and something woodsy, or worse, like a library. Unlike Mason's, which reeked of sweat and testosterone. Plus, Caspar flew her to places Mason couldn't afford—not that Natalie had been interested in travel until recently—and spoke to her history-loving heart in ways Mason never seemed able to connect with.

But he could try. "What are you hunting for this time?"

"An old copy of a Lewis Carroll story."

Books. His Achilles' heel. Her catnip. He had no idea who Lewis Carroll was, but he wasn't about to admit that to Natalie. "No wonder you're excited."

She nodded. "I just feel bad that I'll already have to ask for time off from Harry."

His brow crinkled. "Who?"

"Harry." Her features smoothed, as if she wasn't bothered by him but tired of him. Of them. "Owner of the Golden Key."

"That little bookstore you just started at?"

"The one and only." She leaned back as their server delivered their lunches. "The good thing is, Harry knew ahead of time I'd need a flexible schedule. Still, I feel really bad taking the job and immediately missing days."

Mason twirled his spaghetti around his fork. She'd feel even worse when he told her they could very well be moving again.

"What?" Natalie's voice landed someplace between accusation and dread.

Mason looked up to find her staring directly at him. "Hmm?"

"Don't *hmm* me, Mason Lyle. You have that look."

"What look?"

Her fork clanked as she dropped it on her plate and wiped her hands on her napkin. "The one that says you have something to tell me that you don't want to say." She studied him a moment before a harsh breath puffed through her nose, and she shook her head. "We're moving again, aren't we." She tossed the napkin onto the table and rose. "Unbelievable."

"We aren't moving." The words rushed from him, halting her escape.

She lowered herself onto the cushioned booth. "No?" Her right eyebrow arched, an expression he'd once found endearing. Right now, however, he wanted to smooth it back in place.

"I've been invited to talk to the head coach of a Division III school. That's all."

"Where?" Her fingers tightened around the napkin she'd picked up to twist.

He cracked his knuckles. "Utah."

She didn't even flinch. In fact, she went so still, it was unnerving. "Are you going to the interview?"

"Of course." He'd be crazy not to.

After a long moment, she spoke. "Just like that? No discussion?"

"We are discussing it. Right now."

A humorless laugh escaped her. "That's our problem . . . well, one of them, Mason. You think this is a discussion."

Her comment bothered him. "You're kidding, right?" He paused to suck in a deep breath. Frustration wouldn't help here, so he removed it from his voice in hopes she'd hear him. "You took the job with Harry without so much as a word in my direction that you were thinking about it. Not to mention the work with Caspar that's carted you all over tarnation and now to France—a trip I only heard about this morning. But you're upset because I agreed to an interview in Utah?" He shook his head. "It's hard to have a discussion when only one of us is talking."

"Or when only one of us is in the room." As fast as her retort erupted, her expression softened. She tapped her fingernails together. "Sorry. Communication between us could be better, particularly on my part, but Mace, my choices include travel, not relocation."

"This interview doesn't guarantee a move."

"And if it leads to one?"

"Then we'll move." Sooner than they'd planned, so he understood her possible frustration. Still . . . "It's a college position, like we always planned."

She swiped at the corner of her eye. "Except I thought the plan changed when we moved here, which highlights our biggest problem. We're no longer on the same page, and I think we haven't been for quite some time." Standing, she slung her purse over her shoulder. "I'm going to head home."

He'd anticipated their chat would come as a surprise and that things could possibly get heated, but he never expected she'd feel so differently than him.

"Nat, wait." She often liked space to process, but she didn't have all the information. If she'd just sit back down and take a second with him, he could explain what an amazing opportunity this was and show her some of the houses he'd looked up. The area around Eden Lake would charm her. She just needed all the details and then they'd be back in sync. "You hardly touched your lunch."

She barely paused in her retreat. "It's okay." Weariness rimmed her words like he hadn't heard in her voice before. "I've had enough." Then without so much as a goodbye, she walked out of the restaurant.

⤜ ⤛

She would not cry. She would not cry. She would not cry.

Natalie slammed the door to her car and spun out of the parking lot before tears could fall or Mason could follow her. Ha! As if he would. No, Mason didn't need to pursue her because he no longer needed her. He no longer asked her opinion on job opportunities. Didn't seek out her advice with résumés. Stopped asking her to help him study his playbook or run new coaching ideas with him. It had been easier to overlook his yawning absence when she had the boys to focus on. Now it was impossible to ignore.

This unsettling inside breathed life into old insecurities, awakening the gangly sophomore Mason had once upon a time invited to dinner. That starstruck girl had said a disbelieving yes and quickly fallen madly in love. It had been easy when Mason seemed equally as infatuated with her. Even after graduation and well into his first year of college, he'd visited her as often as she had him. But when his schedule became crazy, she'd picked up the slack.

When his class load grew heavy, she'd driven to him.

When he accepted a job straight out of college, she'd deferred finishing her own program to join him.

When his career aspirations demanded a new location, she'd packed up and followed him.

Because that fifteen-year-old girl still lived inside, wondering what on earth Mason saw in her, and holding on to the fear that if she didn't put in the effort, he would slip through her fingers.

More than that, she loved Mason and truly desired that he achieve his dream. She'd never faulted him for having one. What saddened her was how he chased that dream with more ferocity than he'd ever chased her.

Wetness trailed down her cheeks, and she angrily swiped at it. Stupid tears!

Here she'd thought maybe, just maybe, Mason had invited her to lunch because he missed her company and wanted to reestablish their bond. Her heart ached for connection with her husband. For him to see her. Choose her.

She leeched out a prayer for God to do something before her marriage completely crumbled. Exhaustion weighted her limbs. She was tired. Oh, so tired of existing in this relationship, anxiously anticipating the day Mason would walk away physically, like he already had emotionally. Lately, fear whispered for her to step away first so she wouldn't be the one left behind. She worked to quiet that fear, but today's lunch felt like a death blow to her defenses.

Sniffing, Natalie turned on her blinker and headed toward home, her small office there, and Wilson. Puppy cuddles and work seemed the perfect medicine for what ailed her. She needed to hop online and study Lewis Carroll's penmanship. If they found the book, one way to authenticate it was to prove the handwriting matched.

After they'd talked through their travel particulars, Caspar had circled back to describe the book to Natalie and her friends. Based on his account, it had a gold binding unlike anything she'd heard of or seen before. Carroll had gifted the special keepsake to friends in memory of their young daughter who'd drowned. Not only was it handwritten and illustrated by him, but he'd also left an inscription inside. All those details would help Natalie ascertain if the copy they found was the one Caspar sought.

She still couldn't believe the manuscript might actually be real. In small crowds, rumors of its existence had swirled for years. What a literary find it would be, and she wondered if Caspar was seeking it for someone else or himself. He'd been instrumental in helping Gertie find the Florentine Diamond, and then they'd returned it to the Viennese government. If this was a similar situation, Caspar most likely would have introduced them once again to the person he sought this treasure for. If she had to guess, she'd say this search was for Caspar alone. Because he was a collector? Or did it have sentimental value to him?

Pulling into her garage, Natalie remembered she still needed to call Harry. Hopefully, he'd be as gracious about her schedule as he claimed to be. Sometimes promises were easy to say but hard to keep.

Wilson greeted her at the door, and she ruffled his fur. "Hey, boy." She placed her purse on the hook in their mudroom. "It's good to see you too." Right. She'd need to change him from daycare to overnight boarding, seeing as Mason was flying to Utah—she assumed—this week as well. She headed for her office, Wilson trailing her. He settled at her feet while she made the two phone calls.

Harry was as jovial, kind, and understanding as he'd promised.

Wilson's stay at Camp Bow Wow was booked.

She and Mason remained at odds.

Her stomach roiled. As if Wilson sensed her churning emotions, he snuggled his head on her lap. She brushed her fingers through his fur, the action calming her. His look of complete adoration certainly helped her heart as well.

After a few moments, she kissed his snout. "Lay down, boy."

He obeyed, cuddling by her feet as she fired up her computer and dove once again into work. Distraction was a phenomenal tool for postponing the truth but a dismal failure at erasing it. She couldn't rewrite the state of her marriage all by herself, but she could procrastinate facing reality for a while longer.

Natalie checked her text thread with Brooke and Everleigh. Brooke had sent a GIF depicting happy dancing after she'd claimed victory on a winning bid for a collectible she and Storm Whitlock had been competing over. Natalie had only met the man once, but that one short encounter had provided enough of a glimpse to recognize tension between him and Brooke. Her friend claimed it stemmed from professional competitiveness. Natalie wasn't buying that explanation. Especially not when Brooke declared Storm an off-limits topic yet brought him up often.

Meanwhile, Everleigh sent a picture of her and Niles on his Harley. His favorite pastime had quickly become hers, or maybe it was more about being together that Everleigh enjoyed. The two of them were deliriously happy in love. Must be nice.

No. Natalie's snark wasn't fair. Everleigh was working hard to change her old self-reliant habits and open herself to relationships, and Natalie was immensely proud of her friend. So if she had to contain her green monster whenever the lovebirds were around, she'd paste on her smile and do just that.

Natalie fired off a picture of her and Wilson before returning to her computer to research Lewis Carroll. Most of his history she already recalled from studying him during a college course.

As a child she'd thought everyone possessed the ability to retain word for word what they read. By the time she was seven, she realized that wasn't true. By the time she was twelve, she realized how much it made her stand out—and not in a good way. She'd wanted to be a part of the pretty and popular group, but instead she'd been relegated to the nerdy intellectuals. She'd begun tanking her grades in hopes she'd be let into the tight circle of popular girls. Unfortunately—at least it felt that way at the time—Mom and Dad had found out, thanks to her big brother's tattletaling ways.

While she couldn't dredge up a smile back then, now her lips easily pulled into one as she remembered the way they'd lovingly lit into her. Mom had been fierce in her stance that Natalie possessed a gift from God and who was she to waste it? Dad added the truth that if she had to dumb herself down for someone to like her, then they weren't smart enough to deserve the amazing friend she'd be. They'd both finished on the fact that junior high wouldn't last forever, but confidence could if she learned early how to obtain and keep it. Then they helped her do just that.

Her parents were one of her biggest blessings in life, and she prayed her boys felt the same about her.

Clicking through different websites, Natalie found some samples of Carroll's handwriting. She studied them for the next hour, locking in on every loop and squiggle that made his penmanship his very own. Then she downloaded a few images and air-dropped them to her phone so she'd have examples to compare when they finally located the book. She spent another hour reading articles about the alleged existence of the book but couldn't nail any new details of its description beyond the ones Caspar had already provided.

Her stomach rumbled, reminding her she hadn't eaten much lunch. Her body might be asking for food, but her appetite remained nil. She microwaved a cup of soup, then took Wilson for his evening walk. Afterward, she packed her suitcase for tomorrow night's flight.

She made sure to be in bed before Mason came home, and he didn't comment on the early hour. They both rose and went to church on Sunday, plastering on smiles for their friends, even while tension bubbled underneath. When they arrived home, they tucked away in their separate corners. She compiled more research in her office while Mason watched sports in the family room.

After his baseball game ended, Mason went for a run while Natalie double-checked her list, added toiletries to her bag, and packed her carry-on. She was in their room when he returned. He leaned against the doorframe, his eyes tracking her movements.

His prolonged silence finally drew her focus to him. His damp T-shirt clung to his chest, and sweat beaded on his forehead. He'd obviously run his hands through his dark hair, because it had that tousled look she loved. Mason had always been attractive to her, especially after a workout. Call her crazy, but the sweat never bothered her. Not when his strength and confidence oozed from every pore too. His dark eyes would capture her with a look that said he was fully aware of his effect on her. Even now, heat flooded her body as memories played before she could stop them.

Only this time as they shared a stare, Mason's expression seemed guarded. "You planning on talking before you leave?" He stepped closer. "Or should I anticipate this radio silence until you get home?"

With a sigh, she placed her folded cardigan over her carry-on. "You've been quiet too."

"Because I was trying to give you space."

He knew she processed best with space, but right now what she craved was closeness with him. How did he not see that?

Her heart pounded, and her tongue stuck to the roof of her mouth. Why was this so hard? She excelled at handling conflict with friends, but she froze when it came to her marriage. Maybe her brothers weren't as far off in their assessment of her as she'd thought.

Mason spoke into the stiffness between them. "Nat, I know this could lead to a change in plans, but I didn't pursue this opportunity. They came to me." He swallowed. "There's no guarantee that they'll hire me, but I have to try. You know I've always wanted this."

She did know that. She'd walked into their marriage with her eyes wide open to that fact, but his choice of pronoun battered her heart. He used to say "we." Or had that simply been what she'd heard when he'd promised to love and cherish her *above all else*?

Her fingers tightened in the soft fabric of her sweater. "You've never said differently, so I understand your decision." A plethora of emotions swirled inside. She'd need to sort through them before figuring out how to convey them, but she didn't have the time. Maybe this trip was coming at the right moment. She picked up her backpack. "I wasn't sure when you were flying out, so I switched Wilson from daycare to boarding for the week."

Following her change in conversation, Mason glanced at their fur baby. "Good idea. I leave tomorrow."

"Can you drop him off on your way?"

He nodded.

Natalie pulled up the handle on her suitcase. "I should go. We're taking off from a private airstrip just outside of Chicago. I'll let you know when we land."

Mason stood in front of her and scrubbed the back of his head. "From zero interest in flying to a globe-trotter in a matter of months." He chuffed. "Who are you?"

His words were light, and he attempted a smile, no doubt because he'd always been able to settle tension between them with his smirk and some sort of quip. Natalie no longer saw any humor in their broken relationship.

"I've been asking the same question about you, Mace." She forced herself to look him directly in the eye when all she wanted to do was hide. "Lately it feels like we want different things."

A deep frown wrinkled his forehead. "You said something like that in the restaurant yesterday, and I'm so confused. Do you want something different? Because I still want the same things."

Did he not see how they'd shifted through the years? His late nights had transitioned from them talking over the dinner table to him alone in his office at work. Rather than sharing strategies for nurturing their boys with her, he shared tactics for winning games with his players. He'd been raising athletes while she was raising their children. In the midst of it all, they'd drifted apart.

"That's not true, Mace. You used to want me." Rolling her suitcase to the door, she paused. "Go to Utah. Chase your dream." How she wished that was still her. "We'll talk when we both get back."

Maybe by then she'd know what to say.

CHAPTER SIX

Luciana Perez, age fifteen
Lekeitio, Spain, 1929

THERE WERE MOMENTS LUCIANA WANTED to remember and moments she wanted to forget.

Her first kiss with Angus Forsythe would remain in her heart forever. Her lips still tingled, and her stomach swirled each time the memory replayed. It created the sweetness against a backdrop of bitter remembrances she longed to ignore but couldn't.

Papi was not the man she thought him to be.

Ever since that night when she'd sneaked downstairs and overheard him in his study, she'd done her very best to spin a story that would make sense of the scene. But as her friendship with Adelheid and her brother, Otto, had developed, it had become impossible to write off their continued discoveries. Papi wasn't a simple vigneron, tending to the grapes in their fields. He also tended to people's jewels, artwork, and collectibles, including for Empress Zita, her dear friend's mother.

While there remained much Luciana didn't know about this side of her father, what she had witnessed hurt her heart. The papi who read stories of Alice to her and her little sisters looked nothing like the man she'd seen in dealings with strangers. That man possessed a sternness and chill that, had she not been the recipient of his soft side, would frighten her. In truth, at times fear did threaten, but Papi never once used that persona with her, her little sisters, or Mamá.

Would he though? If he caught her in his study sneaking glances at the black journal he scribbled his notes in? She didn't want to find out, yet she'd promised Adelheid she'd check if the transaction that had occurred today involved the Florentine Diamond. The yellow jewel was precious to her friend, and each time Papi met with the empress, Adelheid worried her mother had sold the jewel. As of yet, she had not. The empress had parted with many of her crown jewels, but so far she'd maintained possession of the diamond she'd promised Adelheid would wear on her wedding day.

Luciana tiptoed into Papi's study. When she'd turned thirteen, Papi and Mamá had allowed her to have her own room. The freedom made it easier for her to sneak around at night, as her new location moved her farther from her parents while also providing proximity to the back staircase.

Moonlight filtered in through the windows behind Papi's desk, casting the room in an ethereal glow. As she moved to open the drawer that held his journal, her eyes caught on a book on Papi's shelves. *Alice's Adventures Under Ground*. She crossed to it and ran her fingers along the golden spine. It had been years since this book had sat on her bedside table. When she'd moved to her new room, evening story time with Papi hadn't accompanied her but rather remained in the nursery with her little sisters, who never chose to hear about Alice's adventures. Eventually, Papi had placed the book here in his study. He said he was keeping it safe for her to hand down to her firstborn one day.

Perhaps it was experiencing her first kiss, knowing she stood on the cusp of adulthood, childish adventures having long been tucked away, that forced nostalgia to overtake her tonight. She pulled the cherished book from its slot and cracked it open. Her fingers trailed over words she didn't need to read. They were a part of her. This book remained as special to her as it did to Papi.

She tugged the bookmark free from its slot in the spine and pressed her fingertips into the small holes carved in the gold. Would Papi miss the book if she brought it back to her room?

A tap at the window jolted her heart practically out of her chest. She slammed the book closed and twirled around. Angus's face peered through the panes of glass.

Luciana quickly shelved *Alice's Adventures* and raced to Angus. "Angus Forsythe!" she whispered. "What are you doing here?"

His grin sent her stomach tumbling and her heart racing, but this time not out of fear. "Coming to see ye, of course." His thick Scottish accent rolled over her as he motioned for her to open the window.

She did, and he climbed through. Luciana darted a glance toward the door to ensure she'd closed it. "If my papi catches you . . ." She shivered, unable to think through the thrashing they'd likely both receive.

"He will no'." Angus spoke in his charmingly confident way. "But if he did, it'd be worth it. Ye shouldn't have to sneak around all alone." His hand took hers. "I told ye I care for ye, and that means I'm here to help. No matter the cost."

This boy . . . No, at almost eighteen, he was nearly a man. They'd been friends for years, ever since his family had moved here from Scotland. His fair, freckled skin and red hair stood in stark contrast to all her other friends, and he was often teased for it. He never seemed to mind. Angus was proud of his heritage and maintained his thick brogue, even though she highly suspected he deepened it on purpose whenever he spoke to her. She'd long believed he saw her as a little sister, especially with the terrible way he pestered her, though never about the birthmark on her cheek like other children often did. Mamá told her his teasing meant something else, and recently Angus had proven Mamá correct—much to Papi's chagrin. He did not believe Angus good enough for her.

Luciana could not dream of anyone better.

These past months, Angus had shown up in more and more hours of her days, and not to bother her, but to listen. He'd walk alongside her on the way home from school and offer to carry her books. He'd join her beneath the giant oak out front, helping her hang laundry. And one afternoon when he'd found her crying in the vineyards, he'd coaxed from her the truths about Papi. Today he'd seen her on her way home from Adelheid's, and she'd revealed her plans for tonight. She'd never thought he'd join her.

She feared what Papi would do should he catch them in here.

Her hands went to his shoulders. "You should go. I never should have opened the window."

His fingers encircled her wrists, and he removed her grip but maintained his. "Have ye already looked at the journal?"

She shook her head.

"Then show me where it is, and I'll look." When she hesitated, he released one wrist so he could cup her cheek. "Ye are no longer alone, Luciana. I will carry this burden with ye."

She didn't know she was capable of love like this, but Angus had claimed her heart, and with each word he captured more territory. "Over here." Clasping his hand, she led him to Papi's desk and handed him the journal.

Angus opened the worn book and turned to where the final entry was listed. His fingers traced the words. "It mentions an emerald ring but nothing about a diamond."

Relief broke the tension in Luciana's shoulders. "Oh, thank goodness. I worried so about Adelheid's feelings should it be the Florentine. She's very much attached to that piece."

Angus's attention remained on the journal as he paged through it. "Nearly all the lines in here are full. Jewels. Paintings. Sculptures."

"That's not his only journal." She'd read others through the years.

His eyes met hers as he closed the book. "Ye've never asked him about any of this?"

Luciana shook her head.

"Perhaps there's an explanation ye've no' thought of." Angus once again cupped her cheek. "The vineyards can be fickle. This may very well be how yer papi has cared so well for yer family throughout the years. Ye've never gone hungry or wanted a roof over yer head." He looked around the room. "In fact, the roof he's provided is the nicest in town."

Luciana was well aware that Angus's family endured more struggles than hers. Their immigrant status here in Lekeitio, along with their lack of money, made them a target by many, including Papi. Though they were hard workers, they'd yet to achieve even a quarter of the status her family possessed.

Meanwhile, Angus's paternal grandparents had found great success in America and repeatedly coaxed Angus's father to join them in a small town called Kenton Corners. Their last letter mentioned a need for help maintaining their business, along with the promise of building a large home for him. They'd already bought a parcel of land, should Angus's father decide to move his family.

Angus vowed that no matter what, he would stay here in Lekeitio with her.

She gripped his shirt and settled her forehead against his chest. "I would rather my papi be the man I thought he was than have a beautiful roof over my head. A home is made by the people inside it, not the structure around them."

"Aye, 'tis true." He pressed into his accent. "But as a man, I want both for those I love." He waited for her to look at him, and when she did, he smiled. "It is my promise to ye, Luciana. Ye will no' want for either. I'll give ye both a man ye can always believe in and a shelter from all yer storms—a beautiful one at that."

People would tell them they were too young to make such promises, but looking into his eyes, Luciana believed each word he spoke. With that belief came the fierce resolution that she would marry Angus Forsythe no matter what anyone said, including Papi. Because like Papi had taught her, it was her story, and she could write it however she chose.

CHAPTER SEVEN

NATALIE WASN'T SURE IF SHE was coming or going. Her mind had been spinning since walking out her front door yesterday . . . That was only yesterday, right? Flying overnight, time changes, and jet lag only compounded the fuzziness in her head. How she'd left things with Mason certainly didn't help either. It was hard to focus on anything when it felt as if one's twenty-two-year marriage was ending.

"You sure everything is okay?" Everleigh asked from across the small table they'd settled at for lunch. "You've been uncharacteristically quiet."

They'd landed a few hours ago, driven the forty-five minutes north to their hotel, and dropped their luggage before heading out to explore. They hadn't made it much farther than a quaint outdoor café, where deep-green iron tables and aromas of sweet and savory food beckoned them to stop.

"Not that it's a bad thing," Brooke added, though she softened her words with a tiny smile.

Natalie, in turn, plastered on a large grin and stuffed down her emotions. She appreciated her friends, but Colmar, France, was a once-in-a-lifetime trip, and she refused to mar it with her personal struggles. "We were all quiet. It was an overnight flight."

Laughter bubbled from Brooke. "Truth." She stretched, and the cap sleeves of her collared blouse pulled tight. Tiny white polka dots covered the black snug-tailored shirt, which she'd tucked into slim black pedal pants. In the past few weeks, she'd maintained her dark color palette but had thrown herself completely into this vintage look. The sleek ponytail she preferred fit this facade as well, as it had her denim and leather phase. "But I think Everleigh's referring to the time since we woke up."

"Exactly." Everleigh leaned back as a waitress filled her water glass. "Typically you'd have an itinerary for us today, along with running commentary on all the scenery."

Natalie perused the square. Old Town in Colmar possessed a fairy-tale feeling, with cobblestone streets and half-timbered Renaissance houses in an array of subdued colors. Farther along, those houses lined La Lauch, a canal that snaked through the streets where Old Town met Little Venice. Flowers spilled from boxes attached to the black iron fence bordering the water, and many people rode bikes with wicker baskets attached to the handlebars.

Birds chirped around them. A warm breeze swayed their white tablecloth. Children's laughter echoed through the streets. This was truly one of the most magical, beautiful places she'd ever seen. If she could clear her head of her troubles, maybe she'd create enough space to appreciate being here.

Natalie stiffened as her eyes landed on a familiar-looking dark-haired man disappearing around a corner. Okay, her head must be as troubled as her heart, because there was no way she'd just seen the Matt she'd met at the Golden Key. Her eyes had to be playing tricks on her due to the questions lingering in the back of her mind, but all her mental energy centered on solving the problems of her marriage, not the mystery of Matt.

"Nat?" Everleigh prodded.

"Sorry." She dragged her attention back to her friends and what they'd been teasing her about—being the coordinator of their little group. "I was simply waiting until you two were sufficiently awake enough to appreciate the knowledge I'm about to drop on you." Her spiel was cut short by their waitress delivering bread and olive oil, but as she walked away, Natalie resumed. "We are currently in the heart of Colmar. Once we finish with lunch, we can walk ten minutes to the small bridge over La Lauch and—if there's not too long of a line—take a canal boat ride. It's supposed to be one of the best ways to see the city."

"And there's the planner we all know and love." Brooke tore a piece off the baguette at their table and dragged it through seasoned olive oil. "Go on. Dazzle us with more knowledge."

"I need to hold some details for the boat ride."

"What?" Brooke widened her bright-blue eyes. "And step on our tour guide's toes? You're way too polite to do that."

"She's not wrong," Everleigh added.

Natalie settled into her chair, thankful she'd been able to distract them—and herself. "A person's occupation determined the color of their house. For instance, fishermen had blue houses and butchers had red." She pointed to the creamy house behind Everleigh. Its brown shutters had hearts carved into them. "And the shape in the shutters created a secret message."

Everleigh, puzzle master that she was, perked up. "How so?"

"Hearts like that one meant a single woman lived there and was looking for love."

Brooke scoffed. "No thank you. What shape meant happily single?"

Natalie's heart tightened. She couldn't envision a world where she'd place the adjective "happily" in front of that term.

"Hey." Everleigh swung back around, and her laser-sharp blue eyes focused intently on Natalie. "You look a little green."

"Yeah," Brooke agreed. "You've gone Kermit on us."

"Told you something was bugging her," Everleigh low-key mumbled to Brooke before speaking louder. "Spill."

Their lunch arrived at that exact moment, causing the perfect interruption. Their waitress just earned herself a huge tip. It grew exponentially when the woman inquired if anyone wanted fresh Parmesan on their entrées. Natalie gladly accepted and let her go to town on grating it over her salmon risotto.

As their server retreated, Natalie scooped a bit of her dish into her mouth. Heavenly.

"Go right on and enjoy. We have no place to be until tomorrow morning." Everleigh pulled her brown waves into a ponytail and shed the light layer she'd worn to lunch. Then she dug into her own entrée, a bowl piled high with spaghetti and meatballs. She appeared perfectly content to sit here for the foreseeable future.

Natalie could be equally as stubborn. She'd raised two boys. Stubbornness, at times, was the only thing that got her through the day. "Does the plan remain to meet the butler of Mr. Hollis's estate at ten tomorrow?"

"It does." Brooke nodded. She'd been the one to set the appointment. "I'm very curious as to what we'll find. From what the butler said, Mr. Hollis was a bit of a pack rat."

"You mentioned that after speaking with him," Everleigh noted. "I wish Niles and Gertie had been able to join us. I think we could probably use the extra set of hands."

Gertie had come down with the flu over the weekend, and Niles had agreed to stay home with her. Natalie knew their friend hated being left behind. Adventure ran in Gertie's blood. "How's she feeling?"

"Tired and cranky," Everleigh said.

"Poor Niles." Natalie knew what it was like to take care of a cranky sick person. Mason became a giant baby whenever he caught a virus.

"Poor Gertie. Niles's bedside manner is severely lacking." Everleigh tapped her foot at a bird hopping nearby. "Burt said he'd stop by and check on them both."

Gertie's old FBI partner was not-so-secretly in love with her. "I have no doubt he'll spoil her rotten." Natalie both admired and envied the attention Burt lavished on Gertie. It had been far too long since Mason had treated her with such thoughtfulness. If he even showed an ounce of the care Burt heaped on Gertie, Natalie might be optimistic about her and Mason's future. As it was, she had more confidence in Burt's chances—which wasn't saying much. "Think there's any hope for him to win her over?"

Everleigh shrugged. "It's possible. I mean, the Bible says faith, hope, and love abide together. Burt seems to possess all three, especially when it comes to Gertie."

"Along with patience. It's his biggest virtue, I think." Brooke pushed away her empty plate. She treated eating like an unnecessary task that simply had to be completed. "I can't imagine waiting for anyone as long as he's waited for her."

"Unrequited love is definitely not fun." The words slipped from Natalie before she had enough sense to stop them.

"Annnd, we are back to you needing to spill." Everleigh settled her elbows on the table. "If you want to make it to La Lauch and that canal ride, you should start talking."

"I think I liked you better when you weren't invested in this relationship," Natalie mumbled.

Brooke straightened. "The sweet one shows her saucy side."

Natalie groaned. "I'm sorry. I—"

Everleigh held up her hand. "No apology necessary, Nat. It's obvious something's bugging you, and you took enough of my salty attitude this spring. You never held it against me, and I'm not going to with you either." She turned and smiled at Brooke. "See, I'm learning."

Brooke rolled her eyes. "Only time will tell."

Those two acted like sisters. Laughing one moment, bickering the next. Time truly would tell where their relationship landed, but based on what she'd been seeing, Natalie believed good things lay ahead for them.

For her and Mason? Not so much.

She pulled in a long breath. "I think my marriage is over."

That silenced them both. Well, at least for a few seconds.

"Over, over?" Brooke clarified. "We know things have been tense for a little while, but what happened?"

Appetite gone, Natalie pushed her plate away. "Mason is interviewing for a coaching job in Utah. He didn't ask me what I thought or if I was okay moving again sooner than we'd planned. He simply assumed I'd follow him."

"You don't want to move?" Everleigh asked.

Natalie shook her head. "No." She watched a young couple stroll past hand in hand. She honestly couldn't remember the last time Mason had reached for hers, but she could remember the first time he'd entwined their fingers. She'd felt safe. Cherished. Special . . . Secure.

It had been years since she'd felt that sense of groundedness with him.

"Nat?" Brooke prodded with uncharacteristic concern in her tone.

"Sorry." She tried to shake off her melancholy, but it wasn't going anywhere. "It's not actually about relocating. It's . . ." She paused. She'd spent practically the entire nine-hour flight here focused on her and Mason. Acknowledging her thoughts out loud somehow made everything feel real, but ignoring truth didn't turn it into a falsehood or make it disappear. "When we moved back to Kenton Corners, he promised we'd be there at least three years. He's breaking his word because his career is more important to him than I am. He's choosing it yet again over me, and I'm tired of coming in a distant second." Her stomach churned as bigger fears mounted.

Everleigh gripped Natalie's hand. "Did you tell him that?"

Natalie shook her head. "I know I need to, but I'm not sure it'll change anything. Mason has made it abundantly clear what matters most to him." She glanced down at her wedding rings. Dirt clouded the diamonds, and scratches marred the gold. How long had it been since she'd cleaned them? She sighed. "And I shouldn't have to beg to be noticed by my husband."

"Telling someone how you feel isn't begging for anything," Everleigh said.

"You certainly haven't had any problem telling me how you feel," Brooke added.

"That's different." Natalie clicked her nails together as she spoke.

"How?" Brooke challenged.

"I don't know, but it just is." Except she did know. Her eyes misted as she faced the answer she'd uncovered on the plane.

Growing up with three brothers and raising two boys, Natalie didn't have a problem speaking logically and confidently into stressful situations to defuse them. She'd learned to separate her emotions and handle what was in front of her. Same when it came to her work. She possessed confidence in spades when a circumstance required head knowledge. But when it came to her heart? All she felt was vulnerable and shaky.

Her silence with Mason was a protective measure. What if she found the courage to tell him how she felt, and he still chose his career over her? Or admitted that he wanted to move on without her?

From where she sat, ignorance might not be bliss, but it did feel safer somehow. Except maintaining this status quo hadn't prevented her from feeling bruised and battered inside.

If only she held a guarantee that talking to Mason would make things better, not worse.

❖ ❖

Natalie wrapped her robe tightly around herself and watched as the sun broke over the horizon in Colmar. Restless, she'd slipped onto her tiny balcony in the early morning twilight with a cup of tea and a packet of the complimentary biscuits. Temps had dropped from their high in the mid-seventies yesterday to the fifties overnight, but she preferred the cooler weather. It reminded her of her favorite season—fall. Summer was simply a speed bump on the way to all things autumn. Give her cozy drinks, cardigans, and thick blankets any day of the year.

Yesterday, after she had spilled her guts to Brooke and Everleigh, her friends had done their best to help sidetrack her sticky emotions by exploring every corner of the city. They'd walked and shopped and sampled several versions of *Kugelhopf*, a brioche-based bread studded with rum-soaked raisins and baked in a special Bundt pan. The delicious treat was a delicacy in this Alsace region of France, and her favorite slice had been from the Gilg Pastry Shop in Little Venice.

Her carb-loving heart had loved indulging in a treat she'd taken a break from (bread and her middle-aged middle were not friends), and the afternoon proved a successful diversion. Then night had arrived, along with too much silence. She'd spent most of the dark hours staring at the ceiling. Was her marriage truly on the brink of ending? If so, how would she tell her parents? How would she and Mason tell the boys? What would holidays and birthdays look like?

She nibbled on the dry biscuit, hoping it would soothe her rolling stomach. How far she and Mace had journeyed from those teenagers once tossed together like the hero and heroine of her favorite romance trope. Mason Daughtry, the star senior of the football team, who'd been forced to accept tutoring help from her, a lowly underclassman. They'd spent months together studying, and the day his second-trimester grades arrived—clinching the fact that he'd graduate—he'd picked her up, twirled her around, and asked her to a celebratory dinner at Olive Garden.

That night they'd talked about everything except school, and at the end of the evening, he'd walked her to the door and kissed her. Her. Natalie Riggs. Nerdy captain of the debate team. Library volunteer. History geek. They were such opposites, yet he claimed he was falling in love with her.

She'd naively believed him, and her heart had leapt with his. All these years later, her heart still belonged to him, but her naivete was gone. She could no longer pretend not to see the truth of the state of their relationship.

She sniffed. This felt suspiciously like grief, and she supposed it was, because something was dying—her marriage. And along with it, the future she'd imagined. This wasn't the fairy-tale ending she'd thought she and Mason would reach, but this also wasn't a story she was writing alone. She and Mace were coauthors with different visions. His had tunneled until all it included was the pursuit of a college position. Hers had grown to include new adventures and friendships. Places where she was needed and wouldn't be left behind.

Their paths had diverged, and she needed to find the courage to ask if his would curve to meet hers again or if he planned to continue along on his own. Living in the unknown hadn't made her worry disappear—it had allowed it to grow. Mason's answer could very well hurt, but she'd reached the point where a known pain seemed more manageable than this buzzing, open-ended anxiety.

With a sigh, she finished her now-cold tea. There wasn't anything she could do about her marriage now, so she'd set it aside and focus on the task in front of her. She wasn't meeting Brooke and Everleigh for another two hours. They planned to have breakfast and then drive to Mr. Hollis's home and begin exploring. Hopefully, by the end of the day, they'd find the copy of the book they'd come for, though there was a minute possibility that it no longer resided in the home. The butler continued to warn them of what a pack rat Mr. Hollis had been, but Natalie couldn't envision the job would be all that difficult. If she could find missing textbooks or socks within her teenage boys' rooms, she could certainly find a rare edition of a Lewis Carroll book inside a collector's home.

With time to kill, Natalie decided to shower and explore the city some more. Supposedly, this town had been used as inspiration for the animated version of *Beauty and the Beast*, right down to the fountain Belle perched on in the opening scene. Maybe she would find that place on her map and head there. After all, book-loving Belle was one of her favorite characters, so how could she be this close to such a sight and not visit it?

Natalie headed for the bathroom. She quickly showered and wrapped herself in a towel. Steam billowed in the tiny room. Ugh, there wasn't a fan in here, and she'd start sweating if she didn't get rid of this hot air. Opening the bathroom door, she opted to remain in only her towel until after she dried her hair.

After sticking in her earbuds, she pressed Play on her latest audiobook and fired up her hair dryer. Between the book and the whirring noise, she never heard the man entering her room, but she caught sight of him out of the corner of her eye.

Screaming, she hurled her brush at him.

"Agh! Nat! It's me!" Her intruder held both hands up in the air.

Heart pounding, Natalie stood with her hair dryer aimed at him and blinked rapidly. Her brain couldn't catch up with her eyes. The last person in the world she expected to see stood stock-still in her hotel room—in France—with a rumpled polo shirt, wayward hair, and sleep-deprived eyes. Oh, and another red mark from her on his face, only this time on his cheek.

She turned off her dryer. "Mason?"

CHAPTER EIGHT

MASON BENT TO RETRIEVE HER brush. "If I give this back to you, do you promise not to chuck it at me again?" He wasn't kidding when he said she could teach his pitchers a thing or two. His wife had amazing aim. "Or your phone?"

"Mason?" she repeated, because apparently it was the only coherent word her mind could conjure. The small towel wrapped around her slipped, and she fisted it against her chest.

Mason's eyes trailed over her, and he swallowed. It had been a long time since he'd seen Nat in so little. Heat tightened his abdomen, and his pulse raced. The desire to step forward and greet her with the kind of kiss meant to drop that towel nearly overwhelmed him. But Nat hadn't kissed him like that in over a year. Used to be she couldn't get enough of him. Now he worried she'd had her fill. While his libido pushed him to move, he held back.

Instead, he offered her a smile. "I know you hate wet hair. Why don't you finish getting ready, and I'll hang out on the patio." He motioned toward her sliding glass doors before heading to them.

Based on the sound of the bathroom door closing, it took Natalie another ten seconds before she snapped out of her daze. He'd meant to surprise her. Mission accomplished. He hadn't meant to freak her out. Mission failed.

Exhausted, he dropped into one of the wicker chairs, leaned his head back, and closed his eyes. His body hadn't caught up with the flight here. Truth be told, his mind ran in overtime, trying to catch up as well. A day ago he'd been sitting at the airport, waiting for his flight to Utah to board, when the university called and told him not to come. They were going another direction and didn't want to waste his time. It was like sacking the quarterback before he'd even had a chance to pass the ball. The loss hurt more than his baseball team's defeat in the semifinals last week.

He'd planned to go home, until he remembered his house was empty. Then Nat's demeanor as she'd left replayed in his head, only this time it hit differently. Worry niggled inside that a third loss could very well be on his horizon. So he'd changed his game plan and hopped a plane here, unsure of what he'd find but desperately in need of a win. Especially where his wife was concerned.

What would it take for her to be proud of him? For her to look at him as if he had something to offer her again? He'd never be her equal, but he missed being valued by her.

The patio door slid open, and Natalie joined him. She hadn't straightened her hair. Instead, her natural waves hung loose and free, his favorite look on her. Lately she'd been wearing her hair like that again. It reminded him of the girl who used to adventure with him. The one he'd entice to try new things. That girl had lived a little more loudly than this Natalie, or at least the Nat she'd become over the past two decades. Her subtle shift back to her old self had happened when she'd met Caspar and the other women she now worked alongside.

What plagued him was the fact that they'd been able to resurrect a side of her he'd watched slowly die. Why hadn't he been enough to sustain it?

"Hey," he greeted her.

"Hey." Her gaze tracked to the city landscape rather than holding his.

While the strained silence was new, this awkward feeling remained familiar.

From the first moments of their relationship, he'd known he couldn't keep up with her intellect or even nourish it, but he could feed her adventurous side. The first time she'd scaled the rock wall at his gym and rang that bell . . . the massive grin on her face and joy in her laughter . . . he knew—her wins were his sweetest victories. He'd worked hard to help her experience more and more of them, but somewhere along the way, something had shifted.

As their joint adventures diminished and her career grew, it became apparent that Natalie's best successes happened without him by her side. He'd stepped back so she could thrive, no longer attending work functions, business trips, or award ceremonies with her, where he'd proved more a hindrance than a help. But he'd never intended for this much space to stretch between them. Somehow they needed to find a way to address the gap before it widened and became impassable.

Even now, rather than sit by him, Natalie crossed to the iron railing on her balcony and leaned against it. She faced him, no doubt waiting for an explanation as to his presence. One that had unintentionally scared her.

He offered her a smile. "Sorry I frightened you. I did knock before entering. I even called your name."

"I had earbuds in."

"I figured." She wore them every morning.

Her eyes narrowed with a look of confusion. "How did you get into my room?" She paused, then, "And what are you even doing here?"

He did his best not to read into her question, but it pummeled his largest insecurity—was he an embarrassment to her? Not ready to face her answer, he swallowed his question and answered hers instead. "I tried having the front desk call up, but you must have been in the shower, so I called the number you left for John, since he made the booking. He connected with the front desk, then they checked my ID and gave me a key."

"Seriously? What if your ID was fake? You could be a killer."

He snorted. "You read way too many of those romantic suspense books."

"Thrillers," she corrected.

"Romantic thrillers then," he conceded. "With unrealistic heroes who always save the day."

"They're not unrealistic."

"Right. Every man has six-pack abs, knows tae kwon do, carries a Glock, and spouts mushy words of endearment right before taking out the bad guys."

"That is not—" She gripped the railing behind her. "How did we even get on this topic?"

"You—"

She stopped him with both her upheld hand and downturned eyes. That expression on her face . . . it was the one she wore when she was unsure about something. "Why are you here, Mace?"

He worked his jaw as he glanced over the view from her balcony. Her curiosity wasn't unexpected, nor was the fact that she hadn't leapt into his arms upon arrival. But he hadn't anticipated her uncertainty. Was she unsure of them? Or his presence here with her new friends?

Whatever the cause, he couldn't blame her for feeling insecure, because he felt it too. His throat tightened, and he fought the voice inside telling him to play it cool. *Don't be the first to be vulnerable.* He silenced it. He hadn't flown halfway around the world to stay quiet, and not laying himself bare ran a greater risk than exposing his feelings.

"I came for you, Nat." His eyes held her hazel ones, and the gold lines in them shimmered. The swirl of greens, brown, and gold had captured him the very first time she'd looked at him. That attraction had grown as they'd sat shoulder to shoulder in their high school library, studying. He'd been in awe of her intelligence and a little jealous of how easily learning came to her. What did a girl like her see in a jock like him? Yet somehow he'd won her over. Twenty-seven years later, he hoped to repeat his teenage success.

He stood and neared her, but he didn't touch her. Rather, he gripped the back of his neck and, for a quick second, focused on the ground before returning to those eyes he still wanted a lifetime to gaze into. Huh. Guess he could be mushy when the time warranted. "I was at the airport, and I somehow found myself on a plane to France instead." Didn't need to share his loss in Utah with her. He only had a three-pack, could toss a half-decent punch, didn't own a gun, and apparently knew a few gushy words, but none of that compensated for his inability to succeed in his career. Not when Natalie killed it at hers. At everything she attempted. She actually had awards on her bookshelves at home, while his trophy cases remained empty. A stark reminder he'd married up.

Her brow wrinkled, like it used to when he'd explain confusing plays she was determined to understand. "You just somehow wound up on a flight here?"

"I . . . I didn't like how we left things. You told me to chase my dream, so here I am." Those wrinkles smoothed as surprise lit her face. He couldn't tell if it was good surprise or bad surprise, and the fact that she remained silent worried him. "That is if you're okay with me being here?"

His heart rate kicked up, and he tensed as her silence lengthened. All right, maybe showing up uninvited hadn't been his best idea ever, but he had to try. If he was going to lose something else, it wasn't about to be Natalie.

After the longest pause known in the history of the world, in which his stomach knotted and sweat beaded between his shoulder blades, Nat spoke. "Yes, Mace. I mean, I'm still fighting off the shock, and I have a lot of questions, but I'm okay with you being here."

His pulse regulated then spiked when a small smile tugged on her lips. In it he caught glimpses of the same cautious hope welling in him.

"How about I call down for room service? I know you hate airplane food, so you've got to be starving."

"You don't have to meet your friends?"

She waved him off even as she moved toward her room. "They'll understand if I miss breakfast."

And she most likely wasn't ready for him to horn in on them. Sure, she'd invited him on her Vienna trip last month as a courtesy, but she knew he'd been headed into playoffs and would have to say no—the best answer for them both. Accompanying her on some swanky trip overseas where she'd be photographed and interviewed by government officials— even if it were done quietly—wasn't a scene he'd add anything to. Quite the contrary, he'd detract from it, and he wasn't about to do that to her again. One time at an important awards gala had been enough. He'd not forgotten that night, the name mix-up that had highlighted how out of his depth he'd been there, or the look on Natalie's face.

His goal here in France was to pursue his wife while not embarrassing her.

He hoped he was up to the task.

⇨ ⇦

Natalie set down her phone. She'd texted Everleigh and Brooke right after placing a room-service order. Yes, they both understood, but they also had questions. Lots of them. She couldn't answer them because she had her own, only one of which she'd already asked Mason—why had he come?

She was still chewing on his response—both verbal and nonverbal— because he'd seemed to shrink a little when she'd asked, though he'd quickly recovered. Mason possessed a bold confidence she'd never seen in anyone else, so she had to have read him wrong.

His soft confession that he'd come for her soothed the ache she'd been carrying for so long. Her sore heart remained tender, and she fought against the fear to believe for change. What was broken between them couldn't be fixed with one sentence, but his grand gesture rivaled that of the heroes he'd made fun of. Maybe they weren't at the end of their story after all. She joined him again on the deck

His eyes flickered over hers. "You get a hold of your friends?"

"I did." This time she took the seat across from him. "We have a little over an hour until we have to meet them in the lobby."

"We?" That hint of insecurity she thought she'd spied earlier returned. "You sure you want me to tag along? I can just wait here at the hotel."

"You came all this way—you might as well help." She clasped her hands over her abdomen.

"I came for you," he corrected.

There was so much to unpack in those few words. She reached inside and pulled out the first piece. "About that. I have to say I'm a bit confused. You turned down Vienna for a White Sox game, but you have an interview of a lifetime, and you miss it to join me in France? I don't get it."

Mason looked so genuinely perplexed that for a second Natalie thought she had spoken a different language. He straightened on his chair. "What are you talking about? I tagged out of Vienna because I wanted to make sure the guys were ready for their playoff game."

"But you had tickets to a White Sox game and said how it was their best season."

"It is their best season," he acknowledged. "But I didn't stay home for them."

"You're telling me if it weren't for the playoffs, you'd have come to Vienna?" His hesitation said it all. She sniffed. "Exactly."

Mason didn't seem to appreciate her one-word response. "You're telling me you truly *wanted* me to come to Vienna?"

"I invited you, didn't I?"

"That's not an actual answer, Nat," he challenged.

Room service knocked on the door before she could answer.

He sighed. "They're conveniently fast."

Rolling her eyes, Natalie went to let them in. The arrival of breakfast allowed for some breathing room between them. Once the attendant had delivered the food to their patio and ensured they had everything they needed, he left them alone. Mason waited for her to sit before taking his own seat. They both dug into their meals, neither breaking the silence that again stretched between them.

Finally, Mason set down his fork. "How are we on such separate pages about this?"

"Honestly? I feel like we've been in completely different books lately."

The edge of his lip picked up. "Different playbooks."

"You would move us into a sports analogy."

"Just trying for a level playing field since we were talking about heroes and thrillers earlier." When she didn't laugh, he sobered. "How'd we get here, Nat?"

This wasn't a conversation she expected to have in France, but he'd come all this way. She could dig out that courage she'd been hunting for earlier and verbally meet him here.

Sucking in a breath, she plunged. "We drifted apart." She'd alluded to the fact with him multiple times, but now she laid it out there directly. Giving voice to those words made their problems feel all too real. Especially when Mason's face crumpled worse than that time in college when he'd thrown an interception that had cost his team their division title.

Natalie blinked back sudden tears.

Mason reached across the table and took her hand, the move surprising her, but she didn't pull away. "We're not apart now. We're both sitting right here."

"I . . . I don't know, Mace." She peeked up at the sky, doing her best to rein in her ping-ponging emotions. Gently she pulled her hand away. "I mean, you showing up here is sweet, but is Utah just on pause? Or when we get home, are you still going to pursue it?"

He glanced out over the skyline of Colmar, where the sunshine filled blue sky. Birds called from rooftop to rooftop, and below, people of the town began their day. A few trills from bells on bikes made their way up to them, and the yeasty scent of fresh bread from the bakery down the street wafted in the air. Natalie absorbed the moment, reaching for the peace it conveyed even as her stomach roiled at Mason's silence.

Finally he returned his focus to hers. "I want to coach at a college level—you've always known that about me. I don't know where that will wind up being, but . . ."

"You won't give up pursuing it." But could he balance things better? Place her above the pursuit of his career, or at least still bring her alongside him while he chased down his success? Because this feeling of being left behind hurt.

"Is it really so awful that I want to be successful at what I do? I would think you'd not only understand that desire, but it would make you proud of me." He batted away a fly. "I've been incredibly proud of each of your successes."

"So proud that you only came to one of my award ceremonies." The first one. Sure, they weren't nearly as exciting as a ball game, but they were important to her. Mason would toss her a congrats or tell her to enjoy herself as she slipped out the door to attend solo yet again. Maybe he thought that showed his investment, but honestly? It only made things worse. It proved he understood what it meant to her yet chose to not stand alongside her.

Red darkened his cheeks. "Nat—"

"I'm sorry." She cut him off. His chagrined look had her instantly regretting her snappish actions. "That was uncalled for and incredibly unhelpful." She took a deep breath and refocused. "I appreciate your compliment"— though she longed for action with his words—"and of course I want your success."

"But?" Mason prodded, knowing her well enough to understand she had more to say.

She fiddled with her napkin. "I don't want to move again, Mason. I don't want to start over. I like the life I'm building in Kenton Corners. I like being settled. I can't keep chasing your dreams at the expense of mine." Because what would she have left to hold on to when he inevitably left? He was already halfway out the door.

Mason pressed back in his chair, as if she'd stunned him with her words. "I didn't know you felt that way, about giving up your dreams for mine."

"I don't think I realized I did until recently myself." The first time she followed him had felt like following her own heart. She hadn't been able to imagine a world without Mason in it. She'd loved being able to help him. Yet through the years, he'd needed her less and less. Like one of the old, dusty boxes he stowed in the attic and forgot to unpack, she'd begun to feel dragged around from move to move rather than a necessary part of his life he couldn't wait to connect with. If she were in a box marked *NEEDED*, then perhaps another relocation wouldn't feel so daunting.

Kenton Corners offered family, new friends, and a new job. Places and people who welcomed her. For once she wanted to hold on and see where all these new possibilities would take her. Especially since the old ones felt wrung out of all their promise.

They sat in shared silence, each lost in their own thoughts. Where did they go from here?

Mason crumpled his napkin and put it on top of his half-eaten breakfast. "I don't know what the answer is, but I do know I'm not ready to just give up."

"So what are you suggesting?" She didn't want to misinterpret his presence here or his words.

Mason cracked his knuckles. "I'm not sure exactly, but we're both here in France for the next few days. Let's start with being together and see where that takes us."

She offered him a wry look. In his book, being together typically meant one thing.

"I'm not talking about sex," he said. "Though I'm not opposed—"

She narrowed her eyes.

His hands came up. "Kidding."

"I highly doubt that."

Mason broke out his roguish grin with those scintillating eyes. "I am a man." His gaze roamed over her. "And you're still the most beautiful woman I've ever seen."

Heat flooded from her abdomen all the way out to the edges of her body. Sex did not fix problems. Sex did not fix problems.

But if he kept looking at her like that, she'd forget that fact.

She swallowed and glanced away.

Mason cleared his throat. "Anyway . . ."

"Yeah."

How did things go from supercharged to super awkward in two point four seconds flat?

Always the smooth one between them, Mason stood and offered her his hand. When she took it, he pulled her into a hug. A chaste hug. His chin rested on top of her head. "We'll figure things out as we go, Nat. Kind of like we did when we were first dating. I just want to know"—he shifted her away far enough to look into her eyes—"are you willing to see if we can make our marriage work again?"

She'd grown used to being by herself, and yet she'd be lying if she said she didn't miss him. But was he still the Mason she missed? Could they truly rewrite their story?

She wouldn't know if she didn't try, and twenty-two years of marriage deserved their best attempt. The last thing she wanted was to live with what-ifs. "I am if you are."

"I am."

She nodded. "Then I am too."

CHAPTER NINE

NATALIE PLACED HER HAND ON Mason's shoulder. Only one of them needed to face the firing squad staring their way, and she volunteered as tribute.

"Mason, this is Everleigh Wheaton and Brooke Sumner." She kept her hold on him as he shook their hands. "Everleigh and Brooke, this is my husband, Mason. He's going to grab our car from the valet."

Mason glanced down at her. Yes, she'd called an audible, but she'd anticipated he'd understand why and roll with it. His downturned lips and wounded gaze surprised her. Shouldn't he be thankful she wasn't submitting him to Everleigh's and Brooke's questions?

Whatever was going on behind his mahogany eyes disappeared with a blink. He accepted the ticket Natalie had passed him. "Guess I'll be outside." He headed for the glass exit doors.

Suddenly, reviving this marriage didn't seem as optimistic as it had upstairs. They used to be able to read each other's thoughts. Complete each other's sentences. Now they weren't only in different books—they were in completely different genres.

"Are you going to seriously stand there in silence?" Brooke's voice broke through Natalie's thoughts. "Because they're fast here with the valet."

"And our curiosity is killing us," Everleigh said as her phone rang. She checked the screen. "It's Uncle Maddox. I can call him back."

Natalie glanced out the doors at Mason as she mentally scribbled together enough of a recap to satisfy her friends. "Apparently he was at the airport and hopped a plane for France instead of Utah. He said he didn't like how we left things when I told him to chase his dreams—meaning the job offer. He listened and chased his dream—meaning me."

Everleigh's hand went to her chest. "Okay, that is sweet."

Brooke scoffed. "Saccharine sweet." She snapped her teeth together. "Like, I think I just got a cavity."

"You need to fall in love," Everleigh declared with her hands on her hips.

"No thank you." Brooke's lips puckered in distaste. "What about Utah? What about your marriage? Does he want to work on things? Does he even realize things need work?"

With her hand in the air, Everleigh stopped Brooke's litany of questions. "Geez, Brooke, how about you let her answer one before launching more at her?"

They both stared Natalie down.

"I don't know about Utah, but he's here instead of there. I told him I didn't want to move. He says he does want a college job, but he also wants to work on things. We've agreed to try to see if we can figure things out."

A black SUV pulled up by the door, and Mason waved for them. "Our car is here." Natalie left her friends standing in the lobby.

Warm air greeted her as she exited to the circle drive where Mason and their SUV waited. He opened the front passenger door. "They okay with me tagging along?"

"Honestly? I didn't even get the chance to ask them." She stopped, one foot in the vehicle and one on the brick pavers. "They had too many questions about you showing up in France. It's why I sent you out here so you wouldn't have to endure their curiosity. Though I don't think I've quenched it. Sorry."

His head tipped. "That's why you told me to grab the car?"

"Yes." She noted how his shoulders relaxed. "Why did you think?"

He shrugged his answer as Brooke and Everleigh approached, and he opened the passenger door for them.

Everleigh climbed in, but Brooke walked around the hatch. "You assume you're driving because you're a man?"

Mason didn't skip a beat. "I assumed I was driving because you sent me to get the car." He hopped in beside Everleigh. "But I don't mind being a passenger."

Once they were all inside, Brooke punched in the address of Mr. Hollis's home. It would take thirty minutes to drive there, and Natalie used the time to fill Mason in on their objective.

"From what Caspar said, the copy has a tightly woven green cloth binding with gold lettering for the title and a gold spine. He also said Carroll wrote a note inside, along with his signature."

Brooke peeked into the rearview mirror. "Mr. Hollis's butler warned the house is in disarray, but we're welcome to look through things. He hasn't had time himself to go through all that's there. It seems Mr. Hollis was quite a collector."

"Of everything," Everleigh said.

Mason shifted in his seat. "It can't be that bad, can it?"

Brooke laughed. "I've been through enough collectors' estates to know that yes, it can be that bad."

Natalie faced forward. "Let's hope that isn't the case here."

Twenty minutes later they pulled up a long drive to a towering brick home. Rounded turrets with black pointed tops anchored both ends, with another column in the center. Long three-story sections connected the circular towers, and gray stones flanked all the windows. A fountain stood in the middle of the courtyard outside the main entrance, water flowing from the fairy statue at the heart of it.

Everleigh peered out the window. "This place is huge."

"Massive," Natalie agreed.

They parked beside the fountain and walked up the wide steps to knock on black double doors that stood taller than Mason's six-foot-three height. Footsteps approached from the inside, and the door creaked open.

"Ahh, you've arrived." Mr. Hollis's butler grinned, showing off two wide front teeth. "Please come inside." He executed a small bow as they entered, then closed the door behind them. "Follow me." With long, even strides he crossed the foyer. At the first intersection of hallways, he turned left.

Natalie shared a glance with her friends and felt Mason's hand gently touch her back. They stepped farther inside, and shadows enveloped them. Dark-green brocade wallpaper covered the two-story walls. A golden chandelier hung overhead, and it matched the thick, scrolled frame of the grand mirror leaning against the wall to their right. An Oriental rug with emerald and amber tones covered most of the onyx-stained wood floor beneath their feet. But the largest attention stealer proved to be the stacks of, well, clutter that created narrowed passageways in all directions.

"We better move, or I have a feeling we'll get lost." Brooke hustled after the butler.

Everleigh followed her.

Mason's breath tickled Natalie's neck as he whispered, "Is this what you've been doing the past few months? Heading into strangers' questionable homes?"

She turned her head so she could catch him in her peripheral. "I never went alone."

"Right, because serial killers never take more than one victim at a time."

"Traditionally, no, they don't." She headed after her friends.

"That was sarcasm, Nat." Mason followed, his hand still on her. "How did I miss that this was what you were doing?"

"You knew I was going places I'd never been."

"Yes, to museums and town halls and . . . and . . ." Mason lost words when he was flustered. "Public places."

What she couldn't understand was what had him flustered now. "Halstead Manor isn't a public place," she tossed over her shoulder.

"I know. Let's talk about that."

Ahead, the butler must have gone up a flight of steps, because she caught sight of Everleigh and Brooke just before they disappeared onto the second floor. "Seriously? You want to talk about this now? Why?"

"Because *now* is when I realized how sketchy this job is and that I should have been asking questions all along."

Feet on the first step, Natalie turned and found herself nearly eye level with her husband. "Maybe trust my judgment. I've been using it to make decisions on my own for years now."

If they hadn't been standing so close, she would have missed his slight recoil.

Ugh. She hated when she acted ugly, but all those unpleasant feelings she'd been holding inside bubbled to the surface. It was as if their acknowledgment that things between them weren't good had given her permission to start voicing them.

Only she needed to do it in a nicer way. And in the right place, which wasn't here.

"I'm sorry." She brushed her hair behind her ear. "That didn't come out right."

He arched his brow. "You sure about that?"

"I didn't say I didn't mean it, only that I didn't say it in the nicest way."

"Thanks for the clarification." His tone didn't exactly sound grateful. He sucked in a deep breath, then slowly released it. "Apparently we have more to work on than I realized."

"Maybe so, but this isn't the time or place."

"Agreed." He motioned to the stairs. "Let's catch up with your friends."

She turned and led the way, because finding Brooke and Everleigh sounded much easier than her and Mason finding their way back to each other.

Upstairs they followed the voices through another hallway filled with so many items that only a narrow pathway remained. Three doors down they entered a room on their left. It was the first space without clutter lining each wall.

"Glad you could join us," Brooke greeted.

Everleigh nodded to the butler. "This is Archibald Clement."

"Please call me Archie." The old man spoke with measured tones, and his hands clasped the edges of his brocade vest.

Not a lock of his shockingly white hair stood out of place. He had a tall, wrinkled forehead and an elongated, square chin, which somehow suited his thin frame. His clothes fit him impeccably. He wore a white long-sleeved shirt under his vest, and dark-gray pleated trousers to match. Natalie's favorite part, however, was the navy-and-white paisley ascot tucked around his neck.

"I thought you'd like to see Mr. Hollis's office first."

Interesting that it was the one place in the house that seemed to be kept in order. What encouraged Mr. Hollis to do in here what he seemed incapable of with the rest of his house?

"It took me all month to clean this one room out." Archie's words provided an answer, along with nixing her fleeting belief that what they'd come to do would be easy. "When I received the call about your help, well, you can see why I was quite happy indeed."

Archie explained his system and how he was organizing all the estate items to either throw away, donate, or ready for a sale. "You can leave your things in here, if you'd like, while you work." He crossed to an ornate buffet underneath the large window overlooking the garden. "I set some tea and pastries out for you in case you grow hungry before lunchtime. Feel free to start in any room you'd like. Many hands make light work."

Before they could respond, he exited on the heels of another slight bow.

Mason turned to Natalie. "Basically, we're free labor then?"

"As far as he's concerned, yes, but Caspar is paying us."

"Even if you don't find the book?"

Brooke stepped past him to the door. "We'll find it." She nodded down the hall. "I'm going to start in the room we passed at the top of the stairs." Then she stuck in her headphones and headed that way.

Everleigh grinned. "I think I'll work with Brooke. Make sure nothing falls on her."

"Be careful she doesn't tip anything over on *you*," Natalie cautioned. She wouldn't put it past Brooke when Everleigh showed up in her space. Everleigh was determined to wiggle her way back into Brooke's good graces, and Brooke wasn't making it easy on her.

With a laugh, Everleigh disappeared into the hall.

"And what about us?" Mason stood by the buffet with a croissant in hand. "Where should we start?"

"Anywhere, I suppose." Where they started didn't matter as much as where they'd finish. "This entire place is a mess."

He popped the last bite into his mouth and quickly swallowed it. "That's an understatement. If we don't go in with a game plan, chances are we'll miss something."

"Oh?" Natalie crossed her arms. "Do you have a game plan then, coach?"

"Since they're working upstairs, how about we start downstairs. We can begin in the room off the front entry. We'll start in one corner and work across the room in an orderly fashion." Dust danced on the sunbeams behind him, and he swiped at his nose.

Natalie dug in her purse and handed him a bottle of allergy pills before taking two herself.

"Thanks. You always come prepared."

"I'm a mom. It's what we do."

He motioned for her to precede him from the room. "Being a mom highlighted the trait maybe, but you've always been that way. Snacks, Band-Aids, tweezers—if someone needed something, you had it." They descended the steps. "I even remember that time you whipped out dental floss at prom."

So did she. "Made me real popular with the other teens." They'd called her fanny pack a granny pack.

"Made you popular with Ross Evans."

"The guy had spinach in his teeth. I couldn't let him walk around like that all night. People were making fun of him."

"You never could stand someone being teased. It's one of the things I admired about you."

She noted his use of the past tense and turned to say something, when her foot snagged on one of the boxes in the hall. She pitched forward, and Mason reached for her. His strong arms steadied her and didn't let go.

"You okay?"

"Yeah." She looked around them. "This place is hazardous. How did Mr. Hollis live like this?"

Mason glanced around too. "I don't think he saw a mess. I think all this stuff was like his security blanket."

The boxes and piles lining the hall narrowed in on her. "The same blanket that makes one person warm can suffocate another."

With a chuckle, Mason led her into the room on their right. "Come on."

"Oooh!" How had she missed this? "It's a library." Natalie pushed on her tiptoes to see over boxes. Bookshelves reached to the ceiling on three of the four walls. Ladders attached to the shelves, the kind one could use to slide along and reach for their next read. Although with all this clutter, they weren't accessible. The fourth wall had a massive stone fireplace reminiscent of the one in Halstead Manor.

"I know." Mason stood beside her, just inside the doorway. "It's why I suggested starting here. We are looking for a book, right?"

"Right." And there were hundreds in here. If the fountain in town resembled the one from *Beauty and the Beast*, then this library was from the same movie. At least she envisioned it would be if they could clear it out. "I can't believe he kept this room in such disarray."

Mason didn't argue with her. "How about we start in that corner. I think there's a window over there. Maybe we can unbury it, and this place won't resemble a crime scene any longer."

"It's going to take more than that."

An hour later they hadn't cleared a quarter of the space. They'd managed to unbury the window, then had thrown open the curtains and spent nearly a minute sneezing. She hated to think what would have happened if they hadn't taken Benadryl.

Mason started clearing a path to the bookshelves while Natalie searched the titles. As she reached the final shelf, the box Mason moved jingled.

He opened it. "Silver bells."

"Too bad it's not Christmastime." Natalie climbed a ladder to peruse the books stacked along this section.

Mason returned to where they'd started their room search as Christmas music flooded the air.

She peered down at him. "Did you honestly put on carols?"

"That surprises you?" He hummed along while opening boxes.

Mason loved all things Christmas. If she agreed to it, he'd put the tree up September first. "It's June."

"And?"

"And how about something more appropriate?"

Ten seconds later "You're a Mean One, Mr. Grinch" started playing.

Natalie glanced down to find his lazy smirk filling his face. She rolled her eyes. "*Seasonally* appropriate."

"Ah." He tapped his phone, and the music switched to a ballad from the eighties. "Better?"

"Much."

Other than inappropriately timed Christmas tunes, they shared a similar taste in music. Anything late eighties or early nineties (other than rap) was their sweet spot. Mason's current playlist kept them moving for another hour, when a gong sounded throughout the halls.

Natalie straightened from a pile she'd been weeding through on the floor. "That's a unique way to call people to lunch."

"He could use a Tarzan call and I'd respond. I'm starving."

The thought of Archie bellowing like Tarzan dissolved her into giggles. Also, her husband possessed the eating habits of a teenager. All food was good food, and he existed in a constant state of hunger. "You're as bad as the boys."

"Please." He motioned for her to step into the hall ahead of him. "I heard your stomach growling a half hour ago."

Inside Mr. Hollis's office, they found Everleigh and Brooke seated around a table Archie had set for them. They had already dug into the steak lunch. Mason held her chair out as Natalie sat.

"Did you two have any luck?" she asked her friends.

They looked from Mason to her before Everleigh cleared her throat. "Um, none. How about you?"

Natalie heard the double meaning in her question, but she wasn't going to speak with them in front of Mason. Her paltry answers about his presence hadn't satiated their curiosity earlier. No doubt their interest had grown as she'd worked with him downstairs. They were like two reporters salivating over their next big story, and the second they had her alone, they'd pounce. All the while, Mason sat obliviously beside her.

He reached for a roll and slathered marmalade over it. "Nothing in our room either, but we're maybe only halfway through it."

Her friends conveyed their understanding of her silence and momentarily tabled their subtle inquisition. Some would look at their prying as intrusive. Natalie found it endearing. It had been a long time since she'd had friendships like theirs.

Brooke laid her napkin on her lap. "We're going to be here for weeks." Streaks of dust covered her black shirt. "Caspar had no idea what he was signing us up for. This is the proverbial needle in a haystack."

"I just wish we knew why this was so important to him," Everleigh said.

"He didn't tell you?" Mason asked.

Natalie shook her head. Though she had tried to figure it out. "I've been attempting to find other families besides Alice Liddell's that Lewis Carroll was close to. History tells us that he gave a copy of one book to her, so logic says if this other version is real—"

"Which is the one thing Caspar has said." Everleigh cut in. "That what we are looking for does exist."

"Yes." They had no reason to doubt him on that point. There'd be no sense purposely sending them on a wild goose chase. "And if he gave one edition, so to say, to a family he admired, then whoever received the copy we're after must have also been close to him. If I could discover who his friends were and trace their family lines, perhaps I'd see the name Caspar. That would not only give us his connection to the book but also reveal his identity."

Brooke leaned forward, intrigue on her face. "And? Any luck?"

"Because that's a brilliant connection to make," Everleigh said. A high compliment from the puzzle queen.

"Unfortunately, not yet. I'll keep looking though."

"Good." Everleigh ran her hand along her water glass. "We have to also consider that Caspar could be after it for someone, like he helped Gertrude with the Florentine Diamond. But then why not tell us who that person is?"

"I wondered the same thing, but all I can come up with in that scenario is that Caspar likes his secrets," Natalie said.

Brooke pushed away from the table to stretch out her legs. "I still think he knew more about the location of the diamond than he told us. Like he was leading us along on that entire hunt." They'd tossed that theory around several times in the last few weeks. "Maybe he'll do the same thing here."

"Unless this time he really doesn't know where the item is." Mason's deep voice added his two cents, but his focus remained on his steak as he cut another slice. "Could be he simply wants this book for the money."

Archie chose that moment to return. "Can I get anything for anyone?"

"A map to where the book is?" Brooke responded dryly.

Archie stood beside their table. Leaning in, he refilled their water goblets. "Mr. Hollis would have enjoyed you. Salt was his preferred seasoning."

Laughter erupted over the table.

"Did he just call me salty?" Brooke watched Archie return the leaded glass pitcher to the buffet.

"I believe so," Natalie said.

Brooke crossed her arms and scrunched her eyes under furrowed brows, but the amusement lining the edges of her frown softened her attempt at looking perturbed.

Circling back to their conversation on Caspar, Natalie pointed to Mason. "You might be right."

He straightened on his chair. "I am?" Then set down his knife. "About what?"

"That this might be a completely different case this time around. It could be about money, not about helping someone." She clicked her nails together. "If we do find the copy and it's legitimately an original, it would be worth several million."

"If it's still here," Everleigh said, "we'll find it."

"And all of this supposes Mr. Hollis truly purchased the book and brought it here," Brooke added.

"He did, on both accounts, I assure you." Archie replenished the bread basket on the table, and the scent of yeast wafted up from it. "I remember it quite clearly."

"Out of all this jun—er, collectibles here, you remember that one book?" Brooke asked.

"I do, miss." Archie nodded. "I had the pleasure of accompanying Mr. Hollis when he attended the estate sale where he acquired it. He made many purchases that day, but the Carroll story was one of his favorites."

"And you're sure it's remained here all this time?"

"Mr. Hollis would never have parted with it." Archie stood stalwartly beside the table. "It wasn't unusual for people—sometimes rather unsavory people—to offer him money for items he'd collected. But he was far more attached to his things than he ever was to his finances, though he had great quantities of both."

"Unsavory people?" Everleigh questioned.

Archie nodded. "Yes, well, one does run into all sorts when he's a collector."

"I can attest to that," Brooke agreed.

Natalie noted Mason's concerned gaze landing on her, but before he could say anything, Archie spoke again.

"In truth, I will struggle to release his treasures when the time comes, especially his books. Those I might not part with. Mr. Hollis loved several as if they were his children. I feel it's my duty to look after them now in his stead."

"Yet you allowed us here to search for this one, knowing we'd like to take it home with us?"

Archie smiled. "Why, because I also believe Mr. Hollis would delight in any of his cherished stories returning to their rightful owner. In this case, your Caspar knows who that is."

CHAPTER TEN

MASON STRETCHED HIS NECK, RELEASING a moan as the tension popped from his muscles. Eight hours of sorting through one man's junk had not led him to any treasures. They'd be back at it at nine tomorrow morning, and he was seriously asking what he'd gotten himself into. Scratch that. The past twenty-four hours had him wondering what his wife had gotten *herself* into.

He settled onto the bed while Natalie showered off the dust from the afternoon before they headed to dinner. Had he honestly become so out of touch with her that he'd missed the details of this new job? Or had Natalie glossed over them? Either way he was aware now, and they needed to have a conversation about if she should continue working for Caspar.

The running water shut off, and he could hear Nat moving around. Within minutes she joined him in the room. She'd donned a pair of wide-leg jeans, a fitted T-shirt, and one of her cardigans. He often teased her about her collection of sweaters, but secretly he loved her in them. Especially when she wore one of his. Her peony scent would linger on the threads for days.

Though, come to think of it, he hadn't smelled that scent for some time. He sniffed the air. "Did you change perfumes?"

She lifted her brow. "Reed and Hunter gave me perfume for Christmas. I've been wearing that."

She didn't add the *since then*, but the words spoke loudly in her expression. Apparently he had been checked out for some time.

Natalie rooted through a small bag and pulled out a necklace. She continued digging for more jewelry, and he scooted to the end of the bed to sit close by her. "I know I mentioned it earlier, but I'm a little leery of all Caspar has you doing. I'm not sure it's safe."

She slipped on an earring. "There is nothing unsafe about this job."

"You wouldn't mind our boys traipsing around the globe, going into strangers' homes, looking for things unsavory people want?"

Natalie secured her other earring, then started working on her necklace. "Unsavory people?"

"Archie's word, not mine." And he'd tensed at the picture his mind supplied in response. "I'd have much rather he said—"

"Delightful? Delectable? Delicious?"

"Thanks, Miss Merriam-Webster, for your arsenal of word choices."

"Actually, it'd be Miss Roget."

Having no clue what she was talking about, he sighed and crossed his arms. Why did he always feel about one hundred IQ points lower around her?

She leaned on the dresser and faced him, addressing his silence as if she understood the reason for it. "Those were synonyms. *Roget's* is to thesauruses what *Merriam-Webster* is to dictionaries, so I'd be Miss Roget."

"Good to know." Maybe one day he could speak Natalie's language. "The point I was trying to make, though, was that you don't really know what you're getting yourself into with Caspar. You don't even know who he is."

"I've worked for him for three months and been perfectly fine, Mace. Plus, the paycheck I brought home covered practically all the boys' tuition this year." She returned to fiddling with the clasp on her necklace.

"Here." He stood and wrapped his fingers around hers. "Let me." She stiffened for a moment, then released her hold on the chain. Turning, she pulled her hair up and out of his way. A strand tickled his cheek, and he did his best not to be affected by her nearness. Or the new scent she wore that suited her even better than the peonies had. There remained a softness underlying the more predominate scent that he couldn't place, but it had a spiciness to it. Strong, yet not cloying. "There." He affixed the clasp, then turned her to face him. "The paycheck was nice, but you're more important to me than our bank account. I want to know you're safe."

Her brown eyes warmed, and the desire to kiss her stirred. How long had it been since he'd kissed his wife? Too long if he couldn't remember. He dipped his head.

With her palm against his chest, she gently pushed him away. "We should get going."

Might as well have doused him with cold water. He'd hoped this trip would lessen the distance between them, but it felt like she'd just added another mile. He sucked in a deep breath. "Right. Lead the way."

They met up with Brooke and Everleigh in the lobby and walked to a nearby café. Once they'd settled and placed their orders, the conversation turned to Archie's comments over lunch.

Brooke placed her sunglasses on the table. "I called John so he could put us in touch with Caspar, but it seems Caspar is currently unavailable. I filled him in, and John says Caspar never mentioned knowing the original owners of the book to him either. He's going to ask him the next time they talk, but that will be a couple of days."

"Based on what Archie said, Caspar *is* having us retrieve this for someone he knows," Everleigh reiterated. "Unless he misunderstood something Caspar told him."

"And if he didn't, why wouldn't Caspar have given us the same information?" Brooke asked. "Like he did with the diamond and Gertie."

Natalie clicked her nails together. "That's the question of the hour."

"You guys really don't know anything about this man, do you." The more he thought about this situation, the less he liked it.

"Not really," Everleigh offered. "But he's been up front with us from the start that there'd be unanswered questions while working for him. It's part of the reason he hired John too."

"Who's John?" He'd heard the name but nothing about the man.

"A lawyer who handles the business end of things while also ensuring everything Caspar asks us to do is on the up-and-up." This from Brooke.

"Unless John's on the take." If this Caspar's pockets ran as deep as they seemed, it wouldn't be hard to *encourage* people to cross the line for him.

"He's not." Natalie shook her head. "We checked into him."

Her response gave Mason a measure of relief. Natalie was an extremely capable woman, and because of his confidence in her, he'd dropped his guard. Didn't inquire about her new job, what it entailed, or any of the travel accompanying it. However, the more he learned about Caspar, the more his protectiveness grew. He should have been asking these things months ago.

Everleigh glanced at him across the table. "Plus, we've got Gertie. She's retired FBI." Said so simply, yet in a tone that promised Gertie let nothing slip past her.

"How's Gertie feeling?" Natalie effectively switched topics before Mason could ask any further questions.

"Better." The breeze picked up, and Everleigh slipped on her jacket. "Niles says she still has a pretty harsh cough, but it sounds like he and Burt are taking good care of her."

"I'm sure Burt is happily spoiling her," Natalie said.

He looked her way. "Who's Burt?"

"Her old FBI partner," she answered.

Everleigh grinned. "Who's not-so-secretly in love with her."

"Ah." Mason nodded, hoping they wouldn't venture much further into the girl talk. Unfortunately, they did. Conversation of Gertie and Burt flowed over appetizers. The main course was all about Niles and Everleigh's new relationship. Dessert brought relentless teasing of Brooke and someone named Storm, which, come to think of it, matched her facial expression right now. While Mason was learning a lot, he wasn't looking forward to the inevitable turn toward—

"Natalie said you two were high school sweethearts." Brooke held up a forkful of cake and tossed Nat a look.

Uh-oh. He was escaping this table before it fully turned toward him.

"We were." He pushed his nearly empty dessert plate away. "The benefit of knowing someone that long is you also know their favorite things. Which is why I'm going to have to steal Natalie away from you for the rest of the night."

Her big brown eyes looked up at him, confused. "You are?"

But he also sensed a hint of relief in them. She didn't want the topic switch either. "I am." He held out his hand.

"Have fun, you two." Everleigh waved.

Leaving the remainder of her dessert behind, Natalie didn't take his hand, but she did stand. "Lead the way."

She followed him down the street. Once they'd moved out of view of her friends, she stopped him. "Sorry Brooke swung the spotlight onto us. I shouldn't have needled her about Storm."

"No worries." He'd seen it coming.

"Thanks." She rubbed her thumbnail, a sure sign her emotions whirled. "For providing an escape."

"Glad to come to the rescue." He tossed the words out without thinking, but as they reached his own ears, their simple truth settled inside. He wanted to be her hero in the big and small things. Instead, for years now, he'd felt like the awkward sidekick.

"It was nice."

Her response was so soft, he nearly missed it. Her gaze flitted over his face and landed on his lips before swinging to his eyes. Man, if he didn't know better, he'd think she wanted him to kiss her, but the last thing *he* wanted was a repeat of what had happened earlier in their room. He'd completely misread that situation.

So instead he chuckled. "What kind of name is that anyway? Storm."

Natalie blinked, clearing away whatever it was she had been thinking. "Right? I've wondered the same thing." She started toward their hotel.

"Hold up." He stopped her. Yes, he'd provided a fast getaway from probing questions, but there really was something he wanted to show her.

Her eyebrows dipped. "What?"

"We're going this way." He nudged his head in the opposite direction.

She pointed the other way. "Our hotel is that way though."

"But Fontaine Schwendi is this way." When she didn't move, he added, "Unless you've already seen it?" Maybe on her first day here before he arrived. *Beauty and the Beast* was her favorite Disney princess movie, and he'd painstakingly scanned a tourist brochure on his flight here. Between pictures and the few words that hadn't remained a jumbled mess, he'd picked up enough to know that the movie town's animation was based on this place—right down to that fountain. Of course, she'd know that and would want to see it, which meant she probably—

"I haven't." She studied him. "I'm surprised you know about the fountain."

Right. She would be stunned by that. "I do read on occasion, Nat."

His tone was a bit harsher than he'd intended, but with each failed play tonight, his insecurities raced to the surface.

She frowned. "I know you do, but typically it's about sports. Not travel destinations."

"Because we never travel." Scratch that. "At least I don't. Your passport is filling up lately."

Her frown deepened. "I invited you to Vienna."

"You knew I couldn't come."

"We're really back here again?" She tossed her hands in the air. "I wouldn't have invited you if I didn't want you to come. Why is that so hard to believe?"

"Oh, I don't know. Maybe because you seem more relieved by my absence than put out by it when I miss events with you." Another bonus of being married so long was the ability to read each other all too well.

Except Natalie looked confused. "What on earth are you talking about?"

"Come on, Nat. We both know I don't fit in with your crowd."

"What crowd? The other middle-aged moms trying to figure out what's next in life?"

Now his forehead crinkled. Natalie always had focus and a plan. She knew where she was going, how to get there, and when she would arrive. And unlike him, she obtained her goals. Natalie never failed at anything.

The look of defeat on her face said otherwise. It was such a foreign expression that it froze him for a moment. How had they gotten to a place where he didn't know her struggles? Where every other word they spoke seemed to poke at each other's sore spots?

He wanted that to change. To not only be her hero but her champion. Her protector.

Mason reached for her, and her gaze shifted over his shoulder. She stiffened, then took a step past him. "It can't be."

He turned, trying to figure out what she'd spotted. "What can't be?" All he saw were crowds.

Whatever captured her attention, she followed down the street. Mason stayed on her heels as she hustled over the cobblestones. She dashed toward an opening between buildings, but as she turned down it, she halted.

Mason stopped shoulder to shoulder with her. "What did you see?"

"Not what. Who." Her gaze darted over the people in the narrow alley. Finally, she turned to look at him. "This is the second time I thought I saw a man I met in Kenton Corners."

This had his attention. "You met a man?"

His tone provoked an exasperated look from her. "A customer at the bookstore. Briefly."

"He apparently made enough impression that you thought you saw him here in France. Twice." Which tensed his muscles.

She sighed impatiently. "Because he asked about Halstead Manor, which is tied to Caspar, who is why I'm here." She turned and retraced her steps.

Caspar. Again.

He followed her, his muscles now tense for entirely different reasons.

※ ※

She had to be seeing things. Matt from Kenton Corners was not here in France. It hadn't been him the other day, and it wasn't him now.

Yet she could not get his face out of her mind. He'd been staring straight at her until her gaze had connected with his. Except if it was Matt, he hadn't seemed affected in the least by her noticing him. Rather, he'd held her look for a long second before disappearing down the alley she'd raced toward.

Could it have been a fellow tourist who simply resembled him? Absolutely.

But her gut said otherwise.

She made her way back to where they'd left Brooke and Everleigh, and Mason silently remained close to her side. His jaw clenched, and he surveyed the throng around them. That demeanor mirrored the stance he took when he watched defensive teams line up against his offense. Ready for the play and already contemplating the next call to keep his team in the lead—and safe.

Brooke and Everleigh stood on the sidewalk outside the restaurant where they'd enjoyed dinner. They watched them approach.

"That was a fast sightseeing trip," Brooke noted.

Everleigh fiddled with the Rubik's Cube attached to her sling bag. "We saw you heading back this way, so we waited." Her forehead crinkled as she took them both in. "What's wrong?"

"Nat saw some guy who she thinks is following her." Mason's attention swiveled around them. "How about we head back to the hotel?"

Natalie grasped his arm to stop him but kept her eyes on her friends. "I'm not sure what I saw." The more she replayed the moment, the more she doubted herself. "Do you remember how I asked John about Stew's Crew because of that guy Matt?"

"Yeah." Brooke nodded.

Natalie explained the past few minutes, and her friends' concern mirrored that of Mason's. She didn't want them to worry, because that made her feel like she should also worry. "Look, I'm sure it was just someone who looked like him. It's crazy to think that this Matt would show up here in France."

Brooke snapped her gum. "As crazy as someone following Everleigh?"

"What?" Mason's brown eyes sparked. "She had someone following her too? Why didn't you tell me that?"

For so many reasons, starting with they barely talked anymore. Now wasn't the time to lay that info out there though. "Because Niles handled it, and we're fairly certain it was her past employer."

"Fairly?" Mason gripped the back of his neck.

Everleigh nodded. "Niles never found anything that directly connected Palmer—my old employer—to the car following me, but I haven't seen anyone since we returned from Vienna."

"I think we should call John so he can fill Caspar in when he's finally able to speak with him." This from Brooke.

Disbelieving laughter choked from Mason. "Unless Caspar is already aware. Maybe he's the one who has people watching you all."

"He hired us. Why on earth would he have people following us?" Natalie asked.

"Oh, I don't know? Maybe he doesn't trust you?" Mason tossed his hands in the air. "You certainly shouldn't trust him. You know nothing about the guy."

"I know he's followed through on everything he's promised," she threw back at him.

Everleigh stepped closer to them. "Okay, let's take a breath." Her gentle touch landed on Natalie's shoulder, and she gave a soft squeeze, reminding her Everleigh was on her side. That she understood underlying tension ran between Natalie and Mason. Keeping her hand on Natalie, Everleigh addressed him. "Caspar has never given us a reason to distrust him. Yes, he's been mysterious, but he's done everything he can to assure us that he is on the up-and-up. I think our best next step is to bring him in the loop as soon as we're able, but I'll also fill in Niles and Gertie. If something wonky is going on, one of them will figure it out. Meanwhile, let's head back to the hotel and keep our focus on why we're here."

Another snap of gum from Brooke. "To clean out a dusty house in hopes we find a book that's worth millions. We're regular Indiana Joneses."

This pulled laughter from them all, even if it sounded tired.

They returned to the hotel and agreed to meet downstairs at nine the next morning. Everleigh promised to connect with Niles, and Brooke said she'd loop in John. With the looks they gave Natalie before slipping away, they were handling those items so she'd have time to handle the tension between her and Mason.

Mason followed her inside their room. He silently toed off his shoes while she stepped onto the balcony. Rather than turn on the TV to find a game to watch like he normally would, Mason joined her outside. He stood beside her at the railing and leaned against it. "Why didn't you tell me any of this stuff when it was happening?"

"It didn't seem noteworthy." And they so rarely spoke, when they did it was only bullet points of necessity—a bill due, something broken in the house, the boys' needs . . . They shared their mutual to-do list and that was about it.

Mason's brows lifted. "You in possible danger isn't noteworthy?"

"No. Because I never worried that I was."

His eyes pointed to where she clicked her nails, then returned to hold her stare.

She stopped the nervous habit, but before she could refute his silent argument, her phone rang. Pulling it out, she smiled. "It's Hunter. He's FaceTiming." She slid her finger over the screen, her smile growing as her boys' faces appeared in separate boxes. They'd conferenced her into their call. "This is a nice surprise."

Hunter's grin was all Mason. "We were talking and realized neither of us had heard from you, so we thought we'd call."

She loved not only her relationship with her boys but that the two of them had their own strong connection. "I'm glad you did."

Mason leaned close. "Me too."

Hunter's and Reed's eyes widened, but it was Reed who spoke. "Dad? What are you doing there?" The way his expression changed, and that his attention bounced between the two, said he was fully aware of the strain in their marriage. She'd done her best to hide it from the boys, but Reed was especially attuned to people's emotions. Probably why he was going into psychiatry.

Hunter piggybacked his question. "Yeah. Aren't you supposed to be in Utah?"

Beside her, Mason shifted like he did when he was uncomfortable. "I came here instead."

Was he already regretting that decision?

"Nice." Hunter nodded his approval.

But deep creases lined Reed's forehead. "How's that going?"

She heard the subtext in his question, and she wanted to reassure him, even if her answer rang untrue in her own ears. "Fairly well."

That wasn't a complete lie. She and Mason had agreed to work on things.

Her response seemed to satisfy him, because her boys launched into recaps of their past week. They circled back to France and spent another few minutes talking about museums she needed to see, the architecture in town, and the history of Colmar. Mason listened but didn't say much until they all gave their goodbyes.

Reed looked pensive. "I'm glad you're both there. You needed the time together."

"Yeah, so have fun," Hunter said. "Make it a second honeymoon, and remember why you fell in love way before you had us guys."

Mason shared a look with Natalie. They'd hidden nothing from their sons.

"We'll try," Mason said.

"Promise?" Reed asked.

"Yes," they answered in unison.

This wasn't only about keeping their marriage together—it was about keeping their family together.

Natalie pocketed her phone and sighed. "They've picked up on the tension between us."

"They have." He cracked his knuckles. "They're not little anymore, and even when they were, they never missed much."

"True." The boys who'd clung to her legs now had lives of their own. They'd grown up and were giving their parents advice. Immense pride in who they were becoming bubbled inside, but oh, did she miss them.

Mason crossed his arms. "You did a good job with them. They've turned from boys into a couple of great young men."

"It was a joint effort." Suddenly tired, she settled onto one of the chaise lounges. Golden-hour sunshine shimmered down at the perfect angle and temperature for relaxation.

Mason took the chaise beside her. "Yeah. In the sense that I provided for their needs, but you? You provided everything they needed."

There was a wistfulness in his voice, or was that sadness? She angled so she could see him. "What are you talking about?"

"You understand them better than me. You speak their language."

Her brow crinkled at the absurdity of his comment. "English?"

"Literature. History. Art. They'd pick a museum over a ball game any day of the week." He shrugged. "That's your arena."

"I didn't realize we had separate zones when it came to our kids."

His eyes widened before he released a long sigh. His hand rubbed the hair on his nape. "No, you wouldn't." He twisted his wrist to see his watch. "You look tired, and there's a soccer game starting soon. Think I'll head inside and watch that while you rest."

She didn't stop him. Attempting to work through things while exhausted never ended well, and Mason processed best while watching a game. Maybe they could pick things back up in the morning, because this conversation didn't feel over. In fact, it felt like the beginning of one they desperately needed to have. Seemed they'd both been holding things inside too long.

Standing, she stretched, then walked to the railing and peered over the city. Her mind returned to the man she'd seen in the street earlier. The one who looked like Matt. She sighed—the problem with her stellar memory was that it could be trusted to recall every single detail her eyes observed. Which meant either Matt had a doppelgänger . . .

Or he'd followed them here.

CHAPTER ELEVEN

IF THE PAST TWO DAYS had solidified anything, it was that she and Mason worked well together on anything *but* their relationship. They'd managed to clear several rooms on the first floor of the Hollis estate, while Everleigh and Brooke continued working on the upstairs. She and Mason had not, however, managed to clear up any of the misunderstandings between them. Of course, to do that, one of them would need to broach the issues fraying the edges of their marriage. No easy task when she didn't like creating conflict between them and Mason didn't like failure.

"Room number four hundred and twenty-seven," Mason joked as they stared into what Archie claimed had once been a study.

Natalie stepped inside. "One of us has to find that book soon, or Brooke's right. We'll be here forever."

Mason moved to the opposite corner of the room. "Same plan as before? I'll meet you in the middle." After the library, they'd decided rather than starting on the same side together, they'd work inward from opposing sides.

"Sounds good." Natalie scooted between the wall and large piles of vinyl records to reach her corner. Mr. Hollis could have opened his own music store with the number of LPs, cassette tapes, and eight-tracks in here. Not to mention several antique radios and record players stored in the center of the room.

Four hours later she could navigate more freely. They'd moved the broken radios to a bin outside. Archie would donate them to a business that collected old parts for people who restored similar pieces. All the tapes, eight-tracks, and records had been organized for the approaching estate sale. Progress was being made, but with *Alice's Adventures* still unlocated, success remained elusive.

Natalie sat cross-legged on the floor. "Hopefully, Everleigh and Brooke are having better luck."

"We're not," Everleigh said from the doorway as she and Brooke joined them.

Mason nodded his hello before picking up a box. "I'm going to run this to the bin outside." He disappeared into the hall.

"I just heard from John." Everleigh held up her phone and wiggled it. "He still hasn't connected with Caspar."

Brooke plopped beside Natalie on the navy-and-gold Oriental rug. "I'm beginning to think that Archie's a whole lot smarter than I gave him credit for. He took advantage of the fact that we wanted that book—which I'm betting he actually knows isn't here despite what he's said—so we'd tackle his workload for him."

"He's definitely shrewd enough to do that, but I don't get lying vibes from him." Everleigh picked up one of the records from a pile in the corner. "Ooh, Abba's first release. I'm going to ask him if I can take this back to Gertie."

Brooke nudged Natalie's leg. "Did you come across any Ella, Louis, Nat, or Duke?"

"You like jazz?" Having ridden in Brooke's car, Nat figured all Brooke listened to was classic rock.

"I have eclectic tastes." Brooke's clothing choices adhered to that statement, so it made sense, Natalie supposed, that her music would too.

Natalie pointed Brooke toward another stack of records. She walked to it and picked up the top album, talking as she studied it. "What are we going to do if at the end of all this, the book isn't here?"

"Hopefully, Caspar will have another lead," Everleigh said. "Though I sort of figure if he sent us here, we'll either find the book or a hint of where to look. He hasn't been one to direct us down a dead-end road."

Natalie clicked her nails together as she ruminated on the past few days. What had they missed? Because Everleigh was right. When they'd searched for the diamond, Caspar had been like a silent force guiding them along the way. Although, just because he'd done that before didn't mean this time would be the same. Perhaps Caspar was as lost as they were when it came to this search. "Here's to hoping, because I checked all the normal sites a book like that would have popped up on, and as far as everyone I've connected with knows, its existence is still only a rumor."

"And I called my contacts." Brooke paused to take a deep breath. "Even Storm." Her lips twisted, like she'd tasted vinegar. "None of my runners or collectors have seen or heard of it either, though several said they'd be extremely interested should we find it and prove it's legit."

Mason returned while Brooke was talking. Archie accompanied him.

"I bumped into Master Daughtry in the hall and inquired if you'd looked through the ledgers in the library. He said you hadn't."

Natalie stood. They'd finished the library yesterday morning, but she hadn't discovered anything other than classic titles in there. Many were special editions with stunning covers and gold-edged pages. In fact, Hollis's collection was so amazing she'd happily extend her trip just to spend the next week holed up in that room, reading. "What ledgers?"

Archie tugged on the bottom of his vest. "Come along. I'll show you."

With a quick shared glance between Mason and her friends, Natalie followed Archie down the hall, the others trailing behind.

They entered the library, and Natalie paused simply to admire it once again. With all the mess removed, she could appreciate the beauty. Sunlight bathed the space from where they'd pulled back the emerald-green velvet curtains on two massive windows. Dust swirled around the wood floor and across the inlaid medallion. Overstuffed chairs with muted fabrics but colorful pillows provided plenty of places to curl up and read or entertain visitors.

"This might be my favorite room in the place," Natalie whispered, more so to herself.

Mason stood close enough to hear. He smiled at her across his shoulder. "Have you ever met a library you didn't like?"

Laughter puffed from her. "True." She always felt at home surrounded by stories. "This one feels special though. The woodwork in here. The light fixtures on the walls. The furniture and those huge windows with the seats built into them. It feels like something from a storybook."

"*Beauty and the Beast?*"

She'd made him rent and watch the Disney animated movie with her when they were dating. He'd endured watching it one more time when the boys were little. She'd been unable to convince him of a third viewing, even though she'd seen it at least a dozen times. Still, he knew that of all the fairy tales she'd read or watched, it was her favorite.

"Exactly," she said.

"We need to make sure you see that fountain before we leave here."

His deep voice rumbled over her with those warm tones that at one time had turned her to mush. There was something about his cadence, when he'd drop it low and slow only for her ears, that assured her he'd fulfill whatever he promised.

Was today's offer an olive branch after two days of awkwardness between them?

She accepted it. "I'd like that."

"Nat, come see this." Everleigh motioned her to where she stood beside a desk with Archie and Brooke. She reached down and pulled a book from the open drawer and handed it to Natalie. Beside her, Brooke paged through another.

Natalie accepted the bound navy rectangular hardback and flipped it open. She read the cursive entries on the first page. "Is this a listing of items Mr. Hollis sold?"

"Yes. Though rare, if he found someone he deemed suitable and could convince himself to part with the piece, he recorded the transaction in these." Archie opened another drawer. "If I remember correctly, there are ten of them. Five per drawer."

Natalie looked to Mason. "How did we miss these?"

"I didn't." Mason's lips tipped down. "I paged through them, but since they didn't match the description of what we were looking for, I continued cleaning out the room."

Brooke closed hers. "You came across ledgers detailing items Hollis sold and didn't think to tell us?" She arched one brow.

Mason's neck grew blotchy red. "Sorry." He shoved his hands into his pockets. "It wasn't the Carroll book."

"But it might tell us where that is," Natalie said. "Thank goodness Archie said something, or we would have missed this possible lead."

Mason shook his head as he looked at the floor. He brought his eyes back to hers. "I'm sorry I overlooked them." He glanced over his shoulder.

"I offered to carry a few heavy items outside for Archie. You guys seem to have things handled in here. I'll go do that so I don't hold you up when you're ready to leave."

The dejection on his face. He'd taken her comment all wrong. "Mason—"

He didn't stop. Natalie nearly followed, but she worried that with emotions running high, any conversation would dissolve into more miscommunication.

Archie caught her eye. "I'll see to him, miss." Then he followed Mason out the door.

Ledger in hand, Brooke moved to one of the couches. Everleigh remained standing close by Natalie. "Things are still strained between you two, aren't they?"

For a split second Natalie contemplated lying, but what good would it do? "Yes." She tucked a loose strand of hair behind her ear. "Honestly, I don't even know where to start. So much is built up between us, I'm not sure we can see past our issues to fix things. We just keep stepping on each other's toes." Like she'd just done with her rash comments. Her mouth had spoken before her brain had caught up. All she'd meant to convey was her relief that they hadn't missed anything. Instead, her words had pressed against Mason's insecurities about his reading abilities. She hadn't intended her remarks to be accusatory, but he'd received them as such.

Everleigh's fingers went to her ever-present Rubik's Cube. "This is an amazing room, isn't it? I mean, the whole house is great, but I'm guessing this is your favorite spot."

"It is."

"Pretty sad that Hollis couldn't use the space because it was filled with too much junk. It's like he held on to all the wrong stuff."

Natalie heard the change in Everleigh's voice. Her friend was a nurse and used to doling out medicine.

Seemed that was what she was doing now as she continued speaking. "Until you and Mason cleaned this space out, no one could see the beauty still here underneath it all."

They stood in silence for a moment before Natalie spoke. "You've grown a lot these past months."

"I did some of my own cleaning." Everleigh squeezed Natalie's shoulder.

"And made some really good friends who handed out advice when I needed it." Then she stepped over to join Brooke on the couch.

Natalie looked around the room. In her life God often used the simplicity of everyday things to speak to her, and it felt like between Everleigh's words and this space, that was what he was doing now. Maybe she and Mason did resemble this room. Holding on to the wrong junk and needing to let it out so they could see the beauty of what lay between them again. If any beauty remained.

Thing was, she needed to determine what was junk to release and what were real issues that needed to be worked through. She'd held on to things for so long, she wasn't sure anymore.

Lord, help me discern it all. Because she didn't want to give up on her marriage, but she also didn't want to keep going the way things had been.

"No way." Brooke jumped to her feet, pulling Natalie from her thoughts and to her side. "Look." Brooke held her open ledger in one hand and a golden lapel pin in her other. Roughly one inch by one inch in design, the pin was shaped like a book, with the word *Custos* engraved on top. "I noticed a bulge in the back cover, so I pried back the leather and found this hidden underneath." Tipping the book toward them, Brooke showed off the small compartment. "This pin was nestled in there."

Opposite the concealed slot, the final page lay open. Everleigh looked at it. "I don't understand. It lists the book but doesn't say he sold it." She traced a line of numbers written inside the compartment that had stored the pin. "And why the code?" She bent closer. "It's a pretty simple one too."

Simple for Everleigh. Not for most others.

"Because he didn't sell the book." Natalie held out her hand. Brooke passed the pin to her, and Natalie was surprised by its weight. Intricate scrolls wove along the perimeter, encircling the word engraved there. At its edges small lines created what appeared to be pages, giving the pin a 3-D appearance. Until this moment, Natalie had thought what the pin represented to be a rumor. Based on the look on Brooke's face, the same could be said of her. "Is this what I think it is?" she asked Brooke.

Brooke nodded. "I think so."

Everleigh looked between them. "I'm so lost. One of you two talk."

Natalie glanced back at the writing on the page. She tapped the code that had caught Everleigh's interest. "We'll talk while you solve this."

Because she had a feeling it would tell them where to go next.

❧ ❧

A bead of sweat slipped down Mason's temple, and he swiped it away. This was the last piece of furniture Archie needed moved. And honestly? The manual labor had done him good.

"Thank you, Master Daughtry." Archie stood on the steps to the Hollis estate, and he squinted in the afternoon sunshine. The expression seemed out of place on the incredibly proper man. "You've been quite the help these past few days."

Of course Archie would feel that way. Mason thrived with physical work, and that was all Archie had needed from him. But if they were to ask Natalie the same thing, she'd note his shortcomings.

Blowing out a breath, Mason scrubbed his hand through his hair. He still couldn't believe those stupid ledgers were something Natalie was interested in. He'd given them a cursory glance when he'd run across them, but he hadn't been able to read the chicken scratches inside. Dyslexia was hard enough when words were printed, but trying to decipher an old man's cursive? Those things might as well have been written in Greek. No way he'd hand them to Natalie and remind her of his weaknesses. Especially when they so obviously weren't the storybook they sought.

Archie descended the steps and walked to Mason. "I apologize for not mentioning the ledgers to you and your wife earlier. I honestly believed the Carroll book to still be on the premises. As I mentioned before, Master Hollis didn't part with things he loved easily." The edges of his lips tipped up, which Mason had come to learn was the largest smile Archie produced. "Unfortunately, so many things became important to him that he couldn't discern which was of greatest significance anymore, and it seems quite possible that in all that clutter, he let go of what he loved most."

"That could easily happen with how much was in there." Mason nodded. "Even with all the donations you made this week, this will still be one massive estate sale."

Archie looked around at the furniture stacked on the lawn. They'd moved pieces out here to free up space for crowds to walk inside. Still, each room remained fully staged.

"It will be that," Archie agreed. "For all he collected, Master Hollis couldn't take any of it with him. These pieces will go to other homes, and once they're done with them, they'll be passed on again until they eventually wear out. That's why I've always valued words." Archie faced Mason. "Kindness. Encouragement. Wisdom. There's no expiration on those things. They linger. They can be passed on for generations and never wear out."

"The same is true of words said in anger, doubt, or ignorance." Mason still carried conversations he'd had with his family, teachers, and even Natalie. The recent moment upstairs would be another difficult one to shake off.

"Ah," Archie said as he tugged on the bottom edge of his vest. "Yes. The person using them must do so carefully, but also the recipient should only collect ones from trusted individuals. You'd never purchase an item from a thief. Neither should you accumulate words from someone un-trustworthy." A fly buzzed around Archie's head, and the man didn't even flinch. "But if they come from someone trusted, then you must look closer to discern if they should be held on to or released. The Lord's good Word tells us that the wounds of a friend can be trusted. Either their words are necessary for our growth, or—if created in haste—they can be healed through forgiveness and reconciliation."

With his tailored vests, his puffy sleeves, and that strange handkerchief thing around his neck, Archie wasn't the type of guy Mason typically approached, but it turned out Archie was one of the most approachable people Mason had ever met.

"Thanks, Archie. You've given me a lot to think about."

"All part of my job."

"I didn't realize your job included counseling."

"Then you've not employed a butler before."

With a chuckle, Mason offered his hand. "I have not, but after this week with you, I'm thinking I should. It has been a pleasure."

Archie accepted his handshake. "The pleasure is mine, sir." He released his grip. "I must return inside. The house won't ready itself."

Mason settled onto one of the bar stools he'd brought outside earlier. He'd left Kenton Corners on Monday feeling like a quarterback running onto the field determined to win a game he'd been losing. But since he'd arrived in Colmar, all he'd done was fumble. The confidence he'd felt when stepping onto that last flight to France no longer beat inside his chest. Instead the looming sense that he didn't possess the ability to turn things around hovered over him. Made him want to give up.

But giving up guaranteed a loss, and he'd already determined Natalie wouldn't become one.

He started for the steps just as she exited the front door. She descended as he ascended, and they met in the middle. With her on the stair above him, they stood nearly eye to eye, though he still had about an inch on her. "Hey," he said.

"Hey."

Sunshine warmed the back of his neck, and he rubbed against the tension lingering in his muscles there. When had vulnerability with his wife become harder than facing down a championship game?

Easy. When he realized he had more to lose if this game plan went south.

"Nat, I—"

"Mason, I—"

They laughed as their voices clashed.

"You first," he said.

She hesitated, clicking her nails together. "I, um, I was just going to apologize for how I acted inside. I understand why you didn't say anything about the ledgers." The clicking stopped, and she reached for his forearm, her touch and her look promising she truly did understand. It had been Natalie who'd first realized Mason was dyslexic, and she'd been the one to ensure he graduated both high school and college. No doubt as soon as she'd looked at the books herself, she'd recognized his difficulty in reading them.

Still, feelings of inadequacy welled inside. He hated that she saw his weaknesses, especially when she had such strength.

"Thanks." His talk with Archie continued to play in his mind. If he wanted to move forward, then he needed to let go of the words spoken inside earlier. Especially with Nat's sincere apology, of which he could offer his own. "And I'm sorry I ducked out. Sometimes I feel every one of my shortcomings around you, and I let it get to me." He'd also let it come between them by way of distancing himself from her. Throwing himself into anything else that could make up for his deficiencies.

She studied him. "What do you mean 'every one of'?" Her head tipped. "Mace, you might struggle to read, but you're an incredibly amazing man who has a myriad of other strengths."

That was her kindness talking in place of honesty. He knew the truth, and it was time they both spoke it rather than continuing to leave it unsaid. "None that compare to yours. Or the boys."

Her forehead crinkled. "You hinted at that the other day when they called, but you're going to have to fill me in because I'm lost as to what you mean." She took his hand and tugged him to sit on the steps with her.

The sun had warmed the stone, and a breeze rustled through the trees in the yard. Squirrels chattered as they scurried around, and a few bees buzzed along the flowers lining the stone walkway below them. Natalie patiently waited for him to bare his soul, but he was completely out of practice with that kind of sharing. They'd been at surface level for so long, it felt awkward to dive deeper.

Yet, if he couldn't be honest with her then where did that leave them? Nowhere good based on the past several years and their current relationship status.

He cracked his knuckles. "It's no secret that the boys received your DNA when it comes to intelligence."

She nodded. "They did well at school, but you always said you hoped they wouldn't face the same struggles as you."

"Absolutely." He still felt that way. "What I didn't expect was how difficult it would be to watch the three of you bond over things that make no sense to me." The gap seemed to grow with each of the boys' birthdays. "I always thought my sons would want to toss a ball with me or watch a football game. Instead they went to museums with you and watched documentaries about history. Those things are completely out of my element."

She looked at him with such compassion. "They tried including you, but you never wanted to come along, so they stopped asking."

"Because I was a fourth wheel. I had nothing to contribute to your conversations, and it wasn't anyone's fault. It just was what it was." Mason looked out over the yard. He clasped his hands together and rested them between his bent knees. This next part was hard, but he needed her to know why he'd stopped showing up. "I figured the best way to not be an embarrassment to you and the boys was to stop tagging along to things with you."

Natalie straightened, and a puff of air shot out her nose. "You've never been an embarrassment to me." Her words held such deep conviction, he nearly believed her.

But he couldn't pretend he hadn't once witnessed the exact opposite from her—even if she hadn't meant for him to catch the look he could still recall on her face. "I know you would never say that to my face or even to anyone else, but, Nat, I saw your reaction at your first awards ceremony. I clearly embarrassed you in front of your colleagues."

The space between her eyebrows pinched. "What are you talking about?" Then her ivory skin smoothed. "Do you mean when Ryan made a dumb jock joke because you misheard him?"

Of course she remembered. She'd probably wanted to crawl into a hole or shove him into one that night. He'd left her side to grab her a drink and had returned at the tail end of a conversation. Her coworker mentioned having once seen Anna Kournikova play, or so that was what Mason had thought he heard. Excited for once to participate in the conversation, he'd mentioned she'd been one of his favorite tennis players.

Except they'd been talking about a Broadway play based on a novel by some writer Mason still couldn't recall, not the former Russian pro tennis player.

"That's the night." He'd never forget it.

"Mace." She squeezed his hand. "If you saw any expression on my face that night, it was out of concern for you, not embarrassment. I was so angry with Ryan for how he treated you. It was an easy mistake. Anna Karenina versus Anna Kournikova. Especially when you'd missed half the conversation." Her cheeks flushed, much like that night, but her explanation provided a new perspective to the redness. "I went to our boss the very next morning."

"You did?" He struggled to replay the moment through this fresh lens.

"Mm-hmm." Her thumb rubbed the back of his hand. "I probably should have told you that, but I didn't say anything when it happened, or afterward, because I could see it made you uncomfortable and *I* didn't want to embarrass *you*." Now she shook her head. "Is that why you stopped coming with me to all my events?"

"I thought it was what you wanted."

"All I ever wanted was you by my side. It's why I married you."

Her words began to soothe the raw places inside.

"And here I thought you stopped coming because I wasn't important to you anymore." She blinked rapidly. "That pursuing work was your priority." She paused, her hand flattening against her chest. "Not me. Especially compared to your next goal. You wanted your next achievement more than you wanted me."

Mason sat there, stunned. They needed to fully unpack what she'd just said, but the most important thing right now was for her to know her belief—one his actions had helped to create—was miles from the truth.

He placed his hand on her knee. "You are the *most* important thing to me, Nat, and I'm sorry if I ever made you feel differently." With a slight squeeze, he continued. "And just so you know, even though I wasn't there, I couldn't be prouder of all the amazing things you've done. You amaze me."

A tear slipped from her eye, and he brushed it away with his thumb as he placed a soft kiss against her hair. They sat for a few moments, lost in their own thoughts. They'd drifted further than he'd realized, and he'd hurt her more than he'd known. This one interaction didn't fix everything, but much like how small moments had built a wall between them, dismantling that barrier would happen in small moments too.

"We've really made a mess of things, haven't we?" he asked.

She pressed her forehead against his shoulder. "We have." Her breath warmed his skin beneath his T-shirt. "Making assumptions and not talking through them isn't exactly the best approach to a healthy relationship."

"Yeah. Isn't it what we've taught the boys *not* to do?"

She chuckled as she straightened. "Good thing they take our advice, even if we don't."

Comfortable silence enveloped them. He couldn't remember the last time they'd sat like this. There was no rush to fill in the quiet space between them. Rather, it felt like he'd just gained yardage and was on the verge of turning this game around.

He looked over to find her watching him. "What are you thinking?"

"That it means a lot that you're here."

There was a tenderness to her words he hadn't heard in a long time.

"I really thought Utah was going to break us apart, but you choosing to come here, us talking so openly, it gives me hope we can fix us."

His stomach clenched. He was grateful for God calling an audible that pushed him to France, and right now he wouldn't change a thing. But Natalie needed to know the full story. He offered a quick silent prayer that his explanation would be received well.

He tapped his foot against hers. "I'm glad I'm here too, Nat." Hopefully, they'd both still feel that way after he clarified her misunderstanding.

"Ever been to Boston?" Everleigh's voice abruptly broke the moment as she burst through the front door and raced down the steps toward them.

Brooke descended beside her. "If not, get ready to check it off your list."

Natalie stood and turned. Mason took a second to gain his bearings as he rose too. He leaned his lips close to her ear. "We need to finish this conversation."

She turned, her mouth brushing softly across his in a peck. Nat hadn't kissed him in months, and the surprise of the movement coupled with the warmth in her gaze practically made him miss her two-word verbal response. "Most definitely."

Was his wife flirting with him? Because while it had been a while since he'd seen the action from her, that felt an awful lot like innuendo. His body warmed, and he welcomed the cool breeze. There remained a lot for him to say before he could respond to her the way he wanted.

"You decoded the message?" Natalie's full attention had turned to her friends.

Mason struggled to dial into the conversation. Especially since he seemed to be missing key information. "What message?"

Everleigh lifted a ledger while Brooke held up a pin of some sort. One shaped like a book.

"This pin was hidden in that ledger," Brooke explained.

"Behind it was a message written in code," Natalie added.

"Which I just solved." Everleigh bounced on her toes in excitement. "It turned out to be a Latin phrase and a location. *Custos Verborum* and Boston."

"Keeper of the Words." Natalie practically breathed the phrase in awe. She looked at Brooke. "Then it's real?"

For someone who seemed to always play it cool, this information had Brooke looking like a kid in the candy store, already hopped up on sugar. "Seems to be."

What was going on?

As if sensing he was lost, Natalie turned to Mason. "We think Hollis sent the book to an underground bookstore in Boston. That's why none of my or Brooke's contacts knew its whereabouts."

"An underground bookstore?" That was as foreign a thought as his wife knowing Latin, but she'd translated the phrase without missing a beat—or pulling out her phone to use Google Translate, which he'd have done.

Natalie nodded. "It's kind of like a secret society for people who want to share unique copies of books, preserve original manuscripts, or save ones that others think should be burned. Brooke and I have heard rumors of such places, but we've never actually been to one."

"And you think that pin links to such a place?"

"I do," Natalie said. "Especially hearing that phrase along with it. In all the rumors floating around, the pin and phrase remain a part of each one. Until now I never knew what the pin looked like, nor have I seen physical proof any of this existed."

"If you've never seen it, how do you know it's real?"

"We don't." Brooke responded before Natalie could. "Not for sure anyway, but it's a lead, so we should chase it down."

"Which is going to be tough. There are a lot of bookstores in Boston." Everleigh typed on her phone.

Natalie nodded. "And we should check them all out, especially the oldest ones. But there's one in particular that might be the place to start. It's called Brattle Book Shop, and it's one of the largest antiquarian bookshops in the country. It's been in the Gloss family for years, and the current proprietor, Ken Gloss, is a genius when it comes to antique and rare books. He's appraised for Harvard, the FBI, even *Antiques Roadshow*."

"I've heard of him," Brooke said.

Everleigh took the pin from her. "Sounds like someone who might be familiar with this and even a *Custos Verborum* himself. His place could house the underground bookstore."

"Right. Like a speakeasy. Some hidden entrance that we need to know the secret knock for it to open." Brooke knocked on a pretend door. "Hopefully, he'll tell us what it is."

"Isn't that what the pin is for?" Mason asked. "Kind of like wearing your team's logo so strangers know you're both fans."

Natalie grinned at him. "Exactly. Let's hope when we find the place, that'll be enough to get us in the door."

Everleigh continued down the steps toward their car. "My guess is John will have our plane ready for us to fly to Boston tomorrow. We should head to the hotel and pack up."

Brooke followed her, and Mason took a step down before he realized Natalie lingered on her step. "Nat?"

She nibbled her lip. "I know you already gave up a lot to be here and that you still have responsibilities at home even if it is summer. I understand if you need to fly home instead of to Boston."

A boatload of work did sit on his office desk. Summer training had started, and soon there'd be tryouts. There also remained a lot for him and Natalie to iron out. Yes, he had responsibilities he couldn't shirk, but he also had people in place who could help cover them while he reprioritized his life. He'd let the things that were most important slide, and he'd nearly lost them.

Lost her.

"If you really want me there, I'll be there," he said.

"I really do."

He clasped her hand. "Then I guess we're going to Boston."

He just hoped the rest of their conversation about Utah wouldn't slam shut the door that had creaked open between them.

CHAPTER TWELVE

Luciana Perez, age thirty-eight
Lekeitio, Spain, 1952

THE LOWERING SUN OVER THE vineyards provided the perfect backdrop to this family party. Luciana looked out across the dirt, vines, and plump grapes Papi would soon harvest. Tonight, however, he'd had their servants place long wooden tables in the yard and cover them with white linen to celebrate her return. She could not believe it had been nine years since she'd dined with her siblings and parents beside her.

Angus captured her attention from where he sat on Papi's right. She'd been placed to her father's left, providing a perfect view of her handsome husband, who beamed brightly tonight. His familiar smile hadn't dimmed since she'd told him they were expecting nearly six months ago. Her stomach jolted as their child in her womb rolled, and Luciana placed her hand on her belly. After years trying to conceive, then tearfully releasing the dream of motherhood, she still could hardly believe she was pregnant. Every day she marveled at the gift of God growing inside her.

Her little sister, Marisol, leaned close. "It's wonderful, isn't it? To feel your child move?"

She'd never grow tired of the sensation. "I cherish it."

"I cherish having you home." Marisol squeezed Luciana's hand under the table. "I've missed you."

"And I, you."

When Luciana had left nine years ago, Marisol had been single. Months

125

later her sister had met Raul Bolivar, fallen in love, and married. Now Marisol and Raul had five children—four girls and, finally, a boy. After hearing their story, Luciana had struggled to be joyful rather than jealous of her little sister. Why had so much happened so quickly and easily for Marisol, when Luciana had faced one struggle after another?

She looked again at Angus. He was worth every hardship and all the years she'd waited to marry him.

"Friends and family." Papi stood, wineglass in hand. A slight breeze blew open his white linen shirt, and sunlight caught the gold charm hanging around his neck. The pendant's sparkle rivaled that of his smile. "Thank you for joining me this evening to celebrate the return of my eldest." He bestowed an adoring glance on Luciana before sweeping his focus across the small crowd seated around the three long tables. His gaze finally rested on Mamá at the opposite end from him. "It is with great joy Camilla and I welcome Luciana and her husband home. So please eat, drink, and be merry, for while we do not know what tomorrow brings, today has brought rejoicing."

Around the table glasses clinked as the servants brought platters of roasted vegetables, fish, and pasta. Plates were piled high as conversation flowed. Luciana observed the festivities. She and Angus had stepped across the threshold of Papi's home only last week, and she still grappled with how much had changed in such a short time. Papi might liken her return to that of the prodigal child in the Bible, but Luciana believed her story more closely resembled Jacob's.

When Angus had proposed to her at eighteen, Papi had refused to give his blessing. Angus didn't have the wealth or lineage that Papi approved of for marrying his oldest daughter. When Papi realized how deeply Luciana loved Angus, he'd offered for Angus to come work for him with the promise that one day he could have Luciana's hand in marriage.

An honorable man, Angus agreed to tend the vineyards, but he refused to step into Papi's other world of business. It was this same nobility of heart that had caused Angus to insist they wait to marry until he received her father's blessing. As such, the same quality that drew her to him kept them apart. For fourteen long years Angus worked for Papi with the ever-dangling promise of marriage. Had her best friend, Adelheid, not lost the love of her life, perhaps Luciana would still be waiting to marry hers. Yet when she received Adelheid's letter that Will had died, Luciana knew life was too short to continue waiting.

She and Angus approached Papi, who refused yet again to allow them to marry unless Angus agreed to carry the mantle of the Perez family. The next day, she and Angus ran away to elope.

They didn't have the same luxuries her home with Papi provided. Meals were hard to scrounge together, yet they never felt hungry. Warmth was hard to find in winters, yet they never felt cold. Money was hard to accumulate, yet they never felt in want. They had each other. That was enough.

All they longed for was a child, and finally God answered their prayers.

Through hooded eyes, Luciana watched Angus dig into his plate of food. He'd changed since she'd told him she was pregnant. What had seemed like enough in their home these past nine years no longer sufficed. He'd talked of returning home to her family and their shelter. Luciana had refused to agree. Then Angus had arrived home two weeks ago with a letter from her mother and father, pleading with them to return home. Angus would work the vineyards once more. Papi apologized for his behavior that sent them away. He missed her, and he wanted to know his grandchild.

She'd become so emotional with this pregnancy, and Papi's words caused endless tears. She missed her family, and she longed for Angus to not feel the pressure of fatherhood. Moving home made sense. Last week they'd arrived on the same doorstep they'd left from nine years ago and were welcomed with open arms.

"I know it's hard to eat when you haven't much room in your stomach, but you should try to have something." Marisol pointed to Luciana's empty plate. "How about some fish? The protein will be good for you and the baby."

"All right." She reached for a fillet, and as she did, she caught sight of Raul staring at Angus. Her brother-in-law ground his jaw, anger simmering from him. The two men sat side by side, but as Angus turned to speak with Papi, he missed Raul's scowl.

Luciana leaned close to Marisol. "Is Raul unhappy with Angus?"

Marisol cast a glance toward her husband before meeting Luciana's eyes. "He's fighting a bit of envy that Papi placed Angus close to his side. He hasn't had to share Papi in all the time he's been a part of the family."

Luciana motioned toward their other brothers-in-law, Sebastian and Nicolas, who were married to their younger sisters. "Do they not count?"

"Truthfully?" Marisol shrugged. "No. You know that Papi is full of tradition. With you gone, I've been the eldest, and as such, Raul was in line to carry on the Perez family line. He's worked with Papi since we married, and their relationship only grew stronger when Santiano Junior was born."

Papi had longed for a son himself, but he'd been blessed with four daughters and then ten granddaughters. Last year when Marisol had her son, she'd named him after Papi, with Raul's insistence.

"You've told Raul that Angus and I want nothing to do with Papi's business, right? Angus is happy to work the vineyards." While the Perez family was known for their wine making, Papi's true profession of buying and selling priceless—and often stolen—artifacts, jewels, and antiquities was a well-guarded secret. One Luciana had discovered at a young age and her sisters learned of as adults.

"I have, though he is doubtful Papi feels the same."

"It does not matter how Papi feels. Angus and I made our feelings known when we agreed to return home."

Marisol merely nodded, though her expression remained guarded.

Luciana squeezed her sister's hand once again. "You have nothing to worry about, nor does Raul."

Before she could respond, Papi clanked his knife against his glass. "It is time for gifts." All attention swiveled to him, and Papi picked up a small wrapped package from beside his plate. He handed it to Luciana. "This is for you and my soon-to-be grandson."

"Papi." Luciana fought the desire to observe Raul or Marisol's expressions. Still, she felt her sister stiffen even as Luciana admonished Papi. "We do not know that we're having a son."

"I *do* know." Papi's smile grew wide. "It is the fulfillment of God's promise to me. A son from my eldest to carry on the Perez family line."

Luciana's brow crinkled, and she sought Angus out across the table to reassure him they remained on the same page. Their child would not inherit Papi's business. Yes, they'd reconciled with her family, but only to repair their tattered relationship. Angus's full attention, however, rested on Papi, and the look on both of their faces caused her muscles to tense.

That tautness grew as Raul, Marisol's husband, glowered in his place beside Angus.

Papi handed her the gift. "Open it."

Setting aside her unease—pregnancy had caused varying emotions, surely that was all these were—Luciana accepted Papi's gift. She untied the ribbon and removed the brown wrapping, tears welling in her eyes as she glimpsed what Papi had given her. *"Alice's Adventures Under Ground."* She gently rubbed the woven green cover, creased with age, as wonderful memories floated through her mind.

"For you to read to him." Papi spoke with the gentle voice he'd used when he'd read to her as a child. It had been so long since she'd heard that tone. "As I once read to you."

Scooting close to him, Luciana pressed a kiss to his cheek. "My son *or daughter* will love it as much as I did. Thank you."

From his other side, Angus repeated their gratitude. "Yes, thank ye. We will be sure to carry on yer traditions."

Pounding his fist on the table, Raul shoved back his chair and stomped away. Marisol excused herself. "I will check on him."

Papi lifted his hand. "Sit, Marisol. Raul will come back. He's simply overheated."

Marisol looked from Papi to her husband, then back to Papi before settling into her seat. "I'm sure you are right."

"Of course I am." Papi motioned to everyone. "Please bring your gifts as we enjoy dessert."

One by one family and friends blessed Angus and her with gifts for their child as the servants brought out *bizcocho*, a sponge cake she'd have each birthday. As twilight descended, Papi and Mamá walked their guests out. Luciana hugged her little sisters, who went to collect their children from the nannies. Raul had not returned, but Marisol assured them he would be fine.

Angus collected their gifts. "This abundance surprises me."

"My family has always been generous." Though often stipulations were attached to their generosity. While neither Angus nor Papi had said as much, she now worried that was the case with their return home. "Angus," she began, nerves nearly stealing her voice, "you aren't helping Papi with anything other than the vineyards, are you?"

Angus's hands stilled around the small teething beads he was adding to their basket, and his jaw tightened. Not in anger—that emotion rarely played across his face. This sentiment was steely determination. "I'm helping yer Papi with anything that will give us the life ye and our child deserve."

For the past six months he'd fixated on all the things they lacked, while she'd reminded him of all they possessed. Their lives were full, yet suddenly he counted them as empty. "We already have that."

Papi chose that moment to rejoin them. He picked up the worn copy of *Alice's Adventures Under Ground*, but rather than add it to their basket of gifts, he pressed it into Angus's hand. "You will care for it until it's time to pass it on to your son."

Angus nodded. "I will."

Luciana looked between them both, completely lost as to whatever was transpiring between them. Papi clapped Angus on the back. "Good. This has long been a treasured book of my family." He looked to Luciana. "For you especially. It makes me incredibly happy that I am able to pass it on to you now. I feared this day would not come."

With her inability to conceive, so had she. There were many stories she hoped to pass on to her own children. Yet today, with her heart pounding a familiar rhythm that had started on that night so many years ago when she'd sneaked away to read from *Alice's Adventures*, she feared this was no longer a story she wanted to tell her little family.

CHAPTER THIRTEEN

WITH THE EXCEPTION OF BRINGING home a newborn, Natalie couldn't remember ever being this tired. She hadn't slept well this week, which wasn't entirely unusual since crossing the threshold of forty. She'd endure weeks where sleep eluded her until exhaustion finally claimed her. It seemed, between the lack of solid rest and the physical work of cleaning out the Hollis estate, that fatigue had finally come calling.

"Oh no you don't." Mason hauled her upright from where she'd slumped onto the bed. "We're only dropping our suitcases in here, then we're meeting Brooke and Everleigh downstairs." The plan was to start exploring Boston tonight.

Natalie groaned. "You go and take notes for me." She remained limp. If he wanted her out of this bed, he was going to have to put some muscle into it.

Unfortunately, she'd married a coach who still considered himself an athlete and worked out like one. Normally, she'd admire the payoff of all his hard work. But as he lifted her to a sitting position, she mentally badmouthed it.

"Come on," Mason encouraged. "You'll thank me later."

"Highly doubtful."

This twelve-hour travel day wasn't helping anything either. All she wanted to do was sleep. "It's eleven o'clock in Colmar. That's past my bedtime."

"But it's only five o'clock in Boston." He refused to relinquish his hold on her arms. "I know you want to see some of the bookstores that are still open this evening."

"They'll be open again tomorrow."

They sat at a stalemate, in which Natalie kept her eyes closed. After a long moment, she heard Mason's sigh as he let go of her. Ha! She knew she was more stubborn than him.

Natalie snuggled onto the bed, not bothering with the blankets, as their hotel room door opened and closed. She drifted off so quickly she never heard it open again.

A freezing cold lump slid down her back, and she jolted upward, reaching for the slippery culprit. "Mason!" She screamed as her husband stood back and chuckled. "You did not just pour ice down my back."

"Guilty." He held up an ice basin. "I have more if you need it."

"I didn't need the first cube."

"Could have fooled me."

Her eyes narrowed in on him. "You know I have a long memory."

His dimple deepened. "Yeah, I do." The way he said the words seemed like something about them hurt, but he blinked the strange emotion away too fast for her to dissect it. He shook the bucket of ice, and the cubes clanked against the metal. "Maybe I should make this worth the payback I'm sure will come my way."

"Don't you dare."

He set it down. "I won't, but only because your friends are waiting."

"Ugh." She groaned. "Don't remind me." She stood and stretched, then reached for her sling bag. "All right, let's go before I decide an ice bath is a small price to pay for sleep."

"Ha." Mason's phone rang, and he glanced at the screen, then looked to her. "It's Trey. I should take this, since I've been out of pocket."

After their talk on the steps yesterday, the tension between them had loosened. They still had a lot to work through, and both their emotions remained tender and easy to inflame, but at least they were talking again. As such, she understood how important it was that he know she wanted him around.

"I'll wait."

"You're sure?"

When she nodded, he answered and moved across the room. Based on the side of the conversation she could hear, Trey was checking in on when Mason would return and catching him up on a few things happening around the school. Natalie unzipped her suitcase to start unpacking, when something Mason said captured her attention.

". . . not your fault." He rubbed the back of his neck as he stared out their large window overlooking downtown Boston. "Winters in the mountains would have been a bear anyway."

The disappointment in his voice gutted her. Did Mason consider it her fault that he'd lost out on Utah? Was he regretting his decision?

She brought her toiletry bag to the bathroom and returned for her curling iron and hair dryer.

Mason said goodbye to Trey, hung up, and turned to her. "Ready?"

"Mason, if you need to fly out to Utah—"

He grimaced and held up his hand. "About Utah." Someone knocked at their door, and he sighed. "Go ahead. We can talk later."

She hesitated, but the knock turned to pounding. Sighing, she strolled to the door and opened it to find Everleigh and Brooke standing there. "I thought we were meeting in the lobby."

"We were." Brooke brushed past her. "Until John called and said he'd finally gotten a hold of Caspar, who wants to speak with us."

Natalie met Mason's eyes, and he moved toward the round walnut table in the corner of their room. He shrugged, but intrigue was written all over his face. Natalie stepped back as Everleigh entered, and they all congregated around the table. Brooke set her phone in the middle and answered just as it started to ring.

"I have them all here, John," Brooke said.

"Good. Let me conference Caspar in then."

A bit of rustling and then Caspar greeted them. "Hello, everyone. I trust your flight to Boston went well?"

"It did." Natalie scooted closer to the table. "Though we're all a little tired."

"I've no doubt." A pause filled with clicking filtered across the line. "John told me some of what's happening, and I think it's time I give you more information." This had them all leaning forward. When they remained silent, Caspar continued. "You might recall Jerrick Perez from his aid in finding the Florentine Diamond."

Jerrick's mother, Luciana, had been Archduchess Adelheid's best friend, and it was Luciana's journals—loaned to them by Jerrick—that had produced clues leading them to the diamond.

"We remember him," Brooke said. "We also remember his family isn't exactly aboveboard."

Due to her work within the antique world, Brooke had been familiar with the Perez name. But it had been Gertie and her past within the FBI's Gem and Jewelry Theft department who'd confirmed the Perez family both collected and fenced priceless items, though they hadn't been active in years.

Mason's questioning gaze swung to Natalie's. She held up a finger, hoping he'd understand she'd fill him in as soon as the call was over.

"That is all in their past," Caspar reminded them. "Yet because of his family's reputation, Jerrick does prefer to keep a low profile. Which is why he asked to have you retrieve the book for him rather than do it himself. Not to mention, he has some health issues, if you also recall."

"And you didn't tell us it was for Jerrick because . . ." Everleigh prodded.

"It wasn't necessary information at the time."

"You didn't think that was *necessary* information?" Mason palmed the table. "To let my wife know she was recovering a book for a criminal?"

"John told me you'd joined us, Mason. It's a pleasure to meet you." Caspar's automated voice didn't allow for warmth, though his words conveyed the feeling. "And to answer your question, like I already stated, no, I hadn't thought it applicable to the job at hand. However, now that John has briefed me on new developments, I felt the need to bring everyone up to speed."

"How kind of you." Sarcasm coated each of Mason's words.

Natalie reached for his arm and gave it a squeeze. "Why is this book so important to Jerrick?"

"Because his mother read it to him as a child."

Brooke frowned. "Then why on earth did he part with it?"

"He didn't. Not intentionally." That was all the explanation he offered, though he did continue. "It took some time, but he eventually tracked it to the Hollis estate."

"You've told him it wasn't there?" Brooke asked.

"Yes, he's been made aware. He's hopeful you'll locate it there in Boston."

Mason sat forward. "What about the man Natalie thought she saw following her? I already had my concerns, but now knowing more about this Jerrick guy, I'm definitely worried."

"I'm looking into that. While I can't promise there's no connection, I can promise Jerrick has ensured your safety."

"That's not very reassuring," Mason scoffed.

"I understand. Which is why I'll also understand if you would like to end this job here."

Natalie shared a look with her friends. "The man I saw in France definitely looked like the Matt I met, but it was from a distance and in a crowd. It could have been someone bearing a strong resemblance." Which sounded more plausible than Matt having followed them to another country. "We're already here." She looked to Mason. "With you, and you have our backs. Plus, it sounds like Jerrick does too, *if* someone even needs to have them."

"Nat." Mason drew out her name, clearly aware of where she was headed but not convinced of her direction.

"I'm just saying we might as well see what Boston has to offer as far as answers."

Brooke nodded. "I agree."

"Me too," Everleigh added. "From what Gertie has said, the Perez family was a big player in their day, but it's been decades since that was the case. We could be jumping at shadows on the wall."

Mason cracked his knuckles. "And if we're not?"

"I assure you, if I find out that you're not, I'll pull you from the job myself." This from Caspar.

"Then I'm still in," Brooke said.

"Me too," from Everleigh.

Natalie held Mason's gaze until he leaned back in his chair with a deep breath. "We are too."

"You'll keep me in the loop, John?" Caspar asked.

John gave a decisive nod. "Always."

"Then I look forward to hearing what you find there in Boston."

They said their goodbyes and hung up. The conversation had pushed away any vestiges of fatigue, and Natalie jumped into the business at hand. "I mapped out the bookstores we can check yet tonight. Brattle Book Shop closed at five thirty, so we'll have to go there tomorrow. There are three others within walking distance that stay open until eight." She placed a map of the surrounding area onto the table between them.

"Your idea of walking distance and mine might be different." Everleigh's finger traced the line Natalie had made on the map.

Brooke studied the paper. "That's more than I thought we'd find."

"I expanded my search to anything fifty years or older, and they have to deal with used and new books." She'd spent the plane ride home crafting this list. Some bookstores she'd already been familiar with. Others were new to her. "I'm still most interested in the Brattle, but I figured being generous in my parameters meant we hopefully won't miss anything."

Mason shifted beside her. "And the plan is to simply walk into these places and casually show off the pin until someone says something?"

"Pretty much." That was what made this hunt hard. Sort of like picking the right marble from a bag when blindfolded. "Even if the actual location we're looking for isn't one of these stores, it's likely one of the owners could have information to share with us. This is at least a place to start."

→ ←

The only luck they'd had last night was when the line at Mike's Pastry only took ten minutes to get through. The popular bakery on the North End served cannoli that was easily worth three times that wait. Natalie's stomach rumbled simply thinking of the thick ricotta cream with the crispy shell encasing it. Luckily, they'd walked enough steps to offset the extra calories.

"You're wishing you'd gotten an extra cannoli for this morning, aren't you?" Mason leaned against the mirrored elevator wall.

The doors dinged and opened, and they stepped onto the second floor. "How'd you know?"

He dipped his head near hers in a conspiratorial gesture. "Because I was thinking the same thing."

She laughed.

They crossed the lobby to the escalator that would deliver them street level. Today they'd grab the T, Boston's public transit, and ride it farther into the city. There were three more bookstores downtown to check.

Natalie held the railing of the escalator and faced Mason as they descended. "If we strike out today, I'm not sure what our next step will be."

"Good thing you're with a guy who's familiar with striking out."

She snorted. "Please. You hit every ball ever pitched to you, and baseball wasn't even your strongest sport."

"You have a faulty memory. Pretty sure I struck out more often than hit homers."

"Homers. RBIs. Base hits." She shrugged. "Those are all I remember."

"Seriously?"

"Seriously." They stepped off at the bottom, and she grabbed his hand to move him out of the way of the people behind them. She tugged him to a stop. "I know you struck out sometimes, Mace, but I chose to focus on your successes."

He cracked his knuckles. "I figured you only saw the failures."

"Because that's what you see." Her hand went to his chest, and she pressed over his heart. "I'm sorry I stopped cheering you on and helping you see what an amazing man you are. I want to do that again, but you have to believe it for yourself too. Believe in the gifts and talents God placed in you, and understand they're worth celebrating, even if they look different from the person's next to you."

His hand massaged the back of his neck. "Sometimes I think God skipped over me when he was handing out gifts and talents."

"Oh, Mace. He didn't. I promise."

"How do you know?"

"Because I see them in you." She could count off the list, but that wouldn't convince him. His hurting heart needed something more. "Ask him to show you all the amazing things he's placed inside you. He will, and I'll be right here reinforcing them as he does. I never should have stopped." His heart beat beneath her fingertips, and her eyes latched on to his. She'd missed him more than she'd realized. Missed being his partner. She shared blame in the distance between them.

Mason reached out, and his fingers skimmed over her cheek to tuck a strand of hair behind her ear. Heat flared in his eyes as they flickered to her lips. This was the part of the story where the heroine leaned in for her long-awaited kiss, and she'd happily follow the script.

Except as she pressed up on her toes to reach her husband's mouth, he shifted and pressed his lips against her forehead. Her lips met his neck, and her hands slid along his ribs as she steadied herself. She peeked up to find uncertainty on his face.

"Nat, about Utah."

Her insides twisted at the abrupt change in topic. "Are you regretting your decision?"

"No, Nat. I will never regret choosing you. But—"

"If you two are done canoodling, let's get this show on the road." Brooke interrupted from just inside the glass doors.

Mason growled, and Natalie sniggered as she faced her friend. "Canoodling?"

Brooke moved to allow another couple through the doors. "I thought you'd appreciate my extended vocabulary."

"I do." Holding his hand, Natalie started for the door that Brooke was now exiting.

Mason didn't move, and she turned to find him watching her in earnest. "Go out with me tonight? Just you and me."

Warmth infused her. "Are you asking me on a date?" They hadn't gone on an official date in months. Possibly all year. Sure, they'd had stilted dinners together or seen a movie, where the car ride had remained silent, but they hadn't actually dated in far too long. With him standing there asking her now, that look of uncertainty still on his face, she was almost as nervous as when he'd invited her on their first date.

He nodded. "Dinner and time to talk?"

"I'd like that." She pulled him toward the door. "Let's get going before they leave without us."

Outside, Everleigh and Brooke waited on the sidewalk in the morning sun. Everleigh's brunette waves hung loose against her shoulders, while Brooke had swept her blond hair into a sleek ponytail. The forecast called for another afternoon of blue skies and upper-eighties temps, so they'd all donned shorts and T-shirts.

They crossed the parking lot and two streets on their way to the Charles/MGH stop on the T. After all the miles they'd walked yesterday, they'd agreed to use public transit to travel the longer stretches today. They boarded the subway and headed toward Downtown Crossing, the stop nearest Brattle Book Shop. After a short walk, they arrived at the historic location.

With its massive number two yellow pencil over the door and large glass windows, the storefront was iconic in its look. But it was the multiple book carts situated in the shadow of the towering brick buildings beside Brattle Book Shop that made it particularly unique. Especially with the black-and-white mural of some of the world's most influential writers covering one of those walls.

"I have a good feeling about this place." Brooke stood on the sidewalk as she surveyed customers perusing the outdoor offerings.

"Me too," Natalie said. "I'm hopeful Ken is in today. Either way we need to check out the third floor. It's where they keep the rare books."

Everleigh patted the bag around her waist. The lapel pin resided inside it. "Let's go."

They made their way inside, and Natalie stopped. Wooden shelves met metal shelves, and even a few had glass doors, preventing easy access. Every surface held books of varying colors, textures, heights, and thicknesses.

"Wow." She crossed to a section and ran her fingers over the spines as she read each one. Many titles were familiar. Some weren't.

"You could spend all day in here, couldn't you?" Mason asked from beside her.

She nodded as she walked along reading titles. "Oooh, she's a new author I've heard great things about." Natalie tapped a name. "I want to read her debut but haven't had a chance." She trailed her finger across more spines. "So many books, so little time."

Brooke joined them after speaking with someone at the small checkout desk. "I know it's practically a travesty, but we don't have time to look around. Ken's supposedly on the third floor, and he's leaving soon for a meeting."

The only thing that could pull Natalie from the marvel of this space was the enticing promise of what another could hold. But if at all possible, she'd be back. "All right, let's go."

They climbed the stairs to the third floor and walked the aisles to find Ken tucked in by one of the windows overlooking the street. He was speaking with another customer about a book in his hand.

While they waited, Everleigh grabbed something from the shelf beside her. "I have got to get this for Niles."

Natalie arched her brow at the title. "*Winnie-the-Pooh*?"

"Trust me, he'll adore it." With a sweet grin, Everleigh cradled the book against her.

Natalie started to prod for more details when the customer with Ken left, and the owner turned to them. With white hair, a prominent nose, and a welcoming grin, the older gentleman seemed to enjoy his job and his patrons. "Can I help you?"

Brooke stepped forward. "We're hoping you recognize this." She nodded to Everleigh, who tucked the copy of *Winnie-the-Pooh* under her arm to pull out the pin.

Ken's expression smoothed from curious to impassive. "Are you hoping I can appraise it for you?" His voice held a hint of a Boston accent, though not nearly as thick of one as Natalie expected.

"We're hoping you're a *Custos Verborum* and could help us locate a book we're seeking." Natalie's gut said the direct route with Ken would be the best one. If this society was real, Ken Gloss had to either know of it or be a part of it.

He studied them for a long moment before his wide-set blue eyes glanced once again to the pin. He held out his hand. "May I?"

Brooke passed it to him.

He walked to a desk in the back, where he picked up a magnifying glass. He inspected the pin closely, then looked at them. "Where did you obtain this?"

"From a Mr. Hollis's estate in Colmar, France."

Ken set down the magnifying glass and returned the bookmark to Brooke. "Cressa Gathin. Old Corner Bookstore."

Then he turned and strolled away.

CHAPTER FOURTEEN

"Wait!" Natalie called to Ken's retreating form.

He stopped and turned, but rather than speaking, he merely lifted his brows and dipped his square chin.

"The Old Corner Bookstore is a Chipotle now." The words tasted nowhere near as satisfying as the restaurant itself. The Old Corner Bookstore had once housed Ticknor and Fields Publishing and put out such greats as *The Scarlet Letter*, *Uncle Tom's Cabin*, and *Walden*—and that only named a few. While the brick building itself still stood, it now served people's stomachs rather than their minds, a fact that upset Natalie. She was all for burrito bowls, but not when they replaced such historic sights.

Across from her, Ken's cheeks lifted as his smile reappeared. It emboldened her to continue. "*Cressa* is Greek for 'gold.' I'm willing to bet if I look up *Gathin*, it'll tie in somehow too."

Beside her, Brooke already had her phone out, and she tapped on the screen. "Yep. One of its meanings is 'storyteller.'"

Ken didn't confirm or deny his words. Instead he merely clasped his hands together. "You have all the information you need to seek what you're looking for." With a nod, he departed.

Natalie looked at Mason and her friends. "Anyone hungry for Chipotle?"

"I love tacos, but we just finished breakfast," Everleigh said. "I am, however, hungry for answers."

"Me too," Brooke said.

"Me three," Natalie agreed.

Mason waved his hand toward the stairs. "Guess I'm 'Me four.'"

In under ten minutes they walked the three blocks to where the Old Corner Bookstore used to be. With sunshine streaming from a blue sky overhead, sweat rolled between Natalie's shoulder blades. Somewhere in the past few years, she'd developed a Goldilocks approach to weather. If the thermometer dropped below fifty, it was too cold. Above seventy? Too hot. *Just right* fell between those two numbers, and today was unabashedly an outlier. She needed more deodorant.

Brooke reached the door first and pulled it open. "Still cannot believe this place isn't home to books anymore."

"It's criminal." Natalie stepped through, the scent of spicy meat and warm tortillas greeting her.

The restaurant had just opened, and the teenager behind the counter looked up from where he was stocking ingredients. "Can I help you?"

Everleigh stepped forward. "We're wondering if Cressa Gathin is working?"

The kid shrugged. "Uh, no one by that name works here."

Brooke had wandered to the far side of the room, where tables met a display. "Guys?" She beckoned them over. "Come see this."

A small grouping of stories and book-related objects paid homage to the history of the Old Corner Bookstore. Natalie perused the items until her gaze caught on what Brooke undoubtedly wanted them to see. A small gold statue of Harriet Beecher Stowe held up one side of a row of novels that extended to meet another gold statue of Louisa May Alcott. The titles in between these unique bookends were all ones that had been published in this very spot.

"Gold storytellers." Brooke pointed to the statues.

Everleigh pressed up on tiptoes. "I don't see any inscriptions on them." She ran her gaze over the wood shelves. "Or anything carved into the shelf itself. Is he watching us?"

"The kid?" Mason asked.

"Yeah."

"Nope."

Everleigh picked up one of the statues, looked it over, then replaced it before reaching for the other. "Nothing."

Natalie studied the titles, her eyes latching on to the Charles Dickens offering. "That's strange."

"What?" Brooke asked.

"Well, they used familiar titles for everyone but Dickens. For him they used *A Dinner at Poplar Walk*, which, while it's his first published work, was published in a magazine. They did eventually add it into a collection of his works, but to my knowledge it was never published as a stand-alone."

Brooke squinted. "Think it means something?"

"It has to," Everleigh answered. "We just have to figure out what."

"You're the puzzle solver," Brooke said.

"But she's the literary scholar." Everleigh pointed to Natalie.

Except Natalie had no clue what any of this meant.

Mason stood beside her, hands in his pockets. "How about we head out into the fresh air, walk a little bit, and talk out what you all know." They looked at him, and he shrugged. "Movement helps me think. Figured it might with you all too."

"He's not wrong." Everleigh brushed past him.

Natalie grabbed his hand and squeezed. They stepped into the late-morning sun. Across the street, a small space with red bricks, statues, and metal benches beckoned them. Crossing over, they stayed silent as they chewed on the pieces of info they'd collected.

"Why Dickens?" Brooke questioned after a moment.

"It's got to be his name or the title." Everleigh pulled out her phone. "Maybe there's a street or restaurant that uses one or the other. The title does mention dinner, after all."

Everyone followed suit and pulled up Google Maps on their phone. Natalie zoomed in on the area around them. Thirty seconds later, she froze. "I think I know what it's referencing." She held out her phone. "Fleet Street."

Brooke's eyes widened. "Dickens used that street in several of his novels."

"Well, he actually used London's Fleet Street, but yes." Excited, Natalie nodded. "There's a small section a few blocks from here called Fleet Street."

"It's worth a try. Let's go." Everleigh headed in the direction of the subway station.

They hopped back onto the T and rode that to North Station, then walked east to Fleet Street. A little over a block long and situated between brick buildings, Fleet Street was an offshoot of the Freedom Trail.

"This is crazy," Brooke said as they walked farther east.

"We've done crazy before." Natalie studied the buildings. "Just keep an eye out for anything with Dickens's name on it or that might relate to *A Dinner at Poplar Walk*."

Everleigh's focus swiveled up and down the street. "A restaurant, another bookstore, even a plaque that says something about him."

"Or a poplar door?" Mason's question reached from behind them. They all stopped and turned around to find him staring at an antique wooden door beneath a brick arch. He pointed to it. "My grandpa used to work with wood, and I'm not positive, but I'm pretty sure that's poplar."

Natalie had forgotten about how Mason had spent his weekends as a child on his grandpa's farm. He'd never gotten along well with his scholarly dad or brothers, but his grandpa had understood Mason. When they weren't tossing a ball or working the cornfield, they'd been in his grandpa's woodshop building furniture. Mason often said those were some of his favorite days growing up.

They joined him, and Natalie looked at her friends. Brooke motioned for her to check out the door. Natalie stepped up to it. There was no address or markings denoting what stood behind this entrance tucked under the arch, but the wood was encased in ornate decoration. A band of black iron with intricately carved scrolls created the framework. Her eyes roamed the beauty of the design. The craftsmanship was stellar. If she was part of a secret society, she'd commission something exactly like this.

"Look." Everleigh pointed over Natalie's shoulder.

Natalie squinted to see what she referred to, but she hadn't a clue.

Everleigh nudged her aside, scooted in close, and crouched for a better view. She unzipped her bag and pulled out the pin and held it beside the door's casing. "The scrollwork matches what's etched on the pin."

Now Brooke stood close too. "You're right."

Lines of concentration creased along Everleigh's brow, and she tipped her head as she studied the ironwork. Her fingers traced its dips and curves as she ran them along the perimeter of the frame. When she reached the oval knob, she paused. Her focus slid to the doorbell inches away and its large matching plate. She leaned in. "Gotcha," she whispered. Then she pressed the pin into an opening in the scrollwork. The aged black iron snugly cradled the miniature golden book. A perfect fit. As it clicked into place, bells tolled inside.

Natalie gasped. Everleigh straightened. And Brooke shared a wide-eyed stare with them both. Footsteps approached from the other side of the entrance. Overwhelming nerves and curiosity swelled, and Natalie's heartbeat pounded in her ears. Mason moved close and grasped her hand as the door creaked open.

A woman in a plum sweater opened the door and greeted them with a wide, toothy smile. She appeared to be in her early sixties, judging by the wrinkles bracketing her mouth and the few strands of gray hair streaking through her black bob. Her green eyes roamed over them. "And who, might I ask, are you?" Warm curiosity rolled through her question.

An ornate gold chandelier illuminated the foyer, casting away the shadows formed from the windowless space. Behind her a black staircase rose toward the second story.

Natalie's perusal was interrupted by Everleigh's response. "A small group who've heard you might have books of interest to us. Possibly even one in particular." She'd removed the pin from the slot in the doorbell.

The woman's palm stretched out. "Might I see what you hold in your hand?"

With a nod, Everleigh passed it to her.

Wrinkled hands turned the pin over, and then, similar to Ken earlier today, she donned the glasses dangling on a pearl strand around her neck and held it closer for inspection. After a long moment, she returned the trinket to Everleigh. "How did you acquire this?"

"We helped clean out an estate owned by the late Mr. Hollis."

As if his name was the final key, the woman's grin widened along with the opening doorway as she stepped back. "I invite you in." When they didn't immediately move, she waved her hand. "Come now. Every adventure begins with a first step, and I believe you're here as part of a grand one."

And with that they stepped inside.

Underneath her feet, a black checkerboard floor spread from evergreen wall to evergreen wall. Ebony trim encased closed doorways, and oil painted portraits of distinguished men and women lined the walls. Opulent bronze frames wrapped themselves around the paintings, but it was the subjects that captured Natalie's attention.

"Hemingway, Twain, Christie."

They flowed down the hallway, where it grew too dark to see from this vantage point.

Mason leaned in. "Who?"

"Authors." She held tight to his hand. There was something strangely satisfying about having him here with her. Living out an adventure with him by her side only made this moment sweeter. What she'd thought dead might actually be starting to blossom.

The woman in front of them halted abruptly and turned. "Dear me. I all but forgot to introduce myself." She bowed with a flourish. "I'm Kit Warmond." Then she spun around and continued down the dim hall to a black-painted door with a shiny gold knob and hinges, but it was the gold emblem embossed in the center that confirmed they'd found the right place.

"It matches." Everleigh held up the pin.

Kit looked over her shoulder. "Of course it does. That's why you're here, isn't it?" She opened the door and descended the long circular stairway behind it. Bright lanterns illuminated the way to a room filled with books.

"Follow me." Kit's voice echoed from the bottom.

Brooke took the first step of their little group. Everleigh stayed on her heels. Natalie looked to Mason, who simply shook his head.

"I can't believe this is what you've been doing all this time."

"Oh, it hasn't been anything like this. I mean, some of it has, but we haven't bumped into anything nearly this exciting."

He grinned, his expression warming. "I have a sneaky suspicion your love of books is helping nudge this discovery above the others."

"Okay. Maybe." She started downstairs. "But can you blame me?"

"Not one bit." Mason's fingers grazed her arm as his hand skimmed the railing she held on to.

Natalie reached the concrete floor and paused to take in the sight. Old stone walls formed the small space, which couldn't be more than twenty by twenty. The staircase dropped visitors directly in the middle of the room, where glassed-in bookshelves lined three-fourths of the perimeter. On the wall across from them was another glassed-in case filled with quills, inkpots, old typewriters, and other finds she had no doubt belonged to authors she'd recognize. The air down here drifted by with a chill but didn't feel damp.

Kit stood beside the lone leather club chair in the space. "This is your first visit in such a place, isn't it."

"What makes you think so?" Brooke asked.

Kit smiled. "Your look of awe. Not that there isn't always a hint of marvel in our guests, but there's something special about the wonder of that first visit. First experiences can never be replicated, nor should they be forgotten, especially the extraordinary ones." She clasped her hands together. "Now you wander. Then we'll chat." With that, she settled at her desk and her full attention turned to the work stacked there.

With a shrug that said they might as well obey, Brooke broke from their circle to peruse the room. Everyone else followed suit, but Natalie stood there in the center. She inhaled the familiar scent of worn pages bursting with stories waiting to be told. Peering around, disbelief settled in at some of the titles on the shelves. Her eyes landed on a pile of papers bound together with a cover page on top, and her breath caught in her chest. "Is that Hemingway's lost manuscript?"

Kit followed the direction of Natalie's gaze. "Ah yes. That's the only draft of his World War I novel."

Natalie addressed her friends, who watched the interaction. "His first wife, Hadley, packed up all his work to take to an editor, but the suitcase disappeared on the train as she traveled from Paris to meet him. It was never recovered."

"Until now," Kit said. "One of our Finders recently unearthed the case."

Natalie picked up on the terminology. "I've heard rumors of Keepers of the Words before, but I've never heard about Finders."

"Rumor allows for partial truth that masquerades as the whole. One must never believe speculation without asking for the veracity of the information."

Beside Natalie, Mason's brow crinkled. She reached over and squeezed his hand as Kit returned to her work. Mason had never been one to use big words, but that didn't mean he wasn't smart. Until recently she hadn't realized how much he believed otherwise, and no doubt Kit's unique vocabulary threatened to reinforce those feelings. Natalie wouldn't say anything to him here in front of everyone, but reassurance could come in silent ways. Which was why she maintained her hold on his hand.

Kit, it seemed, had said her piece and now waited on them. Natalie spoke into the quiet of the room. "So there are Finders and Keepers. What does each do?"

"And which are you?" Everleigh added.

Lifting her gaze to them, Kit's green eyes sparkled. "Questions. I do love them, and those are quite good ones." She clasped her hands together. "Finders locate books. Keepers maintain them, and we have different Keepers for each genre." Her wide grin spread. "As for me, I am merely a cog in the wheel."

"A cog? How so?" Natalie asked.

"Finders locate the books, send them to me—the Authenticator—to log, and then I mail them on their way to the correct Keepers." She moved to the shelves. "We have Keepers of British literature, American literature, children's literature, and so on."

"Is that what this society does?" Brooke asked. "Find and care for priceless manuscripts?"

"That, and also books that are threatened with extinction. The written word itself is priceless, but there are many stories people no longer want told, be they fiction or nonfiction. We safeguard both so history can be preserved." She strode to the Hemingway papers. "But we also are collectors who feel strongly about how pieces should be cared for and reputations maintained. Hemingway wasn't proud of his early work and—like many writers—wouldn't want his rough drafts in the public's hands. Yet they shouldn't simply be tossed into a rubbish bin."

"Absolutely not," Natalie agreed.

Everleigh had strolled the room while Kit spoke. Now she faced her. "We're actually looking for a specific book that someone with this pin had as a part of his collection. The notes he left pointed to the fact that it could be here with you. But I didn't see it."

Kit opened a drawer on the small desk in the room. "Each pin has a number hidden on it that corresponds to its Finder. It's what I searched for when you arrived. Yours did indeed belong to Mr. Hollis." She pulled out a leather binder and flipped through pages. "What story are you seeking?"

"An original copy of Lewis Carrol's *Alice's Adventures Under Ground*," Natalie noted before briefly explaining the past few weeks and what led them there. "I know we're not technically a Finder or a Keeper, but I promise you—I know the importance of books. I'm a historian, and I've helped preserve many antique titles. We're hoping to return this one to its rightful owner, who'll cherish it."

"Hmm." Kit studied her. "Perhaps you should be the one to hold on to the pin now that Mr. Hollis is gone." As if she'd spoken a thought that she'd intended to remain internal, Kit shook her head.

"Could we see the book?" Everleigh asked. "It must be here."

"Hollis wouldn't have pointed us here if it weren't," Brooke agreed.

"Assumptions are as faulty to rely on as rumors." Once again Kit clasped her hands together and her thumbs twiddled as she nonchalantly stood among them.

Brooke seemed to be losing her patience with the old woman, but Natalie found her fascinating. Perhaps because she and Mason had recently learned how misleading assumptions could be. They'd allowed theirs to pull them apart. Yes, truth lived in some of what they'd believed, but it had been buried underneath all their incorrect suppositions. They'd had to dig below what they'd allowed themselves to incorrectly believe to finally start dealing with the real issues between them.

Natalie faced Kit. "Did Mr. Hollis send you the book?"

Her green eyes sparkled. "That he did."

A thread of excitement spun between them. "Then can we see it?" Everleigh repeated.

"Oh dear, I'm afraid that requires another journey." Kit crossed her arms and tapped her finger against the crook of her elbow. "For the book is no longer here."

CHAPTER FIFTEEN

IF THERE WAS ONE THING Mason hated, it was seeing his wife disappointed. She'd gone from absolute delight with their discovery on Fleet Street to crestfallen with Kit's announcement that the book they sought had been mailed to the Keeper of children's literature, who could be found at Moat Brae in Scotland.

According to Kit, Moat Brae was not only home to the National Centre for Children's Literature and Storytelling, but it was also the birthplace of Peter Pan. The home and gardens that had inspired J. M. Barrie to write the classic tale still stood, and they'd been transformed to a magical location for little book lovers' imaginations to grow. "It's the perfect place for the Keeper of children's literature to stash the priceless books sent to him," Kit had declared, then revealed the location.

Mason had watched Natalie's excitement resurrect. Of course she'd been familiar with the home, and of course she planned to immediately travel there. Unfortunately, Kit's next revelation divulged that the Keeper was on vacation and wouldn't return to Scotland until the middle of next week.

Patience wasn't one of Natalie's natural virtues, the fact made abundantly clear by her mood as they returned to their hotel. They'd situated themselves in his and Natalie's suite and dialed John, who patched in Caspar.

"It looks like we'll return to Kenton Corners for a few days before heading to Scotland," Everleigh said.

"I'd really hoped we could go directly from here." Natalie slumped into the corner of the couch.

"Me too," Brooke said. "Though honestly, I could use some time at home. There's a job that needs my attention."

"And I have a man who needs some of mine," Everleigh added with a grin.

Brooke rolled her eyes.

"Kit said she'd connect with her Keeper to let him know you're coming?" John asked.

"Yes," Natalie said. "And to let him know it's okay that we take possession of the book."

Caspar's automated voice broke in. "I find it very kind of her to offer help. She didn't have to do that."

"The whole idea of the society is to ensure these books are well cared for. Everyone we've run into feels that way, and they're happy that this book will return to the family it originally belonged to."

"Jerrick will need to find a way to thank them."

"With his connections, maybe he can find a book they're still looking for and gift it to them," Natalie suggested.

"Possibly," Caspar responded. "What do we know about the Keeper you'll be meeting?"

"Not a lot." Brooke snapped her gum. "Kit said his name's Terrance MacLeod. He works at Moat Brae and has since it opened as this acclaimed literary destination. In fact, from what she said, he had a hand in making it such."

Everleigh consulted her iPad. "Seems Terrance grew up in Dumfries, Scotland, and loved the history of his town and the house. He and his wife are staples of the community and live a rather simple life."

"Other than being part of a secret society," Mason noted.

Natalie tucked her legs underneath her. "Yes. Other than that."

Still on-screen, John leaned toward his camera. "It appears there's nothing more we can do for a few more days. I have your plane scheduled for ten a.m. tomorrow. With the time change, you'll be home just after lunch. Does that work for everyone?"

After they all confirmed, John waved goodbye and disconnected the call. Brooke stood and stretched. "What do you want to bet Caspar is connecting with Jerrick right now to see if he can find a way to thank Kit for her help?"

"No doubt," Everleigh said. "Being a Perez means he most likely has more contacts in the antiquities department than all of us combined." She stood as well. "What does everyone feel like for dinner?"

Mason cleared his throat. "I'd like to take my wife out just the two of us."

Everleigh's expression morphed into that look most women wore when they watched the end of a sappy movie. "Aw. That's sweet." She turned to Brooke. "Guess it's just us then."

"Lucky me." Brooke started for the door, Everleigh on her heels. "You two kids have fun, and we'll see you in the morning."

After they were alone, Mason turned to her. "I made us reservations at Union Oyster House. It's the oldest restaurant in town, so I figured you'd want to eat there." Her love of history knew no bounds. "And before you ask, I made sure they had something other than seafood on the menu." Because she was allergic to shellfish.

He was rewarded with her pressing a kiss to his cheek as her hand squeezed his thigh. "That was incredibly sweet, and it sounds perfect." She lingered in his space, and her eyes searched his. "I'm really glad you joined me on this trip."

So was he. Every day a little more and more, especially when she looked at him with that fiery spark in her eyes again.

Mason inhaled her floral scent, his nerves firing at the feel of her pressed against him. Her fingers massaged his leg. All he had to do was dip his mouth to hers, and he had a solid idea of where things would lead. He craved her more than the dinner they'd be late for if he sank into what she offered.

Oh, his wife was a temptation he'd happily give in to. One taste of her lips couldn't hurt . . .

Except he hadn't come clean to her. Natalie was operating under false pretenses, and he refused to take advantage of their fragile trust. He wanted to strengthen their connection, not test if it could take another hit. Sleeping with her before he cleared up the miscommunication between them wouldn't be fair.

But he didn't want her to think he didn't desire her. At least that was what he told himself as he gave in to one kiss. Sliding his hand into her hair, he drifted his thumb along the soft skin behind her ear and pulled her close. He nipped softly at her bottom lip before diving into the sweetness of her. His Natalie.

Her hands wrapped around his neck, and she made that soft little sound in her throat that always tugged out his smile. Heat grew between them, and his palm slid to her waist, diving beneath the edge of her shirt to rest against her silky skin. Man, he'd forgotten the power of an everyday kiss on the couch with his wife.

As her hands slid under his shirt, he broke away while still clearheaded enough to do so. Peppering small kisses along her temple and forehead, he caught her hands and brought them around to her lap, where he maintained his hold. "If we keep this up, we'll miss our reservation."

"Is that a bad thing?"

Her smile just about had him forgetting that he was trying to be a good guy here. He pulled them to their feet and dropped one last lingering kiss on her lips. "We've got all night. Let me take you to dinner."

She coaxed him toward the bedroom. "I have a better idea how to spend the night."

He resisted. "There is nothing I'd love better than joining in on that suggestion, but we have to talk first."

She stepped close, pressing into his space. "Talking is so overrated." Her lips found the side of his neck.

He leaned his head back, giving her access even as his brain worked to remember his goal. "Trying to be a gentleman rather than a rogue." And she was making it nearly impossible. "Like that Darcy character you love so much."

Her lips drew away from his skin. "Did you just make a *Pride and Prejudice* reference?" Her breath fanned over him in soft puffs. "Maybe talking isn't so overrated."

He laughed. "You're killing me here, Nat."

She pushed up on her toes so she could reach his jawline. "That certainly wasn't my plan." Her mouth went to his ear, where she whispered exactly what her ideas were.

Lord help him, but he needed to do what was right rather than what was enticing.

"Nat." He pulled back, his voice husky. "We really need to talk." He felt her lips lifting in a smile as she continued her assault. "About Utah."

That had her pausing, and he fought against yanking the words back. But if they were going to wind up in bed together tonight, it would be after everything between them was clear. He'd allowed interruptions to prevent this hard conversation for long enough, and while they'd been legitimate distractions, he refused to let this become one.

Natalie peered up at him. "Utah?" She allowed him to lead her to the couch, and as they resettled there, she asked, "Did they call again?"

"No." He cleared his throat. If only it were that easy of an explanation. "Remember I said we still needed to talk about them?"

Fine lines wrinkled across her forehead. "Right. Okay, what did you want to say?" She reached over and brushed her fingertips across the hair at his temple. "I know it was hard for you to turn them down."

His stomach roiled. He hated this situation. Hated how he'd unintentionally misled her. He needed to simply rip the bandage off. So he looked her straight in the eye and cleared the air. "I didn't turn them down. Utah rescinded their offer before I came to France."

Those lines on her forehead deepened, and a few more spread from the corners of her eyes. It was as if the information he'd dropped was sinking in and the meaning of it growing. "Wait." She shook her head and pulled her hand to her lap. "The job offer with Utah was pulled?"

He nodded.

"Before you had a chance to interview?"

Another nod.

"You didn't choose to fly to France instead of Utah? Because Utah wasn't even an option at that point?" Her voice remained level and calm, but he knew her well enough to know a storm brewed underneath her tranquil surface.

"It was my choice to fly to France, Nat. I got on that plane for all the reasons I told you."

"Just not the one you let me believe," she scoffed, and added space between them.

He deserved her frustration. "I didn't mean for the miscommunication to occur. If you remember, I did try and bring Utah up to you a few times, but we kept getting interrupted. It's why I wanted to make sure nothing stopped us from talking about it tonight—which was incredibly hard with you kissing me. Any other time I'd have picked you up and carried you into bed, but I wanted things to be clear between us first."

"Oh. How altruistic of you." His face must have shown the sting of her words, because she held up her hand. "Sorry. It's just, this is catching me off guard."

He hated the hitch in her voice. They'd grown closer over the past week, and he hoped that trend continued. He missed his wife. "I get it. Take your time."

She pushed to a stand and paced the room. He wanted to wrap her in his arms. Assure her that nothing had changed between them in the past five minutes. He'd still chased after her. They'd still made progress and were rekindling things. They were on the path to healing their marriage, and he had every intention of persisting in this direction.

Nat needed a moment though, and he meant it when he'd said to take it.

Finally she looked across the room at him. Moisture rimmed her eyes, but no tears fell. "You did try to talk to me, Mace. I do remember, and I appreciate that you didn't allow this miscommunication to linger any longer." Her cheeks reddened, no doubt as she thought about what he'd paused between them to ensure they talked first. "Thank you."

He stood to hug her, thankful she seemed to understand.

Her strained voice stopped him. "I do have a question for you though."

"Anything." He put his hands in his pockets to quell their shaking. Something in her tone, her expression, said her understanding only went so far.

"If Utah hadn't rescinded their offer, would you have gone there instead of France? Even now?"

Her question punched the air from his lungs. Deceit sprang to his tongue, and he clamped his mouth shut. Natalie deserved a truthful answer. The problem was, if he gave it, he knew he'd hurt her. If they had any hope of forging through the mess their relationship had become, however, then they had to be honest with each other.

Lord, give me the correct words, and allow her to know my heart is for her.

He took a few calming breaths. "You know I've always wanted to work at a college level."

Like him earlier, Natalie wasn't beating around the bush. "A simple yes or no will do, Mason."

"Then yes." Man, did those two words gut him. But was that a terrible thing? To want to better himself *and* his marriage. Couldn't he do both?

One look at Natalie's face said she didn't believe he could. Still, he refused to lie.

Steeling himself, he swallowed the nausea churning inside to finish his response. "I would be in Utah."

✦ ✦

Natalie dug her hands into her hair and tugged it away from her face. Three minutes ago she couldn't imagine feeling this cold, but Mason's words functioned like an ice bath. "Wow. Okay then." Again, she paced.

"But I'm here now." Mason looked like he wanted to approach her.

She held up her palm, stopping him. "Because you had no choice."

"That's not true." He shook his head. "I could have stayed home."

Again, how kind of him. Her mouth tightened. "Honestly."

"Yes, honestly." His voice was the same soothing tone he'd used on the boys when they were little and upset. "We can't make this relationship work if we don't put everything out in the open and speak truthfully."

"Fine." If that was how he saw it. "Then let me be honest with you." Because this little disclosure helped crystallize her feelings. "What I *honestly* want is a husband who will put me first, but it's become *honestly* apparent that you can't do that. I thought with you coming to France, maybe I'd been wrong. Now I know I wasn't."

"Nat."

She stepped away as he approached. "No, Mace. I need some space and time."

He paused. Stilled. Then spoke softly. "Would you prefer I take a walk or you? I'm fine either way but want to give you what you need."

She'd laugh if she wasn't so close to crying. Did he even realize how backward his offer was? The only reason she was asking for space was because he'd put so much of it between them by constantly choosing his career over her. If he'd held her tightly all these years, picked her before his ambition, she wouldn't be the one pulling away now.

He'd give her what she needed to stop the argument but not to fix their marriage.

Suddenly she craved fresh air. "I'll go." She scooped up her purse from the dresser.

"I'll be here when you get back. We need to talk this through, Nat. Remember, we agreed not to ignore issues between us just because they're hard."

With a clipped nod, she walked out the door, rode the elevator to the lobby, and exited the hotel. Heat wrapped around her, no match for the torrent brewing inside. Unable to think of a destination, she retraced their steps from their first night in town. That led her to Charles Street, the quaint cobblestone and brick thoroughfare running through Beacon Hill. Gas lampposts lined the sidewalks, enhancing the historical feel. She didn't slow to enjoy the beauty of the architecture. Crossing Pinckney Street, she glanced down the road to where Louisa May Alcott, Henry David Thoreau, and Nathaniel Hawthorne all had lived. Her furious pace continued. It wasn't until steps later that a sign over a store to her left paused her stride.

Beacon Hill Books and Café.

Over the arched front entry, an iron frame encased a wood carving of a gray squirrel sitting atop a stack of books. She climbed the steps into what had obviously once been a townhouse and stepped into a place that felt as comforting as her own home. It didn't matter the state or town, didn't matter what amenities, didn't even matter how it was decorated . . . bookstores wrapped around her better than her favorite cozy cardigan.

Natalie inhaled the scent of pages filled with grand adventures and moments of wonder. Immediately, calm seeped into her aggravated bones. A staircase ran along the wall to her left, and right in front of her, the clerk smiled.

"Welcome to Beacon Hill Books and Café."

"This place is gorgeous."

Pale-blue walls and blond oak floors allowed for an open feel that late-afternoon sunshine streaming through the large front windows only enhanced. The perimeter was lined with fully stocked built-in bookshelves, while white antique tables held more titles. A fireplace, which no doubt made for cozy fall and winter days, nestled itself along the wall across from the register.

"It was definitely a labor of the heart, rehabilitating this into what you see today. The goal was to create a space where book lovers could spend all day. There's even a café one floor down." The clerk seemed enchanted with not only her job but her environment. "Nonfiction, fiction, and children's all take up the floors above us."

"How many more floors are there?"

"Three." She smiled. "And I highly suggest you take your time on each one, then once you're done, enjoy some tea in the café. Maybe even a tart."

Natalie didn't need convincing. "Thank you." She started up the stairs. Already her blood pressure had lowered significantly. On the next floor the owner had accented the light color palette with a brilliant warm red. Fabric-cushioned areas were built into the wall, which invited customers to relax. After she wandered around and grabbed a few books, she'd take advantage of one of those seats.

An hour later she'd perused the children's section on the top floor and visited Paige the Squirrel, the store's official stuffed-animal mascot, then returned to the fiction section. She meandered the aisles and ran her fingers over some of her best friends. Spotting a title still on her TBR pile, she pulled it from the shelf, then looked to see if anyone stood nearby. What she was about to do would be considered criminal by many.

Seeing she was alone, Natalie gave in to her vice that would likely get her kicked out of every one of her book clubs and reading circles. She flipped to the final chapter. Not one single soul knew she read the end of a novel before deciding if she would read it in its entirety, but she had no desire to begin a story that didn't contain a happily ever after.

The one in her hands did.

Sighing, Natalie grabbed a few more books that captured her interest, then settled onto one of the comfy chairs by a window. Other readers might chastise her over her habit, but there was something comforting in knowing how a story ended. She didn't have to worry about the outcome of the journey. She could rest in the guarantee that when the heroine's tale wound to an end, she'd be loved, secure, and chosen.

Wasn't that what everyone wanted?

It was how she'd tried to write her story, only somewhere along the line Mason had grabbed the pencil and scribbled in his own scenes. Perhaps that was part of their problem. They'd each tried to write their own version of the same story. Natalie leaned her head against the chair's cushion. Now they struggled to combine those adaptations. For all their conversations and shared desire to try to fix their marriage, she and Mason remained at an impasse.

This wasn't a third-act breakup like the books in her hands contained. The kind the hero and heroine could navigate through. This was smack dab in the middle of her life, and it hurt. Real life didn't provide the luxury of paging ahead, but she hadn't thought it necessary. Never in a million years would she have predicted no happily ever after existed for her and Mason.

Now, despite how she hoped differently, she couldn't see an ending where it did.

CHAPTER SIXTEEN

"So that's it?" Mason dragged a hand through his hair. He contemplated getting checked for hearing loss, because surely he hadn't heard his wife correctly. She'd been near silent when she'd returned to their hotel room on Saturday, and he'd continued to give her space. She'd only spoken as necessary during their travel home Sunday morning, then she'd worked the closing shift at the Golden Key that night. Now, as they both were about to leave for their Mondays, she finally spoke to him, but he had to have misheard her. "Twenty-two years of marriage and rather than talk through our problems, you're throwing in the towel?"

"I haven't thrown anything anywhere, Mace." Natalie's voice was resigned, as was her expression. "I just said I don't know what else to do. We want different things."

"Career-wise, maybe, but don't we both want this marriage to work? Which means we can find a compromise."

Sad laugher puffed through her nose. "You're not going to be happy staying here, and I'm not going to be happy constantly moving every time you receive a better job offer. I can't see a compromise that will work. Can you?" No fast answer sprang to mind, and Natalie pounced on his silence. "This past week was a great reprieve, but we haven't truly fixed anything. You'd still choose your career over me."

"Yes, Nat, I'd have gone to Utah instead of France, but that's not me choosing my career over you." He cracked his knuckles. "That's me staying on track with what we both agreed to when we got married. When did me sticking to our plan become a bad thing?"

Moisture built in her eyes. "When it became more important than us. Than me."

He reached for her fingers. "That's not true. You know you're important to me. We can make this work." His stomach bottomed out when she stayed quiet. "Nat?"

"I don't know how we make this relationship work when only one of us sees it's broken." She pulled her hand from his. Her eyes drifted to the clock on their kitchen wall. The one they'd been given as a wedding gift. "We're both going to be late if we don't head out."

Utter disbelief filled him. "We're supposed to just finish our coffees and go to work like this is a normal day? That's it? You tell me our marriage is broken and there's no way to fix it, but enjoy your day?"

"I never said there's no way to fix things, just that I don't know how."

Her clarification helped him calm slightly.

Shifting on her feet, Nat continued. "And I know this was crummy timing on my part, especially with how patient you've been to give me space. I probably should have waited until tonight, but I can't imagine this conversation would feel good whenever we started it." She absently rubbed her thumbnail. "Still, I'm sorry I dropped it on you this morning."

With the gray circles under her eyes, she hadn't slept any better than he had. This was eating at her as much as it was him. "It's okay." Or at least he hoped it would be.

Wilson tapped into the room and bumped up against her leg. Nat reached down and dug her fingers into his fur. "Lorne's still in town, so I'm visiting with him and my parents before my shift at the Golden Key. I can pick up food on my way home."

"I won't be hungry."

A sad smile tilted her lips. "Me either." After one last pat for Wilson, she picked up her purse and left the house.

Mason sat there in the quiet. He'd thought they'd turned a corner. How had things gone so wrong? No answer echoed in the stillness of his home. If anything, the emptiness made him restless. He grabbed his keys from the counter and headed for work.

The familiar musty scent of the locker room greeted him as he made his way to his office. Stacks of paperwork from his assistant coach, who'd been working with the guys all week, sat on his desk. He'd written notes about each teen, their strengths, their weaknesses, and which positions they hoped to fill versus which ones they might be a good fit for. Often, those were different things. Nearly every kid wanted to be the quarterback or wide receiver. Not many wanted to be a nose tackle or kicker. But every single position was necessary for the team's success.

Mason dropped into his chair and dug into the paperwork. His mind threatened to wander, but he forced it to the task at hand. He needed a win, and putting together the strongest team might be the only way to secure one in his future.

He'd made it through half of the stack when Trey popped his head around the corner an hour later. "I thought I saw your light on."

"Got home Sunday." Mason set his glasses on his desk and leaned back in his chair, crossing his arms over his chest. "Catching up on what I missed."

Trey stepped inside and settled into the worn leather office chair across from him. "How was treasure hunting with your wife? Uncover any gems?" He wiggled his brows.

"Funny." Mason had no laughter for him though.

Trey noticed his mood, because his grew serious. "What's wrong? Things didn't go well?"

"Not even close. I'm worried my marriage is over."

Eyes wide, Trey straightened. He remained mute for a long second, then, "Man. I don't know what to say."

"Join the crowd."

"What are you doing here?" Trey poked his thumb over his shoulder. "You need to be out there fixing whatever is broken between you two."

Mason bristled. "You naturally think I'm the one who broke it?"

"Didn't say that." Trey's tone remained even. "There's two of you in the relationship. My guess is you had equal hands in breaking it, but that doesn't mean you can't take the first step in fixing it."

"I flew to France." Had Trey forgotten that huge step?

"Okay. What's next?"

"Nothing. She's made it clear things are unsalvageable."

His friend rested his left ankle over his right knee, crossed his arms, and nailed him with an unrelenting look. "This from the guy who tells his team they don't quit no matter what the scoreboard says. You keep calling plays until the time on the clock runs out."

"It did. This morning."

Trey stood and leaned across the desk, yanked on Mason's arm, and pressed his fingers against Mason's wrist.

"What are you doing?" He tried to pull free.

"Making sure your pulse is still beating." Trey released him. "It is."

"Your point?"

"The clock hasn't run out."

Mason rolled his eyes. "Funny."

His friend towered over him. "I'm dead serious." Trey rarely frowned, and he glared even less often, but the look he leveled at Mason landed somewhere between those two expressions. "Do you love Natalie?"

"Of course I do." He didn't even have to think about it. Loving her was an automatic reflex.

"Is she still breathing?"

"Yes."

"Then time definitely hasn't run out, so stop wasting it."

If only it were that easy. "Like you already mentioned, I'm not the only one in this marriage. And again, Nat isn't so sure we can fix things."

Trey scoffed. "You've never taken excuses from anyone, so don't start taking them from yourself."

"Don't hold back there, friend."

"Don't plan to." Trey looked him up and down and kept right on laying into him. "Your job is to love Natalie like Christ loves the church. That means even when she's running the other way, you pursue her like the treasure she is."

He hated to keep bringing it up, but, "Again. Went to France."

"God only makes one attempt at coming after us?"

It wasn't that simple. "We want different things." Natalie had been right about that, even if he didn't want to admit it.

But that information didn't faze Trey, because he continued to push him harder than Mason pushed his team in the weight room. "Have you two tried to pray—together—about what God wants for you as a couple? Or are you both focused on your own plans?"

Well, then. Nothing like truth bombs when he was operating on one cup of coffee, little sleep, and wrung-out emotions.

Trey pressed his palm on Mason's desk. "Love isn't easy, friend, but it is sacrificial. It's patient. It's hopeful. It perseveres. It—"

"I know the verse," Mason broke in.

"Then maybe act like it." With a clipped nod, Trey turned and walked to the door. Apparently he was done with his impromptu coaching session. He stopped with his hand on the casing. "I'm here if you want to talk or pray, and I'll be praying for you and Nat. If you need to take more time off, I can make sure that happens."

"Thanks."

"It's what friends are for." He left.

His words, however, lingered with a truth Mason had needed to hear. A good friend cared more about helping your life than hurting your feelings. That made Trey a great friend.

Mason pulled out his Bible from his desk.

✦ ✦

It smelled like home as Natalie walked in the door. Either Mom had baked cinnamon rolls, or she was burning her vanilla candle again.

"That you, Nat?" Mom called from the kitchen.

"It is." She toed off her shoes, then followed her nose. Yes. Cinnamon rolls.

Mom looked over her shoulder as she pulled the pan from the oven. "I figured you might like something to go with your coffee."

"More like I'll take coffee to go with my cinnamon roll." Natalie could eat that entire pan, or she could have when she was a teenager . . . and perhaps had. Now one roll alone threatened to add three pounds to her middle. At least it felt that way, but Mom's cinnamon rolls were well worth the cost of the extra few miles she'd have to add to her weekly step count. "Where's Dad and Lorne?"

"They had an early tee time. I expect them back soon."

Natalie settled on the stool at the counter, just like she had when growing up. "How many times have they golfed since Lorne's been here?"

"Nearly every day." Mom grabbed the icing she'd made from scratch. "It's good for your father. He gets antsy sitting around here, while I'm perfectly content to curl up and read a good book."

"Same here."

Drizzling the rolls, Mom sneaked a look at her. "Except recently you seem to enjoy traveling more than quiet nights at home."

"Because home got too quiet." Oops, hadn't meant to let that out. "Besides, I've always wanted to see the world. It just needed to be the right time."

Finished with the icing, Mom dropped the bowl in the sink and added hot water. In silence she washed her few baking utensils before rejoining Natalie at the counter. "How are things going between you and Mason?"

She'd known the question was coming the second Mom had gone silent. Now it was her turn to sit still. Mom plated a roll and poured a cup of coffee, then slid both to Natalie. If she had any hope of enjoying the delicious treat, she needed to get this bitter conversation over, because Mom would wait her out but wouldn't allow her to leave before answering.

Natalie wrapped her hands around her mug. "Not so great." Though she was pretty sure Mom had picked up on that fact. "I think our marriage is over."

Ever grounded and never shocked, Mom simply asked, "Why do you think that?"

"We've grown apart. We want different things."

"Such as?"

"He wants to move for a chance at a college coaching job, and I want to stay." Saying it aloud, it didn't sound as insurmountable as it felt, but again, this wasn't simply about a location change. They could overcome geography. She needed Mom to see it was about so much more. "When we first got married, we were a team working toward a goal. Reaching a college position was something we both wanted for him."

"And now?" Mom asked.

"Now Mason desires his goal more than he does me." He'd all but admitted it during their talk in Boston. "I'm in competition with his job, and the job is winning."

Sunshine spilled across Mom's hands as she held her coffee cup. Those same hands had held Natalie sturdy for years, just like she was no doubt trying to do now. "You believe if he had to choose between his job and you, he'd choose his job?"

"He already has. He flat out told me that if Utah hadn't rescinded their offer, he'd be there right now, even though he promised me we'd be here for at least three years. He's breaking his word."

"Yet you said that him teaching at a college level was a shared goal. Aren't you going back on your word too?"

"It's no longer shared when he's pursuing it on his own now." She couldn't believe Mom suggested otherwise. "He stopped needing me a long time ago."

"Is that him talking or your fear?"

"It's reality talking." One she needed to face.

Steam lifted from Mom's mug. "Then let's listen to all of it, shall we?"

Rather than respond with words, Natalie tilted her head to show her confusion. She had no idea where Mom was going.

"Natalie Renae, you've spent the better part of your life striving to ensure people don't abandon you. It's why you do whatever you can to help, because if someone needs you, they're less likely to leave you."

Natalie blinked back tears. Mom's conclusion struck a chord in Natalie that rang with the sound of truth. "But I honestly do love helping others."

"I know you do, sweetheart, but our greatest strengths can grow from our greatest weaknesses." Mom reached over until their fingers touched. She quietly spoke. "Baby girl, you're wanted. You are loved. You are chosen. I've said those words to you since the moment you were placed in my arms."

"I know." Tears dampened her eyes.

"But do you believe them?" Mom's tenderness made those tears overflow.

"I'm trying to." But maybe she'd struggled with those truths much more than she'd ever allowed herself to see.

The garage door opened, and Dad's and Lorne's voices filtered in. She didn't want to continue this conversation around them. Her emotions were raw, and she needed a moment to process.

Always attuned to her children, Mom stood. "I'll keep praying for this to be settled in your heart." She pressed a kiss to Natalie's cheek. "And for you and Mason. That man loves you, Natalie. Don't let fear rob you of something beautiful just because right now things look ugly. Remember, God makes beauty from ashes."

Natalie swiped at the moisture in her eyes. "Thanks, Mom."

"I'm always here for you." Mom turned to greet Dad and Lorne. "Cinnamon rolls and coffee?"

"Do you even need to ask?" Dad headed for the cupboard to grab mugs. He and Mom worked together in seamless motion.

Lorne settled beside her on another stool. "How was France?" His question was light, but concern lingered in his eyes as he studied her. No doubt he caught her damp eyes, but Lorne wouldn't push her.

"Beautiful." She caught them up on her trip over another cinnamon roll and a refill on her coffee. The only thing she left out was the details on the book they searched for. Those weren't hers to tell.

"A secret society of bookkeepers?" Lorne folded his arms over his chest as he leaned on his stool. "Sounds like a group tailor-made for you."

"I wish I could be a part of them." She took her dishes to the sink. "I also wish I could stay longer and hear more about what you've been up to, but I have to get to work."

Lorne stood and wrapped her in his arms. "My life is not nearly as interesting as yours."

"It's interesting to me." She stepped away to hug her parents.

"I'm here if you need to talk," Mom whispered into her ear.

She gave her mom another squeeze before heading to her car. On her short drive, she connected with Brooke and Everleigh. Caspar had them scheduled on another private flight on Wednesday, and Gertie declared she'd be on it with them. Niles was coming too, which typically wouldn't bother her, but seeing Everleigh and Niles together might currently be a bit to stomach.

⇒ ⇐

Natalie parked in front of the Golden Key, a warm summer breeze skimming her bare arms as she exited her car. The bell over the door jingled as she stepped inside to the strands of instrumental music overhead. Harry's song list often included scores from famous movies, and today he'd chosen *The Sound of Music*. Other than that, the space remained fairly quiet. It appeared there weren't any customers currently, and after a stroll through the aisles, she didn't see Harry either. Natalie peeked into the back room and his office next, but still couldn't locate him. She returned to the store area and called out his name.

"Harry?" She headed for the children's section, knowing his affinity for those books. He wasn't there, but the bookshelves captured her attention. She ran her finger along the spines until she reached the *C*'s. Yep, there it was. *Alice in Wonderland*, by Lewis Carroll. Tipping the book toward her, she pulled the title from its slot. It was a beautiful edition, with a green cover embossed with a gold-scrolled font for the title. A small rabbit graced the corner, and Alice herself stood in the opposite one. Natalie cracked open the pages and inhaled the lovely smell of a new book.

"Ah, one of my favorites." Harry spoke from behind her.

Natalie jumped and turned. "Harry!" She pressed a hand against her beating heart. "I didn't even hear you."

He chuckled. "I've been told I'm rather quiet at times, rather loud at others." He pointed to the story in her hands. "I do believe that book wants to go home with you."

She closed it and placed it back on the shelf. "It is gorgeous, but I already own a copy."

"Can one own too many copies of a classic?" Harry pulled out one with gorgeous flowers blooming across it. Roses spelled out *The Secret Garden*. "This will be my next purchase, and I already own four copies." He leaned in with a tiny smirk and twinkling eyes. "Alas, I've forced myself onto a book budget, or I would have already brought this one home to meet the rest of her friends."

"It is stunning."

"All books are. In their own way." He reshelved that one before bending down to reach for another. *The Velveteen Rabbit*, by Margery Williams. Its spine was cracked, the red leather cover dusty, and its pages jagged. Harry held it out to her, and she resisted a sneeze as she opened it. "Often the most beautiful stories are found in between the most worn pages."

"Fitting thought for this one." Natalie ran her hand over the rough edges.

"You've read it?"

"Of course." It remained one of her favorites. "As a child and then to my own children."

Harry clasped his hands together. "'You become. It takes a long time. That's why it doesn't happen often to people who break easily, or have sharp edges, or who have to be carefully kept.'"

Natalie joined him to finish the famous quote, and their voices blended together. "'Generally, by the time you are Real, most of your hair has been loved off, and your eyes drop out and you get loose in your joints and very shabby. But these things don't matter at all, because once you are Real you can't be ugly, except to people who don't understand.'"

Tenderness softened his features. "That was my wife Tilda's favorite. She always claimed that slightly tattered love is the most beautiful of loves, especially for those who've weathered the tearing together." Moisture filled his eyes. "She was correct."

Natalie reached out and squeezed his hand. His words pressed against her heart, kneading the emotions that had been mixing together all morning. It wasn't simply his loss but her own impending one that dampened her eyes. "She sounds like she was a wonderful woman."

"That she was, my dear. That she was." Harry nodded. "How terribly unfair that we're allowed to choose when we begin our life together but not when it should end. For if I had a choice, I would never have allowed it to be over."

Natalie swallowed the swirl of rising feelings. Harry wished for the choice she had the luxury to make. Was she blind to the beauty her marriage could be with all its worn patches and ragged edges?

Beside her, Harry reshelved the Williams book, then checked his pocket watch. "Why, look at the time. I didn't expect you for another hour. How lucky that you're gifting me extra minutes today." He snapped the golden cover shut on the small timepiece. "I shall use them wisely. After all, time is a most valuable present."

Rather than follow him as he headed for his office, Natalie moved for the register. She needed a moment to compose herself and rein in her thoughts. "I'll head up front in case any customers come in."

"Good. Good." Harry nodded. Today he wore a tan suit with hues of orange creating the plaid pattern on the wool fabric. How did he not suffocate in the summer heat? She could barely handle wool in the depths of winter. Before she could further contemplate Harry's wardrobe choices, he reappeared with his leather messenger bag over his shoulder and fedora on his head. "I'll leave you to it then."

Natalie spent the next few hours dusting shelves and reworking displays. Then she stacked a grouping of hardbacks on the counter that needed to be added to the front window. As she moved to collect a few more, the bell jingled over the door. She peeked around the pile and inhaled sharply.

Matt stood in the entryway. He took off his dark sunglasses and tucked them into the front pocket of his shirt. His eyes roamed the space until they landed on her. He smiled and headed her way. "Natalie, right?"

She smoothed her hands down her slacks to dry her suddenly damp palms. There wasn't one thing that appeared threatening about the man, yet his presence set her on edge. Especially being here alone with all the unknowns hovering over him.

He slowed. "It is Natalie, isn't it?"

Oh. She hadn't responded. Swallowing past her dry throat, she nodded. "Yes. And you're Matt. Though I never caught your last name."

He tipped his head. "Because we didn't exchange them." He held out his hand. "Bolivar. And yours?"

"Daughtry." She returned his handshake. He made her uneasy, but not enough to quell her curiosity.

"Pleasure to meet you again, Natalie Daughtry." He slid his hand into his pocket. "I'm glad you're here today. I stopped by last week, but I didn't see you."

"I was on a trip."

"Oh? Anywhere interesting?" He leaned against the counter.

"Colmar, France." She watched for any reaction out of him. "Ever been there?"

The corners of his eyes tightened ever so slightly, and the edge of his mouth pulled up. His dark-brown gaze took on an air of someone impressed by their adversary. "They have amazing *Kugelhopf.* I hope you tried some."

A nonanswer if she ever heard one. "I did."

They stared at one another for a few seconds. Then he straightened.

"Like I said, I'm glad you're here today. You did such an amazing job pointing me in the right direction of a book last time, and I hoped you could help again."

Her heart rate picked up. Something about his tone and the tension in his shoulders, even while he maintained a casual stance, set her on guard. She probably shouldn't be playing games with him, but she wanted answers to the questions his presence had raised.

"I'll definitely try." She remained behind the counter and near her phone. "Are you looking for another thriller?"

His smile hadn't left, and it felt unnerving rather than genuine. "While I do love suspense, I had something else in mind. I happen to have a fondness for books I read as a child. One of my favorites is *Alice in Wonderland*." He pulled one of his hands free from his pocket and placed it on the counter. He tapped his pointer finger in a slow and steady rhythm. "You wouldn't happen to have a copy here, would you?"

Now her heart rate stuttered. He was definitely toying with her.

Sweat beaded between her shoulder blades.

The bell jingled again. Natalie looked up to see Mason walking through the front door. He offered a cautionary smile that flattened into concern as he took her in. His gaze shifted to Matt, then back to her. In a few quick strides, he joined them at the counter.

Before he could say anything, Matt stepped away. "I don't want to keep you from other customers. I'll come back another time."

He headed to the exit, whistling. They both watched him leave, and the moment the door closed, Mason faced her. "You okay?"

She nodded. "Yeah. Why?"

"Because you're shaking." His gaze went to her hands.

"Right." She squeezed them into fists. "I'm fine."

His look said he wasn't buying her answer.

She sighed. "All right. That was Matt."

Mason whipped around and bolted for the door. He ducked onto the sidewalk but returned within moments. "He's gone." He rejoined her at the counter. "Did he threaten you?"

"No." She nibbled her lip. "But I do think he was in France and that he's looking for the same rumored copy we are. He didn't say so in so many words, but he did cryptically allude to the fact."

Mason dragged a hand through his hair. "You need to quit working for Caspar."

At this, she laughed. "No way."

He leveled a disbelieving look at her. "Something weird is going on here, and it could be dangerous."

She brushed past him to hunt down more books for the front window. "I'll give you the something weird, but I don't think it's dangerous." Even if Matt had raised her blood pressure and suspicion by several notches.

Mason gently wrapped his hand around her arm. "You're smarter than that, and you have great intuition. Can you honestly tell me you feel one hundred percent safe right now?"

Ugh. She had never lied to Mason, and she wasn't about to start.

"I can't." Her hand lifted to stop whatever his open mouth was about to say. "But I also can't tell you that I'm going to stop working for Caspar." She tugged free and headed for the romance racks to finish her project. Mason remained on her heels.

"Why are you here, Mason?" She let the words float over her shoulder.

His jaw worked, and she could see he wanted to say more. Surprisingly, he held up his phone. "Reed's been trying to text you."

Oh. She rounded the counter and dug her phone from her purse. Four missed texts and one phone call from Reed. Two missed texts and one call from Mason. She scanned them. "He got accepted to his program early!" Glancing at Mason, she expected a shared smile but caught a hint of lingering concern instead. His texts had questioned if she was all right. "Sorry. My ringer was off."

"I figured, but in light of this past week, I wanted to be sure." He returned his phone to his back pocket. "You're definitely going to Scotland?"

"I am."

"Then I'm going too."

"Sorry, but no." Stopping in front of the historical romance section, she began grabbing titles.

Mason stood in the aisle, legs braced, arms crossed over his chest like one of his defensive linebackers. Immovable, no matter what hit them.

"Please don't argue with me on this, Mace." She kept right on pulling books. "We've done enough of that, and I'm exhausted."

He stood there for another few seconds before releasing his stance. "Okay."

Then without another word, he turned and left the store.

CHAPTER SEVENTEEN

Luciana Perez, age fifty-three
Lekeitio, Spain, 1967

THIS WASN'T THE FIRST TIME Luciana had eavesdropped on angry voices behind Papi's office door. It also wasn't the first time her heart hurt and her stomach churned at the conversation she overheard. This time, however, the pain sliced deeper because her Angus participated in the altercation.

That pain had originated with their return to this home. How she longed to go back to that decision and make a different one. To ensure Angus did not join Papi's business world outside of the vineyards. Not only that, but Angus had agreed to take up the Perez family mantle when Papi stepped down, and he intended to pass it on to Jerrick one day.

The boy she'd fallen in love with had become the man she could not trust. Yes, he still treated her like a queen, but he also acted like a king drunk with power. He was becoming more and more like Papi. Speaking with less of his brogue. Launching stern words rather than kind ones. Passing down orders he insisted be followed by all those around him. He claimed it was because of his love for her and Jerrick. He questioned why she could not see things as clearly as he did. All she saw was the way he and Papi treated others—with regard only for themselves and their own needs.

Papi had beaten Angus down for years, making him feel as if he were unworthy of her love. Of anything good. It was why they'd run away. She'd thought her love and encouragement had convinced Angus that Papi's words were lies. Instead, she'd only quieted those voices in the years they'd lived away from this place. But the moment he'd discovered Jerrick was on his way, the volume on the voices increased inside Angus. He'd been a prime target for Papi and all he had to offer him.

Angus never counted the cost of what he'd lose. He could only see the accolades, respect, and power he'd finally gained. All she wanted was the man she'd married, but he no longer seemed to exist.

She refused to allow the same to happen to her son.

Luciana jolted as a crash sounded behind the door. Her wandering thoughts had caused her to miss what had just been said. No matter, the argument continued.

"Enough!" Papi bellowed. "My patience has run out with you, Raul."

"As did your love and loyalty the moment your precious Luciana bore you another grandson." Vitriol laced Raul's words. "Santiano Jr. no longer mattered to you, but my son was here first, and he bears your name. He and I deserve to take your place. It was promised."

"The mantle has always been handed down to the eldest," Papi said. "I will not break tradition."

"Tradition was broken when you had no sons. You said as much when I married Marisol and gave you a grandson. *We* were your answer to prayer. *We* were to step into your place."

"I spoke in haste. I should not have rushed God. He had other plans." Papi's voice remained stern but did lower. "I acknowledged this to you. Still, even after Marisol's death, I provided you and Santiano Jr. a place within the family, and I have done my best to give you time to adjust. For fifteen years now I have turned a blind eye to the many ways you challenge me, a gift no one else has ever received. But what you have done today I cannot ignore or forgive."

"I do not need your forgiveness." Raul spat the words.

"Careful," Angus warned.

From her vantage point hunkered by the door, she watched as Angus held Raul's arm in a tight grip, preventing him from advancing on Papi. "Do not make things worse for yourself than they already are. Your son still needs ye."

"Which is why I made my move today." Raul shook free from Angus. "You speak of loyalty for family, but you curse me for caring for mine."

"Undermining me." Papi stepped toward Raul. "Stealing from me has only brought you shame. Marisol would be heartbroken."

Tears leaked from Luciana's eyes. How she missed her sister.

"Marisol believed her son deserved to wear the mantle," Raul said. "If anyone broke her heart, it was you."

The sound of flesh hitting flesh caused Luciana to flinch. Raul was on his knees, and Papi stood over him. Papi glanced at Angus. "You have recovered the book?"

Angus removed something from the inside of his suit coat. It was her copy of *Alice's Adventures Under Ground*. "It was in his suitcase."

She squirmed. When had Raul taken that from the nursery? And why was it important to all these men?

Papi remained towering over Raul. "Stand."

With a glare, Raul obeyed.

Papi stood solemnly in front of him. He held out a thick envelope. "You and Santiano Jr. will be gone by nightfall. I have booked a passage for you to America, and there is enough here to help you start a new life. It is only because of my love for Marisol that I do this, but that grace ends today." He crushed the envelope to Raul's chest. "If you make another attempt to steal from me or harm my family, you will only know my wrath."

Raul gripped the envelope. "Santiano Jr. is your family. Allow him to stay."

"No. Your venom already infects him, and his temper grows daily. The lies you've fed him will only turn into his truth when I send you away. If he remains here, he, too, will try to undermine me, Angus, and eventually Jerrick."

"He loves Jerrick as a brother."

"And you claim to have loved me as a father." Papi would not budge. "Yet you betrayed me." He shook his head. "You both must go." He delivered the words with absolute finality.

Remorse and anger created a strange mix of emotions on Raul's face, but he said nothing as two more men, who'd been standing by Papi's desk, grabbed him on either side and walked him toward the door.

Luciana ducked into the library, like she had so many years before. She swallowed the urge to run to Papi's office and beg him to allow her nephew to remain. When Marisol had passed away ten years ago, Luciana had taken Santiano Jr. under her own care. She'd raised him and Jerrick as brothers. That they'd be torn apart broke her heart.

It was true in the past year that she'd witnessed a change in her nephew, but both boys were in the throes of their teenage years. Even Jerrick had become surly at times. Still, she could not picture anything that would come between them.

Yet she'd also never anticipated the changes in Raul, Angus, or Papi. It was as if something heavy hung over their family, waiting for its chance to soak into their lives.

In the hall, shoes scuffled as the men escorted Raul to his room. Angus followed, his cool voice echoing into the library, where she'd left the door slightly ajar. "I will see to it that Santiano packs his things as well. A car will come for you both in an hour."

More and more Angus sounded like Papi rather than her warm, loving husband.

Luciana wrapped her arms around her middle. Perhaps it was a good thing that Santiano would be separated from the family, because—staring at the future through the lens of the past—she desperately wished the same thing for her own child before he, too, became a voice she no longer recognized.

CHAPTER EIGHTEEN

AT 7:00 P.M. ON WEDNESDAY, Natalie handed off her suitcase to the steward of the private plane Caspar had chartered for them, ensured she had her blanket and neck pillow, and headed for the steps to board behind the rest of her small group. Everleigh and Niles were helping Gertie, while Brooke patiently waited next in line.

Natalie hadn't seen Mason all day. He'd left early this morning before she'd awoken, and he hadn't returned home after his workday. Or if he had, they'd missed each other, as she'd hitched a ride with Brooke to the airport before dinner. She and Mason had at least said cordial goodbyes last night. Things remained stilted between them, and they hadn't talked through any solutions or next steps. They remained at a painful standstill.

Though yesterday's conversations with Mom and Harry nudged at her. Perhaps some things from her past weighed on her current emotions more than she'd realized. Yes, she wanted to come before Mason's career—and she should—but there might also be fears at play in her heart that were impacting their marriage. And maybe, just maybe, all these hardships they faced were part of God's grand plan to bless them with a marriage more beautiful than they could imagine. Or at least these trials could be if they allowed God to work in the midst of them.

"Coming?" Brooke peered down at her from the top step.

"Yes." Natalie shook off her distracting thoughts and hustled onto the plane. She didn't want to be the one to delay them. As she ducked into the aircraft, she peered down the small aisle to see which of the few seats remained open. She came to an abrupt halt. "Mason?"

Her husband looked up from a seat at the rear of the plane. The one beside him remained open, and he patted it.

She brushed past her friends, who were doing their best to feign interest in their own conversation and not the drama unfolding in their confined space. Natalie stopped in front of Mason, confused and not wanting to read into his unexpected presence on another trip. Hope ceased to be kind when proven false.

"I thought we agreed you weren't coming along." Yet she wasn't upset he was here. Quite the contrary.

"I believe I only agreed not to argue with you about my travel status." He relaxed an ankle over his knee, as if he hadn't a care in the world. "And I held to my word. Instead I brought my argument to John, who then spoke to Caspar. Seems you neglected to tell them about seeing Matt again."

"You saw Matt?" Brooke leaned around her seat, accusation in her pinched features.

"I . . . yes. I planned on speaking with you all about it on the plane ride." She turned back to Mason. "Thanks a lot."

"You're welcome." He clasped his hands over his abdomen. "John and Caspar both agreed it was a good idea for me to accompany my wife on this trip. Especially since I have concerns they also share." His finger tapped against the back of his other hand. "Though Caspar assured me the situation should be safe, he understood my desire to remain by your side."

"Why the sudden change of heart?" To everyone else listening, her question would sound aimed at his decision to tag along rather than stay home, like they'd supposedly agreed. But did Mason understand she meant so much more?

Tenderness softened his features, and an earnestness shone from his warm brown eyes. "My heart hasn't ever changed where you're concerned, Nat."

Everything shifted inside. Goodness, she loved this man. Wanted to be with him forever. Which meant they needed to flip the script. Instead of seeing things as impossible to fix, they needed to see each obstacle as impossible to break them apart.

"Oh, let the man tag along," Gertie piped up from her seat.

Niles joined in. "I definitely wouldn't mind a little more testosterone around here." He oofed as Everleigh smacked his abdomen. "Not that I don't enjoy traveling with all you lovely women."

"Yeah, you better add in some endearments, Yogi," Everleigh teased.

He leaned over and smacked a kiss against her lips. "Beautiful, brilliant, bold."

"Ugh, enough." Brooke slumped in her chair and peeked again down the aisle. Her blue gaze offered support as it met Natalie's. "It's whatever you want."

Mason took Natalie's fingers gently in his grip. "Nat, I know I've messed up. I also know we might want different things, and we need to figure out how to navigate all that." His hold tightened. "But I also know I'm not letting you run any further away from me than you already have, especially not when there's a possibility you could be in danger." His thumb ran over the back of her hand. "Definitely not when our marriage is in danger. I'm not letting you go."

She tightened her hand in his. "I guess you better buckle in then."

The steward stood near the stairs, ready to close and lock them. "We're ready if you are."

Looking at her husband, she could see they both were ready to move forward. "We are." She settled beside Mason, realizing in that moment her emotions were calming too. These past few days had felt like a breaking point, but somehow they'd become a mending point instead. What hadn't torn them apart was indeed making them stronger.

The stairs were pulled into place and locked. The steward took his seat in the cockpit with the pilot. The engines roared to life.

Natalie looked to her husband. "You're incredibly stubborn, you know that?"

"Then it should come as no surprise to you that I refuse to give up on our marriage."

She wrapped her arm around his as tears welled in her eyes. "Me either, but I don't know how to fix things, Mace."

"One step at a time, just like you always told the boys to approach things."

"I did say that, didn't I?"

He softly smiled. "You did."

The plane kicked into high gear, forcing them into their seats as it lifted from the tarmac. In front of them, everyone enjoyed conversation. Something about Gertie's ex-FBI partner, Burt.

Mason pressed his mouth to her ear. "Has she agreed to date him yet?"

"Burt would definitely like to be her boyfriend, but no, she hasn't green-lighted him." She opened her phone and pulled up a picture of Gertie and Burt together. Gertie faced the camera, but Burt only had eyes for her. "How can she say no to him? Look at how he looks at her. That is a man in love."

"You always have been a sucker for romance." Mason glanced at her phone screen before digging into his backpack. "Speaking of which, I got you this." He hauled out the debut of the author she'd pointed out in Boston. "I checked first to make sure it had a happy ending before I bought it. I figured you'd finally have the time to read it on the plane ride."

Her heart did a little swoop in her chest. Mason not only heard what she'd said that day, but he'd walked into a bookstore. For her. What spoke loudest, though, was he'd read the end of the book when reading was notoriously difficult for him.

She accepted his gift. "Thanks, Mace. That means a lot."

They held each other's stare. Wasn't that love though? The tiny everyday moments that proved you knew a person better than anyone else. The little gifts that meant so much because they cost you more than money.

Mason broke their shared stare first. He reached into his backpack and hauled out his iPad and AirPods. "I'll let you read. My guess is you'll have it finished before we land." He turned on his iPad. "I'm going to watch some TV."

He'd shown up on this plane for her. Even in the midst of their brokenness, he was still pursuing her. Protecting her. Yet he wasn't forcing his presence on her. Rather, he offered a getaway of sorts within the confines of this small space.

She cracked open her book. The author's opening line was as tantalizing as people had said, but Natalie's attention strayed to her husband. She could sit here and become completely lost in the building romance between two characters she'd anticipated reading about for the better part of a year.

Or she could use this time to work on rebuilding her own real-life romance.

Natalie glanced again at Mason as he pressed Play on some documentary about a soccer team in the UK. She'd gladly finish out her life never having watched a soccer game, but she'd once felt the same way about football, until her teenage heart had fallen in love with Mace. Same with baseball. And zip-lining. And hiking mountains. When had she stopped allowing him to introduce her to new things?

Mason turned to find her staring at him, and he paused his show. His dark brows scrunched over those big brown eyes. "I got the right book, didn't I? I thought that was the author you mentioned, and the clerk said people have been raving about it, but she pointed out a few other new authors too."

His rambling concern zinged warmth through her stomach. "It's the right book." She motioned to his screen. "But I was wondering if maybe I could watch that with you?"

Surprise flashed across his face, but the astonishment quickly morphed into a tender smile. "Of course." He handed her his left AirPod.

She popped it in. "You might have to explain some of the game to me."

"Some?" he challenged with a teasing tone.

"All right. All of it." Their faces were so close that their noses almost touched, and she could see the golden lines sparking through his irises.

"Happily."

Mason pressed Play, and she leaned her head on his shoulder.

Who knew she'd fall in love with soccer? Or, at the very least, the Wrexham team featured in the documentary. She'd have binged all the episodes if not for Mason's suggestion they turn it off and try to get some sleep on their overnight flight. That had been a wise choice, because they hit the ground running once in Scotland.

Their plane had touched down right outside of Glasgow a smidge before 10:00 a.m. local time. They'd driven an hour and a half to Dumfries and now stood outside Moat Brae. She was tired, but if she hadn't slept a good chunk of the flight, she'd be exhausted. So she should be fine, even with the six-hour time difference.

Especially visiting places such as this. The drive alone had already proven breathtaking once they'd made it outside the city. Crystal blue skies and rolling green fields provided them with plenty of moments to ooh and aah. But something about this place felt magical.

Right in front of her was the home that had inspired J. M. Barrie to write *Peter Pan*. "I can't believe we're here."

Everleigh stood nearby, with Gertie sandwiched between her and Niles. "We've certainly had the chance to say that a lot lately."

Brooke slipped on her sunglasses and strolled to the short black iron railing flanking the original entrance, while Everleigh leaned in close to Gertie to describe the area. Mason stepped shoulder to shoulder with Natalie, and they stared up at Moat Brae. He reached over and squeezed her hand. "Pretty cool."

The mere fact that he understood her excitement testified to how deeply her husband did know her. He might not share her delight or understand it, but he was here. How many times in the past years had she wished for a moment like this? She tightened her fingers around his. "Yes, it is."

They stood in a small parking lot on the edge of a row of buildings creating a barrier between them and the River Nith, and Moat Brae held the end spot in line. A two-story Greek revival–style villa with a raised basement that dipped below street level, the home remained much as it had been when Barrie had visited as a child. A symmetrical row of twelve-pane windows ran five across along the top floor, providing plenty of places to look out over the town. Polished red ashlar stone blocks gave a soft orange tint to the facade. Whoever had remodeled the home into this museum had carried that color into the new opening that they'd built on the left. The main entrance remained, however, with its pillars holding up the triangular covering over the massive door.

Brooke headed for the glass entry. "I think general admittance is through here, but I want to check out the original entry once we're inside. There's supposed to be a dome they refinished with a glass sunroof." They followed her to the front desk, where she stepped up to the counter. "We need six tickets for today, please."

"For the home, garden, or both?" the young woman asked.

Brooke swept a glance over her shoulder. They all shrugged. "Both? We're hoping to see Terrance MacLeod. We were told he works here?"

"He does. He's out in the garden, so you'll definitely want tickets for there." She tapped the screen in front of her. "Though I would have suggested that anyway. You can't come to Moat Brae and not take a walk through our garden." She handed Brooke the tickets, a smile on her lips and twinkle in her eye. "Fairies live out there, you know. You might even see Tinker Bell herself."

"One can hope." Brooke accepted the slips of paper and turned to hand them out. The tone of her response spoke to indifference, but Natalie spotted wistfulness on her face. "Shall we start in the garden and try to find Terrance? We can meander through the house afterward."

Everyone agreed, and they crossed to the exit leading to the garden. They stepped into a small, rounded courtyard of vibrant green grass with a border of pebbles creating a walkway. Beyond that, tall trees grew among patches of lawn that stretched to the River Nith. Wildflowers in a rainbow of sizes and colors hid a wooden pirate ship and small tree houses, and if one looked closely enough, tiny oxidized statues of Neverland characters.

"Does anyone see Terrance?" Gertrude asked, oblivious to the beauty around them. Natalie had a feeling that even if Gertrude could see it, she'd still be focused on finding the man.

"No," Natalie answered.

They'd looked up pictures of him on his social media sites, and Kit had confirmed they had the correct man. She'd also said she'd let him know they were coming.

"Maybe we should split up." This from Niles. "Everleigh, Gertrude, and I can head that way"—he thumbed over his shoulder, then pointed past Natalie—"and you three can go that way."

"Sounds good." With a nod, Brooke started off. They had their phones on them, and Caspar had paid for overseas service. "Whoever finds him first, text."

They started down a brown pebbled path, the tiny stones crunching under their feet. Mason hadn't said much, but he remained alert. Natalie had a feeling that rather than look for Terrance, he was looking for any signs Matt had followed them. He fell in step behind her and Brooke.

Midway along, Natalie stopped. "Look. It's Wendy and Pan." She stepped into the grass and crossed to the statue hidden among white flowers.

Brooke studied the petals of the blooms. "They look like bells."

"They do, don't they?"

Mason remained on the path. A warm breeze ruffled the tree branches above him.

Natalie ran her hand over the statue. "I always loved this story and their friendship. How Pan took Wendy on an amazing adventure and how she took care of him." As she spoke, the obvious parallel to her and Mason sprung to mind.

But Brooke moved beyond the statue to the trunk of a willow tree a few feet away. She knelt. "She was my favorite." Natalie joined her to see whom she referred to. Tinker Bell peeked out from a hollow section in the trunk. From the safety of her hidden location, the fairy watched Wendy and Peter. Brooke traced the edges of Tinker Bell's wings. "You'll probably find it offensive, but I dog-eared every page she was on."

"You read *Peter Pan*?"

Brooke looked at her. "I cop to one of the worst offenses in a book lover's world, and you're more surprised I actually read a children's book?"

Brooke hadn't shared much about her childhood, so yes, Natalie was surprised. However, she knew better than to say as much if she wanted her to keep talking. "I'm trying to politely ignore that little detail so we can remain friends."

This won her a snort of laughter before Brooke turned serious again. No. Not serious. Pensive. "I never thought it was fair that she was Peter's friend first, and then when Wendy came along, he forgot all about her."

Much like her own musings sank deeper than the surface of the story, Brooke's seemed to do the same. Though she doubted her friend even realized she was revealing a piece of herself. "That did kind of stink."

Brooke looked over at her. "Yeah. It did, didn't it." She stood and offered Natalie a tiny grin that said maybe she was aware she'd pulled back the curtain on herself a few inches. "Let's go find Terrance."

They rejoined Mason and continued on their way. As the path curved to its end near the River Nith, a middle-aged man, with white hair sticking out under his flat cap, knelt in a flower patch, pulling weeds. With his slight paunch, medium height, and round face with thick mustache, he matched the photos they'd seen of Terrance. He glanced up as they approached, his welcoming grin tightening his jowls. "Good afternoon."

"Good afternoon," Brooke replied. She stopped a foot from him. "Are you by any chance Terrance MacLeod?"

"Now if I say I'm not, are ye going to disagree with me?" A teasing lilt softened the edges of his Scottish brogue.

"Yes," Brooke said.

"Aye, then since ye already know the answer, I needn't give it." He pushed to his feet and worked off his gloves. "I thought there were more of youse coming."

Mason stood beside them, arms crossed over his chest. "You were expecting us?"

"Of course. Kit filled me in." He rubbed his chin. "Best be finding yer friends so I only have to tell this once."

Natalie tipped her head about to ask more questions, when Brooke pulled out her phone. "Huh. My text won't go through."

"Service is nae good here in the garden." Terrance moved his wheelbarrow a few feet to another section. It was apparent he wasn't talking until they were all present.

Brooke sighed. "I'll run them down. You stay with him in case he wants to wander off." She hustled off in the direction they'd come.

Terrance had donned his gloves once again and resumed pulling weeds. Mason cast Natalie a glance, and she shrugged. Terrance looked up from his spot in the dirt. "Cannae let the weeds get out o' hand or yer troubles grow insteada yer contentment."

She met Mason's gaze again, and this time he shrugged. At least she wasn't the only one caught off guard by this man. She hadn't thought about what to expect when meeting him, but this certainly wasn't it.

Terrance motioned to a small spade still in the dirt where he'd been working when they found him. "Do ye mind?"

Before Natalie could grab it, Mason retrieved it. "Are you the only gardener here?"

"Aye. And all-around handyman." Using the spade, Terrance dug out what appeared to be an especially stubborn weed. "Yer friends are coming." He nodded to the path behind them.

By the time Brooke, Gertie, Niles, and Everleigh joined them again, Terrance had won his battle. He tossed the thick green stalk with long roots into his wheelbarrow and stood once again. "I didnae hear from Kit until youse were already on the way, or else I would hev told youse not to come."

That wasn't the opening she wanted to hear. It sounded suspiciously like this might be a fruitless venture. "You don't have the book?"

"I dae not." He tugged off his flat cap and wrung it between his hand. "I let my weeds grow till all I had wis troubles. Seems now those troubles are catching up with me."

It was Gertie who broke the lingering silence. "You sold the book."

"Aye." He nodded. "I didnae think anyone would know. Once Kit logs them, I protect them."

"Selling them isn't protecting them," Brooke challenged.

His head jerked up, and he looked right at her before scanning them all. "I only sold to people who also cared for the books."

"Books?" Plural? "How many have you sold?"

Terrance's cheeks pinkened. "My bonny is sick, and I . . . I have no' been good with our money. I thought I could replace what I lost afore it was missed, but . . ." His voice trailed off.

Mason stepped forward and placed his hand on the man's shoulders. "Your weeds."

Terrance nodded.

Again, silence permeated the space between them. Natalie didn't want to condone what he'd done, and no doubt there'd be consequences for him when it came to Kit. Maybe even legally, though she didn't know who actually owned the books, so was it even stealing? All she did know for sure was, "We've hit another dead end."

"Have we?" Gertie asked.

Everyone looked her way, but it was Niles who wore a matching smile to his aunt. "Not necessarily." He turned to Terrance. "You said you only sold to people you knew would care for the books, which implies you knew your customers. Does that mean you know who purchased *Alice's Adventures Under Ground* from you?"

Anticipation rose in Natalie's chest and grew as Terrance nodded.

"Aye," he said. "That I dae."

CHAPTER NINETEEN

"Follow me." Terrance laid his gloves in his wheelbarrow and started down the path.

With a shared look, the group fell in step.

"Where are we headed?" Gertie asked.

Everleigh guided her with a hand along the small of her back. "I have a feeling to where he keeps the books."

"Yer feeling would be right." Terrance led them to a wooded area, where he brushed back long branches of a fir tree. They ducked under them to find a paneled door on the side of Moat Brae. Carved into the dark oak was a picture of Neverland, complete with a pirate ship sailing a night sky. Terrance pulled open the entrance and flipped on a light that illuminated the small hallway.

Another door came off this hallway, this one carved with the same book that had been on Kit's door, leading to her basement of treasures—the same one that matched the lapel pin they'd found at Edwin Hollis's estate. Terrance turned the knob and pushed. The hinges creaked as a trove of stories opened in front of them. They stepped inside, the scent of old leather and paper permeating the room.

The walls and ceiling were painted a deep navy tone, like the night sky when it overtook the daytime. A few golden stars appeared on the ceiling, and Tinker Bell peeped around one end of a bookshelf. Peter Pan peeked around another. An Oriental rug filled with shades of gold and midnight blue covered the dark wood floor. There were no windows in here, yet there seemed to be plenty of light.

Childhood books that had been Natalie's favorites filled the shelves around her. How wonderful that in this birthplace of youthful dreams, magic, and Pixie Dust, such sweet memories would be preserved. Seeing the titles, she ached to know which ones Terrance had sold. What other books should be sitting here? She hoped he truly had given them to people who would understand their worth.

Once again Everleigh took time to explain what they saw to Gertie, while everyone else explored. Terrance, meanwhile, crossed the room to an end table beside a leather armchair. Natalie strolled to the nearest bookcase and picked out *The Velveteen Rabbit*. The story's words of wisdom that she'd recently shared with Harry remained in her heart and mind. Yes, the years between her and Mason were worn, but she was beginning to understand that was what made their marriage real too. And wasn't that better than them both pretending?

She opened the book, already aware by its unique cover that this had to be a special edition. Sure enough, on the inside was a signature from the author herself, along with the illustrator's autograph. As Natalie flipped carefully through the pages, she could see that they were all hand drawn. She looked over to Terrance. "This isn't a reprint. These are actual drawings by William Nicholson, aren't they?"

"Aye, that they are." Terrance smiled.

It was like being lost in her own Wonderland. "Unbelievable. What other treasures do you have here?"

Across the room, Gertie smiled. "Don't let the librarian get started with books, or she'll be like a math teacher and numbers. She'll go on for infinity."

Her pun elicited a collective groan, but it also brought them all back to why they were there. Terrance removed a journal from the drawer of the table he stood beside. The journal reminded Natalie of the ledger that Mr. Hollis had kept in the library at his estate. Terrance opened it and ran a finger along the pages before shuffling over to Brooke. Since she had done most of the talking in the garden, he must think she was the leader of their small group.

"Here." He handed the journal to her. "This will tell ye where the book is. I may no' be proud of what I did, but I did keep good records."

Brooke consulted the page, and much like Terrance, she ran her finger along the columns. After scanning through a few, she stopped. "Here it is."

Natalie peeked over her shoulder and squinted as she read the entry. Her heart quickened with the location. She looked up at Terrance. "This isn't that far from here."

"Nae, it's no'."

"Where is it?" Everleigh asked.

Natalie couldn't stop the smile that spread over her face. "A place called Booksellers' Row in London. I've heard of the street and always wanted to go there, and it looks like now we will."

"Where in London?" Niles asked.

"Close to the West End."

"Aye." Terrance nodded. "I hand delivered the title. There's a collector who owns a bookshop all about *Alice in Wonderland*. He promised to take good care of her. Made her a part of his personal collection."

"It's not on display?" Mason asked. "And no one else knows it's there?"

Terrance looked down at his hands. His brow furrowed, and Natalie could tell this wasn't easy for him. "I've told no one else. I did me best to do right by me bonny but also right by the book. I do believe in protecting these stories, but I also needed to protect me bonny." He looked up at them and blinked moisture from his eyes. "I love what I do, but I love her more."

"Understandable." Gertie moved from where she was to where she heard Terrance speaking and clumsily reached for his hand. Terrance met her halfway, and she gave him a squeeze. "Is this person someone we should let know we're coming for the book? Or would it be better to surprise him?"

"I've already spoken with him about ye, and while he is sympathetic with yer plight, he's not quick to part with the book. In fact, he told me to save ye a trip and tell ye not to visit."

Brooke straightened. "Well, that's not a possibility."

"I thought ye might say as much, but I had to do me part." Terrance motioned for the journal. Brooke returned it, and he placed the book back in the drawer. "I'd be thankful if ye let me talk to Kit myself. She deserves to hear what I've done from me."

"Of course," Natalie said. "You didn't have to be honest with us or point us in the right direction. Allowing you to speak with Kit yourself is the least we can do to repay you."

"Thank ye," Terrance replied. "Spend as much time in here as ye'd like. I have weeds I need to finish pulling." With that he shuffled away.

Everleigh faced them. "What now? Do we call Caspar to book us a flight to London? We are still going, aren't we?"

"We might need a game plan first," Brooke said.

"Easy," Gertie said. "I've learned through my years that everyone has a price. If Jerrick wants this book, he's willing to pay for it, and he has the means to do just that." She paused, working her lips, as if chewing on her next words. "I just wish I knew why this book was so important to the Perez family. Because I'm not buying that it's only of sentimental value."

Mason stepped to Natalie's side. "Me either, and not knowing makes me uncomfortable. Especially with this Matt character out there."

"After hearing what he said to Natalie at the bookstore, I agree." Niles backed Mason. During the flight, she'd filled everyone in on her interactions with Matt. Niles's jaw had worked, as if he chewed on the information. Now, he shared a look with her husband. "I think there should be a phone call to Caspar, and he needs to give us any remaining information he has. He can arrange a flight to London for us, but we need to be aware if there's anyone else that will be there. And why this book is so important."

"If he even knows himself," Brooke said.

"He does," Gertie said. "Trust me. Caspar is a smart man. There's no way he went into this blind."

Everleigh stood to the side of Gertie. "Then why hasn't he told us?"

"Ah." Gertie tapped her cane on the floor. "Now that's the question we all want answered."

"Why do I think it's a question he won't answer?" Mason muttered.

"Guess there's only one way to find out." Brooke hauled out her phone. "Ugh. That's right—we're in a black hole as far as cell service goes."

"Back to the parking lot?" Everleigh suggested.

Natalie agreed it was time to press Caspar for more details, but she wasn't ready to leave this beautiful space. There was so much more exploring to do.

Mason took one look at her and spoke up. "You guys go ahead—we'll catch up."

＊ ＊

Natalie watched her friends leave the room and head to the parking lot to call Caspar. Mason waited until she turned his way. "I hope it's okay that I told them to go on ahead. It just seemed like you weren't quite done being in here."

The smile she'd worn since they'd stepped into the room hadn't dimmed. "I'm not. I'm fine with them filling me in on what Caspar says. This might be the only chance I'll get to be in this room, and I want to see what all is here."

Mason settled into the leather chair, propped his feet on the matching ottoman, leaned back, and closed his eyes. "Then take all the time you'd like. I'm in no hurry. If they want to even drive back to the hotel without us, we can always use public transit to get back."

It took a second, but then he heard her feet shuffling around. Once he figured she was enthralled with the books, he opened his eyes to study her. Watching Natalie in her element was something he hadn't done for a long time, and he realized in this moment how much he missed it. He'd allowed fear of being an embarrassment, along with his wounded pride—both misguided due to an unspoken misunderstanding—to keep him away. No more.

His strengths might not be hers, but what he'd viewed as his shortcomings actually complemented her weaknesses. Nat was brilliant, and he'd thought her light would cast him into the shadows. But he'd discovered in the past few weeks that his ability to put together a game plan had kept her focused in this hunt. His ability to look outside the box ensured they'd found the door they needed in Boston. He'd had patience to share when she'd had none. He helped her find endurance when she felt tired. He was starting to see that all the parts and pieces—big and small—that made him Mason were valuable. He'd given his insecurities too much power for far too long.

"Nat?" He waited until she turned to look at him once again. "What do you think about what Terrance had to say about the weeds?"

Her forehead wrinkled. "What?"

Yeah, that had kind of come out of left field. "His comment about needing to make sure they're pulled so that trouble doesn't grow."

She nodded as understanding dawned in her eyes. "I thought it wise."

"Kind of makes you think of our marriage, doesn't it?" Mason cracked his knuckles. "We let those weeds grow, didn't we?"

"We did. But I feel like we're working on pulling them out now."

"Me too." And they couldn't give up until every weed was gone. Which meant yanking out the roots of another prickly subject. "Can I ask you something?"

She didn't even hesitate. "Of course."

"What was it about Caspar that convinced you to say yes to traveling again?" He rubbed his palms together. "Every time I asked, you'd turn me down. He comes along, and you fly off across the world." That still stung.

While he'd never been able to offer her trips like she experienced now, he'd still tried to keep their adventuring spirit alive. He'd tried to book weekend getaways, even though they weren't extravagant. He'd tried overnight stays at local hotels. But she would nix even day trips. He could never figure out if it was because the trips weren't enough or if he wasn't enough.

Natalie tipped her head, studying him. "Mace." She joined him to sit on the arm of the chair. "It had nothing to do with you and everything to do with me. My fears." With her this close, the soft, spicy scent of her perfume reached him. "I didn't travel with you because I didn't want to leave the boys when they were younger. I was worried if something happened to us, they'd be orphans."

His eyes immediately latched on to hers as understanding clicked into place. He sighed and shook his head, as if he couldn't believe he'd missed this connection. "Because you're adopted."

She nodded. "I never think of my parents as anything other than Mom and Dad. They're who took me home from the hospital, and had they not told me I was adopted, I'd never have known it." Natalie contemplated her next words. "My parents love me as their own, and I've never questioned that. But I think deep down, the knowledge that I was adopted bothered me more than I realized. I couldn't leave the boys." She fiddled with her fingernail. "And I struggled to believe you weren't going to abandon me. There's always been this little voice inside, one I pretended to ignore, whispering that my birth mom left me for something else. Something better that she loved more than me. I think I worried others would do the same—even you." Chin dipped, she peeked up at him. "When I felt you growing distant, I pulled away too. I'd rather be the one walking away than the one left behind again."

"Nat." With one hand, he took hold of hers. With the other, he cupped her cheek. "I will never walk away from you."

"Even if the perfect job comes along?"

Her question arrived with a teasing lilt, but he understood the seriousness of the moment. More of Terrance's words returned to him. Nothing was more important to that man than his wife. Not even the work he loved so much. Reminded Mason of something he had said weeks ago to Trey. It didn't matter how many games he won if he lost the most important one. Even more true when it came to his wife. "I still want a college position, but not if it means losing you. I don't know how we find a solution. I just know we need to."

She placed her free hand on top of his, sandwiching theirs together. "I love your ambition, Mason. I just don't love feeling second place to it."

"I'm sorry I made you feel that way." Her skin warmed his. "I just wish you would have told me sooner instead of keeping it all inside."

"I'll work at telling you how I feel if you work at keeping me a priority."

"Stop those weeds before they grow?" He grinned.

"Exactly."

He gave her fingers a squeeze. "How about we table any remaining discussion until you've had time to explore this room?"

"You know me so well."

CHAPTER TWENTY

While the phone call to John had gone through, he had been unsuccessful in conferencing Caspar into it. John suggested that they enjoy Moat Brae as long as they were there, and he would continue to try to reach Caspar. He'd connect with them once he was successful. As such, they'd taken the afternoon to explore every nook and cranny of this enchanted place. Natalie spent most of her time in the secret library, relishing each moment with editions she had never seen before and most likely would never see again. Using the ledger, she also took a mental inventory of books that should have been in the room but were absent.

By the time they returned to the hotel, Gertie was exhausted. They ordered a quick dinner from room service, ate together, then went their separate ways. Natalie and Mason returned to their room and opened their laptops to work side by side. He put in headphones to listen to emails pertaining to tryouts. She compiled a list of the books Terrance had sold, and the locations and names of the buyers that she'd seen in the ledger. She wasn't quite sure what she was going to do with the information, only that she had some strange desire to know where those titles had wound up.

About an hour later her phone dinged. "Everleigh wants to know if we want to come down and work on a puzzle with them." Another ding, and she looked at her screen again. "She also says 'fair warning.' Niles is catching up on some of his own work and has a phone call later with Burt, so it would just be us girls. But you are more than welcome to join us."

Mason put away his AirPods. "I'll come."

After all the conversation they'd had recently about him putting work first, he most likely felt that was the only answer he could give. But what man wanted to put a puzzle together with three women? His willingness sure was awfully sweet though. "Mace, you don't have to join us. Stay here and finish up your work."

"You sure?" His fingers drummed the table.

"Definitely." She stood. "Unless you have a burning desire to hear how sickeningly sweet Niles is, how incredibly annoying Storm is, followed by the third degree on our relationship."

"Uh, nope. I'm good. I'll stay here and take advantage of the quiet room to dictate the email responses I need to send."

"Wise man." She slipped her feet into her Birkenstocks and headed for the door. "Not sure how long I'll be, but if you get bored, just text."

"Is that an offer to entertain me?"

With a saucy grin, she sauntered to the door. "I'm sure I could find plenty of ways to keep you occupied." She slipped out the door before he had a chance to respond, then stood in the hallway as her heart raced. Would Mason follow through on her suggestive invitation? Did he even see it as one? Her seduction tactics clearly were rusty, but flirting with her husband was a pastime she missed.

She also missed where flirting led. Her body warmed with memories. She and Mason had always been good together. In the early years of their marriage, she couldn't imagine sex not being a part of their relationship. Now it had been—she gulped—over a year? Wow. Okay. She'd been so fixated on the distance between them that she hadn't even realized how much time had passed since they'd been intimate. And here she was, casually tossing out the idea of sex like it was a regular thing between them.

She sucked in a breath. Crud. What if Mason did text? Suddenly she felt as awkward as a teenage girl waiting for her first kiss. Not to mention, she hadn't even shaved her legs in two days.

Gah! Mason probably sat on the other side of the door blissfully oblivious to their loaded parting words. Shaking her head, she headed down the hall and knocked on Everleigh's door, beyond ready for a distraction.

"Come on in."

Natalie stepped inside to find Brooke on the couch of the suite Everleigh shared with Gertie. On the coffee table in front of her were puzzle pieces they'd already begun to separate. Natalie settled onto the floor, sat crisscross applesauce, and willed her wayward thoughts away. "Are we separating edge pieces first?"

"I am," Brooke said. "But the puzzle queen over there has her own method."

Everleigh reclaimed her seat beside Brooke on the couch. "You do it your way, and I'll do it mine." In front of her was a pile of pieces all the same color.

"Where's the box so I can see what it's supposed to look like when we're done?" Natalie asked.

Brooke laughed as Everleigh smiled and fished the box out from under the coffee table. She handed it to Natalie.

Natalie furrowed her brow. "Is this a joke?"

"I asked the same thing," Brooke said. "And she just looked at me with that dreamy grin and said something about Niles knowing her so well."

Practically verbatim for what Natalie had said to Mason only a few hours earlier in the library. And just like Mason had shown he knew her, the fact that this box had no picture on it definitely said Niles knew Everleigh well. She loved puzzles and was gifted at doing them. She also loved challenges. He'd managed to provide both.

"It's a very sweet gift, Everleigh," Natalie said.

Brooke paused in her study of the puzzle pieces in her hand. She turned that probing gaze on Natalie. "You're sounding a lot less jaded. Plus, you have that same dreamy grin. Are things with Mason looking up?"

Everleigh joined in with Brooke. "You definitely seem cozier with him, but I haven't wanted to probe."

"I have." Brooke remained straight to the point. "I can't stand Storm, but you two bring him up every chance you get."

Natalie leaned on her palms. "Because it's obvious there's something between you two, but you refuse to acknowledge it."

Brooke's cool blue eyes grew icier any time Storm's name entered the conversation. Right along with her voice. "I fully acknowledge each and every time that there is something between us. Animosity."

"That's where Niles and I started. Look at us now." Everleigh fit two pieces together. "We're just like these two puzzle pieces."

Appalled didn't even begin to describe Brooke's expression. "Ew. That will not be Storm and me." She shivered. "Ever."

"Methinks the lady doth protest too much," Everleigh said.

That line from Hamlet was often misquoted. "Actually, it's 'The lady doth protest too much, methinks,' but I wholeheartedly agree." Natalie shared a conspiratorial look with Everleigh.

With a groan, Brooke dug her fingers into her hair and yanked it away from her face. "Listen. Storm and I go way back. We grew up like brother and sister, and then he stabbed me in the back. So the only thing he is to me is a bad memory. Maybe a cautionary tale. But he has never been—nor will he ever be—a romantic prospect." She turned to Natalie. "On to you and Mason."

It was painfully obvious that Storm still took up room in Brooke's heart and that she wished she could serve him an eviction notice. It was also obvious that Brooke didn't want to talk any more about him.

Natalie went along with the topic change. "Mason and I still have a lot to work on, but it finally feels like maybe we're both headed in the same direction again."

Brooke snapped her gum. "And that's what you want?"

"To save my marriage?" Natalie nodded "Yes. If we can make it work, that's exactly what I want. I just wasn't sure it was possible anymore. But the more we've talked, the more we've realized that we allowed misunderstandings and baggage from our pasts to play into how we perceived each other."

Brooke stared at her. "You have the most stable past out of all three of us."

"I do, as far as it goes with my family. We're close knit, and they love me very much. But . . ." She sucked in a deep breath, preparing to divulge something she rarely shared. Something she rarely thought about because she thought it hadn't affected her. Yet the more she dissected her relationship with Mason and her insecurities there, the more she was realizing she had been shaped by what she'd always considered an innocuous event. "I'm adopted."

Both her friends' eyes widened. Everleigh's mouth parted. "How did we not know this about you?"

"Because I don't often think about it. It's only recently that I realized it's played into my life more than I knew." It was a discovery in process. "My parents are the only mom and dad I've ever known, and I couldn't ask for better ones. They've been open with me from the very start, and I've never felt the need to figure out who my birth parents are. But I suppose I do have some abandonment issues that I haven't really wanted to face."

Brooke blinked rapidly. "Understandable."

They sat together in the silence. This was yet another moment of their friendship stepping into deeper levels. Goodness, these girls were beginning to mean so much to her. Before they could say anything else, Gertie's bedroom door opened.

"Darn jet lag is preventing me from getting my beauty sleep." Gertie's cane tapped the floor as she worked her way into the room.

Everleigh jumped up to help her. "Were we too noisy?"

"Not at all. I was listening to an audiobook." She allowed Everleigh to lead her to a chair, which she settled in. "It was all about the history of glue. It was really sticking with me."

"Gertie." Brooke groaned as Natalie and Everleigh laughed.

Everleigh dropped a thin blanket over Gertie's legs. "Can I get you anything?"

"No, I'm fine dear." Gertie leaned her cane against the chair. "I figured it was useless for me to keep tossing and turning in there. Thought I would come out and see what you were up to."

"Just talking about relationships and putting a puzzle together." Brooke started sorting pieces again.

Gertie smiled. "Ah, similar things. You spend a lot of time figuring out how to fit your pieces together with someone else's until a beautiful picture is created."

Everleigh settled on the couch. "I'll definitely be spending a lot of time on this puzzle. Your nephew gave me one where I have no idea what the finished product is supposed to look like."

"Even more like a relationship." Gertie folded her hands over her stomach.

Natalie loved how Gertie saw the world and the wisdom she shared in tiny bursts. She was thankful for the woman's friendship. For all the new friendships in this room.

They worked together in relative silence for a few minutes. As Brooke focused on a corner of the picture, she looked over to Gertie. "What can you tell us about the Perez family?"

If the question caught her off guard, Gertie didn't show it. "From my time with the FBI?"

"Yeah," Brooke said. "You haven't ever really filled us in on the details that you collected from then."

"Because there's not much to tell. They were a very elusive family." Gertie hauled in a deep breath. She looked as if she were reaching for old memories. "The little information I amassed during that time pointed to them dealing heavily in stolen goods. Like you already know, they located and sold items for collectors."

Everleigh leaned forward, placing her elbows on her knees. "Sounds familiar. Kind of like the book collectors we just discovered."

"In some ways, yes. But I don't think their secret society dips into the illegal arena."

"Like the Perez family?" Natalie asked.

"Exactly." Gertie nodded. "We could connect them to several stolen pieces, and we had suspicions of them moving others. But we were never able to make anything stick."

"And then they just went radio silent?" Brooke looked down at the picture they were creating, then back up to Gertie. "That just seems strange."

"It was strange. There were rumors about a fracture in the family, but if that were the case, I would have expected one of the sides to carry on the family business." Gertie grabbed her cane and tapped it on the floor. "All we know for sure is that since 1991, the family has been quiet."

"As far as you know," Brooke said.

"As far as we know," Gertie agreed.

On the table, Brooke's phone rang. She looked down. Looked back up at them all. "Maybe this call will tell us more." She held up her phone, which showed John's name, then swiped the green icon to answer.

"John said you needed to speak to me." Caspar bypassed his typical greeting and went straight to the matter at hand. "That the book isn't there, and the person who has it might not want to part with it."

"That's what Terrance told us," Everleigh replied.

Natalie leaned toward the phone. "He sold it to a bookstore owner in London. We plan on going to speak with the man, but Terrance mentioned he'd refuse to relinquish the book."

"And you're wondering if he might be swayed by a monetary offer?"

"In my experience, everyone has a price," Gertie said. "And if this book is important to Jerrick, I have no doubt he can afford to discover what that price is."

Natalie turned to study Gertie. Something in her voice spoke to familiarity. Was she more acquainted with the Perez family than she'd let on? Brooke must have sensed the same thing, because she'd turned a searching gaze her way as well.

"Speaking of Jerrick," Brooke said as she swung her focus back to the phone. "We're wondering why the book is so important to him."

"It reminds him of his mother," Caspar replied. "I told you that."

"Yes, and while that might be true, we feel it's only a partial reason," Everleigh said.

John cleared his throat. "They believe someone else is looking for the book."

The normal clicking sound came over the line, and they waited for Caspar's words. "Yes. Mason mentioned you had another visit at the bookstore, Natalie."

"I did." Natalie tapped her fingernails together. "Matt came into the bookstore again and made a comment about *Alice in Wonderland*. It just all feels too coincidental."

"Have you seen him there in Scotland?"

"No. And I'm still not convinced he's who I saw in France." She didn't want to cause unnecessary drama or worry.

Gertie's wrinkled hand gripped her cane. "Knowing what I do about the Perez family, it's not out of the realm of possibility that this book has more than sentimental value for Jerrick. Or that someone else might be looking for it." She paused, as if contemplating her next words. "I know you've promised the girls are safe, but if there's information we need that you've held back, now would be the time to fill us in."

Silence met them. After a long moment, clicking sounded again and then Caspar's automated voice. "Jerrick is aware that because of the connection this book has to his family, others could be interested in it. If that's the case, and they know you're looking for it as well, then until it's found, they'll continue watching you."

"Does Jerrick know who else would be after the book and why?" Brooke asked.

"He has ideas but no concrete answers. Once I know anything solid, I'll share with you, but it's my belief that the safest course of action is for the book to be found and turned over to Jerrick. If someone else wants it, he will handle things from there once you've been removed from the equation."

Natalie's stomach clenched. "So there is a possibility we're in danger?"

Brooke's and Everleigh's expressions showed their apprehension as well.

"I've taken precautions to ensure you're not alone." Before they could ask more about that, Caspar continued. "I have another call I need to take. John will schedule your flight to London tomorrow. Whatever deal you need to make with the owner to procure the book, make it. I can wire the money to you."

Natalie knew how much some of these books sold for. "It could be several million dollars."

"I'm aware." With that, Caspar said goodbye and disconnected.

John did the same, promising to text them their flight information and to expect that they'd leave in the morning.

As the call ended, Natalie shared a look with her friends. "Well, things just became a whole lot more interesting."

"Indeed," Gertrude said.

This was one book she really wished she could flip to the end, but if she were honest, she was a little afraid to turn the next page and see what it held.

CHAPTER TWENTY-ONE

Luciana Perez, age seventy-seven
Lekeitio, Spain, 1991

"It is time for our son to come home." Angus's declaration rang loudly through the dining room as he entered. Once again, he arrived late to dinner.

Luciana set down her fork. She'd already finished her soup, and Gregory, their butler, had placed her entrée in front of her. Beef Wellington, a typical favorite of hers, though lately she hadn't had much of an appetite.

She looked to Angus. "Jerrick has made his wishes known. We need to respect them."

Angus's mouth tightened into a thin line. She could not remember the last time she'd seen the smile that once captured her heart. He picked up his sherry glass and held it out for Gregory to fill. "It is he who needs to respect the traditions of this family."

"There was a time when we made the same decision as him." She wished they'd held fast to that choice, and she refused to force her son to change his mind. Her heart broke that Jerrick's decision meant he was absent from her life as well. He'd been in America over a decade, flirting with the idea of taking on the family mantle one day and expanding their reach to that continent. During that time, they'd spoken often. Then a year ago he'd abruptly cut away from them, refusing to step into his father's shoes. There'd been no contact since, and while she longed to hear from him, sometimes love required sacrifice.

"I was as wrong then as he is now." Angus extended his hands, like a king showing off his kingdom. "Look at all this life has provided for us. For him. He will not throw it away."

Luciana bit her lip. It did no good to tell Angus how she felt. He'd stopped listening years ago. His entire focus had become providing for his family, yet in doing so, they'd all lost so much. He'd alienated her sisters. Made rivals of Raul and Santiano Jr. Become estranged from their son. Grown distant from her.

All to gain position and wealth.

He claimed it was to provide the stability for his family that he'd never had as a child. Yet the only security she'd ever wanted was his simple love and dedication. Both those things now went toward his never-ending quest for more. More money. More power. More control.

Gregory approached and spoke quietly to Angus, who threw his napkin on the table. Features pinched and jaw tight, he rose.

"Sorry, my dear, but I must go. It appears your nephew is once again making trouble. He is too much like his father."

"Santiano? Is he here?" Luciana pushed away from her dinner, ready to join Angus. It had been years since she'd seen her sister's son. She'd reached out to him after Raul's death, but Santiano had not responded.

Angus held out his palm, stopping her. "He is not, but even if he were, I would not allow you around him. He carries his father's desire to destroy our family. Yet another reason I need Jerrick here. Our son's absence makes us appear weak, and Santiano wishes to take advantage of what he perceives as my lack of an heir."

A fight she'd thought had ended long ago.

"He still argues that he is the rightful successor."

"Then let him be." It seemed the best solution for all of them. "He is a Perez as well."

"But he is not my son!" Angus pounded the table. As the sound reverberated through the room, he took a deep breath. "I'm sorry. I did not mean to shout. There is simply much happening right now, and Santiano easily riles me in his constant bid for control and attempts to steal what is mine. But I've ensured he cannot find what he looks for." He pressed a kiss to the top of her head. "Please finish your dinner and enjoy a quiet evening. You've been so tired lately."

She had been. Sorrow weighed heavily on her bones.

Angus hurried from the room. Luciana stared down at her food.

"Would you like me to reheat it, ma'am?" Gregory asked from his station by the door to the kitchen.

"No." She stood. "I'm no longer hungry."

Concern weighted his features. "A state you find yourself in often lately." His eyes drifted over her, no doubt taking in the weight she'd lost. Gregory missed little about those in his care. "How about I bring some biscuits and tea to the study?"

She often spent her evenings in there, reading. Tonight, however, another room and its books beckoned her. "Bring them to the nursery."

His lips tilted up as he nodded, then disappeared into the kitchen.

Luciana ascended the stairs to the third-floor nursery. She lifted a hand to her chest, surprised how out of breath the familiar climb made her tonight. While her mind had escaped growing older, it seemed her body hadn't been as successful. Soft laughter rippled from her as she remembered the innocence of her youth and the promise she and her friends had made to never grow old like their parents. With a blink on her part, that promise had been broken.

Moving down the hall, she reached the nursery door. It creaked as she opened it. Memories flooded around her, like a movie screen, as she stepped inside. Inhaling, she could almost smell the scent of baby powder and little boy.

She crossed to the bookshelves and ran her finger over the titles, stopping at *Alice's Adventures Under Ground*. She pulled the worn story from its place, happy to have it back. Last month she'd come up here to page through the story, only to find it missing. She'd gone into a panic, but Angus quickly put her at ease by explaining he had borrowed it for a short while. Perhaps it was the knowledge that he'd recently returned it that had her visiting this room tonight. Or maybe it was the desire to be close to her son. Most likely both.

Each book here she'd read to Jerrick, but—much like herself as a child—this had been his favorite. Oh, how her heart had needed those hours up here with him. As Angus began to resemble Papi more and more, and the man she'd married less and less, she could steal away to this little room and hide within the fictional worlds she'd loved as a child and had adored sharing with her son.

She clutched the book to her chest, remembering the day Papi gifted it to her and insisted she one day share it with her child. Some of her most treasured memories were of Jerrick on her lap, listening intently to the adventures unfolding within these pages. She'd hoped one day he'd read it to his own children. Now she wouldn't even know if he had them.

Taking the book, she settled into the rocking chair and cracked it open, revisiting old friends. As she did, a thought formed. While she couldn't bring Jerrick here to her, maybe she could send him a piece of home.

Yes. She would wrap up this book and mail it to him. The gift would allow him to carry on only the best of their memories, and surely he'd want that.

Because she desperately did.

CHAPTER TWENTY-TWO

"I NEED TO KNOW WHAT happens." Natalie dropped her bags on the floor of their hotel room inside The Londoner. They'd landed on a private runway and driven their car here in under an hour, but it still felt too long when she had a show to finish. She and Mason had watched more episodes of the Wrexham documentary, and they only had a few more to finish. Oh, how she hated not knowing the ending to something. Had it not been for Mason stealing her phone, she'd have googled the info. "We can unpack later."

"You don't want to walk Leicester Square? See the statues? Maybe head over to Booksellers' Row, even if the shops are closed?" Due to a conflict with their pilot, John hadn't been able to schedule their plane until late afternoon. By the time they'd actually arrived in London, it was nearing 6:00 p.m. "Or grab some dinner?"

"I'm not hungry, and we can do the rest in the morning." She hadn't expected to get so invested in the soccer team, but the story was more than that. It had focused on the rebuilding of the town, and she'd been hooked.

He chuckled. "Never thought I'd see the day that you picked anything related to sports over stories."

"Me either." The statues in Leicester Square were all well-known characters from the film industry, ranging from Mary Poppins to Paddington Bear to Gene Kelly and more. Not only that, but the square attached to the West End, where popular theater shows played. Booksellers' Row ran in between the two areas. Typically, the attractions around their hotel would be the first place she'd explore. Instead she plopped onto their bed. "Pull up the next episode."

Mason settled beside her, kicking off his shoes. Now that they were in their own room, they ditched the use of AirPods. Natalie still rested her head on his shoulder, however—a move Mason didn't seem to mind.

"As you wish," he said.

An hour and a half later, she dabbed the edges of her eyes.

"Are you crying?" Mason set the iPad down and looked over at her.

"What? No. My eyes are just overly dry from the airplane."

He leveled a suspicious look at her. "They look damp, not dry."

"Because my body is trying to compensate for how dry they were." She blinked rapidly.

"Mm-hmm." His little hum came from deep in his throat as he stood. "Hungry now?"

She stood and stretched too. "I could eat." In fact, she suddenly felt famished.

"Room service?"

"Sure."

They found the menu and ordered, then unpacked while they waited for their food to arrive. Somewhere over the past few days, a familiar comfort level had returned to them. It was a feeling she wanted to protect and grow.

"It's been nice having you around these past few weeks."

Mason stilled beside the drawer where he'd been stashing his T-shirts. After a moment, he closed it and looked at her. "Yeah?"

She sat on the end of the bed. "Yes." Nabbing the blanket decoratively placed over the corner of the mattress, she played with its fringed edges. "I know it's not easy working through all our problems, but I'm glad we're doing it. I want our marriage to work. I've missed you."

He settled beside her, his hand resting on top of hers. "I've missed you too."

Her eyes remained on their joined hands as Mason's thumb rubbed over her wedding band. She remembered him placing it there on their wedding day and how she'd felt so special. Chosen. As if she permanently belonged to him, and her heart had been so full. She blinked up to find him watching her, such tenderness in his eyes. "You're all I've ever wanted, Mace, but you pulled away"—she touched her fingertips to his mouth as he started to speak—"I know we already covered that, and I understand we both contributed to the distance in our marriage. Now I want to close it."

He pressed a kiss to her fingers, then lifted his lips to brush against her forehead. "I'd like nothing more." A knock at their door had him standing. "I'll grab our food."

Natalie cleared off the small table in the corner so there was room for the tray. After signing for their dinner, Mason walked to the mini fridge in the small kitchenette of their suite. "Water or a soda?"

She joined him, grabbing ice for their glasses. "Water please." As she touched the cold cubes, an idea formed that had her suppressing a wicked grin.

Mason snagged her a water and himself a soda. With his hands full, Natalie took advantage of the moment. Nabbing the collar of his shirt, she dropped ice down his front side. "Payback." She vaulted away as he untucked his shirt to release the frigid assault.

Uncontrollable giggles escaped as she watched him struggle. That was until he stilled and slowly brought his gaze to hers. Uh-oh. She hopped onto the bed as Mason picked up his own glass of ice and advanced.

From here she could jump down and run in any direction, depending on his next move. If she couldn't persuade him to put the glass down, that was. "Come on, Mace. Now we're even."

His grin spread, along with that look in his eyes—pure mischief. He took another step.

"Mason," she warned through her laughs. "Don't."

With one smooth hop, he was on the bed too, proceeding toward her with his glass held high. Natalie raised her hands, latched on to his arm, and tried to turn the ice over on him. The man was too strong and too fast. Ice rained down on her, and she cried out with a shiver. Kneeling, she scooped up the handful of cubes from where they'd landed on the blankets and reached for the hem of his shirt. Her hands slid along his abdomen, pressing the ice cubes into his skin.

"Hey!" He toppled and pulled her with him.

Their laughter mingled, and she arched as he pressed a cube along her back. In the same instant she registered the icy cold, her body reacted to the heat of his fingertips against her bare skin. Mason rolled her over, no doubt to ensure she couldn't escape the ice bath he was giving her. But as she sucked in a breath and stilled, he jolted to a halt too. His face was inches from hers, their bodies tangled together in a way they hadn't been for months. Other than the air conditioner and their mingled breaths, the room grew completely silent. So quiet she had no problem hearing her thoughts.

No more distance.

Mason had to hear them too, because he leaned in, his chest pressing against hers as his lips brushed softly across her parted ones. He pulled back and looked into her eyes, a question there that she answered by lifting to firmly close the space he'd added. It was all the response Mason needed before he tightened his hold, his arms a snug cocoon as his mouth went on a hunting expedition. He moved from her lips to her cheek, softly skimming her skin in a way that lifted goose bumps. From there he slipped to the spot behind her ear before dropping along her neck to the sensitive skin along her collarbone, where he knew would draw her gasp. She felt him smile when he heard her inhale. His nose brushed against the hollow there as he spent some time tickling her with his lips.

Natalie pressed her chin against his forehead and drew his head up with a familiar urgency. His eyes lifted, a hunger there before his mouth covered hers like she was the feast made to quench his craving.

They'd been penning a new portion of their story for weeks now. As their breaths and bodies mingled together, her heart filled pages that had been empty for far too long. Words of love and hope, desire and passion, intimacy and trust. Each syllable whispered truth to them both. She'd missed her husband, and he'd missed her too.

➤ ◄

"I think our dinner's cold." Natalie's warm breath brushed his bare chest as she spoke.

His fingers dragged through her hair. "Well worth it. Though I have worked up an appetite." He pressed a kiss against her head, enjoying the feel of her laughter as she lay beside him.

"Another call to room service?" she lazily questioned.

"If I could reach our phone without moving." Because it had been far too long since he'd held her like this, and he wasn't ready to let go. He was one blessed man.

Natalie palmed his chest, as if she were about to straighten. He tightened his hold on her and felt her cheeks round in a smile.

"Let me up. I don't want to be responsible for you starving to death," she said. "Or being too weak for round two."

He slid down, capturing her lips with his. "Not possible." As she returned his fervor with her own, the desire for room service paled beside other, more appetizing options.

Two hours later they'd finally come up for air, showered, and wrapped themselves in the fluffy robes that had been hanging in their closet. Half-eaten plates of new food sat in front of them, as did glasses filled with ice. Natalie poured some water in hers.

"I'll never trust you around ice again," he teased.

"Hey now. I did forewarn you that I planned on retaliating."

"That you did." He dragged a fry through ketchup. "And if that's your idea of a payback, feel free to repay me anytime."

Her eye roll would have been more effective if she didn't also wear a rosy smirk.

As they finished up their meals, Mason dove into all the things left unspoken between them. He'd firmly made up his mind. There was nothing more important to him than Natalie. What he'd allowed to balloon into seemingly big issues had all been popped. Deflated. Floating between them no more. Misunderstandings, hurt feelings, and pride had persuaded him into thinking he needed more. He wasn't enough. Natalie was better when he wasn't around.

He'd been an idiot.

"Unless a college position opens up at Kenton Corners Community College, I'm not changing jobs."

Natalie stopped, carrot stick midway to her mouth. She set it on her plate. "You can pursue your dreams, Mason. I support them one hundred percent. That's never been the problem."

He understood that now. "I know, but I also know you don't want to move again. You've followed me every step of the way, and I didn't realize how much you gave up in doing that. Or how shaky that made you feel."

"I followed you because I love you. As for feeling shaky, that wasn't because of the moves."

True. Her struggle with abandonment was something neither of them had been aware of, but now that they were, he wanted to do everything he could to help her overcome it. Still, that didn't change his part in the near end of their marriage. "Even so, if I'd kept you a priority, your insecurities wouldn't have flared."

"And if I had shared how I was feeling instead of keeping silent, yours wouldn't have either." She reached for his hand. "Bottom line, we love each other and are committed to making this work."

They let a moment tick by before Mason continued. "Something else we can both work on is praying together. We've done a really great job of saying what we both want for this relationship and our future, but we haven't asked God what he wants for us. For our marriage."

"Kind of like trying to reach an unknown destination without any directions."

"Exactly like that." He moved one of his hands to reach for her other. She slipped it into his grip, and he held tight. "How about we start now?"

"I'd like that very much."

For the first time in years, they prayed together. Mason took the lead, a position he'd neglected right along with his wife, but he promised during their prayer that he wouldn't any longer. Natalie finished up, adding her own confessions and promises. Like their marriage bed had earlier, this moment added another strengthening stitch to their reunited hearts.

The rest of the evening they spent cuddled together watching reruns of *Friends*, a show they'd watched while dating. They fell asleep tangled together, and he woke to her ringing phone.

"Nat." He gently nudged her. "Sweetheart, your phone."

She pressed up on her elbow and brushed her hair from her face before reaching to answer. Mason caught sight of her mom's face on the screen.

"Mom?" Natalie's groggy voice spoke. He couldn't hear Brenda's side of the conversation, but Natalie bolted up straight. She cast wide eyes at Mason. "Dad and Lorne were in an accident."

CHAPTER TWENTY-THREE

Though Mom assured her that Dad and Lorne were both okay, Natalie hadn't been able to sleep the remainder of the night. Simply too much was happening in her life for her mind to shut down. Dad's accident. Reconnecting with Mason. The hunt for this book. Layer them together and she might as well kiss sleep goodbye for the foreseeable future. As such, she was showered, dressed, fed, and caffeinated with three hours to go until the bookshops on Cecil Court opened.

Mason still slumbered in the king-size bed they'd shared last night. A smile lifted her cheeks. She'd awakened to his arm around her, something that hadn't occurred for years but remained familiar and comforting. So much so that she'd lain there enjoying his embrace until nature called and she couldn't ignore it any longer.

She tiptoed around her room, ensuring she didn't wake Mason from his deep sleep. Motherhood provided certain skills, like the ability to navigate stealthily so as to not wake a slumbering child. As such, Mason hadn't heard her run the shower or leave for the buffet downstairs. Nor had her return stirred him. She moved to the balcony to read her morning devotion. Outside, sunshine warmed the early morning breeze, and there wasn't a cloud in the sky. The day held a promise that she was ready to unwrap.

Half an hour later, Natalie checked on Mason one more time, but he hadn't moved a muscle. She slipped on her shoes, wrote him a note, and left the room. The bookshops still wouldn't be open, but that didn't mean she couldn't window shop. Maybe she'd also run across some ideas for the next time she had to create the front window display at the Golden Key.

Phone in hand, Natalie meandered toward Cecil Court. While Leicester Square stood steps away, she'd save it and its bronze statues until later today with Mason. For now, she followed Siri's directions to Booksellers' Row.

People bustled around her during the five-minute walk to the mouth of the alleyway, and she stopped once she reached this quaint street to take it all in. Adorable shops with glass storefronts and painted headers lined both sides of the alley. There were antique stores, auctioneers, appraisers, and bookshops. Oh, the bookshops! Each one a different color. All with unique names. So many with rare editions, yet still bursting at the seams with current titles too.

Black iron lampposts stood every few feet down the center of the small footpath, and a few wooden benches allowed for shoppers to rest a while. Possibly even read one of the new adventures they'd purchased.

She'd never seen anything like it. And she had every intention of enjoying the extra time she had here, even if none of the doors stood open yet.

Natalie trekked to the shops to her left first. Any one of these owners would be interested in the book she sought, but Terrance specifically said it was the owner of Alice Through the Looking Glass who had purchased it. Midway through the alley, she reached her destination. Navy blue paint coated the wood casing above and below the glass window and door. Gold lettering announced the name of the bookshop, and Alice paraphernalia beckoned collectors inside.

Natalie looked beyond the full window to the space behind. Funny. It looked messy in there. She ducked for a better view between items and gasped. Was that . . . She squinted. It looked as if someone was lying on the floor.

Swiveling around, she glanced up and down the alley. A few people milled around, but suddenly she felt isolated. What was Europe's equivalent to 911? She hadn't a clue, so instead she dialed the top number in her favorites. It rang several times before Mason's groggy voice answered.

"Nat?"

"Mace, I think something strange is going on."

She heard him move in the sheets and pictured him sitting up, probably confused. "Where are you?"

"I came to Booksellers' Row, and I think someone's in trouble." She repositioned to try for a better look through the window. Yes. That was definitely someone on the floor.

"I'm getting dressed. Hold on." His voice cleared. "Are you alone?"

"Yes. Well, I mean there's other people in the alley but not many." She glanced up and down. No one looked suspicious. She turned back to the shop and saw movement inside. Someone was still in there! She slammed herself flat against the wall. "Mace," she whispered, "I think someone is still in there."

The sound of a door closing registered, as did his breaths. Sounded like he was running. "In where?" Another door. "Never mind. I'm headed your way. Start walking toward the hotel, but watch your back."

"But what if I can see who it is?" She peeked around the white pillar that separated this shop from the one beside it. Whoever was in there was partially hidden by the large painting of Alice that hung from cords dangling from the ceiling. The picture covered the top half of the person, so all Natalie could see was their pants and shoes.

"Nat!" Mason bellowed. "If you can see them, chances are they can see you. Just get out of there."

"Hang on. I'm going to take a picture." She snapped a shot and returned the phone to her ear.

His groan sounded more like a growl. "Walk to the hotel. Now."

"Fine. I'm coming." Her heart raced.

"Don't hang up." Mason's voice shook. "You're still there?"

"I am, and I won't." She hustled toward the main street and was halfway down it when she caught Mason racing her way.

He didn't slow, barreling into her with the force of a man intent on keeping her safe from whatever threat she'd encountered. His arms engulfed her as his head rotated, looking for threats. "I don't see anyone."

"I didn't either," she said into his embrace. "At least not following me."

His chest heaved up and down with his heavy breaths. Then he grabbed her face and lifted it to his. "You're okay?"

She nodded, relishing the feel of his touch.

He pressed a kiss to her forehead, then wrapped her back in his arms. "Don't scare me like that again."

"I won't." Her words muffled against him, and she pulled away. "We need to find help for whoever is inside the store."

Mason stared at her for another long second before nodding. "Right. You're sure someone was on the floor?"

Natalie showed him the picture she took. "I don't know who to call though."

"Let's go back to the hotel."

She hated taking the time to do so, but with no other shops open nearby, it seemed their only option. They jogged back and alerted the front desk to what was happening. The concierge called authorities, and while they did that, Natalie texted their group.

Ten minutes later they all assembled in the lobby, and she filled them in. "We need to go back there and see what's happening." She started for the door before noticing that Mason remained in the center of the lobby, arms crossed. Oh boy, she'd seen that look before. She knew what was coming even before he spoke.

→ ←

Mason had just about had enough. Scratch that. He was past enough. The idea of his wife in danger had pushed him firmly over that line. "I think it's time to tell Caspar you're done." His heart still hadn't returned to a normal pace since her phone call.

Natalie shared a look with her friends, who then stepped outside while she returned to him. "I know this morning freaked us both out a little, but we don't know for sure that what I witnessed is related to the book."

"Nat, come on. What else could it be?"

"An unrelated robbery. There are a lot of valuables in that store. Maybe other shops were hit too." But even as she offered the explanation, she agreed it seemed unlikely. "If it is connected though, remember that Caspar ensured our safety."

"You've never actually seen the man, and you have no idea where he lives. He could be a thousand miles from here." Mason hauled in a breath, trying to calm himself. "He doesn't exactly inspire confidence."

She gripped his bicep, squeezing gently but firmly. "I've got you, and lately you've been inspiring a lot of confidence."

He peeked down to find her sweet grin and those captivating brown eyes fixed on him. She'd stopped just shy of batting her eyelashes, but she'd never needed to add that component, and she knew it. That one look had always been enough.

Groaning, he shook his head. "All right. Let's at least see what we can find out. But if this is linked together, your smile and flattering words aren't going to be enough to change my mind."

"They can't hurt." She slid her hand down his arm until their fingers touched.

Mason wrapped hers in his grip. "I'm more concerned with *you* being hurt."

She tugged. "Come on."

Outside, their tiny group waited for them. They made the short walk to Cecil Court, and as they entered the alleyway, the street bustled—mainly with police. As they approached, one of the uniformed men stepped out to stop them. Natalie weaved through her friends. "I'm the person who notified the police."

He consulted his notebook. "Natalie Daughtry?"

She presented her license to him. He studied it before beckoning her to follow him. When their entire group moved, he stopped them. "Only her."

Mason remained by her side. "I'm her husband." And she wasn't going anywhere without him.

"Fine," the officer said. "But the rest of you stay here."

He escorted them to the doorway of the shop. "We have a few questions for you."

The officer handed Natalie over to a colleague, and she answered everything he asked, but he ignored all of her prodding questions in return. Around them multiple conversations simultaneously took place. Mason's attention split as he listened to each one.

Finally, the officer closed his black pad of paper. "We appreciate your help. If we need anything else, we'll contact you at your hotel."

Natalie leaned around him to see through the open shop door. "The shopkeeper. Is he okay?"

"He's at the hospital being checked out as we speak, but yes, other than a knock on his head, it appears he'll be all right." He held his hand out for Natalie and Mason to return to their friends.

When Natalie didn't immediately move, Mason nudged her along. She acceded, but based on her frown, she wasn't happy about being pulled away from the center of activity.

"Fill us in," Brooke demanded when they were still a few feet away.

People milled about, more to feed their curiosity than to shop the opening stores. Natalie's frown deepened. "I have no clue if this has to do with the book or not. The officers wouldn't tell me anything."

Everleigh stood hand in hand with Niles. "It has to. There's no way this is a coincidence."

Thank goodness he wasn't the only one saying that.

"Where's the shop owner?" Gertrude asked.

"The hospital." Natalie huffed. "Though I have no clue which one."

He did. "St. Thomas."

Natalie jerked her gaze to his. "How do you know?"

Once again what he'd always seen as a weakness, he now noticed for its strength. "Being aware of multiple conversations isn't so great in school, but it comes in handy as a coach on the field and, apparently, when helping my wife search for rare books."

"You were eavesdropping on the police officers." Her face lit with pride, and it stoked heat inside him. The way her gaze flicked to his lips fanned the warmth into a near blaze.

"Maybe." With intention, he dropped his own focus to her lips before dragging it back to her eyes. Yeah. They were on the same page.

"Hate to interrupt your ogling"—Brooke held up her phone—"but we need to get to that hospital." She started toward their hotel. "I have the directions. Let's get the car."

Way to toss cold water on the moment.

Forty minutes later they arrived at St. Thomas. They all agreed that since Natalie had been the one to call in the attack, it made most sense for her to be the one checking on the shop owner. Mason refused to let her go alone. Brooke and Everleigh refused to let them go alone. Gertie and Niles had remained at the hotel, though begrudgingly on Gertie's part, to update John and Caspar.

Brooke dropped Natalie and Mason at the door. "We'll circle around to the park nearby. Text us when you're finished." With a wave, they drove off.

Natalie and Mason made their way to the information desk at accident and emergency, London's equivalent to an emergency room.

The young receptionist finished typing something into her computer before looking up. "May I help you?"

"Um, yes," Natalie began. "A man was brought in this morning who works in a bookshop on Cecil Court. I'm wondering if he's doing okay?"

The woman's face remained impassive. "Your name and relationship to the patient?"

"Natalie Daughtry. I'm not related to him. I'm the person who found him and called the police."

"I'm sorry, ma'am, but if you're not related, I can't give you any information."

Mason intervened. "We completely understand, but would you be willing to ask the man if he would speak with us? My wife is very worried about him." None of that moved the woman into action. He dug deeper. "We're also acquaintances with one of his business associates, Terrance MacLeod. If you just let him know we're here, I'm sure he'll want to speak with us."

Nothing he'd said was a lie. Natalie had been praying for the man's well-being, and laying eyes on him would go a long way in assuring her that he was all right. Plus, Mason had specifically called them acquaintances—not friends—with Terrance, so he wasn't stretching the truth there either.

The woman studied them, sighed, and stood. "I'll speak with his nurse. That's all I can do."

"Thank you," Natalie said.

Mason took her hand as they waited. In such a short time, he'd grown used to having her by his side again. Of all the teams he'd been a part of in his life, this one was his favorite. How had he let himself forget that?

Never again.

The receptionist returned. "Mr. Goodwind has agreed to see you."

Goodwind. The same name Terrance had given them.

They fell in step to follow her to a curtained-off room. Metal scratched against metal as she pulled the curtain back. Mr. Goodwind—the white board on wall indicated his first name was Barry—lay stretched out on a hospital bed, looking perfectly normal, with the exception of the large goose egg on the side of his red-haired head.

He greeted them with a grunt.

The receptionist returned to her desk. Natalie approached the foot of

Barry's bed. "Mr. Goodwind, we appreciate you agreeing to see us. How are you feeling?"

"Like I got knocked upside my head." His tone held nothing cordial in it. Neither did his assessing stare. He wasn't happy they were here, but at least he was talking to them. "You want that book too."

Ahh, there was his confirmation that this was about the book, but Mason wanted to make it abundantly clear. "That's what the person who attacked you was after?"

"Yes. He didn't get it though." This triumph brought a grin to Barry's face. "I don't take kindly to being forced into anything. I also don't care to be in the middle of whatever is going on here. If you want that book, you can have it." The monitor beside him beat a steady rhythm. "For a price, that is."

His request wasn't surprising. Natalie nodded, no doubt leaning into what they'd already discussed with Caspar. "Terrance told us what you paid. We'll have the same amount wired to you."

"Plus ten percent." Barry shifted in his bed. "To cover my medical expenses."

Natalie shook her head. "Five percent. You'll likely not be admitted, and us taking the book means we're also taking any danger that accompanies it." She arched her brow, like she used to do when she was laying down the law with their boys. "We're doing you a favor."

"Fine. As long as you wire it today." He gave her the necessary information.

"Not a problem." Natalie pulled her phone from her pocket.

While she sent a flurry of texts to John, Mason continued to prod. "What did the person who attacked you look like?"

"I have no idea, other than it was a man. He wore a ski mask."

So much for seeing if the description matched Matt's.

Natalie's fingers paused on her screen. "We're all set. My colleague will transfer half now and half once we have the book."

Barry rolled his eyes but didn't argue. He told them how to get into his shop and provided the code for the safe he'd hidden behind a painting of Wonderland. "How do I know you'll keep your end of this bargain?"

"The police are aware of who we are, since we spoke with them this morning. They also know where we're staying. We're not looking at getting arrested in a foreign country, so we're not planning on double-crossing you." Mason nodded to the curtain and started that way. "As long as that book is there, you'll have the other half within the next hour."

"Looking forward to it," Barry called after their retreating forms.

Natalie texted Brooke. And as they stepped outside to wait for her and Everleigh, she grinned up at him. "We make a good pair, you and me."

"We do, don't we." As much as he enjoyed this light feeling between them, he couldn't ignore what they'd just heard. "But, Nat, this is about that book. Everything inside confirmed that fact."

"I know." She clicked her nails together, a sure sign she was anxious. "But we're so close to finishing this. And like Caspar said, once we get the book to Jerrick, our part will be over. Whatever is going on, we'll be out of the equation."

"You won't take another job with him?" Because if he'd had any clue working for Caspar could put her in harm's way, he'd have encouraged her to quit long ago.

"I don't see him asking us to."

"But if he did?" As he spoke, he realized they'd switched roles from their conversation in Boston. At the same moment, he fully grasped how his response had hurt her because it would feel like her choosing her work over him if she said yes. Yet how could he ask her to give up something she loved? Granted, her job brought possible danger, while his didn't. That aside, he could see both sides of the coin.

Her conflicted look showed she'd picked up on the same thing. "We've still got a lot to work through, don't we?"

"We do."

"Let's start with retrieving the book. Then we'll continue figuring out the rest." Natalie held out her hand.

And he took it.

CHAPTER TWENTY-FOUR

THEY ARRIVED AT ALICE THROUGH the Looking Glass to find the store deserted. With Barry in the hospital, the shop remained closed. The officers had finished their investigation and no longer milled about. Natalie stepped to the door and punched in the code Barry had provided, which unlocked the dead bolt.

"I'll wait here and keep an eye out." Mason's focus remained on the street, ensuring no threats watched them. Not that they had a clue who'd attacked Barry, but they definitely had their suspicions.

Brooke, Natalie, and Everleigh stepped inside.

"He's quite the protector." Brooke referenced Mason as she surveyed the small space. "We're looking for a painting of Wonderland?"

"Yes." Natalie took the opposite wall, while Everleigh strolled to the rear of the store. "He wants me to stop working for Caspar after this."

Brooke halted her search and turned to her friend, skepticism on her face. "He can ask you to give up your job, but you can't ask the same of him?"

"His heart is in the right place, but we definitely have some things to work out still."

"I'll say."

"Found it," Everleigh called.

Those two words shut down their conversation as they hustled to Everleigh's side. She'd already moved the painting and located the safe behind it. Natalie consulted her phone and pressed in the combination. With a click, the safe opened. Inside lay a singular item with a gold spine, green cover, and tattered edges. Natalie peeked up at her friends.

"Go ahead," Everleigh whispered as Brooke nodded.

Gingerly reaching, Natalie removed the treasure they'd sought.

Scrawled in black ink across the rough green fabric was the title *Alice's Adventures Under Ground.* The book was worn, not because of age but because of love. This was a story someone had savored, no doubt Jerrick and his mother, Luciana. Possibly even generations before them.

Everleigh leaned in on her left, Brooke on her right.

This didn't feel like a priceless antique as much as a part of Jerrick's history. A cherished keepsake for him. Natalie ran her finger over the cover before opening it. The pages cracked as she did so, and she read the inscription inside.

George and Clara,

May this story remind you of your Alice. Her life, though short, was one grand adventure.

~Lewis

"Just like Caspar said." Everleigh's voice was hushed. "Lewis knew Jerrick's great-great-grandparents."

Brooke straightened. "This is insane."

Natalie continued to carefully flip pages, studying each one. She returned to the words Lewis had penned and traced the letters. Her eyes narrowed in on the swoops, something catching her attention. She reached for her phone just as the floor creaked behind them. Glancing toward her friends, she whispered, "Did you hear that?"

Their wide eyes and tense muscles proclaimed they had. The direction of the noise was from the stock room behind a curtained-off area.

Everleigh closed the safe. "Let's finish looking at that at our hotel."

"Good idea." Natalie handed the book to Brooke, who wrapped cloth around it before tucking the story into the bag slung over her shoulders. "Let's go."

"Oh, do stay long enough to give me that book." The low voice stopped them in their tracks.

Natalie met the cold gaze of the familiar man stepping through the curtain. "Matt."

Everleigh and Brooke stiffened beside her but remained silent. No doubt the gun in his hand also kept them still. She certainly wasn't about to move.

"Mattias Santiano Bolivar, but yes, you can continue to call me Matt." He approached them. "I'm glad to see you remember me." Another few steps had him within a foot of her. "It means we don't need to go through the mess of further introductions." He held out his hand. "The book."

Natalie blinked toward the front of the store, hoping Mason didn't choose this moment to check on them.

Matt followed her gaze. "He remains safe, as do all of you, if you simply give me what is mine."

His comment loosened Brooke's tongue. "It doesn't belong to you."

Matt tipped his head and ushered a low laugh. "There is much you do not know."

Everleigh spoke up. "Enlighten us then."

"That's not why I came." Matt waved his gun. "The book." When Brooke didn't move, his hand thrust out and grabbed the shoulder strap of her bag. With a sharp tug, he pulled her to him.

Brooke yanked against his grip, and Natalie lunged to help her. Matt slammed the gun against her face, catching her on the cheek.

Blinding pain tore through her head.

"Natalie!" Everleigh reached for her as she dropped to her knees.

Brooke continued to wrestle Matt.

The front door opened. "Hey. Look who I bumped into."

Oh no. No, no, no. Mason was walking right into—

"Enough!" Matt's dark tone thundered into the room, stilling voices and movement. With a jerk, he held Brooke in front of him. "All I want is the book."

Mason halted. He looked Natalie's way, and she reassured him with a nod that she was okay. Hoped it was enough to make him stand down. Not do anything crazy, because she could see him calculating plays in his head like he did when his defensive line took the field.

Brooke's eyes latched on to the man standing behind Mason, and her brow furrowed. "Storm?"

His gaze ignored hers in favor of Matt's.

Mason moved toward Natalie.

"Stay there," Matt ordered.

"My wife is on the ground." He took another step.

The cocking of the gun reverberated through the room.

"Mace!" Natalie yelled.

He stilled, concern darkening his eyes to charcoal.

"Just do as he says. Stay there." Natalie's voice trembled.

Matt's gun held steady on Mason. "I'd listen to her."

Mason's hands curled at his side, and his stance shifted into a brick wall. He planned to tackle this guy. Except this wasn't a game, and Matt wouldn't put Mason down with a hard hit. He'd use a bullet.

"Please, Mace."

The muscles in his jaw tightened, but he nodded at her that he'd stay put.

Storm shifted his stare to Brooke. "Give him the book, Brooke."

"It's not his." She hissed through clenched teeth.

Another jostle from Matt. "You've been lied to." He jammed his gun into her side. "Do you really want to die for a lie?" Then he waved his weapon around the room. "Or watch your friends die for one?"

Their stalemate lingered for what felt like several minutes but had to have only been seconds. Brooke reached for the strap of her bag, maneuvering it off her body. "Fine. Take it."

Matt slung the bag over his shoulder and backed away. "Tell Jerrick this has been returned to its rightful lineage." He stopped. "As has the Perez family mantle. He no longer claims the name Caspar. I do. If he challenges me, I will kill him, just as he killed my father."

Then he disappeared through the curtain, leaving them in a stunned wake of silence.

CHAPTER TWENTY-FIVE

QUESTIONS DARTED AROUND THE ROOM, but there was only one Mason needed answered. He slid to the floor beside Natalie and cupped her cheek, gingerly running his thumb over the forming bruise. "Are you okay?"

"Physically." She leaned into his hold. "Emotionally I'm not so sure."

Behind them, Brooke batted at Storm as he checked on her. "I'm fine," she growled at him. "Confused as to why you're here, but fine."

Mason helped Natalie to her feet. "He showed up in the alleyway to check on you." Mason shuddered to think what could have happened if Storm hadn't arrived when he had. "I, for one, am glad he did."

"Fine. He has impeccable timing." Brooke crossed her arms as she surveyed Storm. "But how did you know I was here?" She cut him off as he started to answer. "In London."

The edge of his lip lifted, as if her clarification amused him. "Adam called me the other day. Said he was worried about you and asked if I could check on you."

"I didn't think he was talking to you." She huffed. "And I told him I was fine."

"He clearly didn't believe you." Storm looked around the room. "With good reason, it seems."

"Well, you can see I wasn't lying. You've done your duty, and you can go back home now."

He seemed unaffected by her vitriolic tone. "Think I'll stick around a bit longer." He calmly strolled to the front of the store.

Shoulders lifting in a long sigh, Brooke turned to them. She must have seen the questions on their faces, because she said, "Adam was a partner in a business Storm and I used to own. Any other explanations will have to wait, don't you think?"

Everleigh nodded. "Definitely." She stood beside Natalie. "You sure you're okay?"

Natalie didn't look okay. Her cheek was turning a dark purple, and she winced at the sunlight streaming through the window. Mason held her steady. "I think we should take you to the hospital and have you checked out."

"No hospital," Natalie protested. "I'm okay. I promise. It's nothing a few aspirin won't help." She nodded to the door. "Along with answers to that verbal bomb Matt set off. We need to go back to the hotel and call John. See if he can get us through to Caspar."

"Do you think John knows?" Brooke asked. "That Caspar and Jerrick are the same person? Because that's what Matt was implying, right?"

"That's certainly how I took it." Everleigh played with the cube attached to her belt loop.

"I don't think he does." Natalie pressed fingertips to her forehead. "But we won't know until we ask him."

"That is, if he doesn't lie, like apparently Caspar's been doing," Brooke said.

"About a whole lot more than his name," Mason added. The name thing didn't bother him nearly as much as the accusation of murder.

"He hasn't actually lied," Everleigh said. "He just hasn't revealed everything."

Brooke's eyes nearly bugged out of her head. "You're seriously going to try to split hairs here? Omission and misdirection *are* forms of lying."

Natalie stepped between them. "Can we please handle this at the hotel? After I down a few aspirin?"

Mason took her arm. "Come on." He led her toward the door. "The rest of you can follow or not, but we're leaving." If he had his way, they'd head to the hospital. Once they ensured him Natalie would be okay, *then* he'd take her to the hotel, where he'd tuck her in and keep a watchful eye on her. He understood she wouldn't rest until she had the answers she sought, so instead he'd be here for her to lean on and do his best to help in whatever way she needed.

The walk back remained silent. Brooke maintained distance from everyone, though Storm kept her clearly in his sight. With everything Mason had heard about the man from Brooke, he had expected horns, a tail, and a pitchfork. Looked more like cupid and his arrow had gotten a hold of Storm, because no man hopped an airplane and flew thousands of miles for a woman he detested. That was an act of love—or at the very least, affection—and Mason would know. He'd done it twice now. How did Brooke not see Storm's feelings for her?

It wasn't his job to play matchmaker though, especially right now. There was a whole lot more at stake than any of their hearts.

Half an hour later, their entire group congregated in Mason and Natalie's sitting room, with John on the other side of their FaceTime call. Everleigh took the floor to fill Gertie, Niles, and John in on what they'd missed. As she spoke, Niles paced the long length of the room, frustration rolling off him. Mason understood the feeling. Having anyone held at gunpoint was hard. Having a gun pointed at the woman you love, terrifying.

As Everleigh recounted Matt's parting words, Niles rubbed his palm over his face. "Unbelievable." He strolled to Everleigh and pulled her into a tight hug. "I should have been there."

"I'm glad you weren't, Yogi. You'd have released your grizzly-bear side and gotten yourself shot."

His hands lifted her face from where she'd burrowed into his chest. "And I'm glad you're okay." He pressed a kiss to her lips.

"Very sweet, you two, but hello?" Brooke stood near the windows. Storm leaned against the ledge of another, but Brooke ignored him. "Are we going to talk about the fact that Jerrick is Caspar and, it seems, a murderer?" She stomped to the computer and leaned toward the screen. "How much did you know, John?"

"I'm as in the dark as all of you." He'd rubbed his neck as Everleigh spoke, leaving his bow tie crooked. "More so, because you heard this information firsthand and before me."

Natalie reclined against Mason on the couch. He'd gotten her three ibuprofen and a bag of ice for her cheek. She'd closed her eyes but obviously remained awake because she added her two cents. "Can we believe everything Matt said? There's always a chance he's the one lying to us, not Caspar."

"What would his lies benefit?" Brooke questioned.

"What would Caspar's?" Natalie challenged.

As they battled back and forth, Mason homed in on Gertie, who sat quietly in a chair. Her wrinkled face tightened in concentration as she stared unseeing into the distance. He didn't know her well, but the little he knew said she wasn't often silent.

Everleigh had also noticed. "What are you thinking, Gertie?"

"I think Matt was telling the truth." Her typically unflappable voice shook, and she cleared her throat before continuing. "My team knew the name Caspar linked to the Perez family, but we never unraveled the connection. We only heard tales of a Caspar Perez, who we thought to be long dead. Matt alluding to the fact that 'Caspar' is a mantle would make sense for how we believed the family ran things. We suspected one Perez held the reins and passed them down to another." When it came to the criminal side of things, Gertie's knowledge proved invaluable. "Jerrick must be the current Caspar, but if he killed someone, there had to have been a reason. He might have misled us with his identity, but he's not a cold-blooded murderer."

"Misled?" Brooke scoffed. "Another soft way of describing the situation."

"I'm not happy about the subterfuge either," Gertrude admitted. "But I have no doubt he had his reasons for withholding information."

"How would you know?" Mason had no intention of giving Caspar, Jerrick—or whatever his name turned out to be—the benefit of his many doubts. "How would any of you know if he's a liar or a killer or simply messing with us? You've never met the man."

"Except I have," Gertrude revealed. "I knew Jerrick as a child."

Like earlier at the shop, the air sucked from the room. Niles's forehead wrinkled. "What?" The one word came out low. Quiet. Disbelief wrapping around it. He moved to position himself in front of his aunt. "You *knew* Jerrick? And all this time you've said nothing?"

"He asked me not to."

Now Niles shook his head, as if trying to clear his ears because he wasn't hearing correctly. "You've spoken with him?" His voice strengthened and rose. Everleigh gripped his hand. Whatever transpired in their shared look calmed him marginally. "Fill us in, Aunt Gertie." Tension rolled off him.

Gertie cleared her throat. "Jerrick isn't only a Perez, he's a Forsythe. His grandparents built Halstead Manor, and he'd visit there in summers as a child. Your mother and I would play with him, and he's who originally told us about the Florentine Diamond."

The gem Caspar had initially hired Natalie and her new friends to find. Per Natalie, while seeking it, they'd crossed paths with Jerrick, though they'd never actually met him. Their only interactions had conveniently been through Caspar.

"During our search for the diamond, I put together that your Jerrick was the same as my Jerrick. Then in Vienna, he met with me."

If the mood in the room wasn't so serious, Mason would laugh at their mirrored expressions of pure shock.

Brooke was the first to speak. "You met with him. In person? In Vienna?"

"And—once again—said nothing?" Hurt and frustration mingled in Niles's tone. "We were there with you."

"He asked me to protect his privacy, and he claimed you all were safe."

Now Niles tossed his hands in the air. "He's a criminal!" He stood and paced again. "All this time while we've been questioning if it was safe to work for him, you knew who he was and said nothing."

"I didn't know Jerrick was Caspar." Gertie's jaw tightened. "Or that he was a potential murderer. But I did give him my word. And I also trust your capabilities. Do you think for one second that if I truly believed you—any of you—would be harmed that I wouldn't have said something?" She stamped her cane. "You know me better than that, Niles."

"I thought I did." He looked to the ceiling and puffed out a long stream of air.

Gertie opened her mouth, but Everleigh placed her hand on Gertie's knee. "Just give him a second to take this all in."

"Give us all a second," Brooke scoffed. "Or several."

The room quieted until John spoke. "I think it's best if we call Caspar and get some answers."

"My guess is Matt's father was Jerrick's cousin Santiano," Gertie said.

"He would often visit Halstead Manor with Jerrick as a child, and you said Matt claimed that is his middle name." It was probably a good thing right now that she couldn't see, because hard stares accompanied every one of her revelations.

Brooke snapped her gum. "Makes sense."

"And you did say you heard rumors of a fallout in the Perez family," Natalie reminded.

Mason couldn't help but think of the revulsion on Matt's face when he spoke of Jerrick. "I'd say murdering someone's father qualifies as a fallout."

"But when did the murder happen? And why did his revenge, or whatever this is, take so long?" Natalie looked to Gertrude. "You said they've been silent since about '91."

"Matt looks about my age, so he would have only been a baby back then," Brooke spoke.

John punched a few buttons. "We won't know anything for sure until we speak with Caspar. Who is apparently Jerrick." He muttered that last part as if to himself. With another punch, ringing split the air as John connected their calls.

Mason had a feeling that though they might receive some answers, not enough of them to satisfy all their questions.

⟫ ⟪

Natalie placed a hand against her throbbing head. Her bed sounded more and more enticing, but she wasn't about to leave this room.

The ringing stopped. At least the one attached to the phone. Her ears, on the other hand, might take a while longer.

"I was starting to worry." Caspar's automated voice answered their call. "I thought you planned to speak with the collector hours ago."

"We did." Niles advanced on the phone. "A lot has transpired since then, culminating with a nice visit from a Mattias Santiano Bolivar, who held the girls at gunpoint and then took the book you hired them to retrieve."

"I'm assuming his name is familiar to you," Brooke spoke. "As he also told us a bit about you, *Jerrick*."

The open line stretched, before clicking could finally be heard. "Before I address your understandable questions, is everyone all right?"

"Natalie is sporting a bruise from where he hit her with his gun." Anger rolled through Mason's voice.

Natalie placed her hand on his arm. She appreciated his protectiveness, but she didn't want to swing the conversation her way.

"I'm fine," she said, to which Mason loudly huffed. She squeezed his bicep gently, and his muscles relaxed under her touch. "Please tell us, are you really Jerrick?"

Again, silence stretched over the line. Had he disconnected the call?

Then something they rarely heard when interacting with Caspar occurred. A long, weighted sigh sounded before the automated voice spoke. "I was once. A very long time ago."

"What kind of answer is that?" Brooke asked.

"An honest one."

She opened her mouth, but before she could speak further, Niles stepped forward. "And you know my aunt Gertie."

"I do."

Gertie's lips thinned. She'd been caught between a rock and a hard place and was now being squeezed in its tight grip.

Tapping preceded more words from Caspar. "But she didn't know I now bear the name Caspar. She only knew me as Jerrick, and as I said, I am not that boy anymore."

Niles glanced at his aunt, then out the window as he scrubbed his face. No doubt he struggled that his aunt's loyalty to Jerrick had trumped her loyalty to him. The fact that she'd remained silent on her relationship with Jerrick would undoubtedly take time for Niles to work through.

Based on the body language in the room, they all had a lot to work through. Adrenaline still hung in the air, as did worry for one another. With all the heightened emotions, perspective was hard to find. Perhaps if they'd discovered Caspar's identity and Gertie's connection to him in a less stressful way, the response wouldn't have been so charged. Cooler heads were definitely not prevailing.

"All right, *Caspar*, tell us who this Matt is and why he wants the book," Everleigh said.

"And why he says you murdered his father." Niles's bearlike qualities that Everleigh teased him about were in full force. He'd practically growled his question, and he continued to stalk the room.

"Oh, and also while you're at it, how about cutting out the use of that voice synthesizer now that we know who you are?" Brooke added.

Caspar's throat cleared before two weak, gravelly words answered. "I can't."

"He's sick," Gertie said quietly, silencing Brooke's rebuttal before she could offer it. "ALS."

The amount of new information needing to be digested rivaled that of the food her boys consumed during the height of their teen years. "I'm sorry," Natalie responded, her heart softening at the thought of his diagnosis. "Are you all right?"

"For now. Though I've lost much, there is still much I can do."

Brooke remained stationed by the window, arms crossed. "I'm sorry too. Truly I am. But it doesn't change the situation or our need for answers."

Caspar's familiar clicking filled the space. "Of which I don't have many, though I can speculate." It was obvious he needed the aid of his computer for longer conversations. "I wasn't aware of Matt's existence, but if what he told you is true, then I believe he is the son of my cousin Santiano Bolivar . . . whom I did kill."

Brooke's demeanor darkened. "Explains his anger."

"But not why he wants the book," Gertie said.

"I couldn't care less about that book right now." Brooke stabbed a finger toward Gertie. "You weren't straight with us." Then toward the phone. "He lied to us and is a murderer who stuck us in the crosshairs of some crazy revenge plot."

"I never meant for any of you to be in harm's way." Caspar's automated words remained emotionless as always, but Natalie imagined she heard remorse.

"We at least deserve an explanation as to why we were," she said. "And why you honestly want that book."

"I do carry fond memories of my mother reading it to me," Caspar said. "As for anything else, well, the less you know, the better."

"Seems there's an epidemic of withholding information going around." Arms crossed, Niles leaned against a wall and stared at his aunt.

Gertie's lips thinned into a straight line.

The weight of relationships fracturing in this room was palpable.

"I'm not trying to frustrate you. I'm trying to protect you." Caspar's confession did nothing to lessen the heaviness around them. If anything, it caused more pressure.

Brooke's scoff gave voice to what was written on most of their faces. "Seeing as we had a gun pointed at us, I think you've failed on both accounts."

Always the go-between, John finally spoke. "Maybe we need to take a short break."

"Or a long one," Brooke muttered.

Everleigh jerked a gaze her way. "What are you saying?"

"That I'm not sure I want to continue." A snap of her gum. "Can you honestly say you do? I mean, we accepted from the start that working with Caspar meant we'd be in the dark about some things, but there was an underlying agreement we'd also be honest with one another." She shrugged. "Yet all we've done is broken one another's trust. First you with the diamond. Then Gertie withholding her knowledge of Jerrick. And apparently Caspar with"—she tossed her hands in the air—"well, everything. This isn't what I signed up for."

"Brooke." Natalie took a step toward her friend. She wasn't wrong about any of it, but Natalie hated watching everything crumble right in front of her eyes.

Brooke held her arm out to stop Natalie's approach.

Everleigh faced her friend. "I get it. I do."

Brooke didn't appear to believe her, but Natalie had seen how hard trust was for both of them. It went even deeper with Brooke though. She hungered for connection. Had probably held a dangerous hope that she was finding it within these walls, these relationships. Now that rug felt pulled out from under her once again, just as it had when Everleigh had run off on her own. Brooke had hung in through that debacle, but it looked as if this one might be too much.

Natalie swung her gaze around the room. Everyone looked worn out. Brooke dug both hands into her hair as she studied the floor. "Forget about trust. Forget about the book. About everything else. He's a murderer." Her glance raised to the phone. "Unless you can tell us it was self-defense."

"I cannot."

She looked around the room. "Then how can we work for him?"

"Because there's more going on here. There always is with the Perez family," Gertie said. "These girls can handle whatever it is, Jerrick. They can help you stop Matt."

"It's Caspar, and Brooke is right." Quiet buzzed around the room as they awaited Caspar's next words. "I'll pay you for the work you've done, but leave approaching Matt to me."

Gertrude stomped her cane. "So that's it? You bring us into this mystery, then cut us off before we resolve it? Let a potential criminal walk?"

"*Caspar's* a criminal, Aunt Gertie!"

"I know he had a reason." She thrust to her feet and faced where she heard Nile's voice. "There's more to this story!"

"Guys, please." Everleigh moved between them.

Natalie's pulse raced. What was happening?

Caspar spoke into the tension. "I never wanted any of you in danger," he said. "I'll wire the money into the account. John, you'll handle the rest?"

Somewhere during all of this, John's hair and glasses had become as askew as his bow tie. His appearance paralleled Natalie's emotions. "Of course," he said.

"Then I'll say my goodbyes." A pause, and then, "Please don't allow my shortcomings to break apart the friendships you've begun. Let something good have come from all of this." With that, the line disconnected.

Brooke stood. "I guess that's that, then."

But Gertrude wasn't ready to let things go. "Nope. I can't abide leaving this where it's at." She smacked her leg. "I'm sorry I kept what I knew of Jerrick from you all, but don't allow that to stop us from doing what's right. And don't sell yourselves short. You might not wear a badge, but you all definitely have the necessary skills here, and I've seen them." She smiled. "No pun intended there." Her comment had the result she no doubt intended, as it brought a hint of levity into the room.

"That actually wasn't a pun for once, Aunt Gertie." Niles's shoulders lost a little of their stiffness.

But with a collective sigh, that lightness dissipated.

"It's not only you, Gertie," Everleigh said from beside her. "This entire thing has become a giant mess."

"And based on everything that's happened, running after Matt doesn't sound like a good move," Niles said.

Mason nodded. "I agree."

This could not be happening. Natalie wasn't ready for these people to walk out of her life. Her lungs constricted.

Brooke stood. "It's been real, but I can't say it's always been fun." Nabbing her jacket from the couch, she headed for the door.

No. No. No. "Brooke, please don't leave."

She contemplated the room. "There's nothing here to stay for. Caspar said we're done, and Everleigh's right. This entire thing has become one giant mess. The moment I realized this book search was for a Perez, I should have ducked out rather than settle for Caspar's assurance that their family's illicit past remained there. Whatever is going on is very much in the present, and since he won't give us the full story, I won't stay." Her hands went to her hips. "I don't work for criminals or where there's no trust."

"But I trust you," Natalie said. "All of you." They'd had their hiccups, sure, but her gut said each one of these people was her friend.

Brooke motioned to Niles. "What about you? How's the confidence level with your aunt right about now?"

Hands in his pockets, he met Brooke's gaze head on. "It's taken a hit."

"Niles Samuel Butler!" Gertie said.

"Don't." His focus switched to her. "You've always touted openness and honesty between us. It was the one guarantee I had, even when our relationship was on shaky ground. Finding out you kept something like this from me is going to take a little time to recover from." He rubbed his chin. "And I agree with Brooke. I'm not sure how I feel about the entire Perez angle. I'm going to need a moment with that info too."

There was no joy in Brooke's face. Only resolution. "I rest my case." With that, she exited.

Storm, who'd remained silent in the corner this entire time, pushed off the wall he'd leaned against. Hands tucked into his pants pockets, he strolled across the space. "I'll follow her. Make sure she's safe."

As the door closed behind him, Everleigh wrapped her hand over Gertie's. "I think she's right. A break from all this is the best thing for now."

It wasn't. Not when it felt strangely permanent.

Natalie sat, shell-shocked, as the rest of her friends walked out the door.

CHAPTER TWENTY-SIX

They'd flown home yesterday on the longest, quietest flight Natalie had ever experienced. Typically, the private jets John chartered for them felt spacious compared to standard airline travel. Sunday's plane had squeezed them together figuratively by confining them to one common area with no escape. While they could stretch out their legs, Natalie's companions' forgiveness had remained crammed inside them, along with, it seemed, their words.

Even after they'd landed, few goodbyes were spoken. Everleigh had been kind enough to offer a hollow promise of meeting for lunch at some elusive time in the future, but Brooke's loose nod and fast departure screamed that wouldn't happen. Niles had escorted his aunt into their car, but his worn expression shouted he still battled his emotions where she was concerned.

The only person who'd remained at Natalie's side had been Mason. How quickly life could be upended—both in positive and negative ways. The past forty-eight hours had provided her with glimpses of both.

This morning she and Mason had risen together for breakfast and co-pious amounts of coffee before his return to work. Conditioning for teens wanting to try out for the football team had begun in his absence. He needed to check in, get eyes on the hopefuls, and consult his assistant coach as to which boys made the strongest candidates. Mason also loved to provide pointers at this stage that could swing a boy's chances from likely to be cut to likely to make the roster.

Mason held out his hand for her dishes so he could place them in the dishwasher.

"I can do it." Natalie rose from her seat at the table.

"You cooked. I clean."

His grin flipped her stomach, but his help warmed her heart. Okay, and it intensified his allure.

Mason walked the dishes to the sink to rinse. "You're going to check on your dad this morning?"

"I am." Mom had reiterated he was doing all right, but she'd also said he'd suffered a broken leg. "I'm going to bring them lunch."

He shot her a look over his shoulder. "And cookies for your dad?"

Dad was a renowned cookie monster. "Of course."

"Are you baking them?"

"Yep."

"Your chocolate chip recipe?"

"They are his favorite."

He closed the dishwasher. "Mine too."

She was well aware. "I plan on making extra."

Mason strolled over and tugged her to her feet. He dropped a kiss on her lips before hauling her into his embrace. "Will you call Everleigh or Brooke today?"

"Probably not."

Resting his chin on the top of her head, he squeezed her closer. "I'm glad you're safe, but I am sorry for how everything's worked out."

So was she. People walking out of her life hit on all her insecurities. While she could rationalize this instance wasn't personally about her, that fact didn't lessen the impact on her heart. Especially when a tiny, growing voice continually declared that Brooke and Everleigh didn't have to walk away from her to walk away from Caspar.

"It's okay."

Leaning her away from him, Mason met her eyes. "It's not, but it will be."

For the first time in a long time, that belief felt true, at least for her and Mason. She wasn't as convinced about her and her friends. "Thanks, Mace. For being here. For loving me."

He dipped his face to be near hers. "I'll always be here for you. We're a team."

He chased his declaration with a toe-curling kiss that held the potential to make them both forget they had responsibilities for the day.

Rekindling their relationship had thrown them back into a near newlywed state, and she was here for it.

Mason came up for air. "You are seriously making me contemplate telling them I can't come in today."

She laughed and placed her hand on his chest to nudge space between them. "Go to work."

"Fine." He dropped one parting kiss to her lips before nabbing his keys from the bowl on the counter. At the door, he paused. "Date night tonight?"

"Definitely. What are you thinking?"

His head tipped. "Rock climbing?"

They hadn't been to a climbing wall since before Hunter was born. Much like she'd help Mason in the library, he'd help her in the gym. He'd coach her through each hand and foothold, remind her how strong she was, and help her find a way forward when she didn't see one. Revisiting what had once made them so good together acted like a healing balm to her soul and, she suspected, Mason's. She desired more of those moments and fresh ones to add to them. "Sign me up."

"I'll make a seven o'clock reservation so we can grab dinner beforehand. I'll be home by five." With a wave, he was gone.

Natalie pulled out her baking supplies and whipped up four dozen cookies. She placed one dozen into the glass domed container on her counter, boxed up two to mail to the boys, and placed the last into a baggie to take to Dad. An hour later she'd hit the post office, picked up Reubens from Dad's favorite sandwich shop, and nabbed flowers for Mom.

She stepped into her parents' house to Mom's warm embrace. "Natalie." Mom emptied from Natalie's hands the bags she held. "I saw you pull up. Are these for me?" She inspected the bright bouquet of dahlias—her favorite.

"They're just starting to show up in the flower markets, so I couldn't resist."

"Thank you, sweetheart." Mom strolled to the kitchen, set the cookies and sandwiches on the counter, and grabbed a vase from under the sink. "Sit at the island while I put those in water."

In the living room, a Detroit Tigers game played. Rather than settle onto a stool, Natalie lifted plates from the cupboard. A cheer lifted from the other room. "Sounds like the Tigers are winning."

"Surprisingly, they're playing really well this season. It's nice to see a team make a comeback." Mom arranged her flowers. "How are things with you and Mason?"

Mom's segue wasn't smooth, but she had set it up nicely. "We're doing really well, Mom. Not perfect, but finally headed in the right direction, it feels."

"That's good to hear." Mom placed the vase in the center of the island. "It's even better to see a smile on your face again. Europe was good?"

For Mason and her? "Very good." Unfortunately, not when it came to her friendships. She didn't want that to put a damper on her time with Dad and Mom though.

"Based on that blush, I'd say you two have rekindled things."

"Mom!"

"What? I'm not just your mother. I'm also a happily married woman."

Natalie placed her hands over her ears. "Please stop."

Nonplussed, Mom headed for the living room. Natalie followed, and they joined Dad, who sat in his recliner in front of the TV. He'd elevated his left leg on two pillows, and a black boot encased his foot to his knee. Natalie pressed a kiss to his cheek. "How are you feeling?"

"Fine."

"Don't lie to your daughter," Mom said as she gently swatted him. "He refuses to take his pain pills, and his leg is hurting. I can tell because he didn't even try to get up when I said I was going to mow the lawn."

Dad harrumphed. "I have the good sense to not argue with you. This many years of marriage, a man knows what battles he'll win and those he won't." His nose lifted in the air. "That a Reuben from Jimmy's that I smell?" His gaze drifted to the plastic bag Natalie also carried. "And your chocolate chip cookies?"

"Your sniffer is spot on."

"Think I'll start with the cookies."

"You always made me eat my dinner before dessert." Except on her birthdays. Then she could start with cake. Natalie held out the sandwich but stopped just shy of him claiming it when he winced as he stretched her way. "I'll make you a deal. I'll brew you some coffee and let you eat your cookies first if you agree to take your pain pills."

Dad slumped in his chair. "Making deals with your father. I raised you better than that." His mouth twitched, and his blue eyes twinkled.

She jiggled the cookie bag. "Take it or leave it."

"Fine. You drive a hard bargain, but bring me those pills." As Natalie disappeared into the kitchen, he called, "And three of those cookies."

"Two now. One after you eat your sandwich," she called back.

"The good Lord says to honor your father."

"He also says not to exasperate your child."

Dad's hearty chuckle bounded into the kitchen. Natalie brewed the coffee and returned with everything Dad needed to ensure he was well fed, cared for, and spoiled a little. After he'd polished off two of the cookies, he unwrapped his sandwich and pointed to a gift bag on the coffee table. "Lorne left that for you. An early birthday present."

"Very early." Her birthday wasn't until August.

"Apparently he stumbled across something while he was here, and since he's not scheduled back until fall, he wanted you to have it now," Mom said.

Natalie sat on the couch and picked up the purple bag. She pulled out the tissue paper on top to find a wrapped book-shaped present along with a card. Scrawled across the wrapping paper were the words *Open Me First*, so she carefully did and uncovered what appeared to be a first edition of *The Lion, the Witch, and the Wardrobe*, by C. S. Lewis. She flipped to the copyright page to encounter two exciting discoveries. First, it was an original. Second, it was signed.

"What is it?" Dad asked.

She displayed the book for both Dad and Mom to see.

"You loved that book as a girl," Mom said.

"I still do." Placing it in her lap, she reached for the card to read.

Natalie,

I found this book at a shop in Chicago. They tell me the signature is legitimate, but I've no doubt you'll know for sure. Either way I couldn't pass up a first edition of one of your favorite stories. Happiest of birthdays.

Love, Lorne

He wasn't wrong. Whether the signature proved to be authentic or not, she'd cherish this book. Returning to the title page, she held the story close and examined the signature.

"What are you doing?" Dad asked.

"Inspecting Lewis's autograph." Every line, dot, and squiggle. She was highly familiar with his handwriting, and this looked genuine.

A buzzing began in the back of her head. One that reminded her of suspicions raised in London that had fallen by the wayside when everything imploded. She stood. "I have to go."

Mom stood too. "Is everything okay, sweetheart?"

"Yes." She gave them quick hugs. "I think so." Her mind whirred. "I mean, yes. But there's something I need to check on."

"All right." Mom walked her to the door. "Do you and Mason want to come for dinner this week?"

"Sure. Call me with what day works best," she replied before hustling to her car.

Once inside she pulled up Lewis Carroll's signature on her phone. Not that she needed to, because it lived in her brain. Sure enough, the photo in front of her only confirmed what she thought to be true. Still, she had questions.

Pulling up John's number, Natalie pressed Dial.

He answered after only a few rings. "Hello? Natalie?"

"Can you still get a hold of Caspar?"

A pause. "I can. Why?"

"Because I need to speak with him." Another pause, which she spoke into. "I believe the book Matt stole was a counterfeit."

CHAPTER TWENTY-SEVEN

Luciana Perez, age seventy-seven
Lekeitio, Spain, 1991

SHE THOUGHT SHE'D HAVE MORE time. Yet much like the rest of her days, she learned God's plans were different than her own. Now she was oh so tired. Weariness and pain ached inside her bones, but even more so in her heart. The story written throughout her years had changed from a fairy tale to a heart-wrenching one of loss. Her home, once filled with the voices of family, echoed with emptiness.

Angus's death last month at the hands of her nephew had gutted her.

But the loss of Jerrick to the hate that consumed this family left her heartbroken. How she wished to change things, but cancer was winning the battle over her body.

"Father Torres said to thank you for your recent contribution to the orphanage." Gregory tucked a blanket around her. For many years the butler's care for her had been borne more from friendship than duty. He opened a bottle and shook out a pill.

Luciana took it from his hand. "Please make sure when I'm gone that you sell everything and give it to the church." She'd already ensured there remained a special gift for Gregory. Other than that there was no one left. Her siblings had long since died or moved on from the craziness of this life. Angus, Raul, and Santiano were dead. And Jerrick sat in jail. It only seemed fitting that all Papi had worked for now went to those who truly had need.

Yet she couldn't quiet the sadness inside. While Papi had ensured they attended services weekly and he'd been generous with the church, the faith that had seeped into her soul had never managed to touch his. His generosity, no matter how great, couldn't save him. He'd sought the wrong treasures. Christ wanted his heart, not his money. She'd prayed daily for Papi to understand that truth, but if he had, it would have been in his final breaths.

"La Iglesia de Vida is blessed to have you." Gregory capped the medicine bottle and returned it to her bedside table. He'd taken to administering her pain medication every four hours. "Is there anything else I can get you, ma'am?"

"No. Thank you, Gregory. You've been wonderful." Her voice felt as weak as the rest of her body.

"You make it easy." Tears glistened in her old friend's eyes. Yes, he'd been paid to be here, but through the years they'd developed a kinship. "I'll let you rest."

A sudden fear that if she closed her eyes, this time they wouldn't reopen, had her calling out to him. "Gregory, wait." She coughed as he turned. "Would you please visit Jerrick? Let him know I love him. That I wish . . . I wish I'd done more for him."

If she could go back and do things differently, she would. But life offered no do-overs, only regrets that forced change. Unfortunately, that change arrived too late to save Jerrick from the consequences he now faced.

Hindsight chided her, speaking hard-earned wisdom she was unable to practice now, with Angus dead. She should have voiced her concerns. Told Angus how she truly felt about him following in Papi's footsteps rather than letting the years pass silently as they'd drifted further and further apart. Perhaps it would have made a difference and saved their marriage. Their family.

Their son.

Her attempts to protect Jerrick had failed. She'd taken him to spend summers with Angus's parents in America. There at Halstead Manor he could simply be a child. Run free with friends who knew nothing of the Perez family. After her sister Marisol had passed away, Santiano had accompanied them too. He and Jerrick were raised more as brothers than cousins.

But the ugliness of her family had still found them both, and it made no sense to her.

Jerrick had been clear that he wanted nothing to do with the Perez family dealings. Still, he'd flown across the ocean to avenge his father's death. Now he sat in a jail cell, with Santiano's blood on his hands. Jerrick refused to see her, so she'd receive no explanation.

The pain medicine took effect, pulling her into its deep sleep, where she had the strangest dreams. Daniel, Jerrick's oldest friend, sat in a chair in the corner of her room. His grandparents had been close friends with Jerrick's, and the boys' friendship had been forged during their summers at Halstead Manor. Daniel had been like another son to her.

Like with Jerrick, it had been years since she'd seen Daniel. His deep voice reached her as he read something familiar. Something about a girl who'd drunk a potion and shrunk. Luciana smiled. Alice.

"I remember her," she croaked out.

Daniel's eyes lifted from the book to meet her gaze. "And I remember you." It was then she noticed he held a small bundle in his arms. Daniel stood and came to her, turning so she caught sight of round cheeks, rosy lips, and the sweetest nose.

This was indeed a strange dream because Daniel held her baby son in his arms. "Jerrick?"

Soft laughs, then, "No. This is your grandson."

She felt moisture on her cheek, and her voice failed her. Or was she speaking? She hadn't a clue right now.

Daniel spoke again. "I've been reading to him from *Alice's Adventures Under Ground*. I found it in the study and remembered how much you and Jerrick loved that story."

How could that be? She'd mailed that book to Jerrick weeks ago.

Angus had been livid when he'd discovered it missing. He'd accused Santiano of stealing it. There'd been a fight, blood, then everyone was gone.

Confusion swirled in her mind, yet she didn't want to wake up. Not when Daniel lay the sweet bundle beside her in bed. She turned her face to nuzzle Jerrick's.

But no, Jerrick wasn't here. He was at . . . "Halstead Manor."

Daniel's fingers touched her arm. "It's all right. Jerrick has given me the authority to carry out your wishes. Gregory will ensure the sale here happens with this estate, and I've hired someone to ensure everything in the manor there is sold. All the proceeds will go to the church, though Jerrick has asked that we not sell the manor itself for now."

That was good. He'd have a place to live when he returned from . . . Something squirmed in her arms. Soft. Warm. She inhaled the scent of baby powder as a coo met her ear. Or was he already here?

Luciana blinked open her eyes, unsure of when she'd closed them. Yes. Jerrick was here. Oh, she missed her son. How she wished she could return through time and pry her family from her father's grip. She'd wanted to avoid more conflict, but her silence had not prevented a rift from occurring. If only she'd spoken up and fought for her family. Now time permanently stopped healing from happening on this side of heaven.

Jerrick stirred, his cheek brushing against her nose.

"Keep him safe," she whispered, speaking to herself.

But it was Daniel who answered, gripping her fingers. "I promised Jerrick I would, and I make you the same promise."

Good.

She could finally rest.

CHAPTER TWENTY-EIGHT

NATALIE SAT IN ONE OF the leather armchairs in Halstead Manor's study. She'd left Dad and Mom's house two hours ago. It had taken John that long to reach Caspar and arrange a phone call. John had wisely held back Natalie's counterfeit theory, aware that Caspar could take the information and not the meeting. Instead, John stressed the extreme importance for Natalie to speak with him. Finally, Caspar had acquiesced.

She'd briefly contemplated calling Brooke and Everleigh, but with no concrete evidence at this point, she held off. Open-ended questions and vague information had helped lead to the dissolution of their team. Until she had proof to back up her assumption, she'd leave them out of it.

John sat at his desk and pressed Dial on his phone. Caspar answered on the second ring. "Natalie?"

"I'm here. Thank you for agreeing to speak with me."

"John mentioned it was important. Are you all right?"

She hadn't intended to worry him. "I am. We all made it home safely and haven't seen any sign of Matt."

"Good. I don't think he'll bother you now that he has what he wants, but it would be prudent for everyone to remain vigilant for a while."

"We will." She and John shared a look.

"What can I help you with?" Caspar asked.

Natalie clicked her nails together. "I believe it's me who can be of assistance to you."

"Oh?"

Taking a deep breath, she plunged. "But first can you tell me any identifying markers about your copy of *Alice's Adventures Under Ground*? Other than the inscription that's on the inside from Carroll?" Better yet, "Or do you happen to have a photograph of it?"

A long pause preceded Caspar's automated response. "Why do you ask?"

"Curiosity."

A hoarse chuckle filled the line. "I have no doubt it's more than that, but I'm sorry to say I don't have a photo. My family wasn't one to take many." Neither of them spoke for another moment. "You suspect a counterfeit."

She wasn't surprised her questions had led him there. "I do. Is it possible your family had one made?"

"Anything is a possibility when it comes to my family," Caspar said. "That, however, is a strong one." A few familiar clicks, then, "Were there any tears in the pages? My mother tore one as a child when she tried to jump into the story, hoping to journey to Wonderland."

Natalie closed her eyes and replayed the movie strip in her mind of those few precious moments she'd held the book. The memory remained so sharp she could see every detail with absolute clarity. She opened her eyes. "Every page was intact."

John's foot tapped the wood floor, but he remained silent.

"It would seem highly likely, then, that the book Mattias has is indeed a counterfeit." Caspar agreed with her hypothesis.

"Which means we can still find the real one for you." A solid reason to call Everleigh and Brooke with a common goal to work toward. They all possessed curiosity in spades. Surely that would trump their frustrations with Caspar. It was, after all, what had led them to accept his original invitation to this house.

But Caspar was having none of it. "Absolutely not. I don't want you girls anywhere near Mattias."

"We wouldn't be. He thinks he has the real deal, so he won't even be a part of the equation. His quest has been satisfied."

"No."

"But—"

"No!" Caspar's thunderous voice spoke. A real voice.

Her eyes flew to John's, whose were as wide as hers felt.

More words came through the phone, but these returned to the computerized version. "I appreciate you passing on this information, but as I already decided—this is where your journey ends."

The call disconnected.

She and John remained staring at each other in disbelief. He broke the strained silence. "You're not going to stop looking, are you?"

"No. I'm not."

➤- ◄

Mason stood across from Natalie as they donned harnesses at a new rock-climbing center nearby their house. Her greeting when he'd arrived home to pick her up hadn't lacked warmth, but it had lacked focus. She'd been distracted, and that distance had grown on their drive here. It wasn't unusual for Natalie to become lost inside her head when she processed information. Something must have happened today, and he'd thought he could wait her out. His curiosity, however, could not.

"All right. Spill."

She clipped her buckle and waited for the loud crowd leaving to pass by them. "Sorry. I know I've been preoccupied. I didn't want to ruin our date."

"Sharing your thoughts with me will do the exact opposite, Nat."

Removing an elastic band from her wrist, she tugged her waves into a ponytail. "I realized today that the book Matt took isn't the real one."

Not what he'd expected, but Natalie knew her stuff, so whatever had led her to that conclusion, he wasn't doubting it. Even so, over the next few minutes, she filled him in on her thought process and her afternoon—including her phone call with Caspar. Mason wasn't thrilled she'd touched base with the criminal again, but he understood why. Natalie wasn't one to give up easily. A fact he was thankful for, or their marriage could have ended long ago.

He wasn't as keen on the idea that her ambition, in this case, kept her centered on what could be a dangerous task.

"If Caspar told you to leave it alone, don't you think you should listen?" Mason questioned.

"I'm not going to go after Matt, but I do want to discreetly ask a few more questions of some people."

"Like who?"

"Archie, for starters. Remember he said he was with Mr. Hollis when he purchased the book from the estate sale. I'm curious where exactly that was, because it makes a significant difference if the book was purchased directly from Caspar's family estate or someplace else." Someone rang the bell at the top of one of the walls. "And it's not like Caspar is going to tell us himself now."

"Because each possible location the book's been gives us a potential owner who could have had it forged."

"Exactly. I didn't reach Archie, but I did leave him a message." They stepped away from the wall so others could climb it. "I also called Kit to see if she has located any of the books Terrance sold."

Mason furrowed his brow. "Why?"

"Because if she has and they're also forgeries, it's a strong possibility Terrance could be our culprit."

"If that's true, why would he have sent us after one of his copies?"

"In hopes we wouldn't realize it wasn't real? We'd be satisfied and stop asking questions about what he'd been doing. He could possibly even continue his scam. We know Alice wasn't the only book he hawked." She fiddled with her carabiner. "If he needs money as badly as he claimed, selling forgeries multiple times would allow him to line his pockets faster and deeper." Her lips swished to the side. "I know I'm reaching for possibilities, but Everleigh taught me that sometimes thinking outside the box is where solutions are found."

Mason stood firm in front of her, arms loosely folded across his chest. "Maybe you should call her. Another set of eyes and all?" Because that forlorn look on her face every time she mentioned her friends was killing him.

"Not yet."

Her familiar stubborn tone stopped him from arguing further. There was no point. "What did Kit say?"

She shrugged. "I'll know once she returns my call."

He clapped his hands together. "Okay then, how about we climb while you wait?"

"Sounds good."

Enthusiastic wasn't the word he'd use for her response, but he knew it wasn't personal. And that, he mused, was progress. A month ago he'd have interpreted her body language and tone as lack of desire to be around him. Possibly even embarrassment toward him. Tonight, rather than push him away, her actions pulled him in close. He wanted to help her unravel the mystery in front of her. Or at the very least, pass the hours while she waited for answers.

They stepped to the wall as Mason's phone rang. Natalie caught sight of Trey's name on the screen. "At least one of us is receiving calls." She motioned toward the front desk. "Go ahead and take it. I'll grab us some waters."

He hesitated, but as she backed away, he went ahead. "Hey there."

"Hey." Tiny voices in the background said Trey was at home with the kids. "I know it's after hours, but I wanted to call because I just got off the phone with my friend in Utah. Seems the man they offered the job to isn't taking it, and no, I don't know why. He asked if you'd still be interested and plans on giving you a call. Thought I'd give you a heads-up."

Though Mason had been at the school the past two days, Trey had been in district meetings, and they hadn't been able to catch up. "I appreciate that."

Trey hesitated. "All right, I wanted to give more than a heads-up."

"I kind of figured." At the front desk, Natalie asked one of the workers for water bottles. Her ponytail swung off the back of her head. She wore a tank that showed off her toned arms and athletic shorts that highlighted her sculpted legs. While she complained of extra padding in her middle, gray running through her hair, and new wrinkles carving lines on her face, all he saw was the girl he had fallen in love with. Any extra pounds reminded him of all her body had done to give him their sons. Where she saw wrinkles, he saw laugh lines. Her gray hair testified to the years he'd been blessed on this earth with her by his side—and he prayed for decades more. They'd matured together. Raised their children and made a home. Faced hardships and were coming out stronger. There wasn't a woman on this planet more stunningly beautiful than his wife.

"Mason?" Trey's voice yanked him back to the conversation.

"Yeah. I'm still here. Sorry."

"It's all right." Kids scuffled in the background. "Sounds as crazy wherever you are as it is here. Anyway, I was just saying that I know you really want this job, but I'm not sure this is the right time for this move. I hate saying that because I'm aware what a college position means to you, but I'm always going to root for you and Nat first."

Which was one of the many reasons he was Mason's best friend. They'd need to catch up soon, but Nat was headed this way. Mason turned around.

"So am I." Though he'd done a lousy job these past several years. "You got nothing to worry about. They can call, but I'll politely decline."

"Things are going better with you and Natalie then?"

His mind went to their time in Europe. "Better than better. I'll fill you in later when we both have time."

A child's shout filled the background. "Looking forward to hearing all about it." A beat. "The non-romantic stuff that is. I don't need recaps on the rest."

"Wouldn't dream of it."

They hung up, and he turned to find Natalie standing close by. "Everything okay?"

"Perfect."

She held out one of the bottles. "I heard you say something about declining something."

"Yeah." He wasn't going to hold anything back from her. "Seems Utah is still looking for a coach, and they might call me." Before she could put words to the surprise he saw on her face, he continued. "That was what you heard me say I'd decline."

She reached for his hand. "Mace, you should at least take the call."

"I will. To politely decline their offer."

"That's not what I meant."

"I know." He tugged from her grasp so he could hold her instead. Support her. Like he should have been doing all along. "We're staying here. Together. Now, are you climbing first, or am I?"

She blinked rapidly. "I don't want you giving up your dream."

His thumb drew over her skin. "I'm not. I'm clinging to it with everything I have." His grip tightened, and he hoped she understood what he was saying. Based on the way her free hand swiped at a stray tear, he guessed she did. "The right time and place will come along, and we'll make that decision together. Right now I want to keep focusing on making *us* strong, not my career."

"I love you, Mace."

"And I love you. Very, very much." One more quick kiss and then he stepped to the wall. "Time me so we know how much I beat you by."

She laughed and leaned into the rope. "Belay on."

They took turns climbing until their muscles grew weak. After Nat conquered the highest wall, he encouraged her to try the slant that mimicked an overhang. She dominated it, and the triumphant look on her face was more rewarding than him besting his record time. Sitting side by side in the corner of the gym, they each finished their second water bottle.

"You did great." Mason brushed sweat from his forehead. "Keep it up and maybe one day you can entertain the idea of beating me."

"Funny man." She stood and stretched, then sneaked a glance at her phone.

"You would have heard it ring."

"I know." She slid it into the pocket on her shorts. "Patience is not my current strong suit. I know they're in different time zones, and Archie has the estate sale and Kit is buried in books—ones I could spend hours with myself. But it is extremely difficult to wait for them to call."

Mason hung his arms over his bent knees. "You'd love to work with her, wouldn't you?"

"Kit?"

He nodded.

"And get to track down and care for novels most people will never encounter?" Her eyes lit. "Um, yes please."

He chuckled and stood too, placing his hand on the small of her back as they strolled toward the parking lot. "I could see you traipsing through the world, uncovering secret manuscripts like the Indiana Jones of the literary world."

"My dream job." She winced as the words escaped, no doubt thinking about their earlier conversation on his dream job.

Mason stopped beside their car, hand on the door to open it for her. "Don't."

Her forehead wrinkled. "Don't what?"

"Apologize." He brought his other hand around to bracket her against the car door. Then he waited until her entire focus rested on his. "Joking around with you is one of my favorite things. I love how we're back at that place again, so don't overthink it. I know your heart, Nat." He dropped a kiss on her lips. "I hope you know mine." He remained close, his mouth brushing hers as he spoke.

She slid her palms up his chest and around his nape, linking her fingers together. Heat flared between them. "I do." Her nose nudged his. "Know what one of *my* favorite things is that I'm super grateful we're doing again?"

The flames built toward an inferno. "No. Tell me." He played along, loving the feel of her fingers toying with his hair. His mind worked out the fastest route home.

"Doing dishes together. I've really enjoyed—"

Mason dropped his mouth to that ticklish place in the crook of her neck, and laughter peeled from her. "Hey!" She playfully shoved him. "What happened to joking around being one of your favorite things?"

"It's right up there with tickling you." His hands went to her sides. "Especially in retaliation for teasing me."

"Teasing you?" The words came on puffed breaths as she wiggled under his assault. "Oh, did you think I was going to say—"

"You know I did."

Her fingers found his face, and she dragged his mouth to hers, surprising him with a ferocious kiss. "That, Mr. Daughtry, is my most favorite thing." Another kiss. "Take me home?"

She didn't need to ask twice.

CHAPTER TWENTY-NINE

SHE'D THOUGHT FALLING FOR MASON the first time had left her breathless, but there was something about a bruised and battered love finding healing that stole her breath in the best of ways. The past few days had launched new hardships at her, but waking up in the security of her husband's arms softened their blows. If restoring their marriage was the only real thing they found while on the quest for this book, then it would all still be worth it.

But she sure did hope they could track down that story.

Wilson stirred by her feet as Mason joined her in the kitchen, showered and dressed. "What are your plans for the day?"

Before she could answer, her phone rang. She immediately recognized the number. "It's Kit."

Mason settled beside her and nodded for her to answer. He reached down to pet Wilson as she put Kit on speakerphone. "Hey, Kit, thanks for getting back to me."

"Of course. I very much enjoyed meeting you. I feel like we're kindred spirits."

Most people would gloss over the friendly term, but Natalie recognized the phrase from *Anne of Green Gables* and took it as the high compliment Kit undoubtedly meant it to be. "As do I. Which is what provided the hope that you might be able to help me out."

After enjoying their favorite pastime last night, she and Mason had sat up and talked for hours. They wanted to lessen any chance of Matt discovering he possessed a fake, so they agreed that the fewer people who knew of the possible counterfeit book, the better. With Archie she could withhold details, but for this conversation, she'd need to tell Kit.

"If I can, I will," Kit said. "Tell me then, how might I be of assistance?"

"We located the copy of *Alice's Adventures Under Ground* that Terrance sold." She paused. "It was a counterfeit."

Kit inhaled sharply. "And you wonder if he had something to do with it? If he maintained the original and sold a counterfeit?"

"I do. Possibly with more than one book." At least it presented a theory she had to run down. "Have you located any of the others he sold and, if so, had time to inspect them?"

"I've found three of his buyers. Unfortunately, two of them had immediately turned around and sold the books again, and they were not as meticulous in keeping notes as Terrance." Sadness edged her voice. "But we shall prevail. If we found them once, we'll find them again."

"I've no doubt."

"Though I am now down one Finder with the loss of Mr. Hollis and one Keeper with Terrance being relieved of his position." She clicked her tongue. "Nevertheless, that is not why you called." A drawer shut on Kit's side of the line. "The one book I have reclaimed, an original copy of *The Little Prince* with handwritten notations by Saint-Exupéry himself, is quite real."

"I'm glad to hear that." Even if it didn't lead her toward the answers she sought.

"I promise that when I do find the others, if anything is amiss, I shall let you know."

"Thank you." Outside the window, squirrels raced around the yard. Wilson's tail wagged, and Mason stood to open the door so Wilson could chase them. "Would you also be willing to put feelers out to your contacts? See if anyone knows of artists able to re-create books like these? Or if anyone has heard of a copy of Alice circulating out there?"

"Of course. I'll let you know if I hear anything."

They hung up, and Mason squeezed her hand. "It's just a start. You still have to hear back from Archie, and who knows what Kit's contacts will tell her. Don't give up. There's lots of time on the clock yet."

His presence and encouragement buoyed her spirit. "Thanks, Coach."

"Anytime."

Mason headed to work for the day, leaving his delicious scent in his wake. She needed to buy another bottle of his cologne. Forget about burning one of her candles. She planned on spraying that fragrance throughout the house. Tapping her lip, she glanced down at the sweatshirt she wore, as a memory of their dating days flickered. She ducked down the hall to their bathroom and found his cologne. When Mason had been in college and she'd lived hours away, she'd grab samples of this scent from the department store and douse her pillow and clothes with it. She'd been a tad heavy handed with the amount back then. Today she sprayed a hint on her collar, feeling the giddiness of a teenager in love mixed with the maturity of a woman who'd plumbed the depths of that emotion.

Returning to the kitchen, Natalie poured herself another cup of coffee, settled at the counter, and dove into her laptop. She perused all the regular sites on the off chance the book would pop up. After lunch she took Wilson for a walk, finished laundry, and cleaned out her closet as she contemplated her next step. Midway through the purge of her jeans that no longer fit, the call she waited for finally rang.

"Archie," she answered.

"Miss Daughtry, it's such a pleasure to hear your voice."

"I feel the same toward you." She imagined him in the hall with his white cravat tied perfectly and his black suit coat pressed to perfection. "How did the estate sale go?"

"Wonderfully. Mr. Hollis would have been sad to see his belongings leave but happy to know he was able to help others. We're making a sizable donation to one of the shelters in town."

"I'm sure he'd be pleased." Natalie extricated herself from her pile of jeans and settled on the edge of her bed. "I appreciate you returning my call. I wondered if you might be able to help me?"

"After all the help your group bestowed upon me, I'd be most pleased to return the favor."

She hoped him able.

"Could you tell me where the estate was that Mr. Hollis purchased *Alice's Adventures Under Ground* from?"

"Why of course. It was in Lekeitio, Spain. A quaint little town along the Basque coast of the Bay of Biscay. The estate itself had quite the land, and I can see it clearly, though forgive me—I forget its name. Funny when I so easily recall the town's name."

Natalie gripped her phone, disbelief causing her hand to shake. She, Brooke, and Everleigh had visited Lekeitio on their quest for the Florentine Diamond. They'd gone to Jerrick's residence—though it hadn't been an estate. They also hadn't met him that night. He'd claimed he was sick and had his housekeeper meet with them. Knowing now what she did, his claim of illness had been one of the few truths he'd shared.

"Is there anything else you remember about the estate? Anyone you might have met there? Or the family names?" Questions raced through her mind as she tried to put together pieces, or at least collect enough for Everleigh to string together. "Other items at the sale?"

"Hmm . . ." Archie took a moment. "We didn't meet any of the family who owned the estate, but I do now recall that while Mr. Hollis looked through the library, I chatted with the family's butler."

Of course he would have done that.

"A rather pleasant man named Gregory. He noted Mr. Hollis's love of books and mentioned it was a shame we'd missed their American estate sale, because his mistress's library in that home was even larger. He spoke of some of the titles he'd recently mailed there, including *Alice's Adventures Under Ground*." Archie made a clucking sound. "I thought he must be mistaken since we were purchasing the book along with others that day, but with the extensiveness of the sale he was handling, his confusion seemed understandable."

Natalie sat straight. "Do you know the name of their American home?"

"I'm sorry, ma'am. He told me, but I can't recall."

The idea forming seemed both wildly impossible and terribly logical. "Could it have been Halstead Manor?"

"Why yes! That's it." Excitement laced his words.

Her pulse jumped higher as another conversation resurfaced in her mind.

"Miss Daughtry?"

"Yes. I'm still here." But her mind was in a million other places. "Thank you, Archie. You've been incredibly helpful."

"It has been my utmost pleasure." His impeccable manners continued even as she rushed him off the call. He was a wonderful man. "If you need me for anything else, please don't hesitate to call again."

"Thank you." She disconnected and beelined for the kitchen, where she'd left her car keys. Her mind remembered everything it encountered in great detail—that was one of her strengths. Except she didn't put pieces together as quickly as Everleigh or perhaps she'd have seen sooner how the ones she held possibly fit together. What Archie had shared only made her theory more probable.

Caspar's family owned Halstead Manor, which, by Archie's account, at one time had an extensive library. But she'd already known it held a large collection of children's stories long before Archie told her.

Slot that together with the knowledge that Mr. Hollis purchased what turned out to be the counterfeit in Lekeitio, Spain. Yet a butler claimed he'd mailed the book to Halstead Manor. If that were true, the book he'd mailed wasn't the counterfeit. It was the real one.

Which meant she might know exactly who owned *Alice's Adventures Under Ground.*

CHAPTER THIRTY

NATALIE WALKED THROUGH THE DOOR to the Golden Key as Mason held it open for her. While driving, she'd called him to share her thoughts and ask for his in return. He'd immediately agreed her speculation feasible and promised to meet her here. She'd arrived five minutes before him and had waited in her car.

Natalie stopped in the entryway. "I'm so nervous that I'm sweating."

He palmed her back, infusing her with his steadiness. "I thought women didn't sweat—they glistened."

She glanced at him to find his dimples on full display. His attempt to defuse her nerves didn't work, but it did make her incredibly thankful he was here.

Behind the counter, Harry waved as they approached. "Why, this is a pleasant surprise." His bushy mustache wiggled as he spoke, and his eyes glowed with a warm welcome.

Natalie attempted to calm her beating heart. There was a strong possibility that Alice had made her way here to Harry's collection, but strong possibilities offered no actual guarantee. She tempered her excitement with that knowledge.

"How are you, Harry?" she asked as she joined him.

"Good, good." He tugged on his gray vest. Varying shades of pink created today's plaid pattern, and he'd added a floral bow tie and pocket square that highlighted those tones. "I see you've returned from another of your adventures. Was this one successful?"

Natalie shared a look with Mason, who answered, "Jury's still out."

"Oh?" Harry set down the book he'd been reading. *The Velveteen Rabbit*. Definitely his favorite. "I hope it returns soon with a fruitful result."

"Actually," Natalie said as she leaned on the counter, "I wondered if perhaps you could supply exactly that."

His bushy brows drew together. "And how would that be?"

"You mentioned once that you'd purchased several children's books at Halstead Manor years ago."

He smiled. "That I did." Memories surfaced in his eyes. "That family loved reading. Luciana would come in once a week with her son to peruse our books when she was in town. She purchased practically an entire library herself." That lined up with what Archie had said. "When I heard she passed, well, I just knew that she'd want those stories to be well cared for."

Natalie wasn't sure if she should be excited or concerned. After all, Harry only intimated that he'd acquired the books he'd sold to Luciana. That didn't include *Alice's Adventures Under Ground*, which meant this could go either way. "Did you happen to purchase other titles from her? Besides the ones she'd bought from you?"

Harry bounced his gaze between Mason and Natalie. "Why, I bought nearly every single story in her nursery. I couldn't leave any behind." He leaned close. "And might I say, she had an extensive compendium."

"Collection," Natalie whispered to Mason, who nodded. "Harry, would one of those books have been *Alice's Adventures Under Ground*? Perhaps an original copy signed by the author himself?"

Harry glanced around the quiet shop as he wiggled his mouth back and forth. It was quite an ask she'd posed to him. He would know the worth of the book, yet if it had remained in his possession, then he'd decided to protect it, not profit from it.

If, however, he'd sold the novel, then they'd be back to square one.

And all this speculation hinged on if he'd obtained the book.

His fingers played with the chain to the watch in his pocket. "The only known copy of such a book resides in the British Museum. I assume you know that."

Something about his wording prompted her to continue pushing. "Known copy, yes, but I'm searching for one that's merely been a rumor, though I've strong reason to believe its existence is quite real."

"That would be quite a find." Harry's beard twitched as he swished his lips again. "Quite a find indeed."

"Yes, it would. One Luciana's son has been seeking."

His beard stilled. "Jerrick?" Harry watched her closely. "Do you know him?"

"I do." Her answer felt shaky, as she didn't believe she truly knew Caspar.

After a long moment, Harry shuffled around the counter before beckoning her toward the back of the shop. "Come. Come."

Without hesitating, she and Mason followed. They ducked into the back room, where Harry led them to the armoire where he hung his coat and she hung her purse whenever they worked. He opened its double doors, pushed aside his other suit coats, and pressed against the back wall. With a creak echoing their very own Narnia moment, the wooden panel swung open on hinges to reveal a secret room.

Was this where he disappeared to whenever she couldn't find him?

Natalie gasped. "Harry! This is amazing."

Floor-to-ceiling bookshelves lined three of the four walls. There was even a ladder attached to them. A massive rug covered the concrete floor, and leather club chairs with blankets draped over the arms beckoned readers to curl up. Overhead, a skylight allowed sunshine to stream into the space. And trinkets that paid homage to his favorite childhood stories perched alongside the books.

Harry stood behind her. "One magical thing about being forced to grow up is we obtain the ability to breathe life into our childhood dreams—if we don't forget them or believe ourselves too old to still live within their walls."

She turned to him. "The moment you doubt whether you can fly, you cease forever to be able to do it." The words from *Peter Pan* came unbidden.

His lips lifted above his bushy beard. "Truly. Truly." With a clap of his hands, Harry scurried to the right. He seemed to know exactly where he was headed, and he moved so effortlessly that it took Natalie by surprise how quickly everything happened. After all, it seemed the moment deserved more pomp and circumstance than his hurried return to place in her hands the very book she'd been seeking.

She'd traveled thousands of miles only to find what she'd been looking for had been right here all along.

"Is this the book?" Harry questioned when she remained silent.

Natalie opened the worn cover, aware that Mason stood behind her. He placed a hand on her shoulder and squeezed as they read the inscription Lewis Carroll had penned. The same exact words written in the counterfeit, except here the signature matched what she knew to be his. Yet to be certain this was the authentic copy, she carefully flipped the pages until she located the proof. A tear on page 10 made by little Luciana's excited attempt to hop into the story.

Glancing up at Harry, she found him watching her. "This is it," she said on a breath of excitement.

"It was fortuitous timing, most assuredly, that allowed me to purchase this book. It arrived at the manor just as I was loading my vehicle. The executor asked if I'd like to add it to my pile." Harry played with the chain on his watch. "I nearly fell over, that I did. He had no idea of its worth, and I couldn't very well leave it to chance that someone would happen along who did. Luciana was my friend, and I knew what that copy must have meant to her."

Natalie brushed her fingertips over the old, inky words. "So you kept it all these years?"

"Why, of course, of course. What else would I have done but care for it?" he said, as if the story were alive and it had been his duty to keep it that way. "It was obvious to me it had been well loved."

"That it had." Natalie closed the pages and pressed the book to her chest. "Which is why Jerrick's been searching for this." For she fully believed that though more was at play, this precious treasure meant the world to Caspar.

Harry nodded. "Then you must take it to him."

And just like that, her search was over.

But a million questions remained.

CHAPTER THIRTY-ONE

"ANY RESPONSE?" MASON GLANCED HER way as he flicked on his blinker.

After leaving the Golden Key, Natalie had called John, who'd said he'd set up a time for them to—hopefully—meet with Caspar at noon tomorrow. Then she'd phoned Everleigh and Brooke, but her calls had gone to their voicemails. She'd left them both a message and was painfully awaiting their response.

Natalie held her phone in her right hand, wishing for it to ring. "Not even a text." An old fear whispered that she wouldn't hear from them, and she worked hard to silence that voice.

Mason reached over and laced his fingers through hers. "They didn't walk out on you, Nat. It's the situation they need space from, not you."

"I know." They passed by gas stations and stores. She recognized this street, but she didn't know where they were headed. All Mason had said was she needed a good surprise to end her day on. "I'm starting to grasp that I can't let my emotions rise and fall on other people's actions. I can't let whether or not they love me determine my worth or security." She turned her face, resting her head against her seat, and looked at him. "The only one who gets that place in my life is God, and he'll always love me. Always be there for me."

Mason's fingers tightened around hers. "So will I."

She brought their joined hands to her mouth and kissed his. "That's all I need."

Her confession sank into her core and firmly settled there. Her life wasn't exactly where she wanted it to be, yet for the first time in a long time, peace blanketed her.

Her phone rang, and she pulled it out to silence it. "It's Kit."

"Answer it."

Natalie tapped the screen and put her on speakerphone. "Kit, it's Natalie and Mason."

"Why, good evening to you both." Her singsong voice rolled over the line. "I won't take but a moment of your time, if that's quite all right with you?"

Natalie shared a look with Mason and shrugged. "Of course."

"As you well know, Natalie, I'm in need of a new Finder and Keeper. A thought keeps buzzing in my head, and I've learned to listen to the bees when they buzz. They do so often know what they're talking about."

Natalie had the sneaking suspicion that Kit enjoyed playing the character she'd created for herself. It suited her, so Natalie didn't mind going along. "Oh? And what are they saying?"

"That you would make a prodigious Finder."

Goodness, the offer felt made for her. She loved the thought. But there was something—someone—she loved even more.

"The idea is intriguing, Kit, but I have a job right now. Two actually, and adding another might be too much." Her and Mason's relationship had to remain a priority for them both. That required time, and she would guard hers as ferociously as she asked him to with his.

"Dear me, but I'm sad to hear it. I'd rather hoped you both would be open to the adventure."

"Both?" Mason piped up.

"Why, yes. You are a team, aren't you?"

Joy bubbled inside and spilled out in laughter as Mason took her hand and squeezed. "Yes."

"Yes, we are." Her voice melded with his.

"Oh good. Now that we have that silliness cleared up, can I convince you to at least contemplate my proposal?"

Natalie glanced at Mason, who shrugged. He pulled the car into Kenton Corners High School and shut off the engine. A new curiosity pulled at her. What was her husband up to? "Can we call you back tomorrow, Kit?"

"I look forward to it."

Natalie disconnected the call as she looked out the windshield. "Did you leave something in your office?"

"Nope." He exited the car, ducked down, and laid his dimpled grin on her. "Come on."

She met him by the hood. He clasped her hand again and tugged her inside.

"What do you think about that phone call from Kit?" she asked.

"That she made us an offer we can't refuse." He spoke the words in a strange accent she was pretty sure wasn't real on any continent.

A chuckle escaped her. "Was that your attempt at Brando in *The Godfather*?"

"Attempt? I nailed that."

"Whatever you say." She followed him, the squeak of their shoes the only sound. The halls were dark, but they both knew them well. After a few turns she guessed where he was taking her. Sure enough, he stopped beside a wooden door with large windows on either side. She tilted her head as he ushered her in. "The library?"

Still silent, Mason led her down the aisles that smelled exactly as she remembered. Old pages, dust, a hint of teenage angst, and wood shavings from the shop down the hall. Light glimmered through the bookstacks, right about at the location of her once favorite table. Tucked into the rear of the room near the eight hundreds and nine hundreds—literature, history, and geography—it had once been her favorite place. When she'd begun tutoring Mason, she'd shared the spot with him.

They rounded the corner, and she sucked in a breath. "Mason," she exhaled softly.

He chuckled. "We're the only ones here. You don't have to whisper."

Flameless candles covered the table, the floor, the shelves all around, casting an ethereal glow throughout the space. He pulled out his phone and tapped the screen. Music drifted from a speaker somewhere nearby, and she melted as she recognized the first strands of "She" by Elvis Costello. From her favorite movie, *Notting Hill*—they'd danced to this song at their wedding.

Still holding her hand, Mason led her to the desk. He leaned against it and pulled her close, until she stood between his legs, then he released her hand to rest his at her waist. In this position, he was able to look her directly in the eye. "What I said earlier in the car? I meant every word." His thumbs hung on her belt loops. "I realized these past few weeks that my priorities had drifted way out of whack. I let my insecurities come between us. I let them push me into chasing all the wrong things to try to prove myself worthy of you."

She ran her fingers over the hair at his temples, brushing it back from his ears. "We both struggled with insecurity—it wasn't only you." It had almost broken them apart. "And you never have to prove yourself to me, Mason. Ever. I love you in your strength and in your weakness."

He dipped his head. "I know that now." Then looked up at her again. "And there's something I want you to know, because I've been keeping a secret all these years."

She tipped her head and wrinkled her forehead. "Um, oh-kay." Her heart rate picked up.

Yet his smile set her prickling nerves back at ease. Goodness, her husband was handsome.

"You've hinted in some of our talks that you thought I only fell in love with you because of what you could offer me. That if I hadn't been forced to be tutored by you, I never would have fallen for you."

"Oh, Mace. I don't believe that anymore. Like we just said about our insecurities—"

His finger went to her lips. "I want to banish that thought once and for all." Then he patted the table he leaned on. "October third of my senior year. It was a Tuesday." He nodded to the chair beside him. "You sat right here. You had on a red sweater and blue jeans, your hair in some twist"—he tugged on a strand—"with just a few pieces touching your neck. And those big round glasses that highlighted your big brown eyes."

"What are you talking about?"

"The day I fell in love with you."

Her heart lurched as he continued talking.

"I'd already seen you in the history class we shared."

He had? "I thought you didn't even know I was in there. At least not until after I started tutoring you."

"I knew."

His deep baritone oozed warmth that melted her muscles.

"You talked to anyone in class—didn't matter if they were popular or outcasts. In fact, you seemed to prefer the outcasts." His assessment was true. "And you were brilliant but didn't flaunt it. I only know because I could see your homework and test scores whenever Mr. Brady returned them. One hundred percent every single time."

School had been easy for her, but she'd recognized that wasn't the case for everyone. She also recognized that God hadn't blessed everyone with the same talents, so why make someone feel small for not having the ones she did?

Mason kept on talking, his hands still at her waist. "But that day in the library, some of my teammates were teasing Becca Marston."

Right. Prom queen extraordinaire. Natalie gulped as the memory of the moment he recalled returned to her as well.

"She'd been awful to you," Mason said. "I'd witnessed it multiple times with my own eyes."

"We weren't exactly friends." Not enemies either. More like a girl and her bully.

"Imagine my surprise when you came to her defense. You put those guys in their place with a few well-placed words. Shut them right up, pulled out a chair, and invited Becca to your table, then sat back down and kept right on studying."

John Thornton's adoring look at Margaret Hale at the end of *North & South*. Mr. Darcy's hand flex after helping Elizabeth into the carriage in *Pride & Prejudice*. She'd always thought she'd swooned at those moments. She hadn't known what swooning was.

Not until this moment.

The intensity of love rolling off her husband. The way his eyes darkened as they flickered over her face, like he couldn't get enough of her. Would never tire of her. But it was his next confession that solidified this as her one true swoon-worthy moment.

"I fell in love with you right then and there, and I haven't fallen out since."

Oh, this man. Natalie pressed into him and touched her lips to his. They'd shared many kisses in this library, but back then they'd had to restrain their passion. As his wife, she could give their desires free rein.

Mason stumbled as she pressed against him but quickly regained control. His hands slipped under her shirt to rest against the skin at her waist, and he returned her kisses with the caress of a man deeply in love with his wife. Desire and adoration lingered in his touch. As her fingertips trailed up his spine, he slowed them down.

"Darlin'." His lips moved against hers.

"Hmm?" She tugged him closer.

"Agh, you're killing me here."

More kisses. "Not exactly my plan."

"Mine either." He groaned. "Nat." He nipped at her bottom lip, his hands wreaking havoc on her senses. "Nat." This time he pulled away enough to look her in the eyes. "They installed cameras in here."

She hadn't thought anything could douse the fire raging inside her.

That did.

Disentangling herself from her husband, Natalie took a step back. Then she grinned up at him. "There's no cameras in our car."

CHAPTER THIRTY-TWO

"Do you think they'll come?" From her spot by the window overlooking Halstead Manor's long drive, Natalie voiced her concern to the other two people in the room.

Mason stood beside her. "They will."

John perched on his desk. "I have no idea."

She turned and paced the room. Yesterday after they'd returned home, Natalie had texted the group yet again and explained how the book they'd found had been a counterfeit but she'd since located the real one. She'd then told them that today she planned on talking with Caspar to see if he'd give them any more answers, and she invited them to meet her at Halstead Manor. In response, she'd finally received a text from Everleigh.

Sorry for the radio silence, there was a lot to process over here. Niles and Gertie are in a decent place, but I'm not sure if returning to Halstead would be best right now. Especially since Niles is still worked up about our run-in with Matt. Will do my best.

Brooke, meanwhile, had yet to respond.

As much as Natalie hated that Everleigh and Brooke might not come, she'd done all she could. She understood that Everleigh's focus needed to be on Niles and Gertie. She also understood that Brooke's response stemmed from old wounds, not the current situation. As someone who needed space herself to process, she'd give them the same grace. But she refused to give up on their new friendship.

"You okay?" Mason asked.

"I am." She reached for his hand and squeezed it. "I love you."

The smile he gave chased away all her shadows. He pressed a kiss to her cheek. "Love you more."

Her anxious heart relaxed. Yes, she missed her friends, but if God could restore her relationship with Mason, then she had nothing to worry about with Brooke and Everleigh.

Just as the clock hands reached noon, tires crunching against gravel reached them through the open window. It had rained earlier, and moisture clung to the air. Natalie hurried over to look outside. "That's Niles's car."

"I'll let Caspar know we're running a bit behind." John lifted his phone to shoot off a text.

Everleigh, Niles, and Gertrude exited his vehicle and dodged puddles as they headed to the front steps. Within moments, they joined her inside.

"Thanks for coming." Natalie greeted them with hugs.

John offered handshakes.

"Sorry we're late," Everleigh said, her eyes flicking to Niles. "It was a very last-minute decision to show up."

"You came. That's all that matters." A breeze gently blew the curtains and filled the room with the scent of damp earth and summer flowers. "Have you heard from Brooke?"

Everleigh shook her head. Unsurprisingly, she was ignoring both of them. Perhaps, like Everleigh, she'd make an impromptu decision to join them.

They agreed to wait another fifteen minutes for Brooke, who remained absent.

"I don't think she's coming," Everleigh said.

Natalie turned from the window where she'd stood watching. "No, I suppose she's not." Disappointment welled, but she'd have to dwell on that emotion later. The rest had come, and they deserved to see what she'd found. After crossing the room, she reached into the leather bag she'd placed on the coffee table. She unwrapped the cloth holding *Alice's Adventures Under Ground*. The fabric draped over her palms, and she held them up, presenting the book resting there to Everleigh.

Her friend's blue eyes widened, and her hands remained at her side. "I feel like I need gloves or something."

"Normally I'd agree, but this isn't a collectible. It's an adventure meant to be shared."

"It looks so fragile though. More so than the one we found in London." Everleigh stepped closer. "The pages are worn, and that binding is loose."

"It's definitely well loved, but I assure you it's sturdy." She caught Mason's eye and couldn't help but smile. "That's how you know it's real."

She'd borrowed from *The Velveteen Rabbit* once again, but stories were a conduit for her emotions. Truth often wove its way through fictional worlds and the lives of characters in a way that painted pictures more vibrant than the Van Gogh *Starry Night* across from her. For some, it was music that did this. Others, art. Still others, nature. But for her it had always been the written word. She even gravitated toward the parables in the Bible.

Everleigh reached out. "All right, then." Book in hand, she walked to one of the club chairs and sat to examine it. As she did, Natalie filled her in on the past few days and what had them arriving at this moment.

When she finished speaking, Everleigh closed the book. "You're hopeful Caspar will tell you the true significance of this."

"Aren't you?" Natalie couldn't believe she was the only hopeful—or curious—one here. "Isn't that why you came?"

"It's why we both did," Gertrude answered. "Niles is begrudgingly here because he refuses to allow either of us out of his sight after the whole fiasco in Europe."

Arms folded over his wide chest, Niles didn't respond with more than a bothered look.

John stood and rounded his desk. "Let me put the call through, and maybe we can get some answers."

"*If* he answers," Everleigh said.

John glanced her way. "He will. I already prepped him that we'd be calling." And based on what he'd told Natalie, done some creative finagling to convince Caspar to speak with them.

On the third ring, Caspar's automated voice answered. "Good afternoon, ladies." As their chorus of greetings responded, Caspar amended, "And gentlemen, based on what I'm hearing."

"Mason and Niles are here, along with Everleigh, Gertrude, and Natalie," John said.

"No Brooke?" Caspar asked.

Natalie hovered near the phone. "I invited her, but it appears she's not coming."

His lengthy pause indicated he was taking in that information. Rather than address it, however, he moved forward. "Well then, how can I help the rest of you?" he asked.

All eyes trained on Natalie, the current spokesperson for their group. "First, there's something I need to know."

"Which is?"

"Why did you kill your cousin Santiano?" It was a bold question, but one she wanted a response to because it would determine her next steps.

"He killed someone dear to me. I know now that it wasn't for me to avenge the death, as only God holds that right, but I did so anyway. It was what I knew. What I was taught." A pause. "My family . . . I bear that cross, and it is one I am attempting daily to shed."

Natalie held no doubts that his answer could be all fabrication, but her gut said he spoke the truth. "And finding your book, that was going to help you do so?"

"Yes."

Everleigh sat forward. "Along with finding the Florentine?"

"That quest accomplished multiple things."

"Like bringing me on board so you could use my connections in the future," Gertrude said, as if reminding him of the conversation she'd claimed they'd had in Vienna.

"Yes," Caspar said. "Though knowing what it meant for you to find that diamond far outweighed other reasons."

Lifting her hand, Everleigh flicked up her fingers as she spoke. "Helping an old friend. Gertrude's connections. That's only two, and you said multiple."

The office chair squeaked as John repositioned himself.

Finally Caspar spoke. "It allowed me to know you could be trusted. Not many would return a priceless treasure upon finding it, yet you did."

Deep laughter ripped from Mason, who'd been silent this entire time. "You wanted to know if you could trust them. Oh, that's rich."

Based on the looks around the room, he wasn't saying anything they weren't all thinking. But despite everything they'd encountered, despite not knowing all the details about him or his endgame, something inside said Caspar could be trusted. She'd felt that all along or she never would have come on board.

Now she trusted that small voice once again. "I found your book."

"My original?" Per usual, Caspar deftly handled the abrupt turn in conversation. "Where?"

"Yes. A bookshop owner in town named Harry White purchased it from the estate sale here years ago. He knew your mother."

"I remember Harry," Caspar responded. Natalie imagined fondness in his voice. "But if that were true, it would have been listed on the log of items sold that day, much like the copy in Lekeitio was listed there. And had that happened, I would have caught there were two copies and realized there was a counterfeit in play."

"A simple oversight." Natalie had thought through the sequence of events, and it was all she could come up with. "The original was mailed by your mother's butler in Lekeitio to Halstead Manor and arrived on the day of the sale here. The executor asked Harry if he'd like to add it to his pile, and from there he must have forgotten to add it to the log."

"Understandable, I suppose," Caspar agreed. "There were many items and most likely many shoppers that day."

A swath of silence covered the room before Natalie dove into another unknown with the hope Caspar would continue extending explanations. "Why did you send us to retrieve this book, Caspar?"

"I already told you. For your protection, the less you know, the better."

"That's hogwash." Gertie wasn't buying his answer. "You knew when you asked them here three months ago that there was an element of danger simply being involved with the Perez family."

"Which I tried to mitigate by keeping the Perez name distant from them," Caspar replied.

"That clearly didn't work," Niles groused.

"We've already established that," Caspar said before more tapping sounded. "I thank you for finding the book, though I did ask you not to continue this pursuit."

Everleigh stood. "No, you asked us not to pursue Matt."

"And in all honesty, Caspar, you brought three very curious women together along with one former FBI agent and sent us chasing after a mystery that remains unsolved to us." Natalie paced the room, shooting a glance at her friends before landing on Mason. They'd spoken about this last night too, and he nodded his support her way. "We are women with connections and skills—which is why you hired us—who can and will continue trying to solve this mystery with or without you." She darted another look to Everleigh to find her smiling in agreement.

Gertrude held her cane tightly and her spine even tighter. "You asked for our help, so let us help you."

"I don't want anyone hurt," Caspar said.

Natalie moved closer to the phone. "Then point us in the right direction to help end whatever this is you started."

Niles moved to behind the couch where Everleigh sat. "It's highly likely that Matt will discover he has a forgery. When that happens, he could come after the girls again in his quest to find the original. Whether you intended to or not, you already placed them in the middle of all this. Now you need to give them a way out."

An audible sigh sounded over the line, but Caspar gave no answer.

Natalie clicked her nails. Everleigh fiddled with her Rubik's Cube. Gertrude drummed her fingers on her cane. The men paced.

Then tapping sounded. "The book holds only half the key to this story."

EPILOGUE

Brooke Sumner gingerly placed the rare Lladró vase into Mrs. Albrecht's Mercedes. "This is going to look stunning in your entryway alcove."

The polished mid-sixties woman's eyes hid behind large sunglasses, but her perfect smile was on full display. "I knew if anyone could find it for me, it was you."

Ha. Take that, Storm Whitlock.

Brooke bit her tongue on her rough rebuttal to offer a much more refined one. She'd learned from a young age how to blend in with the company of whomever she was around. "That means the world to me, Mrs. Albrecht. I highly value your opinion and your loyal business."

The gold bangles on Mrs. Albrecht's wrist jingled as she swept her silver hair behind her ear. "Dear, we women must stay together." She leaned close. "Plus, you rather remind me of myself when I was young and vibrant, and I remember well the man who did me wrong. I simply couldn't continue to work with the one who hurt you."

With effort, Brooke maintained her placid expression. She'd purposely not aired her dirty laundry with anyone—it wasn't her style. Never had been, even though she had bags of it. Mrs. Albrecht was far more observant than Brooke had given her credit for if she picked up on the real reason behind Brooke cutting ties with Storm. To the world she'd proclaimed a desire to go into business for herself. Behind the scenes the story was vastly different.

"Again, your loyalty is unmatched." She pressed in for the hug and air kisses Mrs. Albrecht loved to give, then stood in the parking lot to wave her goodbye. As the Mercedes turned onto Route 66 and disappeared into the horizon, Brooke returned inside. In her pocket her phone buzzed, and she pulled it out to check the screen. Natalie. Again.

Last night Brooke had listened to the voicemail Natalie left her. She'd also read every text this morning. None of it changed her mind about rekindling their working relationship. Having missed the noon meeting, Brooke figured Natalie would firmly receive that message.

Nope. She'd texted three times since then, including this most recent one. Brooke chose to leave these messages unread.

The door chimed as a customer entered. She pocketed her phone and looked up to greet the person until she saw who walked toward her. Instead, she pointed to her entrance. "You can turn around and leave."

Amusement lifted the edge of Storm's lip and sparkled in his eyes, a look that once had the power to send electrical impulses through her stronger than a high-voltage wire. Now it still made her dangerously hot, but for all the wrong reasons.

He'd become her shadow ever since that whole European debacle. Each morning he'd be in the parking lot when she arrived, and he'd walk into the store with her and hang around while she opened. Each evening he'd run the same pattern in reverse. She also thought she'd seen him sitting outside her house a few times, but she refused to ask. She had no reservations, however, in telling him to beat it whenever he let his presence be known.

A move that rolled off him like water off a duck's feathers—never penetrating.

"That's no way to greet your customers." He sauntered toward her.

With his cargo pants and leather jacket, he reminded her of a young Harrison Ford playing Indiana Jones. It wasn't simply his appearance but also the way he carried himself that made the comparison to one of her favorite movie characters so strong that she'd once nicknamed him Ford.

Now she realized his given name suited him much, much better. At least in her world. "You're a competitor, not a customer." She scooted behind the counter.

Storm's glance bounced from the barrier she'd hidden behind to her. Wrinkles fanned from his eyes as they crinkled and lost a bit of their sparkle, but he never loosened his smirk. "I prefer the word colleague."

"That word no longer applies." Brooke busied herself with pretend paperwork.

Storm rested his hands on the counter and waited her out. After two minutes it became painfully obvious he wasn't going anywhere until she further acknowledged him.

"What do you want."

"To apply that word again."

His answer arrived so nonchalantly that she shook her head to clear her ears, because surely she'd heard him wrong. One look at his earnest face said she hadn't. "No."

He shrugged. "Then I guess competitor it is, since I've no doubt you'll see my next job that way."

Ugh. She loathed that he knew how to stoke her curiosity. "Fine. Spill it. You came for a reason, so go on and tell me instead of playing games."

The air conditioner kicked on, its hum a comforting white noise. "Your friends didn't contact you?"

Heat blossomed in her cheeks. "Natalie texted, but I haven't had a chance to read it."

His eyebrow lifted, but he wisely kept his challenge to her lie nonverbal. "You might want to, then. I'll wait."

She held his gaze as she pulled her phone from her back pocket. Her nerves wreaked havoc with the late lunch she'd eaten. Pulling up Natalie's stream of texts, she began reading through the last three she'd ignored. The first asked if she was coming. The second said Everleigh, Niles, and Gertrude had joined her, and they'd all spoken with Caspar. The third tore the breath from her lungs. She looked up at Storm, whose irresistible dimples and blue eyes could once upon a time convince her to say yes to any crazy scheme he suggested.

"They need your help, but they'll settle for mine." He rested his muscled forearms on the counter and leaned in. "So competitors or colleagues? You decide."

ACKNOWLEDGMENTS

As always, writing a book is not a solitary endeavor. And, as always, my first thank-you belongs to God. Every bit of who I am is because of who he is. Anything I achieve is because of his grace and work in my life. All glory to him. Forever.

Next is my amazing family. I am blessed with the best husband and children, and this year our family expanded with the addition of a daughter-in-love. You all cheer me on in your own ways, and I am thankful for each and every one of you. Love you all so much.

Then there are the friendships that push me along with encouragement, prayers, and critiques. Kelli, my Bible Bootcamp girls, Ashley, Kim, Joy, Joanna, and Jessica, you have ALL had a unique hand in this book. You bless my life in so many ways. Thank you.

And, of course, my agent and my editor. Linda S. Glaz, you are a champion of stories, and you never stop believing in your authors. Thank you, agent extraordinaire. Dori Harrell, thank you for all the time you spent editing this story. Your suggestions made it stronger while preserving my voice. Thank you for applying your amazing editorial skills to Natalie and Mason's story.

AUTHOR'S NOTE

ONE OF MY FAVORITE ASPECTS of this series has been placing my own fictional spin on real-life elements. When I began researching for Natalie and Mason's story, I stumbled across an article on Lewis Carroll, and one sentence spurred on my imagination. Those few words hinted at the fact that some believe Carroll truly did have an earlier manuscript of *Alice's Adventures Under Ground* other than the one he gifted to little Alice Liddell. While never proven (and the article has since been removed from where I accessed it), the mere mention of the possibility intrigued me and I knew that this was the book Natalie, Everleigh, and Brooke would search for. From there, I had the joy of discovering locations around the globe that book lovers would be delighted to visit.

With that in mind, the bookstores in Boston (along with Fleet Street) where the group travels to are very real. As is Moat Brae in Scotland and Bookseller's Row in London. And I, of course, had to include Colmar, France, when I learned it was the inspiration for the animated town Belle called home in Disney's *Beauty and the Beast*. However, the Finders and Keepers, along with any location pertaining to them, arose from my imagination. How fun, though, to imagine a secret society of book lovers who find and preserve the most treasured of manuscripts! Though they are not real, if you had a choice, would you be a Finder or a Keeper?

While you decide, I'm diving into research for book 3. I hope to see you return for Brooke and Storm's story and the ending to the Treasures of Halstead Manor.

SNEAK PEEK

The Hidden Key of Brooke Sumner

Jerrick Forsythe, age eight
Kenton Corners, Illinois, 1960

"YOUR FAMILY ARE TREASURE HUNTERS?"

Jerrick Forsythe gazed into the wide blue eyes of his friends Gertie and Amelia Levine. A swell of pride at their awe-inspired question inflated his chest. "Yes." He nodded, his own attention drifting to where his mother stood talking to his grandparents. If she'd overheard his confession, she'd be upset. He'd been taught his whole life not to speak about Paw's work, but what good was it to have such fun information and not share it? Besides, what would it hurt to tell his friends? They lived an ocean away from Paw and his business.

Jerrick leaned close and lowered his voice. "Paw finds treasures for people."

Each summer Jerrick and Mamá traveled to America to visit Paw's parents at their manor. Paw rarely accompanied them, but Jerrick didn't mind. Mamá seemed happier here. She laughed more. Smiled often. Cried less. Jerrick preferred their time spent in America over their home in Spain, where they resided with his Perez grandparents, and he wished they could remain long after summer ended. Especially with the friendships he'd made with other children in the town, like Amelia and Gertie, who often visited the manor.

Gertie's eyebrows scrunched up as her hands landed on her hips. "Have you seen any?"

"No—"

"Then how do you know he's really a treasure hunter?" Gertie challenged.

Amelia placed her hands on her hips too. "Don't be like that, Gertie." She looked at Jerrick with a soft smile. "I believe you. Tell us more."

Gertie's disbelief unsettled him, but Amelia's trust cooled the heat twisting his stomach. Good. Because he didn't like feeling angry at his friend. If he had to choose between the dark looks Paw gave people or the soft smiles Mamá offered, he'd pick Mamá's response every time. He might not be old enough to be a man yet, but he'd already decided he didn't want to be one like Paw.

Gazing across the lawn, he caught Mamá watching, and suddenly his disobedience made him uneasy. "Sorry, Amelia. Gertie is right. I don't truly know for sure. It's more that I wish he were, because wouldn't that be exciting? Much more so than picking grapes in the vineyard." Mamá's family owned hundreds of acres and were known around Spain for their wine.

Rather than looking sad at his admission, Amelia's smile widened. "Then we shall pretend to be ones and go on a grand adventure today." She took his hand and looked from him to her sister. "What are we hunting?"

Gertie never held grudges or remained in a sour mood. She accepted his honest response and moved forward with their fun. "Gold! Isn't that what all treasures are?"

He might not be able to tell them about Paw, but he could use some of the knowledge he'd overheard to make their day exciting. "Art and jewels too."

Jerrick's cousin Santiano strolled from the manor toward them. Since his mamá passed away three years ago, he rarely smiled anymore. Though, like Mamá, he did grin more often when here. Jerrick supposed that was why Mamá begged Uncle Raul to allow Santiano to accompany them each summer.

"I got us more cookies." Santiano handed them each one. His already had a large bite taken out of it, and he added another. "What are we playing today?"

Amelia clasped her hands together. "We're searching for lost treasure!"

Santiano scrunched up his face and looked at Jerrick, then back at the sisters. "There's no lost treasure to be found here at Halstead Manor."

"How would you know until it's been found?" With that, Amelia grasped her sister's hand and raced off.

Before Jerrick could chase after them, Santiano blocked his path. "You know there's nothing here."

Laughter trickled from where Mamá stood by Grandmother and Grandfather. Her head tipped back as the sound poured from her smiling lips. The joyous noise rolled across the lawn, colliding with Amelia and Gertie's glee as they skipped toward the flower beds alongside the manor. In that moment it struck Jerrick what Mamá had once told him. Treasure meant different things to different people. While he couldn't be certain that Paw hid any of his here at the manor, that didn't mean none could be found.

Jerrick tugged his cousin's arm, propelling him forward to join their friends. "Or maybe there's some of the greatest worth."

And perhaps it was time to discover what treasure meant to him.

⇒ ⇐

Present Day

A storm was coming.

And for Brooke Sumner, a storm on the horizon spelled nuisance, not trouble.

Scratch that. It spelled both descriptive words out in thirteen annoying letters: Storm Whitlock. Six feet four inches of muscle, a too-confident smile, and a head full of wavy brown hair she'd like to shave off his head. Because how on earth was it fair for a man to be that distractingly handsome and bothersome all in one breath?

She wasn't quite sure at what point Storm Whitlock had gone from being an annoying brother type to her first crush, but she clearly remembered the day he'd crushed her under that size 13 shoe of his in a devastating act of betrayal. Chosen that criminal Anna Weitz over her. All their years of friendship couldn't compete with his greed, and she'd never seen it coming. His ability to forget everything between them had stung so sharply that she'd cashed in her shares of their business and walked away.

Storm had retained control of the pawn shop she'd worked her tail off to open, and he'd become her competition, oftentimes wearing that infernal smirk of his while he attempted to outbid or outsmart her. All for the underhanded, conniving, slippery eel of a woman he'd partnered with in place of her, which rubbed salt in a still-festering wound.

Brooke promised herself she'd never lose anything to him ever again, and she wasn't one to break promises, unlike the smarmy man himself.

"Fifteen hundred, do I hear fifteen-one?" The auctioneer surveyed the crowd, his words moving at an impossible speed. He pointed deftly to a spot over Brooke's shoulder. "Fifteen-one. Do I hear fifteen-two?"

She lifted her paddle again. "Sixteen." She had no patience for playing Storm's game today, and she had no doubt he was the one raising the stakes behind her. She could smell the top notes of his cologne—black pepper and sandalwood. He wore it strictly to annoy her because she'd been the one to pick it out for him. Like his little reminder that their lives remained intertwined.

She disagreed. Yes, their pasts would forever be linked through shared memories and trials, but their futures needn't be—no matter how hard Storm tried to keep them woven. It had been like losing a limb when she'd cut him from her life, but how could she trust someone who'd proven himself completely untrustworthy?

So she'd cherish her old memories of Storm, because that boy . . . that man deserved her loyalty and love.

But she wouldn't be making any new ones with the person he'd turned into.

ABOUT THE AUTHOR

 Susan L. Tuttle is a best-selling, cookie-loving, cardigan-wearing, and coffee-drinking author of inspirational romance. She lives in the Mitten state, where she met and married her best friend, then had three littles who aren't so little anymore. Since they no longer tolerate her hugs, she adopted a borderdoodle who must endure her embraces. As a former homeschooling mom, she recently graduated her youngest child and now splits her time between running the women's ministry at her church, dating her amazing husband, navigating the sandwich years (adult kids *and* aging parents is quite the combo), and penning stories about ordinary people finding extraordinary love. You can learn more about her at susanltuttle.com.

"Get ready to be awed with mesmeric prose coupled with an intriguing plot. Add in a fun cast of characters, and you have a story that shines!"
—Rachel Scott McDaniel,
award-winning author of *Walking on Hidden Wings*

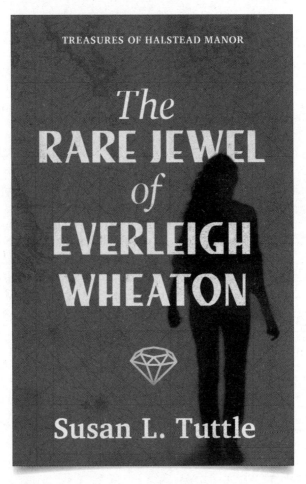

TREASURES OF HALSTEAD MANOR

The
RARE JEWEL
of
EVERLEIGH
WHEATON

Susan L. Tuttle

When Everleigh Wheaton loses yet another job, an enigmatic strange offers a solution to her financial troubles. But she's not about to let he guard down. Life has taught her that trust is dangerous.

KREGEL
PUBLICATIONS